John Milton (1608–74) was the son of a successful scrivener, who supported his extensive education. After receiving his B.A. and M.A. from Cambridge University, Milton spent a number of years on the Continent to round out his education. By 1644, Milton was a renowned poet but he spent more and more of his time on political questions. His pamphlets on the Reformation and republicanism brought him to the attention of Oliver Cromwell, who appointed him to his government. After the restoration of Charles II in 1659, Milton narrowly escaped execution. He spent his remaining years working on such poems as *Paradise Lost* and *Samson Agonistes*.

Edward M. Cifelli, Ph.D., has taught British and American literature for more than thirty-five years and is the author or editor of seven books, including biographies of poets David Humphreys and John Ciardi. A regular essayist on poetry for *Arts & Letters: A Journal of Contemporary Culture*, he is currently at work on a book about Arkansas poet Miller Williams.

Edward Le Comte, professor emeritus of English at the State University of New York at Albany, also taught at Columbia, his alma mater, and the University of California at Berkeley. He has published twenty-two books, including novels and biographies, but his specialty, both in teaching and in numerous influential articles and books, is Milton.

PARADISE LOST
and Other Poems

John Milton

With a New Introduction
by Edward M. Cifelli, Ph.D.
Annotated by Edward Le Comte

A SIGNET CLASSIC

SIGNET CLASSIC
Published by New American Library, a division of
Penguin Group (USA) Inc., 375 Hudson Street,
New York, New York 10014, U.S.A.
Penguin Books Ltd, 80 Strand,
London WC2R 0RL, England
Penguin Books Australia Ltd, 250 Camberwell Road,
Camberwell, Victoria 3124, Australia
Penguin Books Canada Ltd, 10 Alcorn Avenue,
Toronto, Ontario, Canada M4V 3B2
Penguin Books (N.Z.) Ltd, Cnr Rosedale and Airborne Roads,
Albany, Auckland 1310, New Zealand

Penguin Books Ltd, Registered Offices:
80 Strand, London WC2R 0RL, England

Published by Signet Classic, an imprint of New American Library, a
division of Penguin Group (USA) Inc. Previously published in a Mentor edition.

First Signet Classic Printing, December 2003
10 9 8 7 6 5 4 3 2 1

 REGISTERED TRADEMARK—MARCA REGISTRADA

Library of Congress Catalog Card Number: 2003054364

Printed in the United States of America

Contents

NOTE ON THIS EDITION

This edition of Milton's three greatest poems presents a text in modern spelling (but the British rather than the American form of such words as *honour* and *theatre* is adhered to). The more interesting textual variations are given in the footnotes, which also, for the first time in any edition, keep track of the far-flung repetitions of phrases, and the scattered fixed epithets, within (and also to a lesser extent between) *Paradise Lost* and *Samson Agonistes*.

INTRODUCTION

Milton for Our Times

1. Duty v. Enjoyment

Modern-day readers of *Paradise Lost* may feel something like a dreary sense of duty at the prospect of having to spend several hours, days, or weeks with John Milton, the premier spokesman of seventeenth-century English Puritanism. The feeling is complicated for American readers by the connection (real or imagined) of Puritanism to whatever sexual hang-ups have mysteriously managed to persist into the new millennium. What good, new readers may think, can come of getting to know John Milton? What can his version of the Garden of Eden story possibly say to twenty-first-century readers? Is it really worth the bother?

The answer to the last question is yes, of course, but the possibly surprising chief reason is because *Paradise Lost* is enjoyable, not because it is uplifting, if in fact it is, or because it is nearly 350 years old—a detail that engages antiquarians and academics more than general readers. Nor are these readers likely to enjoy the book primarily for its richly imagined version of the Judeo-Christian creation myth. And no amount of professorial assertion about the baroque beauties of Milton's grand style is likely to persuade readers to pick up this formidable English classic. *Paradise Lost* does compel the attention of some readers for all these reasons—and no doubt many others—but the too often ignored simple truth about the book is that it is a great read, with a wonderful, sometimes lusty, cast of characters, a carefully arranged plot, and here and there even a hint of humor—the surefire ingredients of bestsellers even today. *Paradise Lost* is certainly worth the bother.

But is it really enjoyable? Isn't it like all the other "classics" Mark Twain once quipped about as works "everybody wants to have read and nobody wants to read"? Perhaps, but not all classics have such an interest

as *Paradise Lost* does, for example, in romantic love and
sex—not only on Earth, but also in Heaven. (See Books
VIII and IX.) And even among epic poems, this one is
notable for its violent and high-stakes scenes of war.
(See especially Book VI.) Readers have always thrilled
to Milton's heroic superheroes and indestructible arch-
villains, characters who may remind younger readers of
similarly immune-to-harm figures in twenty-first-century
comic books, movies, television shows, and computer
games. (See, for example, how the Archangel Michael
swings his mighty sword at Satan, slashing through "All
his right side" [VI, 327], and how his wounds then magi-
cally heal themselves.) In another vein, it's one kind of
slightly off-center enjoyment to stare openmouthed at
the page over Milton's infuriating habit of claiming biblical authority for his personal brand of male superiority.
It's so blatant and unapologetic as to leave modern-day
readers stunned—and yet it is magnificently balanced by
one of the great moments in *Paradise Lost,* when Adam
loses his priggish ego, becomes fully humanized (at least
for a moment), and deliberately chooses Eve over
Heaven: "if death/Consort with thee, death is to me as
life . . ." (IX, 953–54).

Still another aspect of *Paradise Lost* new readers will
enjoy is the sheer audacity of the thing—not only its size
(twelve books and 10,565 lines in the 1674 edition) but
also its scope. Milton set out to write, as he put it, "things
unattempted yet in prose or rhyme" (I, 16), which, it
turns out, is nothing less than to "justify the ways of God
to men" (I, 26). In an age like the current one, when
poetic ambition is generally satisfied with a one-page lyric,
here is a monumental narrative poem complete with a
full cast of characters and a sustained drama. How can
readers not bow in admiration of a mind that could imagine the architecture of Heaven, Hell, and Paradise—not
to mention the geography of the intellectual and spiritual
landscapes in and between each? There is Milton standing
proud, tall, and stern, with a bold self-assurance born of
theological and intellectual certitudes, announcing his
grand goal. It doesn't matter that he may in the end fall
short, or that modern readers (children of Chaos Theory,
moral relativism, and the Computer Age) may not share

his worldview. It doesn't even matter that Milton was stubbornly, Puritanically, doctrinaire about his story—wasn't Dante guilty of a similar narrowness in *The Divine Comedy*? No, what strikes new and old readers alike when they come to Milton's announced purpose is his breathtaking, irresistible audacity. Wouldn't it be a great thing, readers catch themselves thinking, if he could actually do it?

The grandeur of Milton's language in *Paradise Lost* is often praised, and rightly so, despite some difficulties that need mentioning, but for now, however, note that it is impossible not to be impressed by the stateliness, the formality, and the dignity of Milton's poetry in *Paradise Lost*—all the more striking to contemporary readers when set against the casual informality of the early twenty-first century. For the versification, Milton chose blank verse, the form popularized by Elizabethan dramatists earlier in the seventeenth century, even though the lack of rhyme in an epic poem drew attention to itself. (The point was sticky enough for the publisher, in subsequent printings, to explain that Homer and Virgil hadn't written in rhymes; that rhyme had been added by later poets just to distract readers from "wretched matter and lame metre"; and that anyway all readers with "judicious ears" would agree that rhyme was "trivial" and added "no true musical delight." See "The Verse" preceding Book I.) The blank verse is, in fact, so successful in *Paradise Lost* that there are long portions in which the dramatic action simply takes over, and one of the usual topics of classroom discussion is whether it is indeed an epic or a drama. The debate is no doubt more important to literary critics and historians than to readers, who are, after all, at liberty to enjoy what they please—and the drama seems to please them most. It is in the dramatic sequences that Milton seems most sure-handed as he navigates one ten-syllable line after another, managing in the process to make them (and the characters who speak them) different from one another at the same time that they are similar. Perhaps most amazing is that, despite a distance of three and a half centuries, an overfondness for the baroque, and an American readership that has a slightly different voice box from the British, Milton manages very often to write lines that sound something like the way modern-day English is spoken. No small trick.

But like most language three and a half centuries old, it also presents difficulties to readers coming to it for the first time. The inversions, allusions, and Latinate diction cause most of the problems, but even pronunciation stands occasionally in the way of grasping the sense and the movement of the words. The solution to these problems is to read slowly, work carefully through complicated syntax, re-read particularly obscure constructions, check the footnotes, and even read the words aloud if it seems the ear might help when the eye alone can't get the job done. And don't be afraid to abandon some passages as simply too dense or knotty to follow. This is a long poem, and a few lost passages aren't going to matter in the long run.

Another problem is that many of the more difficult passages in *Paradise Lost* arise from Milton's vast classical erudition, his seemingly endless knowledge of biblical lore, and his use of epic conventions familiar to more of the literary community then than now. Today "epic" is much more loosely used to describe anything that is above the norm in size and scope. It is therefore not surprising that the hardest going in *Paradise Lost* comes when Milton resorts to formula-driven epic conventions and seems to get temporarily lost amid roll calls, catalogues, extended similes, biblical geography lessons, detailed vistas, psychologically telling dreams, and so on. Many will learn to enjoy these sequences in their own right, but at worst they can be silently borne as necessary interludes, temporary interruptions of the narrative and dramatic action. Certainly the ample glories of *Paradise Lost,* like those in the finest grand opera, are worth waiting for.

2. The Glories

The first of these glories, as readers have commented on from the beginning, is the peculiarly human archvillain himself, Satan. When Milton, blind apologist of the Puritan Commonwealth in the 1650s, sat down to write his epic poem on the fall of Adam and Eve in the Garden of Eden, he not only had the unfortunate pair themselves for his story; he also had God, the Son of God, a host of archangels and rebel angels, plus Satan for his dramatis personae. Furthermore, Milton understood the importance of creating a worthy chief antagonist, not just a villain who was larger than life, but one who was complex in his intellectual and psychological makeup. Of course, Milton is consistent in his vilification of Satan—witness, for example, some of the ways he labels him, as the "hellish Pest" (II, 735), the "fraudulent impostor foul" (III, 692), the "wily Adder" (IX, 625), the "Prince of Darkness" (X, 383), and many more. In this sense, Milton never wavers in his indictment of the "Author of Evil" (VI, 262), and yet the character he created is so brilliant, especially in the early going, so articulate, so driven, so almost-human in his frailties that he cannot fail to resonate with modern readers. In some of the most celebrated lines in *Paradise Lost,* Satan, expelled from Heaven and "Chained on the burning lake" (I, 210), with head held high and eyes still blazing, ponders his situation and declares, "The mind is its own place, and in itself/Can make a Heaven of Hell, a Hell of Heaven" (I, 254–55). And then, overfilled with a burning, unrepentant bitterness, he determines that for him at least it is "Better to reign in Hell than serve in Heaven" (I, 263). Satan's passionate misery is deeply felt by readers who either have themselves been defeated and then angrily turned inward for a new and perhaps painful resolve—or can readily imagine doing so. It is after all the human way.

In the early going, before he is shown in all his incestuous ugliness at the end of Book II as the father of the hideous monsters Sin and Death, Satan seems almost the perfect epic hero: imposing, capable of superhuman courage, even in one sense elevated, both in language and sentiments. Milton was clearly walking a dangerous line here, for Satan had to be the ultimate villain, not a sympathetic victim, and although Milton did manage to regain his moral footing and return to condemning Satan, readers will always be struck by Satan's human qualities—his anger and resentment over his defeat, his pride and continuing determination, and his undaunted courage. Is this attractiveness of Satan's adequately explained by Milton's need to create a worthy antagonist for his story? Did he inadvertently raise his archvillain too high

and make him too humanly appealing? Or is it perhaps that
readers identify more often with rebel angels than with archangels? Perhaps the biggest question is why Milton never revised the early Satan to make him less attractive. Of course
that would have required him to tamper with some of his
best writing, so perhaps it was that, in the contest between
good Puritanism and good writing, Milton showed his own
humanity and chose the writing.

Another of the glories of *Paradise Lost* that readers
have commented on from the outset is the complicated
relationship between Adam and Eve, with Milton caught
between black-and-white biblical authority, as he understood it, and the actual complexities of male-female rela-
tionships, perhaps as he had experienced them in his
three marriages. As is the case with Satan, Adam is
hardly a uniformly attractive dramatic figure, and yet he
does have a couple of moments onstage that are very
nearly perfect. The first has to do with sex, the second
with love. In the first, in Book VIII, Adam tells Raphael
with deadpan humor about how he came in a dream to
notice that he alone among all God's creatures had no
female companion: "I found not what methought I
wanted still" (355). So Adam complains to the "Author
of this Universe" (360) about his lack of a "human consort" (392), but God, having fun with the pushy young
Adam, asks what this business about a consort is all
about—after all, He doesn't have one either:

> Seem I to thee sufficiently possessed
> Of happiness, or not, who am alone
> From all eternity? for none I know
> Second to me or like, equal much less.
> How have I, then, with whom to hold converse
> Save with the creatures which I made, and those
> To me inferior . . . ?   (404–10)

A tough question, to be sure. But Adam reminds his
Maker that he has a job to do, to "beget/Like of his like"
(423–24), and how is he going to do that all by himself?
For such work, he says, he is "defective" and requires
"Collateral love and dearest amity" (425–26). So it is sex,
at last, that he is after, though he doesn't quite have the

language to say so. But God, turning convivial and jovially paternal for this father-son moment, replies in good spirits that He has only been teasing Adam, that He's had in mind a partner for him all along, a special gift to enjoy: "Thy wish exactly to thy heart's desire" (451). And He is as good as His word, for after Eve is created from a rib on Adam's left side, Adam finally has true happiness: "The spirit of love and amorous delight" (477). Eve ("Grace was in all her steps, Heaven in her eye" [488]) then gives Adam "nuptial sanctity and marriage rites" (487).

But Milton wasn't finished quite yet with the subject of sex. Adam, finally mated "exactly to [his] heart's desire," confesses to Raphael that this particular pleasure ("Commotion strange" [531]) had been special ("in all enjoyments else/Superior . . ." [531–32])—even for Paradise. Liking it as much as he does, he can't help wondering if there is sex in Heaven: "Bear with me, then, if lawful what I ask./Love not the Heavenly Spirits, and how their love/ Express they, by looks only, or do they mix/Irradiance, virtual or immediate touch?" (614–17). It's a safe bet he is hoping for "immediate touch" over "looks only." Raphael, however, like a father explaining the birds and bees to his son, blushes "a smile that glowed/Celestial rosy-red" (618–19), clears his throat, and starts off, but soon he gets tangled up in limbs, joints, and spirits—and decides to quit with as much of his dignity intact as he can salvage. Before leaving Adam and Eve to their own devices, though, Raphael adds one cautionary note: "take heed lest passion sway/Thy judgement to do aught, which else free-will/ Would not admit" (635–37). Good advice from angels, but always difficult for young men to follow.

3. Fallen or Risen?

Nothing in *Paradise Lost* is further from humor, more solemnly noble in its way, than Adam's decision to join Eve in sin, that is, to turn his back on Paradise—even to accept death and the loss of Heaven as a consequence. Milton opens Book IX, the story of the Fall and the very heart of *Paradise Lost,* with Adam's too-usual smugness toward Eve. He condescendingly comments, "nothing lovelier can be found/In woman, than to study household

good,/And good works in her husband to promote"
(232–34). After the lovers have their first quarrel in Paradise (not over his remark, but over Eve wanting to work a different part of the Garden from Adam), Satan arrives as a serpent, tempts Eve, and seduces her into eating the fruit of the Tree of Knowledge. God has warned that death would follow from eating that particular fruit, but after she eats, not only does Eve find herself quite alive, but she also feels surprisingly good about herself, not just "more equal," she thinks, but "perhaps,/A thing not undesirable, sometime/Superior . . ." (see 816–25). She likes this feeling so much, in fact, that she is tempted not to share it with Adam at all. But after she reexamines the situation and realizes she might yet die, that a new Eve might be created in her place, and that Adam might then enjoy Eden with someone else, she thinks it might be best after all to share. However, when she approaches with her new knowledge and fruit, Adam recognizes instantly that she is lost, that Satan has "Defaced, deflowered" her (901).

But Adam, instead of picking up his earlier theme by bitterly reminding Eve about the purpose of a woman's life being to promote good works in her husband, is suddenly transformed, fully aware, perhaps for the first time, of the depths of love in his own heart:

> How can I live without thee? how forgo
> Thy sweet converse and love so dearly joined,
> To live again in these wild woods forlorn?
> Should God create another Eve, and I
> Another rib afford, yet loss of thee
> Would never from my heart. No, no! I feel
> The link of nature draw me: flesh of flesh,
> Bone of my bone thou art, and from thy state
> Mine never shall be parted, bliss or woe.
>
> (908–16)

Still, he does not eat the fruit quite yet. First he ponders his choices, just as Eve did before him, the human thing after all. The arguments he comes up with, of course, amount to little more than rationalizations, mere intellectual exercises, and they are totally beside the only point that matters—

the flesh-and-bone Eve standing before him. Turning to her, he says:

> I with thee have fixed my lot,
> Certain to undergo like doom; if death
> Consort with thee, death is to me as life,
> So forcible within my heart I feel
> The bond of Nature draw me to my own;
> My own in thee, for what thou art is mine;
> Our state cannot be severed, we are one,
> One flesh; to lose thee were to lose myself.
>
> (952–59)

It's hard not to be proud of Adam here, as he looks squarely at all he stands to lose, yet steadfastly, loyally, devotedly chooses to stay with the woman he loves. It's a human choice, of course, not a heavenly one, yet Adam, in his moment of courage, shines. From Milton's standpoint, he was once again on shaky ground, wavering between his dogma and his art. He could certainly have gone back to temper the nobility in Adam that he had written into the scene, but he let it stand—just as he had let stand the wonderful lines he had written for Satan earlier. He must have liked as much as subsequent generations have this exhilarating expression of the romantic love of Adam for Eve, and one imagines that only later, under the requirement of the story he had set out to write, did he force himself back to condemning them. But regardless of how the preordained story had to resolve itself, there's a strong temptation to think Adam's heart may have been right at his moment of decision—one of the truest and most moving moments in all English literature.

Oh, yes—it's worth every bit of the bother.

"Lycidas" and *Samson Agonistes*

Modern readers may have more trouble with "Lycidas" than with *Samson Agonistes* and prefer *Paradise Lost* to either—and for some obvious reasons. *Paradise Lost* is a literary epic, a form that is no longer written, but which in terms of characterization and plot does not (always) seem so very different from novels and screen-plays. "Lycidas," however, is a pastoral elegy (also sometimes called a pastoral allegory), a form rooted in ancient Greek idylls and classical Roman eclogues; it is a form that has shepherd-poets, invectives against death, flower symbolism, and other similarly remote features—and therefore it is today a largely forgotten ancient form that has no modern counterpart it might sound familiar to. It would be more remarkable if modern readers did *not* have trouble with it.

Written when Milton was not yet twenty-nine, and called by him a "Monody" (itself a dated term meaning "dirge" or "lament"), "Lycidas" commemorates the life of his friend Edward King, who had drowned earlier that same year. And even though it is generally acknowledged to be the finest example of its form in English, readers, like the famously sharp-tongued Samuel Johnson in the eighteenth century, are often impatient with its old-fashioned formulas. "Nothing," Johnson wrote, "can less display knowledge, or less exercise invention, than to tell how a shepherd has lost his companion, and must now feed his flocks alone. . . ." But as dismayingly remote as its form may be, "Lycidas" can still be enjoyed if one accepts it on its own terms and determines on going in to learn about rather than struggle against the form. Learning to love a piece of literature for its odd shape and peculiar mannerisms is at least half the joy of being literate. Of course, one is free as well to be happy if the piece happens also to be short.

Samson Agonistes, however, is another story, for there are moments in this play that are as engaging as any in *Paradise Lost.* Based on the Aristotelian theory of tragedy and modeled on Aeschylus's *Pometheus Bound* and Sophocles's *Oedipus at Colonus, Samson Agonistes* was written as a closet drama, a work intended to be read rather than acted. The story of Samson is from the Bible, of course, Judges to be exact, and it tells the story of an Israelite who is born to a barren woman and pledged to God. Under the terms of the pledge, Samson is not allowed to have his hair cut, but is, however, free to marry a Philistine girl, who tricks him into killing thirty men, which soon escalates into a thousand as he fights with superhuman strength—and the jawbone of an ass. It's at this point that Samson falls for the temptress Dalila, who, on behalf of the Philistine leaders in Gaza, worms the secret of his strength out of him: Samson is then subdued, taken into slavery, and blinded. Unfortunately, all this happens before the play opens. Milton's Samson furiously rages, when it does start, against Dalila's "foul effeminacy" (410) and manages by the play's end to have his mortal revenge against the Philistines on their high holy day, but despite the dignity and disciplined orderliness of Samson's biblically scripted vengeance, it is in the key scene with Dalila (who is onstage for a very brief time) that *Samson Agonistes* comes alive. Sparks always light up Milton's scenes with women.

Samson calls Dalila "My wife, my traitress" (725) and will have nothing to do with her, yet she makes an appeal to him, claiming she is sorry for what she did, frightened too, but most of all, she is moved by "conjugal affection" (739) to see his face one last time. Samson, however, won't be sweet-talked anymore by her "wonted arts," what he calls the "arts of every woman false like thee" (748–49). Dalila defends herself by saying she was weak and suffered from "curiosity." Then, once she knew some secrets, she couldn't help but "publish them"—all, she says, "common female faults" (773–77). He should have known better than to "have trusted that [secret] to a woman's frailty . . ." (783). Samson doesn't give an inch, replying that she was indeed weak—for Philistine gold and lust. But Dalila continues to defend herself well, saying it wasn't gold at all that swayed her, but the appeals of the magistrates, princes, and priests of her country that she steal the secret of Samson's strength—both to protect the Philistines from him in the future as well as to punish him for his past actions against them. Now, she says, she wants to make it up to Samson by seeking his release, but he turns her away one final time and says to the Chorus:

> So let her go; God sent her to debase me,
> And aggravate my folly, who committed
> To such a viper his most sacred trust
> Of secrecy, my safety, and my life.
>
> (999–1002)

It remains a curious truth that despite Milton's ambitious high-mindedness, his frontal attack on the literary, political, and religious problems of his own and perhaps all time, he also had an unerring ear for the sort of dialogue that rings true between men and women, whether they be loving partners, bitter antagonists, or both at the same time. His forms may be dated, but when Milton's men and women talk to (or about) each other, they sound hauntingly modern.

—Edward M. Cifelli, Ph.D.

THE LIFE OF MILTON

The life of Milton is much more fully and intimately known than the lives of his great predecessors—and favorites—among the English poets: Chaucer, Spenser, and Shakespeare. The reasons are three. First, the latter part of the seventeenth century saw the dawning of modern interest in the biography of authors, which was to lead to such spectacular products a century later as Boswell's *Johnson* and Johnson's own *Lives of the English Poets*. No less than five sketches of Milton's life were written between his death in 1674 and the end of the century. Second, he was more than an author: he became a public figure, known for his controversial prose and his service to the Cromwellian regime before he was known as a poet. Third, Milton, above and beyond his thirty-one Familiar Letters in Latin, did not hesitate on occasion to bring himself into his own writings. He did this to an extent that may be measured by the fact that the compilation *Milton on Himself* has two hundred seventy pages of direct quotation.

The poet was a Londoner most of his life. The house he lived in longest was the house in which he was born, at the corner of Cheap and Bread streets, December 9, 1608. His father, also named John, maintained a scrivener's shop there under the sign of the Spread Eagle. Scriveners served as notaries and preparers of legal papers, and could prosper because of their advance knowledge of property transfers. John Milton the elder did prosper, to such a degree that he could retire, first, in 1632, to the suburb of Hammersmith, then, in 1635, to a country estate in Horton—a far cry from his struggling youth. He had come to London from Oxfordshire about the age of twenty-one upon being disinherited by his father, a recusant, "because he kept not the Catholic religion" and was caught reading the Bible.

Somehow, perhaps as a boy chorister at Christ Church, Oxford, the poet's father early acquired training in his

lifelong avocation of music. He composed at twenty "an
In Nomine of forty parts, for which he was rewarded
with a gold medal and chain by a Polish prince, to whom
he presented it" and went on to gain, as a musician of
the school of Byrd, "the reputation of a considerable
master in this most charming of all the liberal sciences."
He was invited by the great madrigalist Thomas
Morley—who composed for *As You Like It*—to contrib-
ute to *The Triumphs of Oriana,* a cantus book honouring
Queen Elizabeth in one of the last years of her reign.

About the poet's mother, Sarah, less is known, the
very form of her last name being uncertain. It is not
known when she was married, or how often. Milton's
only reference states that she had a reputation in the
neighborhood for her alms-giving. In two letters to his
friend Diodati written not long after Mrs. Milton's death
on April 3, 1637, Milton makes no mention of the event,
and when he turned to poetry in the fall of that year it
was to memorialize another friend—in "Lycidas." (Similarly, in the month that Milton's first wife died he wrote
a sonnet to Cromwell. In both cases the conclusion could
be that the poet was turning away from an event too
deep for tears, melodious or otherwise.) The antiquarian
Aubrey reported that Milton's mother "had very weak
eyes, and used spectacles presently after she was thirty
years old."

With his sister and, after 1615, younger brother, the
future poet moved about as a boy in an apartment often
resonant with the sound of the "pealing organ," which
he himself learned to play, with viols and virginals, with
"lute well touched, or artful voice." After going to petty
school, he received private tutoring from a Scotch Pres-
byterian, Thomas Young, whose ally in ecclesiastical
controversy he was to be more than a score of years
later. A canvas now in the Morgan Library in New York
and reproduced as the frontispiece of the Columbia Edition of Milton's works is the most striking as well as the
first of all the portraits, showing an earnest and winsome
boy of ten who was already, according to Aubrey, a
poet: the brocaded doublet and delicate lace collar seem
to symbolize the not yet past glories of the Renaissance,
while the intent eyes and the auburn hair cropped

closely according to the Puritan prescription are mediated by the sensitive chin and lips.

Milton was fifteen when he produced his earliest surviving lines, paraphrases of Psalms cxiv and cxxxvi. By then he was attending that by no means average school a few blocks away, St. Paul's (organized by John Colet, Dean of St. Paul's Cathedral, early in Henry VIII's reign), and brought to this or any poetic task already an abundance of Latin and Greek (he was subsequently to put Psalm cxiv into Greek dactylic hexameters) and at least the beginnings of Hebrew. A fellow pupil was the closest friend of his youth, Charles Diodati, and he seems to have had a fruitful relationship with a teacher there, Alexander Gill the younger, the headmaster's son and eventual successor.

It is important to note the many cordial relations Milton enjoyed (with both sexes) in the course of a life marked by heated controversies. The first of the latter on record developed during his first year at Christ's College, Cambridge, 1625–26—a quarrel with his tutor William Chappell. The result was the student's "rustication" or suspension. He went to London and addressed Diodati a Latin poem, "Elegia I," on the subject, line 16 of which may refer to unspeakable corporal punishment—"whipped him," said Aubrey. Most modern readers are reluctant to believe that Milton underwent this particular humiliation, but there is nothing historically improbable about it. The master of Cromwell's college, Samuel Ward of Sidney Sussex (Cambridge), had the scholars (many of whom, it must be remembered, were just entering upon their teens) whipped in hall when they offended, and as Dr. Johnson (who had his own reasons for believing the story) might have opined, "If Cromwell received the cane, who will deny the same to Milton?" In any case Milton was soon back under a more agreeable tutor, without having missed a term.

He was turning into a proud, serious, reserved young man, whose nickname was "The Lady of Christ's." (Virgil had borne, as Milton would have been glad to remember, a similar sobriquet: Parthenias—"Miss Virginity.") When he gave in assembly the first of a series of required Latin orations (*prolusiones*), on looking around he saw mostly unfriendly countenances, perhaps, he conjectured, because his intellectual interests were different, as he was proudly sure his style was. By the time of the sixth of these prolusions (July 1628), titled "Sportive Exercises do not stand in the way of Philosophic Studies," his popularity has risen, and playful as the elephant's "lithe proboscis" in *Paradise Lost,* he gratefully begs pardon in advance for any comic license contrary to his usual modesty and labours to be a jolly good vulgar fellow. Of more lasting significance is that he overleapt the University statutes ordaining that all the academic discourses should be in one of the learned tongues and broke out into fifty heroic couplets, "At a Vacation Exercise," that ranks with "On the Death of a Fair Infant" as his earliest original English poem. Before going on to scholastic puns, the author soars to "Heaven's door" and grandly declares his ambition to compose epic poems "Such as the wise Demodocus once told/ In solemn songs at King Alcinous' feast." The miniature epic "In Quintum Novembris" (On the Fifth of November—the anniversary of the Gunpowder Plot), was even then one year behind him.

The "Fair Infant Dying of a Cough" was Milton's niece. "O fairest flower no sooner blown but blasted," he begins, and launches into a flurry of conceits, ending with the sage advice that the mother, Anne, should "wisely learn to curb thy sorrows wild" in expectation of an offspring that "shall make thy name to live." Alas, neither of the later children of Milton's sister, Edward and John Phillips, amounted to anything, in spite of having their uncle for a tutor in the 1640s.

The Cambridge student had already mourned in Latin verses the University beadle, the vice chancellor, and two bishops. It goes against the popular notion of inspiration that most of the poetry of Milton's youth, right up to and including "Lycidas," was occasional. On his twenty-third birthday he wrote a sonnet; on the death of old Hobson, the University carrier, he composed two sets of relentlessly punning heroic couplets; he put forth octosyllabics when the Marchioness of Winchester (a Catholic, but the saving grace was that she was said to be leaning to Protestantism) died in childbed (Ben Jonson also commemorated her); and made his English debut in print, anonymously, with "An Epitaph on the Admirable Dramatic Poet W. Shakespeare" in the 1632 Second Folio.

But the greatest poem before "L'Allegro" and "Il Penseroso" was the "Hymn on the Morning of Christ's Nativity," composed in December 1629. Had the author died then, the thin-spun life cut by the blind Fury just after his twenty-first birthday, he would still have held a secure place in English poetry, ranking with Crashaw. The essence of what Hallam called "perhaps the most beautiful ode in the language" Tillyard found to be "not stateliness excusing conceit, but homeliness, quaintness, tenderness, extravagance, and sublimity, harmonised by a pervading youthful candour and ordered by a commanding architectonic grasp." Much in this baroque or "mannerist" masterpiece looks forward to *Paradise Lost,* most obviously the fiends and false deities, "Peor and Baalim" and "sullen Moloch" and the "old Dragon under ground" that "swinges the scaly horror of his folded tail." Christ in his cradle can, like the infant Hercules, strangle this serpent. As will prove so characteristic of Milton's art, classical and Christian elements are held in brilliant tension, as surely as Christmas coincides with the winter solstice or Easter is the name of a pagan goddess.

The young poet was moved by his success to celebrate more feasts, in "The Passion" and "Upon the Circumcision," but these fail, the former being left unfinished. Better are "On Time" and "At a Solemn Music" and even some autobiographical sonnets (along with a canzone) in Italian. Milton had proclaimed in his first English sonnet, "O nightingale that on yon bloomy spray," his willingness to fall in love, and now a black-eyed, dark-tressed, polyglot foreigner named Emilia had inspired him to write in her native tongue. This was evidently an encounter lasting not much longer than glimpses of British beauties commemorated in Milton's Ovidian Latin elegies that also—I, V, and VII—celebrate the rites of spring, what the "Song on May Morning" catalogues as "Mirth and youth and warm desire!" In contrast Elegia VI lays down an ascetic regimen for the epic poet, and Edward Phillips reported that the vein of the author of *Paradise Lost* "never flowed freely but from the autumnal equinox to the vernal."

Before this winter seriousness descended, however, came the twin poems known to every schoolchild (of how little can this be said anymore!). Of uncertain date, with scenery that cannot be pinned down, these belong immemorially to a time when the world was younger; where the eighteenth century went wooden in its imitations perhaps because it was already too old, Milton achieved the perfect matching of art and vitality. L'Allegro means, of course, the Cheerful Man, but he proves to be as far from wanton gaiety, whatever the reel of abstractions at the beginning, as Il Penseroso, the Pensive or Contemplative Man, is far from melancholia. Critics have not agreed whether the poems balance day versus night as in Prolusion I, or two different persons (such as Diodati and Milton), or two moods in one person, or offer a debate between two ways of life, with Milton preferring the latter (as length, at least, would indicate). The best illustration to accompany the poems, both of which "unsphere/ The spirit of Plato," whose idealizing influence lasts until Milton's marriage, is the "Onslow" portrait, in the National Portrait Gallery, of the ruffed author at twenty-one: the delicate aristocratic face comes to us in a believable way for the last time without suffering or distortion.

After receiving his M.A., July 3, 1632 (his B.A. had been won March 26, 1629), Milton left Cambridge to go into rural retreat with his father at Hammersmith-Horton for a period of private study and preparation for his calling that was to last six years and be succeeded by the grand tour of the Continent. It was fortunate that the poet had for a father a man of means and culture (one sonnet of his survives) and understanding, whose qualms about the apparent idleness of his elder son (while the younger was diligently pursuing the law) could be smoothed by addressing him one hundred twenty hexameters, "Ad Patrem" (To his Father), that pointed out that the musician and the poet shared Phoebus between them. Milton did not earn a penny until he was thirty-one, but in the country he followed "L'Allegro" and "Il Penseroso" with "Arcades" and "Comus" and "Lycidas." He kept notes on a vast and systematic program of reading that helped to make him the most erudite of the English poets, rivaled perhaps only by Southey. In the Renaissance the poet was one who knew: there was not the modern invariable dichotomy between "knowing" and "making," between the scholar and the creative writer. Milton had grandly proclaimed in his Seventh Prolusion his Baconian intention of taking all knowledge for his province. However, for his "tardy moving" he was put on the defensive, as by a friend who inquired why he did not join the ministry and charged him with "too much love of learning."

"Arcades" and "Comus" belong to the genre of masques, mythological court entertainments involving song and dance and costumes, of which Ben Jonson wrote thirty-six. "Arcades" (which means Dwellers in Arcadia, the district in central Peloponnesus associated with pastoral, as in Sir Philip Sidney's romance, *Arcadia*) consists of three songs and a recitative in twenty-nine heroic couplets in honor of the Countess Dowager of Derby at Harefield, ten miles from Horton. This lady, whom Spenser had also praised, was the stepmother and mother-in-law of John Egerton, Viscount Brackley, who became Earl of Bridgewater in 1617 and commissioned "Comus" in 1634 for Michaelmas night, September 29, in honor of his installation as Lord President of Wales. The future Puritan was moving in high circles, although it is not known whether he was present for that first performance, at Ludlow Castle in Shropshire, of a piece the fame of which redounded so that Henry Lawes (who composed the music for its songs) had to have it printed (1637): "although not openly acknowledged by the author, yet it is a legitimate offspring, so lovely and so much desired, that the often copying of it hath tired my pen to give my several friends satisfaction, and brought me to a necessity of producing it to the public view." Adapting from the Circe myth, *A Mask* (it was named for its villain, whose Greek name means revelry, only after Milton's death) is a paean to chastity, a topic with which its author was restively and increasingly concerned up to 1642. Where the typical masque was light and short, this one unwinds for a thousand lines, mostly of blank verse (Milton's first, and, except for translations, his last before *Paradise Lost*), with arguments so serious that they were cut for the actual performance. Sir Henry Wotton, who was Provost of Eton, wrote handsomely: "I should much commend the tragical part, if the lyrical did not ravish me with a certain Doric delicacy in your songs and odes, whereunto I must plainly confess to have seen yet nothing parallel in our language."

"Lycidas," dated in manuscript November 1637, was another commissioned poem. It commemorates, as everyone knows, "a learned friend, unfortunately drowned," Edward King (1612–37), the son of a civil officer in Dublin, Sir John King, of an English family. With his older brother, Roger, Edward King had entered Christ's College sixteen months after Milton, after tuition by the famous schoolmaster Thomas Farnaby. On June 10, 1630, King was awarded by royal mandate a fellowship to which Milton, three years his senior, had a superior claim. Milton was at Hammersmith before King took his M.A., July 1633. Besides being a Tutor and Fellow in Christ's, King served as prelector, 1634–35, while qualifying for the Church. During the long vacation of 1637 he arranged to visit his friends and relatives in Dublin, including his and Milton's first tutor, Chappell (of unpleasant memory), who was serving there as provost of Trinity College. He made his will nine days before setting sail. The ship had not been long out of Chester when, as the memorial volume's Latin prose preface says, it "struck on a rock, was stove in by the shock; he, while the other passengers were busy in vain about their mortal lives, having fallen on his knees, and breathing a life which was immortal, in the act of prayer going down with the vessel, rendered up his soul to God August 10, 1637, aged twenty-five." King's alma mater decided on a collection of elegies, perhaps in rivalry to Oxford's *Jonsonus Virbius: or the Memory of Ben Jonson Revived,* 1638, and of course Milton was applied to and in fact given the place of honor, for "Lycidas," signed just with his initials, closes the volume, as if it were well understood that the final and definitive word had been said. Preceding were twelve other pieces in English, of no merit, and twenty-three in Latin and Greek, and the whole was issued from the press in 1638 under the title *Justa Edouardo King naufrago, ab Amicis maerentibus* (Rites to Edward King, drowned by shipwreck, from his grieving friends). King and Milton must have been well acquainted while at college together, although the friendship was not the same as with Diodati. King's surviving Latin ventures into verse, most of them obstetric pieces on royal births, showed little promise that he would ever "build the lofty rhyme." However, Milton's possible lack of deep personal grief on this occasion and King's demonstrable lack of poetic ability did nothing to spoil Milton's primary inspiration that a poet (and a priest, a good shepherd) had died an untimely death and must be greatly mourned.

By the time this volume was published Milton had left Horton for "fresh woods and pastures new"—a fifteen-month Continental tour that took him to France, Italy, and Geneva, and was the crown of his long and elaborate education. Accompanied by a manservant, and aided by references and linguistic facility, he again moved in high circles, starting with Lord Scudamore, Charles I's ambassador to Paris, who "gave me a card of introduction to the learned Hugo Grotius, at that time ambassador from the queen of Sweden [Christina] to the French court." In Italy, where he spent the greater part of his time, the gifted young man was received by a cardinal, Galileo, the librarian at the Vatican, a Neapolitan nobleman who had befriended Tasso and Marini, and sundry belle-lettrists who invited him to read his Latin poetry at their literary clubs and praised it extravagantly. A little talent went a long way in that twilight time of the Italian Renaissance, and there was no end of mutual backslapping among hopelessly minor talents; still, Milton was glad enough to print as preface to the Latin section of his 1645 poems the versified "testimonia" of Salsilli, Selvaggi, Francini, Dati, and Manso. Two of these were addressed poems by the visitor, Salsilli in sickness, and Manso, Marquis of Villa, in return for hospitality, and other literati figured in surviving correspondence.

After journeying from Rome to Naples in January

1639 in the company of an eremite friar who introduced him to Manso, Milton recalled (in his *Defensio Secunda*) that the latter proved "most friendly: for he guided me himself through the different parts of the city and the palace of the viceroy, and came more than once to visit me at my inn. On my leaving Naples he gravely apologized for not showing me still more attention, alleging that although it was what he wished above all things, it was not in his power in that city, because I had not thought proper to be more close in the matter of religion." Milton's stout Protestantism is also the only regret in Manso's two-line epigram, repeating the old Anglus (Englishman)—Angelus (angel) pun of Gregory the Great. Close thoughts, "i pensieri stretti," were exactly what the diplomat Wotton had advised, but one of Milton's character and upbringing had to draw a line between courtesy and hypocrisy, just as he could not but entertain mixed feelings on contemplating Rome itself—the seat of civilization *and* the residence of the whore of Babylon. About his second visit to Rome he had a melodramatic tale to tell. "While I was on my way back to Rome, some merchants informed me that the English Jesuits had formed a plot against me if I returned to Rome, because I had spoken too freely about religion; for it was a rule which I laid down to myself in those places never to be the first to begin any conversation on religion, but if any questions were put to me concerning my faith, to declare it without any reserve or fear. I nevertheless returned to Rome. I took no steps to conceal either my person or my character, and for about the space of two months I again openly defended, as I had done before, the reformed religion in the very metropolis of popery. By the favour of God, I got safe back to Florence, where I was received with as much affection as if I had returned to my native country." *Areopagitica* scores a point apropos of the Florentine interview with the latest person to be referred to in *Paradise Lost*. "I found and visited the famous Galileo, grown old, a prisoner to the Inquisition, for thinking in astronomy otherwise than the Franciscan and Dominican licensers thought." But Catholicism did not interfere with the poet's obeisance to beauty wherever he found it. Thus he addressed the diva Leonora Baroni three Latin epigrams of almost impious praise; the first declares that God or the Holy Spirit speaks in her voice.

While planning to journey on to Sicily and Greece, Milton was led to turn homeward by "the melancholy tidings" of pending civil war. He made his way back in leisurely enough fashion in the spring of 1639, stopping at Lucca, Venice, Lake Leman, Geneva. Lucca in Tuscany would have been of special interest as the ancestral home of his best friend, Charles Diodati. That friend, alas, after entering his father's profession of physician, had died in August 1638 at the same age as Milton was when he wrote "Lycidas." Life had but too well imitated literature. The poet probably first got the news at Geneva, from the uncle Giovanni Diodati, a theologian and translator of the Bible into Italian and French.

This loss hit home so hard that the guise of a Latin pastoral was what the surviving friend, on his return, chose for its expression: he put it at a distance in the most formal way, including a reiterated choral line in which the sheep seventeen times are bid to go home unfed. Significant is the ending of "Epitaphium Damonis," in which Diodati (Damon) is translated to the pure ether that, dying unmarried, he deserves. By his youth without stain he has earned the heavenly rewards of those "which were not defiled with women; for they are virgins" (Rev. xiv, 4).

With this poem of 1640 the first period of Milton's life came to a close, a period of preparation and innocence and perfection in little. Twenty years in the public arena now ensued. From 1641 to 1660, from *Of Reformation touching Church Discipline in England* to *The Ready and Easy Way to Establish a Free Commonwealth,* he exchanged (in the words of his fourth pamphlet) "a calm and pleasing solitariness fed with cheerful and confident thoughts" for "a troubled sea of noises and hoarse disputes." Several of the early pamphlets make promise of poetry: "Readers, as I may one day hope to have ye in a still time, when there shall be no chiding." But it looked as if utopia had to come first. And utopia was dilatory.

Settling down in a "pretty garden house" in Aldersgate

Street, Milton, commencing with his two nephews, took up as a private occupation tutoring. As the clouds of civil war gathered, the first of the troubles on which, as a private citizen, he decided to let himself be heard was the need for ecclesiastical reform. The hungry sheep looked up and were not fed: so he had already concluded in "Lycidas," at a time when Scotland rose against the attempted imposition by Laud, Archbishop of Canterbury, of the Anglican Prayer Book on a kirk that had long been satisfied with Knox's Book of Common Order. Laud took note in his Diary of a charge "pasted on the Cross in Cheapside, that the arch-wolf of Canterbury had his hand in persecuting the saints." The saints were Puritans and Presbyterians, the former named for their desire to purge the English church of corrupt and Romish practices, which appeared to be on the increase under the Stuarts: the clergy were "wooden, illiterate, or contemptible," lazy and "tavern-haunting," the communion table was railed in and icons and kissing of the cross abounded, and confession was allowed, and violation of the sanctity of the Lord's Day encouraged. The archbishop had been offered a cardinal's hat. True Protestants were being harried out of the land—to Holland and America. A proud and tyrannous hierarchy put down individual opposition through the Court of High Commission, the ecclesiastical equivalent of the dreaded Star Chamber that pilloried and trimmed the ears of such doughty antiprelatical martyrs as Prynne, a lawyer, Burton, a clergyman, and Bastwick, a doctor.

The Long Parliament, which had been meeting since November 1640, was turning to questions of church government, and a Root and Branch Bill abolishing archbishops and bishops was up for consideration when Milton made his debut, anonymously, "amidst . . . deep and retired thoughts," as a pamphleteer in May 1641, with *Of Reformation touching Church Discipline in England, and the Causes that hitherto have hindered it: two books written to a friend.* The "friend" may be taken as Thomas Young, the author's former tutor, who in collaboration with four other Puritan divines was arguing in print with Bishop Joseph Hall and now welcomed a vigorous and scholarly ally, who followed this reasoned historical review with *Of Prelatical Episcopacy, Animadversions upon the Remonstrant's Defence against Smectymnuus* (a pseudonym formed by the initials of the five collaborators), *The Reason of Church Government Urged against Prelaty,* and *An Apology for Smectymnuus.*

What did the world of literature lose by a great poet's grimy descent into that arena where victory was not to be had over the adversary without much "dust and heat," if indeed victory was ever to be had, as obscure citations were answered by countercitations, dubious texts were endlessly wrangled over, and history was written to order? The argument, short on light but not on heat, waxed personal, with the Hall party claiming that their opponent, having been "vomited out" of the University, was looking for a "rich widow" to mend his fortunes. To these charges there was no reply but passionate autobiography and ever rougher language, lightened by jests about chamber pots and the stench of the episcopal foot.

Milton knew he was demeaning his genius. "I should not choose this manner of writing, wherein, knowing myself inferior to myself, led by the genial power of nature to another task, I have the use, as I may account it, but of my left hand."

But the poetic vein, the right hand, was evidently not ready, anyway, to flow freely to produce a large work. Milton did try, and he had more leisure in this twenty-year period than is generally realized. Between 1639 and 1641, and from 1645 to 1648, for instance, he entered no public frays and so, presumably, could have written poetry, if other conditions had been right. He kept a notebook in which he jotted down ninety-nine subjects for tragedies. The theme of Paradise Lost heads the list, since the Old Testament is raked through in order, but the brevity and miscellaneousness of most of the entries betray desperation or mere diligence. What could ever have been made (or so we ask, knowing that nothing ever was made) of "The Quails" (Num. xi) or "The Murmurers" (Num. xiv)? A number of topics are brutal or obscene: "Comazontes or the Benjaminites or the Rioters" (Judg. xix), "David Adulterous," "Moabitides or

Phineas," "Tamar" (2 Sam. xiii), "Solomon Gynaecocratomenus" (woman-governed).

What Milton had to go through in order to write *Paradise Lost* and *Samson Agonistes* can only be conjectured, but it is superficial to follow the well-known nineteenth-century biographer Mark Pattison in treating the period 1641–60 as years of deplorable waste, when Milton gave to party what was meant for mankind. "Our wish for Milton is that he should have placed himself from the beginning above party." To which Richard Garnett properly retorted, "We think, on the contrary, that such a mere man of letters as Pattison wishes that Milton had been could never have produced a *Paradise Lost*." Whether in prose or in verse, in *Paradise Lost* or the *History of Britain* or the *Doctrine and Discipline of Divorce*, Milton thought of himself as the counselor and teacher of his countrymen. He told a well-wisher in 1654: "I am far from thinking that I have spent my toil, as you seem to hint, on matters of inferior consequence." He included *Of Education* in the 1673 edition of his shorter poems. There are many connections between his prose and his verse, and Poe, for one, dramatically drew attention to the considerable stylistic merits of the former by preferring it to the latter. The life Milton led, political and domestic, the suffering and turmoil he underwent, the causes he won and lost, entered the long poems of his last period. Nor did he leave behind the equipment he had sharpened in the arena—his scholarship, his gift for satire, his passion.

Meanwhile this good citizen and schoolmaster, having issued the fifth and last of his antiprelatical tracts, having as he there wistfully says "spent and tired out almost a whole youth" in "wearisome labours and studious watchings," deemed it high time to get married, that spring of 1642. Edward Phillips, the elder nephew, tells the scant story of the sudden union of the thirty-three-year-old poet with a girl half his age who belonged to Royalist gentry and whose father owed his father five hundred pounds that had gone unpaid for fifteen years (a far cry from a "rich widow" she!). "About Whitsuntide it was, or a little after, that he took a journey into the country, nobody about him certainly knowing the reason, or that it was any more than a journey of recreation; after a month's stay, home he returns a married man, that went out a bachelor, his wife being Mary, the eldest daughter of Mr. Richard Powell, then a justice of peace, of Forresthill, near Shotover in Oxfordshire, some few of her nearest relations accompanying the bride to her new habitation; which, by reason the father nor anybody else were yet come, was able to receive them; where the feasting held for some days in celebration of the nuptials, and for entertainment of the bride's friends. At length they took their leave, and, returning to Forresthill, left the sister behind, probably not much to her satisfaction, as appeared by the sequel. By that time she had for a month or thereabout led a philosophical life (after having been used to a great house, and much company and joviality); her friends, possibly incited by her own desire, made earnest suit by letter to have her company the remaining part of the summer, which was granted, on condition of her return at the time appointed, Michaelmas, or thereabout."

Whitsuntide had been May 29. But Mary Powell Milton did not come back at Michaelmas, September 29. Another early biographer rounds out the tale. "Nor though he sent several pressing invitations could he prevail with her to return, till about [three] years after, when Oxford was surrendered (the nighness of her father's house to that garrison having for the most part of the meantime hindered any communication between them), she of her own accord came, and submitted to him, pleading that her mother had been the inciter of her to that frowardness."

This authority, the Anonymous Biographer, makes a connection with Milton's thinking about divorce, "the lawfulness and expedience of" which "had upon full consideration and reading good authors been formerly his opinion, and the necessity of justifying himself now concurring with the opportunity, acceptable to him, of instructing others in a point of so great concern." That deserted husband, having no assurance that his disaffected wife was ever coming back, published no less than four tracts on the new center of his interest: *The Doctrine and Discipline of Divorce; The Judgment of Martin*

Bucer, Concerning Divorce; Tetrachordon: Expositions upon the four chief places in Scripture which treat of marriage, or Nullities in Marriage; Colasterion: A Reply to a Nameless Answer against "The Doctrine and Discipline of Divorce."

This ever bolder thinker argued for divorce for incompatibility, grounds then utterly unknown. He achieved a succès de scandale, even being attacked by a preacher before Parliament. Mrs. Sadleir reproved Roger Williams for daring to recommend such an author: "For Milton's book that you desire I should read, if I be not mistaken, that is he that has wrote a book of the lawfulness of divorce, and, if report says true, he had, at that time, two or three wives living. This, perhaps, were good doctrine in New England, but it is most abominable in Old England." This may be a reflection of the rumor that Milton was at one time thinking of taking the backward law into his own hands by marrying a Miss Davis and thus presenting his first wife—and an unsympathetic Parliament—with a fait accompli. Such a rumor, true or not, may have hastened Mary Milton's return.

Also by then she had had an opportunity to see which side was winning the Civil War. The years of the publication of the divorce tracts, 1643–45, were the years of the military conflict between King and Parliament. At first the Royalists had the edge, but the organization and superb generalship and cavalry maneuvers of Cromwell's New Model Army enabled the Roundheads to win decisive victories at Marston Moor (1644) and Naseby (1645). Charles was forced to surrender at Newark in May 1646.

Meanwhile Milton, having begun with championing ecclesiastical liberty, was led to consider other branches of domestic liberty besides marriage—namely education and freedom of the press. On the invitation of a philanthropist and reformer named Samuel Hartlib he gave his rather formidable views *Of Education* (published June 1644). Two quotations are outstanding. "The end then of learning is to repair the ruins of our first parents by gaining to know God aright, and out of that knowledge to love him, to imitate him, to be like him, as we may the nearest by possessing our souls of true virtue, which being united to the heavenly grace of faith makes up the highest perfection." "I call therefore a complete and generous education that which fits a man to perform justly, skillfully, and magnanimously all the offices, both private and public, of peace and war." But the program of learning at the proposed academy—which was to be a combination of school and college—was such as only young Miltons could have been expected to encompass. This pamphlet was followed in November by the now famous but then ignored *Areopagitica: A Speech of Mr. John Milton for the Liberty of Unlicenced Printing,* objecting to the new censorship that Parliament had instituted after abolishing the Star Chamber, a censorship prior to publication that had made it necessary for the *Doctrine and Discipline of Divorce* to be issued unlicensed and unregistered.

During his prose period the poet kept his hand in with occasional sonnets, including a disillusioned "tailed" sonnet "On the New Forcers of Conscience under the Long Parliament." He began with one that bore the deleted title "On his Door when the City expected an Assault" (November 1642), and by the time he had completed fifteen others he had exhibited a considerable range—complimentary, admonitory, satirical, memorial, pleasantly social, deeply personal. At the end of 1645, after, with his wife's return, taking up residence in a larger house in the Barbican, he saw through the press a collected edition of his English and Latin poems. The publisher was Humphrey Moseley, who persisted in specializing in poetry and pure literature in a time of troubles when political pamphlets and sermons were "more vendible." He now called the attention of the discriminating reader to "as true a birth as the Muses have brought forth since our famous Spenser wrote." The little volume has long been rarer than the first editions of *Paradise Lost.* The diarists Pepys and Evelyn were among the early purchasers, and a presentation copy to Oxford got lost; the poet sent another, and with it an eighty-seven-line ode to Rous, the Bodleian librarian, that was destined (except for a couple of epigrams) to be the last of his Latin poems. The portrait of the author that served as the frontispiece of this small octavo was so badly done that Milton took advantage of the bungling engraver's barbarous ignorance by having him inscribe underneath four lines of Greek iambics that made fun of his ineptness.

Nothing is known about Milton's first marriage after his wife lived with him again except that she bore him three daughters (and a son John that died in infancy) and died in childbirth of Deborah, May 5, 1652, by which time the poet was blind. The first two daughters were Anne, a cripple, born July 29, 1646, and Mary, born October 25, 1648. Milton did not get along with his mother-in-law, and it must have been a strain when his wife's family, sequestered from their estate with the fall of Oxford (June 1646) moved in on him. The Barbican house saw, early in 1647, the death of both his father-in-law and his father. On hearing that spring from his old Florentine friend Dati, he sent him a cri de coeur: "a something heavier creeps in upon me, to which I am accustomed in very frequent grievings over my own lot: the sense, namely, that those whom the mere necessity of neighbourhood, or something else of a useless kind, has closely conjoined with me, whether by accident or by the tie of law, *they* are the persons, though in no other respect commendable, who sit daily in my company, weary me, nay, by heaven, all but plague me to death whenever they are jointly in the humour for it, whereas those whom habits, disposition, studies, had so handsomely made my friends, are now almost all denied me, either by death or by most unjust separation of place, and are so for the most part snatched from my sight that I have to live well-nigh in a perpetual solitude."

In 1648 "the false North," as the sonnet "On the Lord General Fairfax at the Siege of Colchester" puts it, displayed "her broken league," when the Scots changed sides and took up arms for Charles in return for his promise to establish Presbyterianism as the sole form of church in England. Cromwell won at Preston, and at last the difficult decision was made to try the King, who had long been playing one faction against another, for treason. A purged Parliament—the so-called "Rump"—gave this legal sanction. At this juncture Milton composed his first political pamphlet, *The Tenure of Kings and Magistrates: Proving that it is Lawful and hath been held so through all Ages, for any, who have the Power, to call to account a Tyrant or Wicked King. . . .* Written during the trial, it appeared two weeks after the King was beheaded outside his palace of Whitehall, an act that forced a groan from even the most republican of the witnesses. The second of the Stuart kings bravely met the same fate as Laud in 1645 and that proud tyrannical agent the Earl of Strafford in 1641.

In the words of the nephew of Milton, "for this his last treatise, reviving the fame of other things he had formerly published, being more and more taken notice of for his excellency of style and depth of judgement, he was courted into the service of this new Commonwealth" by being invited, one month after publication, to serve as Secretary for the Foreign Tongues. This involved being responsible for despatches in the diplomatic language of the day, Latin.

Milton's English was soon called into play again too, for the body of the executed king was scarcely cold when an apology, *Eikon Basilike, the Portraiture of his Sacred Majesty in his Solitudes and Sufferings,* appeared in his name and achieved enormous underground circulation— "there's such divinity doth hedge a king"—going through about fifty editions the first twelve months. *Eikon Basilike* (the King's Book or King's Image) proved such a potent instrument in stirring up sympathy for the royal martyr (who was shown handsomely at his prayers in the frontispiece—by the same engraver who had dealt badly by Milton three years before) that the Council of State gave the order for Milton's *Eikonoklastes* (the Image-breaker). The new official went about this assignment with no great rush of enthusiasm, observing in his first sentence, "To descant on the misfortunes of a person fallen from so high a dignity, who hath also paid his final debt both to nature and his faults, is neither of itself a thing commendable nor the intention of this discourse." The same author was also commissioned to do *Observations upon the Articles of Peace with the Irish Rebels.*

Thus, after having moved into official quarters in

Whitehall, Milton, despite failing health and eyesight, laboured valiantly for the republican regime, writing state letters in Latin and taking on, by assignment, one opponent after another. The most famous internationally of these was not the late King, who, most scholars agree, had little to do with the composition of *Eikon Basilike:* at the Restoration Bishop John Gauden claimed the honor (and rewards) of its authorship. The dangerous new foe was Claudius Salmasius, a French scholar and polymath, who, for one hundred jacobuses from the King's son, blackened the new regime at home and abroad with his *Defensio Regia Pro Carolo I* (Royal Defense in behalf of Charles I), some five hundred pages of vituperation and pedantry. Milton spent his remaining eyesight in preparing his voluminous, point-by-point reply, *Pro Populo Anglicano Defensio* (Defense of the English People).

Whatever the modern reader's disappointment in what seems fantastically abusive, legalistic, outrageously personal, dully grammatical, controversy—Hobbes professed to be unable to decide between the opponents whose language was best, or whose arguments were worst—the learned looked on with fascination at this battle between titans of scholarship in an age that respected scholarship and cared about such a question— as Dr. Johnson still did a century later—as to whether "vapulo," which has a passive meaning, could be used as a gerundive. However, Johnson concluded contemptuously, "No man forgets his original trade: the rights of nations, and of kings, sink into questions of grammar, if grammarians discuss them."

Milton's attitude, needless to say, was different. He alluded in a sonnet to the "noble task/ Of which all Europe talks from side to side." He felt the game was worth the candle—the last gleam of his light. He was satisfied to "have prosperously, God so favouring me, defended the public cause of this Commonweal to foreigners"—who could never read his English works. A modern commentator perhaps captures his attitude when he says, "In some true if incomplete sense he was delivering to the world, in his first and second Defence of the English People, that epic 'doctrinal and exemplary to a nation' to which he had early dedicated his powers.''

Salmasius was basking at the court of Christina, enjoying the favor that the Swedish queen regularly accorded scholars and artists, when, in the spring of 1651, Milton's reply fell on him. If Keats, as Byron thought, was killed by bad reviews, Salmasius did not live long after this either, though against the charge that he died of shame at being worsted in Latin, law, history, logic, and invective is his lifelong record of poor health: the Spa waters (he could no longer face Christina) were perhaps what finished him. (He and Milton were the same age when they died.) He threatened an answer that he never completed (a fragment was published at the Restoration).

What is interesting is the contrast. There but for the grace of poetry and integrity and sturdy good sense, Milton might have gone. There was no lack of energy in either: Salmasius published more than fifty books in such diverse fields as theology, medicine, jurisprudence, and botany, and was particularly eminent as a classical editor and commentator. Milton made a respectful reference to him in the *Reason of Church Government*. In many ways Salmasius was an anti-Milton before he was aware of the poet. Salmasius also began with an interest in belles-lettres, but his father wanted him to study law, and his father prevailed (compare "Ad Patrem"). However, instead of writing the wistful lines, though he did do some Latin poetry—"Were it not better done, as others use,/ To sport with Amaryllis in the shade?"—young Salmasius frankly sported. Both he and Milton married in their middle thirties—and lived to regret it. He and Milton entered the episcopal controversy at the same time (1641), but the one betrayed—for a sizable fee—the principles he had enunciated, so that Milton was able to quote Salmasius versus Salmasius. Salmasius, whose profoundest faculty was his memory, was giddy with his fantastic load of learning; Milton felt within himself the dichotomy of creative writer and critic or scholar, which he found various ways of seeking to mend.

But in 1652, if Salmasius was sulking in disrepute, Milton, awaiting his promised reply (but attacked by others

instead), was blind and a widower, bereft of an infant
son and with three small daughters to bring up. His
blindness had come gradually over a nine-year period,
the left eye failing first. His works contain many references to it, most famously two passages in *Paradise Lost*
(iii, 1–55; vii, 24–30) and the sonnet that begins, "When
I consider how my light is spent" and ends, "They also
serve who only stand and wait." He sent a friend, who
had held out hopes of treatment by a famous Parisian
specialist, a detailed clinical account, but modern stu-
dents of the subject, including ophthalmologists, do not
agree on a diagnosis. His enemies—the enemies of the
government he had wielded his pen for—saw it as a punishment from Heaven. The literary critic is left to wonder about its influence on his three long poems, which
in compensation develop the aural over the visual. Is it
accidental, or dictated solely by subject, that *Paradise
Lost,* that microcosm, that "little world made cunningly," depends for most of its effects—including the
moral—on the alternation of light and darkness? The
last ocular perceptions Milton had were flashes of light.

In 1654 Milton published a work shorter and of better
quality than his first Defense, namely his Second Defense, *Defensio Secunda.* Salmasius had defaulted and
died; his confuter, who had been reserving his strength,
could now attend to another opponent, the author of
Regii Sanguinis Clamor, The Cry of the Royal Blood to
Heaven. The question was, as with *Eikon Basilike,* who
was the author? Milton took it to be Alexander More
or Morus, who in fact was merely the editor; the true
author, Peter Du Moulin the younger, "looked on in
silence, and not without a soft chuckle, at seeing my
bantling laid at another man's door, and the blind and
furious Milton fighting and slashing the air, like the
hoodwinked horse-combatants in the old circus, not
knowing by whom he was struck and whom he struck in
return." The Second Defense is witty at the expense of
More, a Greek professor and theologian with a scandalous private life (including an affair with Salmasius' ser-
vantmaid Pontia) that Milton relentlessly ferrets out,
sparing no punning aMorous detail. But the enduring
interest of the *Defensio Secunda* lies in what is serious—

autobiography and the encomia of the new leaders and their having built for freedom (though that foundation was already slipping, as Milton gave warning signs of realizing). The form was oratorical, like *Areopagitica*. In the words of Hanford, "In the *First Defence* Milton's ardor is in part factitious; he is more the controversialist, using the accepted weapons of the day. In the *Second Defence,* he is John Milton himself, rising in wrath and dignity against the enemies of truth."

Milton also rose in wrath in one of the greatest of his sonnets, "On the Late Massacre in Piedmont," on the occasion of the treacherous slaughter, on April 24, 1655, of a pristine Protestant sect, the Waldenses or Vaudois, that had been living under a toleration treaty in northwest Italy. The fourteen lines are a veritable onomatopoeia of grief and rage. The writer said some of the same things in Latin, as Cromwell promptly responded to the call for help and sent a special ambassador and was in fact ready to go to war.

Meanwhile Milton continued his pen-war with More, issuing *Pro Se Defensio,* Defense in his Own Behalf, but he was gradually obliged—or inclined—to be less active in matters relating to the state and his salary was reduced, as younger men—eventually the poet Andrew Marvell—were called on to assist him. He worked now on his *History of Britain* (up to the Norman conquest), published 1670, and the heretical treatise *De Doctrina Christiana* (On the Christian Doctrine) that first saw the light in 1825 and casts doubt on the orthodoxy of *Paradise Lost.*

He made a love match with a woman twenty years younger and whom there is no reason to believe he had ever seen—much of the pathos of the moving sonnet "On his Deceased Wife" depends on this. Katherine Woodcock became his bride November 12, 1656, only to die less than fifteen months later following the birth of a daughter named after her, and the next month the infant was buried too. These are the bare facts of a marriage that the sonnet "Methought I saw my late espousèd Saint" (it would be his last sonnet) indicates to have been as happy as it was brief. "But O, as to embrace me she inclin'd,/ I wak'd, she fled, and day brought back my night."

There was nothing to do now but to hear of the latest turns of events with increasing concern and start *Paradise Lost*. Cromwell, who had become virtually a dictator (though a reluctant one), "King Oliver," had died (the Latin Secretary marched in his funeral procession), and his son, Richard, proved an incompetent successor. The seeds were sown for the Restoration. Milton's countrymen were "backsliding." He gave them last admonitions, both on the ecclesiastical and on the political front. In 1659 he issued *A Treatise of Civil Power in Ecclesiastical Causes* and *Considerations Touching the Likeliest Means to Remove Hirelings out of the Church*. A year later, after General Monck with his troops had entered London and was about to give the necessary nod of approval to the reestablishment of the monarchy, Milton pleaded for a perpetual "grand council" "of ablest men" instead, in *The Ready and Easy Way to Establish a Free Commonwealth*. In April appeared an enlarged edition of these "last words of our expiring liberty," not so much with the vain thought of stemming the tide "as to confirm them who yield not." There the upbringing of Charles II is glanced at forebodingly, and as it turned out correctly: "What liberty of conscience can we then expect of others, far worse principled from the cradle, trained up and governed by popish and Spanish counsels, and on such depending hitherto for subsistence?" The new king did in fact become a pensioner of Louis XIV.

The second edition of *The Ready and Easy Way* prudently omits name of printer or stationer, but the initials of the author—who was taking his life into his hands—are boldly imprinted on the title page for all to see, with a motto that indicates that, Monck himself being despaired of, the good citizens themselves are now exhorted (but not the mob, the vulgar multitude, whom this believer in the elite distrusted as much as an absolute monarch).

Charles II, restored in May, left it to the Convention Parliament to decide who, such as regicides, should be excepted from the general amnesty he had proclaimed in the Declaration of Breda before he landed. It was touch-and-go whether Milton would suffer capital punishment. Perhaps the damage he had done—or sought to do—was not so known to his judges as he, going now into hiding, believed; moreover, "our author had many good friends to intercede for him both in the Privy Council and in the House of Commons"—e.g., Marvell. That visitation, his blindness, which was much mocked during this period by pamphleteers, may have been thought punishment enough, along with certain heavy financial losses he faced. In June the *Defensio (Prima)* and *Eikonoklastes* were ordered burned, and a warrant went out for the author's arrest, but he could not then be located. A dozen victims went to the gallows ultimately, including Milton's heroic friend Sir Harry Vane, one of history's noblest figures and a great champion of liberty (he had been elected governor of Massachusetts at twenty-two, but, like Roger Williams, proved too liberal for that colony and moved out), to whom the poet (who, by the way, had studied Dutch with Williams) had addressed a sonnet that was published as part of an obituary in 1662. The bones of Cromwell and other already dead associates were "dragged to Tyburn, there to hang for some time, and afterwards be buried under the gallows." Milton was found and taken into custody, but ordered released December 15, 1660. Whereupon he indignantly protested to the Commons (through Marvell) that the sergeant-at-arms had charged him excessive fees during his imprisonment. Nothing is more characteristic of the man than that he thus insisted on his rights, when an ordinary mortal would have been glad to slink away free, though not scot-free, free and alive. Horrible remnants were all around him, including, at the top of Westminster Hall, the grinning head of John Bradshaw, formerly President of the Council of State, who may have been his cousin and who, before he, like Cromwell, frustrated the avengers by dying too soon, had named the poet in his will for ten pounds. Under date of October 13, 1660, Pepys made a famous entry about the demeanor of one of the living victims: "I went out to Charing Cross, to see Major-general Harrison hanged, drawn, and quartered; which was done there, he looking as cheerful as any man could do in that condition. He was presently cut down, and his head and heart shown to the people, at which there was great shouts of joy. It is said that he said that he was sure to come shortly at the right hand of Christ to judge them that now had judged him, and that his wife do expect his coming again. Thus it was my chance to see the King beheaded at White Hall, and to see the first blood shed in revenge for the blood of the King at Charing Cross."

Out of the ruins and out of the darkness Milton brought *Paradise Lost, Paradise Regained,* and *Samson Agonistes*—a long epic, a short epic, and a Greek tragedy, all without rivals in the language. It was a miracle of the spirit—of, he intimated, the Holy Spirit, for he was strong and insistent in his belief in the sacredness of his inspiration.

The Anonymous Biographer tells about his habits of composition. "And he waking early (as is the use of temperate men), had commonly a good stock of verses ready against his amanuensis came; which if it happened to be later than ordinary, he would complain, saying, 'he wanted to be milked.' The evenings he likewise spent in reading some choice poets, by way of refreshment after the day's toil, and to store his fancy against morning." This last statement is confirmed by *Paradise Lost,* iii, 29 ff.

According to Aubrey, *Paradise Lost* was finished in 1663. In any case it was finished by the fall of 1665, when the Quaker Ellwood saw the complete manuscript. It may not have been easy to find a publisher for it; it would not be easy now. It did not come out until 1667.

In that year of possible completion (1663), Milton entered upon his third and last marriage, a *mariage de convenance,* February 24, with Elizabeth Minshull, some thirty years younger. The blind widower was having trouble with his daughters—according to the testimony of a maidservant, Mary said, "if she could hear of his death, that was something," and "his said children had made away some of his books and would have sold the rest of his books to the dunghill woman." The household needed a mistress, and a physician friend supplied a young kinswoman for the purpose. All that is known of her up to her last days—she reached ninety (no risky childbirths for her!)—in her native Nantwich points to her having made a satisfactory wife (though not a good stepmother—perhaps it was impossible to be both) in a marriage that could not have begun very romantically, despite the fact that her hair, like Eve's, was gold. In his nuncupative (oral) will, Milton called her "my loving wife." As for the daughters by the first marriage, they may have been going through just the usual adolescent rebellion. It is a myth perpetuated by a bad painting at the New York Public Library that the three of them were depended upon as amanuenses of *Paradise Lost*— Milton had professionals to help him, and friends who were glad to help him for nothing or for what they could hear from him. We do have a telling bon mot (which was or became a proverb) when the question of his daughters' knowing another language came up: "One tongue is enough for a woman." In sum, our author, however radical, was not a feminist. He did call on two of his daughters to read to him in languages they did not understand.

The family moved to the father's last London residence, "in the Artillery-walk leading to Bunhill Fields." The only change was in the summer of 1665 when his young friend Ellwood found him a cottage at Chalfont St. Giles, twenty-three miles from London, as a refuge from the plague (till the beginning of 1666). That rustic place, still spared invasion by the main road, is the only one of Milton's dozen residences that survives and can be visited. At the village manor had lived the family of Fleetwood, three of whom had signed Charles's death warrant. Now their estates had been taken from them, and they scattered; Milton found no friends to welcome him on his arrival, for Ellwood, having had one of his Dissenter conflicts with the authorities, was in jail.

It is this Quaker who tells in his autobiography an anecdote about the composition of *Paradise Regained,* 2070 lines of blank verse in four books on the temptations of Jesus in the wilderness. Having been shown the manuscript of *Paradise Lost* at Chalfont St. Giles and encouraged to speak freely, he "pleasantly said to" the author, " 'Thou hast said much here of Paradise Lost, but what hast thou to say of Paradise Found?' He made me no answer, but sat some time in a muse; then brake off that discourse, and fell upon another subject. After the sickness was over, and the city well cleansed, and become safely habitable again, he returned thither. And when afterwards I went to wait on him there (which I seldom failed of doing, whenever my occasions drew me to London), he showed me his second poem, called *Paradise Regained,* and in a pleasant tone said to me, 'This is owing to you, for you put it into my head by the question you put to me at Chalfont, which before I had not thought of.' " A completion date of 1666 or 1667 is thus indicated. Milton held it back, however, waiting to see how *Paradise Lost* would fare. *Paradise Regained* was published with *Samson Agonistes* in 1671. Needless to say, modern critics look deeper than Ellwood for the poem's inspiration, which may go back to the days when Milton was calling the Book of Job a brief epic (in *The Reason of Church Government*)—as St. Jerome had done—and to a desire to excel in all the principal forms. The shorter epic, Phillips was already reporting in 1694, was "generally censured to be much inferior to the other, though he could not hear with patience any such thing when related to him." *Paradise Regained* is in a plain style in keeping with the asceticism of its hero and uninvitingness of its setting. It is a debate, with just two characters, Jesus and Satan. Nearly all dialogue, it has been called dramatic and even thought originally designed, perhaps, as a play. There are, however, appropriate outbursts of the virtuoso allusive Milton of yore—he had not lost his old powers. He was proving, as with *Samson Agonistes* (which pioneers with what amounts to free verse), his power to go on to other styles, and must have been impatient with those who expected him to sound always the same.

The former pedagogue also published textbooks. *Accidence Commenced,* a simplified Latin grammar, came out in 1669, and was followed by a Latin Logic in 1672. These are remarkable publications to follow *Paradise Lost* and precede an enlarged edition of the minor poems in 1673. Wordsworth in the sonnet commencing, "Milton! thou shouldst be living at this hour," observed,

"Thy soul was like a Star, and dwelt apart," but the sonnet concludes, with no less wonder, "and yet thy heart/ The lowliest duties on herself did lay." Milton worked on many things during his lifetime, including a Latin dictionary. *A Brief History of Muscovia* was found and published after his death. So were his Letters of State—with the apology that they were interesting for their style. *Paradise Lost* having proved vendible—he received ultimately fifteen pounds for it (the equivalent of two thousand dollars in today's money)—the book-sellers sought him out for anything not too subversive he had lying around. To this is to be attributed the publication of his college oratorical exercises as an addition to his Familiar Letters, 1674: "to fill up the space and compensate for the paucity of the letters" (as the "Print-er's Preface to the Reader" candidly explains).

In that year, the last of his life, a second edition of *Paradise Lost* was called for; he made twelve books, a more epic number, out of the original ten by dividing Books vii and x, adding some necessary connecting lines. He also put out *A Declaration or Letters Patents of the Election of this Present King of Poland.* The year before, after thirteen years of silence as a pamphleteer, he shot a last fusillade with *Of True Religion,* his most anti-Romish tract, amid widespread fears that Charles II (that crypto-Catholic warned against in *The Ready and Easy Way*) was paving the way for popery with his Dec-laration of Indulgence suspending the penal statutes against Catholics and Dissenters; the latter indignantly declined toleration at the cost of its being granted to the former.

Thus the last years of a versatile teacher, who never retired and who barely reached retirement age, were busy and, after the departure of the daughters—they were "sent out to learn some curious and ingenious sorts of manufacture, that are proper for women to learn, par-ticularly embroideries in gold or silver"—outwardly calm. "Of a very cheerful humour," noted Aubrey, "and only towards his later end he was visited with the gout spring and fall: he would be cheerful even in his gout-fits and sing." "He was visited much by learned: more than he did desire. . . . Foreigners came much to see him." Dryden, the poet laureate, who had exclaimed over *Paradise Lost,* "This man cuts us all out, and the ancients too!" requested and received permission to make a rhymed "opera" of the epic. The resulting *State of Innocence and Fall of Man* is one of the curiosities of literary history and was part of a continuing controversy over blank verse versus rhyme.

Milton died around November 9, 1674, of "gout struck in." "He died . . . with so little pain or emotion, that the time of his expiring was not perceived by those in the room." He was buried "in the Church of St. Giles Cripplegate, being attended from his house to the church by several gentlemen then in town, his principal well-wishers and admirers."

As with Shakespeare, Milton's direct line soon died out, although the families of his brother and his sister have gone on into this century. His daughter Deborah Milton Clarke and his long-lived widow expired within a day or two of each other in August 1727. Dr. Johnson wrote a prologue for a benefit performance of "Comus" in 1750 for the poet's granddaughter, Mrs. Elizabeth Foster. She, the last living direct descendant, lingered on poorly till 1754, thereby reaching the age of her grandfather, sixty-five.

—Edward Le Comte

PARADISE LOST

The primary source of *Paradise Lost* is the Bible with all
its commentators (including the rabbinical) and expanders.
It must be remembered that Milton had an audience that
knew one book better than we know any book. One inves-
tigator has counted nine hundred thirteen references from
the Old Testament and four hundred ninety from the New,
but of course what the reader should be fresh on primarily
is Genesis, i–iii, in the King James version (which Milton
often quotes verbatim). The rebellion and battle in heaven
indicated in Revelation, xii, 4, 7–9, and Isaiah, xiv, 12–15,
had been fleshed out in many a patristic or poetical account by Milton's day.

The reader should also be fresh on Homer's *Iliad* and
Virgil's *Aeneid* as the prime epic models affecting the
form and structure and even the story of *Paradise Lost*.
It is better to know these two epics well, for the sometimes surprising recognitions that come, than to have
merely a nodding acquaintance with the multifarious other
influences that make Milton's poem the encyclopedia of
allusions—biblical, geographic, mythological, classical, literary, historical, scientific—that it is.

One of its most useful cultural services today is to acquaint the reader, perhaps even the churchgoing reader,
with Christian theology. One must beware, however, of
concluding that Milton was what we should call a funda-
mentalist Christian: he had to seem to be, to function as
a poet, since poetry is more happily built of the concrete
than the abstract. Did he believe that Sin and Death, palpable shapes, built a palpable causeway from Hell to
Earth? Was he sure of the location of Hell? Did he believe
that Satan personally invented gunpowder and that angels
ever wore armor? Is everything in his poem presented as
gospel truth necessary to salvation? One gets perspective
by asking parallel questions about the poems of Homer
and Virgil, although there was always for Milton a sense
in which he was embodying the truth, while the pagans
dealt with "an empty dream" (vii, 39).

THE VERSE

THE measure is English heroic verse without rhyme, as that of Homer in Greek, and of Virgil in Latin—rhyme being no necessary adjunct or true ornament of poem or good verse, in longer works especially, but the invention of a barbarous age, to set off wretched matter and lame metre; graced indeed since by the use of some famous modern poets, carried away by custom, but much to their own vexation, hindrance, and constraint to express many things otherwise, and for the most part worse, than else they would have expressed them. Not without cause, therefore, some both Italian and Spanish poets of prime note have rejected rhyme both in longer and shorter works, as have also long since our best English tragedies, as a thing of itself, to all judicious ears, trivial and of no true musical delight; which consists only in apt numbers, fit quantity of syllables, and the sense variously drawn out from one verse into another, not in the jingling sound of like endings—a fault avoided by the learned ancients both in poetry and all good oratory. This neglect then of rhyme so little is to be taken for a defect, though it may seem so perhaps to vulgar readers, that it rather is to be esteemed an example set—the first in English—of ancient liberty recovered to heroic poem from the troublesome and modern bondage of riming.

BOOK I

THE ARGUMENT°

The First Book proposes, first in brief, the whole subject—Man's disobedience, and the loss thereupon of Paradise, wherein he was placed; then touches the prime cause of his fall—the Serpent, or rather Satan in the Serpent; who, revolting from God, and drawing to his side many legions of Angels, was, by the command of God, driven out of Heaven, with all his crew, into the great Deep. Which action passed over, the Poem hastens into the midst of things, presenting Satan, with his Angels, now fallen into Hell—described here not in the Centre (for heaven and earth may be supposed as yet not made, certainly not yet accursed), but in a place of utter darkness, fitliest called Chaos. Here Satan, with his Angels lying on the burning lake, thunderstruck and astonished, after a certain space recovers, as from confusion; calls up him who, next in order and dignity, lay by him: they confer of their miserable fall. Satan awakens all his legions, who lay till then in the same manner confounded. They rise: their numbers; array of battle; their chief leaders named, according to the idols known afterwards in Canaan and the countries adjoining. To these Satan directs his speech; comforts them with hope yet of regaining Heaven; but tells them, lastly, of a new world and new kind of creature to be created, according to an ancient prophecy, or report, in Heaven—for that Angels were long before this visible creation was the opinion of many ancient Fathers. To find out the truth of this prophecy, and what to determine thereon, he refers to a full council. What his associates

The first issue of *Paradise Lost* did not have "The Argument" for each book—convenient summaries of the plot such as were customary with long or epic poems. The poet made the addition (which sometimes forms a supplement to the poem worth studying) "for the satisfaction of many that have desired it."

*thence attempt. Pandemonium, the palace of Satan, rises,
suddenly built out of the Deep; the infernal Peers there
sit in council.*

    OF Man's° first disobedience and the fruit°
    Of that forbidden tree° whose mortal taste°
    Brought death into the world and all our woe,
    With loss of Eden, till one greater Man°
5 Restore us and regain the blissful seat,
    Sing, Heavenly Muse, that on the secret top
    Of Oreb° or of Sinai didst inspire
    That shepherd who first taught the chosen seed
    In the beginning° how the heavens and earth
10 Rose out of Chaos;° or, if Sion hill

1–16 The first sentence is typical of the style of *Paradise Lost*—
in syntax, in vocabulary, in multiple-choice allusiveness, and in
"the sense variously drawn out from one verse into another."
The word order is Latin—object first, main verb held in
reverse, with subordinate clauses suspended in between, or
clustered afterwards. Where modern poetry aims to be
colloquial, Milton stands on epic ceremony, aims for the
exalted and magniloquent. 1 **Of Man's** Eve, formed from
Adam's rib; cf. viii, 465 ff., 495 ff. **fruit** not to be taken
literally only, but also in the sense of outcome (compare Eve's
"fruitless" pun, ix, 648; also ix, 1073). 2 **forbidden tree** One
meaning is "the forbidding of the tree," just as the title means
"The Losing of Paradise" and "since created Man" (573)
"since the creation of Man." "Forbidden tree" is the first of
many phrases (like fixed epithets in Homer) to return: x, 554.
mortal taste "deadly taste" and "taste by mortals." 4 **one
greater Man** the Messiah. "For as by one man's disobedience
many were made sinners, so by the obedience of one shall
many be made righteous." Romans, v, 19. 7 **Oreb** Horeb,
"the mountain of God" (Ex. iii, 1 ff., where Moses is identified
as literally a shepherd) in Arabia near Mount Sinai (sometimes
equated with Sinai or treated as a lower spur), where the Lord
appeared to Moses in the burning bush. 9 **In the beginning**
a punning recognition of Moses as the author of Genesis 10
Rose out of Chaos Milton's first heresy, the orthodox view
being that God created *ex nihilo,* that before creation was only
"void" (Gen. i, 2). The identical expression appeared in the
Doctrine and Discipline of Divorce: "the world first rose out
of Chaos" (end of Ch. X).

Delight thee more, and Siloa's brook that flowed°
Fast by the oracle of God, I thence
Invoke thy aid to my adventurous song,
That with no middle flight intends to soar
Above the° Aonian mount,° while it pursues   15
Things unattempted yet in prose or rhyme.°
And chiefly Thou, O Spirit,° that dost prefer
Before all temples the upright heart and pure,
Instruct me, for Thou know'st; Thou from the first
Wast present, and, with mighty wings outspread,   20
Dovelike sat'st brooding° on the vast° Abyss
And mad'st it pregnant: what in me is dark
Illumine, what is low raise and support,
That, to the height° of this great argument,°
I may assert Eternal Providence,   25

10–11 In contrast to the pagan mounts (cf. 15) and springs
are hailed those of Moses, then the Mount Zion of David
the psalmist, and finally Siloa, a pool outside Jerusalem
flowing past the Temple, with the waters of which Jesus
healed a blind man (John ix, 7). The line throughout (cf. vii,
39; ix, 13 ff.) is that a better source, holy, true—a muse
that is none of the pagan Nine but the Heavenly Spirit,
17—makes a greater poem, even as the Jesus of *Paradise
Regained* (iv, 346–47) found Greek and Roman literature
"unworthy to compare/ With Sion's songs." The first
paragraph encompasses the Trinity of God's activities—
Creator, Redeemer, Inspirer. **15 the** Here, as regularly in
his work, Milton, in keeping with the convention of his time,
put *"th',"* to signal that the *e* was not to be counted in the
scansion before the following vowel. Today's reader may be
more distracted than helped by this device; accordingly, the
e has been restored in *th'* and many other words, e.g.,
count'nance, fall'n, Heav'n, wand'ring. **Aonian mount**
Helicon in Boeotia, sacred to the Muses **16 This proud
boast** (compare "Comus," 44–45) echoes Boiardo and
Ariosto ironically. **rhyme** verse, whether rhymed or not **17
Spirit** a monosyllable **21 brooding** a more accurate
translation of the Hebrew than the King James Version
"moved" (Gen. i, 2) or the Revised Standard "was moving."
Sir Thomas Browne spoke of "that gentle heat that brooded
on the waters, and in six days hatched the World." **vast**
wasted, lifeless. **24 height** Milton's spelling and pronunciation were "highth." **argument** The basic meaning is
"subject."

And justify the ways of God to men.°
    Say first—for Heaven hides nothing from thy view,
Nor the deep tract of Hell—say first what cause
Moved our grand Parents, in that happy state,
30 Favoured of Heaven so highly, to fall off
From their Creator and transgress his will,
For one restraint, lords of the world besides?
Who first seduced them to that foul revolt?°
The infernal Serpent; he it was whose guile,
35 Stirred up with envy and revenge, deceived
The mother of mankind, what time his pride°
Had cast him out from Heaven, with all his host
Of rebel Angels, by whose aid aspiring
To set himself in glory above his peers,
40 He trusted to have equalled the Most High,
If he° opposed, and with ambitious aim
Against the throne and monarchy of God
Raised impious war in Heaven and battle proud,
With vain attempt. Him the Almighty Power
45 Hurled headlong flaming from the ethereal° sky,
With hideous ruin° and combustion° down
To bottomless perdition, there to dwell
In adamantine chains and penal fire,
Who durst defy the Omnipotent to arms.
50 Nine times the space that measures day and night
To mortal men, he with his horrid crew
Lay vanquished, rolling in the fiery gulf,
Confounded, though immortal; but his doom
Reserved him to more wrath, for now the thought
55 Both of lost happiness and lasting pain
Torments him: round he throws his baleful eyes,
That witnessed huge affliction and dismay,
Mixed with obdúrate pride and steadfast hate;

26 The normal prose order would be: "And justify to men the ways of God." Cf. *Samson Agonistes,* 293–94. **men** often misquoted as "man," perhaps under the influence of Pope's "Laugh where we must, be candid where we can;/ But vindicate the ways of God to man" (*Essay on Man,* 15–16). 27–33 After the Invocation the Epic Question 36 **pride** key word, key sin, in both the fall of angels and the fall of man. *vain attempt* (44) is deadly serious wordplay. 41 **he** Satan 45 **ethereal** Note the literal use. 46 **ruin** Latin *ruina,* a fall (the same pun is brilliant at iv, 522) **combustion** "burning together"

At once, as far as angel's ken,° he views
The dismal situation waste and wild;   60
A dungeon horrible, on all sides round,
As one great furnace flamed, yet from those flames
No light, but rather darkness visible°
Served only to discover sights of woe,
Regions of sorrow, doleful shades, where peace   65
And rest can never dwell, hope never comes
That comes to all,° but torture without end
Still urges, and a fiery deluge, fed
With ever-burning sulphur unconsumed.
Such place Eternal Justice had prepared   70
For those rebellious, here their prison ordained
In utter° darkness, and their portion set,
As far removed from God and light of Heaven
As from the centre thrice to the utmost pole.
Oh, how unlike the place from whence they fell!   75
There the companions of his fall, o'erwhelmed
With floods and whirlwinds of tempestuous fire,
He soon discerns, and, weltering° by his side,
One next himself in power, and next in crime,
Long after known in Palestine, and named   80
Beëlzebub.° To whom the Arch-Enemy,
And thence in Heaven called Satan,° with bold words
Breaking the horrid silence, thus began:

59 **angel's ken** The original has no apostrophe, an omission
which proves nothing but leaves it uncertain as to whether
"ken" is a noun or a verb. It is a noun in the next use, iii,
622. 63 It was an old conception that Hell, though "teeming
with flame," was "void of light" (Anglo-Saxon Caedmonian
poem, *Genesis B*), a place "where the light is as darkness"
(Job x, 22). Cf. 181–83 and "Il Penseroso" (79–80) "Where
glowing embers through the room/ Teach light to counterfeit
a gloom." The paradox was too much for Milton's eccentric
editor of 1732, Richard Bentley, who emended the epic line to
read, "No light, but rather a transpicuous gloom." 66–67
hope never comes/ That comes to all (others), the greatest inner
torment of hell, as famously indicated in Dante's "*Lasciate ogni
speranza, voi ch'entrate*" (*Inferno*, iii, 9) 72 **utter** outer 78
weltering tossing 81 **Beëlzebub** "God of flies" 82 **Satan**
"the Adversary"

'If thou beest he—but oh, how fallen! how changed
85 From him who, in the happy realms of light,°
Clothed with transcendent brightness, didst outshine
Myriads, though bright!—if he whom mutual league,
United thoughts and counsels, equal hope
And hazard in the glorious enterprise,°
90 Joined with me once, now misery hath joined
In equal ruin; into what pit thou seest
From what height fallen: so much the stronger proved
He with his thunder—and till then who knew
The force of those dire arms? Yet not for those,
95 Nor what the potent Victor in his rage
Can else inflict, do I repent or change,
Though changed in outward lustre, that fixed mind,
And high disdain from sense of injured merit,
That with the Mightiest raised me to contend,
100 And to the fierce contention brought along
Innumerable force of Spirits armed
That durst dislike his reign, and, me preferring,
His utmost power with adverse power opposed
In dubious battle on the plains of Heaven,
105 And shook his throne. What though the field be lost?°
All is not lost—the unconquerable will,
And study of revenge, immortal hate,
And courage never to submit or yield—
And what is else° not to be overcome.
110 That glory never shall his wrath or might
Extort from me. To bow and sue for grace
With suppliant knee, and deify his power
Who, from the terror of this arm, so late
Doubted his empire—that were low indeed;°

84–85 An imitation, such as Tasso had also made, of Aeneas's outburst when he received a vision of the mutilated Hector, "quantum mutatus ab illo/ Hectore" (*Aeneid,* II, 274–75), but there is a piece of Isaiah too: "How art thou fallen from heaven" (xiv, 12). 89 It is made plain, soon enough, that it was not a "glorious enterprise". The Father of Lies, unable or disinclined to complete a true sentence, slips into romantic deception, perhaps even self-deception. 105 ff. The fine words deserve a better cause. 109 **else** besides 113–14 With God this is a joke, v, 721–24.

That were an ignominy° and shame beneath   115
This downfall; since by fate the strength of Gods
And this empyreal substance° cannot fail;
Since, through experience of this great event,
In arms not worse, in foresight much advanced,
We may with more successful hope resolve   120
To wage by force or guile° eternal war
Irreconcilable, to our grand Foe,
Who now triúmphs, and in the excess of joy
Sole reigning holds the tyranny of Heaven.'
  So spake the apostate Angel, though in pain,   125
Vaunting aloud, but racked with deep despair;
And him thus answered soon his bold compeer:
  'O Prince, O Chief of many thronèd Powers
That led the embattled Seraphim to war
Under thy conduct, and, in dreadful deeds   130
Fearless, endangered Heaven's perpetual King,°
And put to proof his high supremacy,
Whether upheld by strength, or chance, or fate!
Too well I see and rue the dire event
That, with sad overthrow and foul defeat,   135
Hath lost us Heaven, and all this mighty host
In horrible destruction laid thus low,
As far as Gods and Heavenly Essences
Can perish: for the mind and spirit remains
Invincible and vigour soon returns,   140
Though all our glory extinct, and happy state
Here swallowed up in endless misery.
But what if he our Conqueror (whom I now
Of force believe almighty, since no less
Than such could have o'erpowered such force as ours)   145
Have left us this our spirit and strength entire
Strongly to suffer and support our pains,
That we may so suffice his vengeful ire
Or do him mightier service as his thralls
By right of war, whate'er his business be,   150
Here in the heart of Hell to work in fire,
Or do his errands in the gloomy Deep?

---

115 **ignominy** pronounced ignomy   117 **empyreal substance**
made of the purest element, fire   121 **guile** the first hint of a
new tack; cf. 646   131 The flatterer echoes the master's lies.

What can it then avail though yet we feel
Strength undiminished, or eternal being
155 To undergo eternal punishment?'
    Whereto with speedy words the Arch-Fiend replied:
'Fallen Cherub, to be weak is miserable,
Doing or suffering°—but of this be sure:
To do aught good never will be our task,
160 But ever to do ill our sole delight,
As being the contrary to his high will
Whom we resist. If then his providence
Out of our evil seek to bring forth good,
Our labour must be to pervert that end,
165 And out of good still to find means of evil;
Which oft-times may succeed so as perhaps
Shall grieve him, if I fail not,° and disturb
His inmost counsels from their destined aim.
But see! the angry Victor hath recalled
170 His ministers of vengeance and pursuit
Back to the gates of Heaven: the sulphurous hail,
Shot after us in storm, o'erblown hath laid
The fiery surge that from the precipice
Of Heaven received us falling; and the thunder,
175 Winged with red lightning and impetuous rage,
Perhaps hath spent his shafts, and ceases now
To bellow through the vast and boundless Deep.
Let us not slip the occasion, whether scorn
Or satiate fury yield it from our Foe.
180 Seest thou yon dreary plain, forlorn and wild,
The seat of desolation, void of light,
Save what the glimmering of these livid flames
Casts pale and dreadful? Thither let us tend
From off the tossing of these fiery waves;
185 There rest, if any rest can harbour there;
And, reassembling our afflicted° powers,
Consult how we may henceforth most offend°
Our Enemy, our own loss how repair,
How overcome this dire calamity,

158 **Doing or suffering** whether we are active or passive; cf. ii,
199   167 **if I fail not** if I am not mistaken   186 **afflicted**
literally, beaten down   187 **offend** attack. Note the rhyme with
183 and the further rhyming of 185, 188, 191.

What reinforcement we may gain from hope,   190
If not, what resolution from despair.'°
  Thus Satan, talking to his nearest mate,
With head uplift above the wave and eyes
That sparkling blazed; his other parts besides
Prone on the flood, extended long and large,   195
Lay floating many a rood,° in bulk as huge
As whom the fables name of monstrous size,
Titanian° or Earth-born, that warred on Jove,
Briareos° or Typhon,° whom the den
By ancient Tarsus held, or that sea-beast   200
Leviathan,° which God of all his works
Created hugest that swim the ocean-stream.
Him, haply slumbering on the Norway foam,
The pilot of some small night-foundered skiff
Deeming some island, oft, as seamen tell,   205
With fixèd anchor in his scaly rind
Moors by his side under the lee,° while night
Invests the sea and wishèd morn delays.
So stretched out huge in length the Arch-Fiend lay,
Chained on the burning lake; nor ever thence   210
Had risen or heaved his head but that the will
And high permission of all-ruling Heaven
Left him at large to his own dark designs,
That with reiterated crimes he might
Heap on himself damnation, while he sought   215
Evil to others, and enraged might see
How all his malice served but to bring forth
Infinite goodness, grace, and mercy, shown
On Man by him seduced, but on himself
Treble confusion, wrath, and vengeance poured.   220

---

191 **despair** Landor objected to the rhyme with 188.   196 **rood**
twenty feet or so   198 The Titans and the Giants both "warred
on Jove."   199 **Briareos** a hundred-armed monster **Typhon**
another monster or giant—his name means "whirlwind" (ii,
541)—assigned a hundred heads by Pindar and located in a
cave in Cilicia in Asia Minor, of which *Tarsus* (l. 200) was
the chief city   201 **Leviathan** cf. Isaiah, xxvii, 1. The fable
about the treacherous whale—a symbol of Satan in the
medieval bestiaries—illustrates what can happen to the "night-
foundered" soul that anchors in sin.   207 **under the lee**
sheltered from the wind

Forthwith upright he rears from off the pool
His mighty stature; on each hand the flames,
Driven backward, slope their pointing spires, and, rolled
In billows, leave i' the midst a horrid vale.
225 Then with expanded wings he steers his flight
Aloft, incumbent on the dusky air,
That felt unusual weight, till on dry land
He lights—if it were land that ever burned
With solid, as the lake with liquid fire,
230 And such appeared in hue as when the force
Of subterranean wind transports a hill
Torn from Pelorus,° or the shattered side
Of thundering Aetna, whose combustible
And fuelled entrails, thence conceiving fire,
235 Sublimed with mineral fury,° aid the winds,
And leave a singèd bottom all involved
With stench and smoke; such resting found the sole
Of unblest feet. Him followed his next mate,
Both glorying to have 'scaped the Stygian° flood
240 As gods, and by their own recovered strength,
Not by the sufferance of Supernal Power.
  'Is this the region, this the soil, the clime,'
Said then the lost Archangel, 'this the seat
That we must change for Heaven, this mournful gloom
245 For that celestial light? Be it so, since he
Who now is sovran can dispose and bid
What shall be right: farthest from him is best,
Whom reason hath equalled, force hath made supreme
Above his equals. Farewell, happy fields,
250 Where joy for ever dwells! Hail, horrors! hail,
Infernal World! and thou, profoundest Hell,
Receive thy new possessor—one who brings
A mind not to be changed by place or time.
The mind is its° own place, and in itself

232 **Pelorus** the northeast cape of Sicily, an island that Diodorus
Siculus supposed had been torn from the mainland by an
earthquake. The volcanic Mount Aetna rose south to a height
of 10,705 feet. 235 **Sublimed with mineral fury** vaporized by
heat 239 **Stygian** Styx, "the flood of deadly hate," ii, 577, was
the best known of the four rivers of Hell. 254 **its** one of the
two places in the poem (iv, 813) where this modern possessive is
used instead of the regular Elizabethan neuter *his*

Can make a Heaven of Hell, a Hell of Heaven.   255
What matter where, if I be still the same,
And what I should be, all but less than he
Whom thunder hath made greater? Here at least
We shall be free; the Almighty hath not built
Here for his envy, will not drive us hence;   260
Here we may reign secure, and, in my choice,
To reign is worth ambition, though in Hell:
Better to reign in Hell than serve in Heaven.°
But wherefore let we then our faithful friends,
The associates and co-partners of our loss,   265
Lie thus astonished° on the oblivious° pool,
And call them not to share with us their part
In this unhappy mansion, or once more
With rallied arms to try what may be yet
Regained in Heaven, or what more lost in Hell?'   270
    So Satan spake; and him Beëlzebub
Thus answered: 'Leader of those armies bright
Which, but the Omnipotent, none could have foiled,
If once they hear that voice, their liveliest pledge
Of hope in fears and dangers, heard so oft   275
In worst extremes, and on the perilous edge°
Of battle, when it raged, in all assaults
Their surest signal, they will soon resume
New courage and revive, though now they lie
Grovelling and prostrate on yon lake of fire,   280
As we erewhile, astounded and amazed;
No wonder, fallen such a pernicious height!'
    He scarce had ceased when the superior Fiend
Was moving toward the shore; his ponderous shield,
Ethereal temper, massy, large, and round,   285
Behind him cast. The broad circumference
Hung on his shoulders like the moon, whose orb

263 Achilles in Hades said, "I would rather be a serf in a poor
man's house and be above ground than reign among the dead"
(*Odyssey*, XI, 489–91). Lucifer, in the second act of Joost van
den Vondel's drama *Lucifer* (1654), had disagreed: "Better the
prince of some inferior court/ Than second, or less, in beatific
light." 266 **astonished** stunned **oblivious** inducing oblivion
276 **edge** pun on Latin *acies,* which has the further meaning of
the forefront of an army; cf. vi, 108

Through optic glass the Tuscan artist° views
At evening, from the top of Fesole,
290 Or in Valdarno,° to descry new lands,
Rivers, or mountains, in her spotty globe.
His spear, to equal which the tallest pine
Hewn on Norwegian hills to be the mast
Of some great ammiral° were but a wand,
295 He walked with, to support uneasy steps
Over the burning marl,° not like those steps
On Heaven's azure; and the torrid clime
Smote on him sore besides, vaulted with fire.
Nathless he so endured till on the beach
300 Of that inflamèd sea he stood and called
His legions, Angel forms, who lay entranced
Thick as autumnal leaves° that strew the brooks

288 ff. Galileo, the first to put the telescope to astronomical use.
Professor at the University of Florence for life, he is represented as
using *Fesole* (three syllables), a hill near the city. Blind, he was
confined in the villa at Alcetri when Milton made the visit
mentioned in *Areopagitica.* 290 **Valdarno** valley of the (river)
Arno, in the lovely upper part of which Florence was situated 294
ammiral the admiral's ship, chief ship 296 **marl** soil; cf. 562
302 ff. The famous simile of the autumnal leaves has precedents in
Homer, Bacchylides, Apollonius Rhodius, Virgil, Dante, Tasso,
and Ariosto. Drayton wrote (*The Barons' Wars,* II, 451), "As leaves
in autumn, so the bodies fell." John Foxe said in his sixteenth-
century *Book of Martyrs* (London, 1851, I, 1000), speaking of the
plague in Italy: "The common people died without number; and
like as in the cold autumn the leaves of the trees do fall, even so
did the youth of the city consume and fall away." *Vallombrosa*
continues Milton's Florentine references, being the site of an
eleventh-century Benedictine abbey eighteen miles southeast, but
promotes the symbolism by meaning "vale of shades" and thus
associating with the valley of the shadow of death: the lost souls
suffering "the second death" (see Rev. xx, 14; xxi, 8) of damnation
are numerous, though it was once spring and summer for them.
They are "abject and lost," the next part of the simile implies, as
the hosts of Pharaoh drowned in the Red Sea after the waves had
parted to let the Chosen People through to safety. The constellation
of the hunter *Orion,* 305, set at the beginning of November, a time
of storms. By proceeding from leaves to sedge to the Egyptian
"chivalry" (cavalry) Milton works back to the first rout of the forces
of evil. "Confusion worse confounded" (ii, 996) is the theme of the
first two books, in contrast to the order that rules in Heaven.

In Vallombrosa, where the Etrurian shades
High overarched embower; or scattered sedge
Afloat, when with fierce winds Orion armed   305
Hath vexed the Red Sea coast, whose waves o'erthrew
Busiris and his Memphian chivalry
While with perfidious hatred they pursued
The sojourners of Goshen who beheld
From the safe shore their floating carcases   310
And broken chariot-wheels—so thick bestrewn,
Abject and lost, lay these, covering the flood,
Under amazement° of their hideous change.
He called so loud that all the hollow deep°
Of Hell resounded: 'Princes, Potentates,   315
Warriors, the Flower of Heaven, once yours, now lost,
If such astonishment as this can seize
Eternal Spirits;° or have ye chosen this place
After the toil of battle to repose
Your wearied virtue,° for the ease you find   320
To slumber here, as in the vales of Heaven?
Or in this abject posture have ye sworn
To adore the Conqueror? who now beholds
Cherub and Seraph rolling in the flood
With scattered arms and ensigns, till anon   325
His swift pursuers from Heaven-gates discern
The advantage, and, descending, tread us down
Thus drooping, or with linked thunderbolts
Transfix us to the bottom of his gulf:
Awake, arise, or be for ever fallen!'   330
　　They heard and were abashed, and up they sprung
Upon the wing, as when men wont to watch
On duty, sleeping found by whom they dread,
Rouse and bestir themselves ere well awake.
Nor did they not perceive the evil plight   335
In which they were, or the fierce pains not feel,
Yet to their General's voice they soon obeyed
Innumerable. As when the potent rod
Of Amram's son,° in Egypt's evil day,

---

313 **amazement** stupefaction, like *astonishment,* 317　314 **deep**
There is MS. authority for *deeps.*　318 ff. Sarcasm is a devilish
trait.　320 **virtue** manliness, also power　339 **Amram's son**
Moses

340 Waved round the coast, upcalled a pitchy cloud
     Of locusts, warping° on the eastern wind,
     That o'er the realm of impious Pharaoh hung
     Like Night and darkened all the land of Nile,
     So numberless were those bad Angels seen
345 Hovering on wing under the cope of Hell,
     'Twixt upper, nether, and surrounding fires;
     Till, at a signal given, the uplifted spear
     Of their great Sultan waving to direct
     Their course, in even balance down they light
350 On the firm brimstone and fill all the plain:
     A multitude like which the populous North
     Poured never from her frozen loins to pass
     Rhene or the Danaw,° when her barbarous sons
     Came like a deluge on the South and spread
355 Beneath Gibraltar to the Libyan sands.
     Forthwith, from every squadron and each band,
     The heads and leaders thither haste where stood
     Their great Commander: godlike Shapes, and Forms
     Excelling human; princely Dignities;
360 And Powers that erst in Heaven sat on thrones,
     Though of their names in Heavenly records now
     Be no memorial, blotted out and rased
     By their rebellion from the Books of Life.
     Nor had they yet among the sons of Eve
365 Got them new names, till, wandering o'er the earth,
     Through God's high sufferance for the trial of man,
     By falsities and lies the greatest part
     Of mankind they corrupted to forsake
     God their Creator, and the invisible
370 Glory of him that made them to transform
     Oft to the image of a brute, adorned
     With gay religions full of pomp and gold,
     And devils to adore for deities:
     Then were they known to men by various names,
375 And various idols through the heathen world.
     Say, Muse, their names then known, who first, who last,°
     Roused from the slumber on that fiery couch
     At their great Emperor's call, as next in worth

341 **warping** swerving   353 **Rhene or the Danaw** Rhine or the
Danube   376 ff. This is comparable to Homer's catalogue of
the ships, *Iliad,* II, 484 ff.

Came singly where he stood on the bare strand,
While the promiscuous crowd stood yet aloof?   *380*
The chief were those who, from the pit of Hell
Roaming to seek their prey on Earth, durst fix
Their seats, long after, next the seat of God,
Their altars by his altar, gods adored
Among the nations round, and durst abide   *385*
Jehovah thundering out of Sion, throned
Between the Cherubim; yea, often placed
Within his sanctuary itself their shrines,
Abominations; and with cursèd things
His holy rites and solemn feasts profaned,   *390*
And with their darkness durst affront his light.
First, Moloch,° horrid king, besmeared with blood
Of human sacrifice, and parents' tears;
Though, for the noise of drums and timbrels loud,
Their children's cries unheard that passed through fire   *395*
To his grim idol. Him the Ammonite°
Worshipped in Rabba and her watery plain,
In Argob and in Basan, to the stream
Of utmost Arnon. Nor content with such
Audacious neighbourhood, the wisest heart   *400*
Of Solomon he led by fraud to build°
His temple right against the temple of God
On that opprobrious hill, and made his grove
The pleasant valley of Hinnom, Tophet thence
And black Gehenna called, the type of Hell.   *405*
Next Chemos, the obscene dread of Moab's sons,
From Aroer° to Nebo and the wild

392 **Moloch** means *king*. 396–99 The Ammonite, a people hated by Israel and subdued by Jephthah (cf. *Samson Agonistes*, 285), had Rabba as their chief city, east of the Jordan. 401–03 See 1 Kings xi, 7; 2 Kings xxiii, 13, 14, *that opprobrious hill* being the Mount of Olives. 407 ff. Aroer was on the river Arnon (399) which entered the Dead Sea at the northern boundary of Moab (406). Nebo in the north was the elevation where Moses took his first and last view of the Promised Land. Abarim (408) was the name of mountains to the west. Hesebon (Heshbon) lay north—all within the tribe of Reuben, as were the other places named as "Seon's realm" (409) (he was the king of the Amorites), territory east of the Asphaltic Pool (411), the Dead Sea, noted for the masses of asphalt or bitumen it tosses up. The fifteen-year-old poet, in his versification of Psalm cxxxvi, noted God "foiled bold Seon and his host,/ That ruled the Amorrean coast" (65–66).

Of southmost Abarim; in Hesebon
And Horonaim, Seon's realm, beyond
410 The flowery dale of Sibma, clad with vines,
And Eleale to the Asphaltic Pool:
Peor his other name, when he enticed
Israel in Sittim,° on their march from Nile,
To do him wanton rites, which cost them woe.
415 Yet thence his lustful orgies he enlarged
Even to that hill of scandal,° by the grove
Of Moloch homicide, lust hard by hate,
Till good Josiah° drove them thence to Hell.
With these came they who, from the bordering flood
420 Of old Euphrates to the brook that parts
Egypt from Syrian ground, had general names
Of Baalim and Ashtaroth—those male,
These feminine. For Spirits, when they please,
Can either sex assume, or both, so soft
425 And uncompounded is their essence pure,
Not tied or manacled with joint or limb,
Nor founded on the brittle strength of bones,
Like cumbrous flesh, but, in what shape they choose,
Dilated or condensed, bright or obscure,
430 Can execute their aery purposes
And works of love or enmity fulfil.
For those the race of Israel oft forsook
Their Living Strength, and unfrequented left
His righteous altar, bowing° lowly down
435 To bestial gods; for which their heads, as low
Bowed° down in battle, sunk before the spear
Of despicable foes. With these in troop
Came Astoreth, whom the Phoenicians called
Astarte, queen of heaven, with crescent horns;
440 To whose bright image nightly by the moon
Sidonian° virgins paid their vows and songs;
In Sion also not unsung, where stood

413 **Sittim** Shittim, the last stop, east of the Jordan, opposite
Jericho, of the Israelites on their exodus from Egypt, where "the
people began to commit whoredom with the daughters of Moab...
and Israel joined himself unto Baal-peor" (Num. xxv, 1, 3)   416
hill of scandal same as *that opprobrious hill,* 403   418 **Josiah** see
2 Kings xxiii   434, 436 **bowing—Bowed** vengeful wordplay   441
Sidonian Phoenician

Her temple on the offensive mountain,° built
By that uxorious king° whose heart, though large,
Beguiled by fair idolatresses, fell   445
To idols foul. Thammuz° came next behind,
Whose annual wound in Lebanon allured
The Syrian damsels to lament his fate
In amorous ditties all a summer's day,
While smooth° Adonis from his native rock   450
Ran purple to the sea, supposed with blood
Of Thammuz yearly wounded: the love-tale
Infected Sion's daughters with like heat,
Whose wanton passions in the sacred porch
Ezekiel° saw, when, by the vision led,   455
His eye surveyed the dark idolatries
Of alienated Judah. Next came one
Who mourned in earnest, when the captive ark
Maimed his brute image, head and hands lopped off,
In his own temple, on the grunsel-edge,°   460
Where he fell flat and shamed his worshippers—
Dagon° his name, sea-monster, upward man
And downward fish—yet had his temple high
Reared in Azotus, dreaded through the coast
Of Palestine, in Gath and Ascalon,   465
And Accaron and Gaza's frontier bounds.
Him followed Rimmon,° whose delightful seat
Was fair Damascus, on the fertile banks

443 the offensive mountain cf. 403, 416 **444 uxorious king**
Solomon, who "had seven hundred wives, princesses, and three
hundred concubines" (1 Kings xi, 3) **446 Thammuz** the
Babylonian vegetation god, equivalent of Greek *Adonis*—
pictured as a river at 450 (which indeed "Ran purple" because
of loose particles of red hematite). In the words of Sir J. G.
Frazer, "The true name of the deity was Tammuz: the
appellation of Adonis is merely the Semitic *Adon,* 'lord,' a title
of honour by which his worshippers addressed him. . . . In the
religious literature of Babylonia Tammuz appears as the
youthful spouse or lover of Ishtar, the great mother goddess,
the embodiment of the reproductive energies of nature." **450
smooth** flowing; cf. "smooth-sliding Mincius," "Lycidas,"
86. **455 Ezekiel,** viii, 14 **460 grunsel-edge** threshold **462
Dagon** Philistine deity; see 1 Samuel v, 4, and note to *Samson
Agonistes* 13 **467 Rimmon** Syrian deity. The Biblical references
are 2 Kings v, xvi.

Of Abbana and Pharphar, lucid streams.
470 He also against the house of God was bold:
A leper once he lost, and gained a king—
Ahaz, his sottish conqueror, whom he drew
God's altar to disparage and displace
For one of Syrian mode, whereon to burn
475 His odious offerings, and adore the gods
Whom he had vanquished. After these appeared
A crew who, under names of old renown—
Osiris, Isis, Orus, and their train—
With monstrous shapes and sorceries abused
480 Fanatic Egypt and her priests to seek
Their wandering gods disguised in brutish forms°
Rather than human. Nor did Israel 'scape
The infection, when their borrowed gold composed
The calf in Oreb; and the rebel king°
485 Doubled that sin in Bethel and in Dan,
Likening his Maker to the grazèd ox,
Jehovah, who, in one night, when he passed
From Egypt marching, equalled with one stroke
Both her first-born and all her bleating gods.
490 Belial° came last, than whom a Spirit more lewd
Fell not from Heaven, or more gross to love
Vice for itself. To him no temple stood
Or altar smoked; yet who more oft than he
In temples and at altars, when the priest
495 Turns atheist, as did Eli's sons,° who filled
With lust and violence the house of God?
In courts and palaces he also reigns,
And in luxurious cities, where the noise
Of riot ascends above their loftiest towers,
500 And injury and outrage; and when night
Darkens the streets, then wander forth the sons
Of Belial, flown with insolence and wine.°
Witness the streets of Sodom, and that night

481 Osiris was a bull, Isis cow-horned, Anubis dog-headed (cf.
"Nativity Hymn," 211–12).   484 ff. **rebel king** Jeroboam
rebelled against Solomon's successor, Rehoboam, and was guilty
of making two golden calves.   490 **Belial** means *worthless-
ness*.   495 **Eli's sons** "were sons of Belial; they knew not the
Lord," as detailed in 1 Samuel ii, 12 ff.   501–02 possibly a hit
at the Cavaliers

In Gibeah,° when the hospitable door
Exposed a matron, to prevent worse rape.   505
These were the prime in order and in might:
The rest were long to tell, though far renowned,
The Ionian gods—of Javan's° issue held
Gods, yet confessed later than Heaven and Earth,
Their boasted parents; Titan, Heaven's first-born,   510
With his enormous brood, and birthright seized
By younger Saturn: he from mightier Jove,
His own and Rhea's son, like measure found;
So Jove usurping reigned. These, first in Crete
And Ida known, thence on the snowy top   515
Of cold Olympus ruled the middle air,
Their highest heaven; or on the Delphian cliff,
Or in Dodona,° and through all the bounds
Of Doric land; or who with Saturn° old
Fled over Adria to the Hesperian fields,   520
And o'er the Celtic roamed the utmost Isles.
    All these and more came flocking, but with looks
Downcast and damp, yet such wherein appeared
Obscure some glimpse of joy to have found their Chief
Not in despair, to have found themselves not lost   525
In loss itself, which on his countenance cast
Like doubtful hue; but he, his wonted pride
Soon recollecting, with high words, that bore
Semblance of worth, not substance, gently raised
Their fainted° courage, and dispelled their fears: 530
Then straight commands that, at the warlike sound
Of trumpets loud and clarions, be upreared
His mighty standard. That proud honour claimed

---

504 **Gibeah** This gruesome tale of a sacrificed concubine is in
Judges xix. In 1667 "door" was plural and "Exposed a matron"
was "Yielded their matrons," and "avoid" was "prevent":
bringing in Genesis, xix, 8.   508 After the Semitic deities the
Greek gods get less attention, and an equation is made
between Ion (ancestor of the Ionians or Greeks) and Javan,
the son of Japhet = Noah's son and Iapetus the Titan.   518
Dodona the oracle (cf. the reference to Delphi, 517) and
temple of Zeus in Epirus   519–21 Defeated by his son Jove,
Saturn fled over the *Adriatic* to Italy (520) and even wandered
to France and Britain (521)   530 **fainted** so the 1667 text; 1674
has *fainting*.

Azazel° as his right, a Cherub tall,
535 Who forthwith from the glittering staff unfurled
The imperial ensign, which, full high advanced,
Shone like a meteor streaming to the wind,
With gems and golden lustre rich emblazed,
Seraphic arms and trophies, all the while
540 Sonorous metal blowing martial sounds;
At which the universal host upsent
A shout that tore Hell's concave, and beyond
Frighted the reign of Chaos and old Night.
All in a moment through the gloom were seen
545 Ten thousand banners rise into the air,
With orient° colours waving; with them rose
A forest huge of spears, and thronging helms
Appeared, and serried shields in thick array
Of depth immeasurable. Anon they move
550 In perfect phalanx to the Dorian mood°
Of flutes and soft recorders—such as raised
To height of noblest temper heroes old
Arming to battle, and instead of rage
Deliberate valour° breathed, firm, and unmoved
555 With dread of death to flight or foul retreat,
Nor wanting power to mitigate and suage°
With solemn touches° troubled thoughts, and chase
Anguish and doubt and fear and sorrow and pain
From mortal or immortal minds. Thus they,
560 Breathing united force with fixèd thought,
Moved on in silence to soft pipes that charmed
Their painful steps o'er the burnt soil. And now
Advanced in view they stand, a horrid front

534 **Azazel** "brave in retreating" (Newton). Milton follows
Cabalist tradition in making him Satan's standard-bearer   546
orient bright   550 **Dorian mood** martial, in contrast to "soft
Lydian airs," "L'Allegro" (136)   554 **Deliberate valour** Milton
is following, right down to this phrase, Plutarch's description
of the Spartans under Lycurgus. "It was at once a magnificent
and a terrible sight to see them march on to the tune of their
flutes, without any disorder in their ranks, any discomposure
in their minds, or change in their countenances, calmly and
cheerfully moving with the music to the deadly fight. Men, in
this temper, were not likely to be possessed with fear or any
transport of fury, but with the deliberate valour of hope and
assurance."   556 **suage** assuage   557 **touches** strains

Of dreadful length and dazzling arms, in guise
Of warriors old, with ordered spear and shield,   565
Awaiting what command their mighty Chief
Had to impose. He through the armèd files
Darts his experienced eye, and soon traverse
The whole battalion views—their order due,
Their visages and statures as of gods;   570
Their number last he sums. And now his heart
Distends with pride, and, hardening in his strength,
Glories: for never, since created Man,
Met such embodied force as, named with these,
Could merit more than that small infantry°   575
Warred on by cranes—though all the giant brood
Of Phlegra° with the heroic race were joined
That fought at Thebes and Ilium, on each side
Mixed with auxiliar gods; and what resounds
In fable or romance of Uther's son,°   580
Begirt with British and Armoric° knights;
And all who since, baptized or infidel,
Jousted in Aspramont, or Montalban,
Damasco, or Marocco, or Trebisond,°
Or whom Biserta sent from Afric shore   585
When Charlemain with all his peerage fell
By Fontarabbia.° Thus far these beyond

575 **infantry** pun on (1) foot-soldiers and (2) diminutive people,
"that pygmean race" (780) (slightly over one foot tall) whom
Homer, in a comparable martial simile, mentions as suffering
slaughter by the cranes (*Iliad,* beginning of Book III) 577–79
Phlegra on an isthmus in Macedonia, site of a clash between the
giants and the gods. Polyneices, the son of Oedipus, besieged
Thebes, as related in Aeschylus's drama *The Seven Against Thebes.*
Ilium, of course, witnessed the Greeks against the Trojans, with
"auxiliar"—assisting—gods on each side. 580 **Uther's son** King
Arthur 581 **Armoric** reference to Brittany (Britain in France)
583–84 Milton ranges from Italy and France to Asia and Africa and
the Black Sea for these places renowned in chivalric romance.
585–87 Milton's source for this passage is unknown. It was not the
famous *Chanson de Roland,* the twelfth-century epic, which was
not discovered and made available until after the French
Revolution. Charlemagne did not fall at Fontarabbia, but legend
has it that forty miles from there, in the Pyrenees, at Roncevaux,
Charlemagne's nephew Roland made a rear-guard stand to the
death when betrayed during the emperor's return from the
campaign in Spain against the Saracens (Arabs, thus perhaps
the reason for Milton's shift to Font*arabbia*).

Compare of mortal prowess, yet observed
Their dread Commander; he, above the rest
590 In shape and gesture proudly eminent,
Stood like a tower: his form had yet not lost
All her original brightness, nor appeared
Less than Archangel ruined, and the excess
Of glory obscured—as when the sun new-risen
595 Looks through the horizontal misty air
Shorn of his beams, or, from behind the moon,
In dim eclipse, disastrous twilight sheds
On half the nations, and with fear of change
Perplexes monarchs.° Darkened so, yet shone
600 Above them all the Archangel; but his face
Deep scars of thunder had intrenched, and care
Sat on his faded cheek, but under brows
Of dauntless courage, and considerate pride
Waiting revenge: cruel his eye, but cast
605 Signs of remorse and passion, to behold
The fellows of his crime—the followers rather
(Far other once beheld in bliss), condemned
For ever now to have their lot in pain,
Millions of Spirits for his fault amerced°
610 Of Heaven, and from eternal splendours flung
For his revolt; yet faithful how they stood,
Their glory withered, as, when Heaven's fire
Hath scathed the forest oaks or mountain pines,
With singèd top their stately growth, though bare,
615 Stands on the blasted heath.° He now prepared
To speak; whereat their doubled ranks they bend
From wing to wing, and half enclose him round
With all his peers: attention held them mute.
Thrice he assayed, and thrice, in spite of scorn,

594–99 This passage worried the original licenser of *Paradise Lost* as possibly treasonous. The archbishop's deputy might have hesitated still longer had he connected this with the allusion in *Eikonoklastes* to "those who, being exalted in high place above their merit, fear all change" (ch. XVI, second sentence). **609 amerced** mulcted (French *à merci*, at the mercy of) **615 blasted heath** The first thought is *Macbeth* I, iii, 77, where also "blasted' means "withered" (612) by lightning. This continues the autumn-death line.

Tears, such as Angels weep, burst forth; at last   *620*
Words interwove with sighs found out their way:
  'O myriads of immortal Spirits! O Powers
Matchless, but with the Almighty!—and that strife
Was not inglorious, though the event° was dire,
As this place testifies, and this dire change,   *625*
Hateful to utter. But what power of mind,
Foreseeing or presaging, from the depth
Of knowledge past or present could have feared
How such united force° of gods, how such
As stood like these, could ever know repulse?   *630*
For who can yet believe, though after loss,
That all these puissant legions, whose exile
Hath emptied Heaven,° shall fail to reascend,
Self-raised, and repossess their native seat?
For me, be witness all the host of Heaven,   *635*
If counsels different° or danger shunned
By me have lost our hopes. But he who reigns
Monarch in Heaven till then as one secure
Sat on his throne, upheld by old repute,
Consent or custom, and his regal state   *640*
Put forth at full, but still his strength concealed,
Which tempted our attempt, and wrought our fall.
Henceforth his might we know, and know our own,
So as not either to provoke or dread
New war, provoked: our better part remains   *645*
To work in close design, by fraud or guile,
What force effected not; that he no less
At length from us may find, who overcomes
By force hath overcome but half his foe.
Space may produce new Worlds; whereof so rife   *650*
There went a fame° in Heaven that he ere long
Intended to create, and therein plant
A generation whom his choice regard
Should favour equal to the Sons of Heaven.
Thither, if but to pry, shall be perhaps   *655*

---

624 **event** outcome   629 **united force** an echo from 560   633
emptied Heaven Satan exaggerates, or prevaricates, as usual.
Only "the third part of Heaven's sons" (ii, 692) rebelled, as
Revelation xii, 4 indicated.   636 **different** A meaning related
to *defer* has been suggested.   651 **fame** Latin *fama,* rumor

Our first eruption—thither, or elsewhere:
For this infernal pit shall never hold
Celestial Spirits in bondage, nor the Abyss
Long under darkness cover. But these thoughts
660 Full counsel must mature. Peace is despaired,
For who can think submission? War then, war
Open or understood, must be resolved.'
    He spake; and, to confirm his words, out flew
Millions of flaming swords, drawn from the thighs
665 Of mighty Cherubim; the sudden blaze
Far round illumined Hell. Highly they raged
Against the Highest, and fierce with graspèd arms
Clashed on their sounding shields the din of war,
Hurling defiance toward the vault of Heaven.
670   There stood a hill not far whose grisly top
Belched fire and rolling smoke; the rest entire
Shone with a glossy scurf—undoubted sign
That in his womb was hid metallic ore,
The work of sulphur. Thither, winged with speed,
675 A numerous brigade hastened, as when bands
Of pioneers, with spade and pickaxe armed,
Forerun the royal camp to trench a field
Or cast a rampart. Mammon° led them on,
Mammon, the least erected Spirit that fell
680 From Heaven; for even in Heaven his looks and thoughts
Were always downward bent, admiring more
The riches of Heaven's pavement, trodden gold,
Than aught divine or holy else enjoyed
In vision beatific; by him first
685 Men also, and by his suggestion taught,
Ransacked the centre, and with impious hands
Rifled the bowels of their mother Earth
For treasures better hid. Soon had his crew
Opened into the hill a spacious wound,
690 And digged out ribs of gold.° Let none admire°
That riches grow in Hell; that soil may best
Deserve the precious bane. And here let those

678 **Mammon** Syriac for wealth   689–90 A curious parody of
creation, to be compared with viii, 465–67, even as 710–11, below,
is the devilish version of 9–10, above.   690 **admire** marvel

Who boast in mortal things, and wondering tell
Of Babel, and the works of Memphian kings,°
Learn how their greatest monuments of fame,   695
And strength, and art, are easily outdone
By Spirits reprobate, and in an hour
What in an age they, with incessant toil
And hands innumerable, scarce perform.
Nigh on the plain, in many cells prepared,   700
That underneath had veins of liquid fire°
Sluiced from the lake, a second multitude
With wondrous art founded° the massy ore,
Severing each kind, and scummed the bullion-dross;
A third as soon had formed within the ground   705
A various mould, and from the boiling cells
By strange conveyance filled each hollow nook—
As in an organ, from one blast of wind,
To many a row of pipes the sound-board breathes.
Anon out of the earth a fabric huge   710
Rose like an exhalation, with the sound
Of dulcet symphonies and voices sweet,
Built like a temple, where pilasters° round
Were set, and Doric pillars overlaid
With golden architrave;° nor did there want   715
Cornice or frieze, with bossy sculptures graven:
The roof was fretted gold. Not Babylon
Nor great Alcairo° such magnificence
Equalled in all their glories, to enshrine
Belus° or Serapis° their gods, or seat   720
Their kings, when Egypt with Assyria strove
In wealth and luxury. The ascending pile
Stood fixed her stately height, and straight the doors,
Opening their brazen folds, discover, wide
Within, her ample spaces o'er the smooth   725
And level pavement: from the archèd roof,
Pendent by subtle magic, many a row

694 **Memphian kings,** e.g., the builders of the pyramids 701
liquid fire mentioned 229 703 **founded** 1674 reads *found
out.* 713 **pilasters** square columns 715 **architrave** the beam
that rests on the pillars 718 **Alcairo** Cairo, ancient Memphis
720 **Belus** chief Babylonian god **Serapis** the Underworld aspect
of Osiris

Of starry lamps and blazing cressets,° fed
With naphtha and asphaltus, yielded light
730 As from a sky. The hasty multitude
Admiring entered; and the work some praise,
And some the architect: his hand was known
In Heaven by many a towered structure high,
Where sceptred Angels held their residence
735 And sat as Princes, whom the supreme King
Exalted to such power, and gave to rule,
Each in his hierarchy, the Orders bright.
Nor was his name unheard or unadored
In ancient Greece, and in Ausonian land°
740 Men called him Mulciber,° and how he fell
From Heaven they fabled, thrown by angry Jove
Sheer o'er the crystal battlements: from morn
To noon he fell, from noon to dewy eve,
A summer's day,° and with the setting sun
745 Dropped from the zenith, like a falling star,
On Lemnos, the Aegaean isle. Thus they relate,
Erring; for he with this rebellious rout
Fell long before; nor aught availed him now
To have built in Heaven high towers; nor did he 'scape
750 By all his engines, but was headlong sent,
With his industrious crew, to build in Hell.
   Meanwhile the wingèd Heralds, by command
Of sovran power, with awful ceremony
And trumpet's sound throughout the host proclaim
755 A solemn council forthwith to be held
At Pandemonium,° the high capital°
Of Satan and his peers. Their summons called
From every band and squarèd regiment°

728 **cressets** hanging lanterns   739 **Ausonian land** Italy in the time
of the Romans   740 **Mulciber** More familiar as Hephaestus or
Vulcan, but Milton uses the name that means the *softener* or *welder*
of metal. He is lame in the *Iliad,* perhaps as a consequence of his
fall to Lemnos in a passage in Book I (588–95) that Milton echoes,
and he uses the incident as an archetype of the Scriptural fall. In
fact the three words "fell/ From Heaven," 740–41, were first used
at 491.   744 **A summer's day** cf. 449   756 **Pandemonium** the
palace of *all the devils* (Milton's coinage; opposite of pantheon, all
the gods) **capital** perhaps *capitol(?)*   758 **squarèd regiment**
squadron

By place or choice the worthiest; they anon
With hundreds and with thousands trooping came   760
Attended: all access was thronged; the gates
And porches wide, but chief the spacious hall
(Though like a covered field, where champions bold
Wont ride in armed, and at the Soldan's chair
Defied the best of Paynim° chivalry   765
To mortal combat, or career with lance)
Thick swarmed, both on the ground and in the air,
Brushed with the hiss of rustling wings. As bees°
In springtime, when the Sun with Taurus° rides,
Pour forth their populous youth about the hive   770
In clusters; they among fresh dews and flowers
Fly to and fro, or on the smoothed plank,
The suburb of their straw-built citadel,
New rubbed with balm, expatiate,° and confer
Their state-affairs: so thick the aery crowd   775
Swarmed and were straitened; till, the signal given,°
Behold a wonder! they but now who seemed
In bigness to surpass Earth's giant sons,
Now less than smallest dwarfs, in narrow room
Throng numberless, like that° pygmean race   780
Beyond the Indian mount; or faëry elves,
Whose midnight revels by a forest-side
Or fountain some belated peasant sees,
Or dreams he sees, while overhead the Moon
Sits arbitress and nearer to the Earth   785
Wheels her pale course: they, on their mirth and dance
Intent, with jocund music charm his ear;
At once with joy and fear his heart rebounds.
Thus incorporeal Spirits to smallest forms
Reduced their shapes immense, and were at large,   790
Though without number still, amidst the hall
Of that infernal court. But far within,
And in their own dimensions like themselves,
The great Seraphic Lords and Cherubim

765 **Paynim** pagan   768 **As bees** a simile made familiar by
Homer and Virgil   769 **Taurus** The sign of the Bull is entered
by the sun in April.   774 **expatiate** walk abroad (Latin)   776
signal given cf. 347   780 **that** Latin *ille,* the famous

795 In close recess and secret conclave sat,
A thousand demi-gods on golden seats,
Frequent° and full. After short silence then,
And summons read, the great consúlt began.

797 **Frequent** in the Latin sense of crowded

BOOK II

THE ARGUMENT

The consultation begun, Satan debates whether another battle be to be hazarded for the recovery of Heaven: some advise it, others dissuade. A third proposal is preferred, mentioned before by Satan, to search the truth of that prophecy or tradition in Heaven concerning another world, and another kind of creature, equal, or not much inferior, to themselves, about this time to be created. Their doubt who shall be sent on this difficult search: Satan, their chief, undertakes alone the voyage; is honoured and applauded. The council thus ended, the rest betake them several ways and to several employments, as their inclinations lead them, to entertain the time till Satan return. He passes on his journey to Hellgates; finds them shut, and who sat there to guard them; by whom at length they are opened, and discover to him the great gulf between Hell and Heaven; with what difficulty he passes through, directed by Chaos, the Power of that place, to the sight of this new World which he sought.

HIGH on a throne of royal state, which far°
Outshone the wealth of Ormus° and of Ind,°
Or where the gorgeous East with richest hand
Showers on her kings barbaric pearl and gold,

1–5 Compare Spenser's Lucifera, Pride (*Faerie Queene*, I, iv, 8): High above all a cloth of state was spread,/ And a rich throne, as bright as sunny day,/ On which there sate, most brave embellished/ With royal robes and gorgeous array,/ A maiden queen, that shone as Titan's ray,/ In glistring gold and peerless precious stone.   2 **Ormus** island that was chief mart for Persian Gulf area **Ind** India

5 Satan exalted sat, by merit raised°
   To that bad eminence; and, from despair
   Thus high uplifted beyond hope, aspires
   Beyond thus high, insatiate to pursue
   Vain° war with Heaven; and, by success untaught,°
10 His proud imaginations thus displayed:
      'Powers and Dominions, Deities of Heaven!
   For, since no deep within her gulf can hold
   Immortal vigour, though oppressed and fallen,
   I give not Heaven for lost: from this descent
15 Celestial Virtues rising will appear
   More glorious and more dread than from no fall,
   And trust themselves to fear no second fate:
   Me though just right, and the fixed laws of Heaven,
   Did first create your leader, next, free choice,
20 With what besides, in council or in fight,
   Hath been achieved of merit, yet this loss,
   Thus far at least recovered, hath much more
   Established in a safe, unenvied throne,
   Yielded with full consent. The happier state
25 In Heaven, which follows dignity, might draw
   Envy from each inferior, but who here
   Will envy whom the highest place exposes
   Foremost to stand against the Thunderer's aim
   Your bulwark, and condemns to greatest share
30 Of endless pain? Where there is, then, no good
   For which to strive, no strife can grow up there
   From faction, for none sure will claim in Hell
   Precedence, none, whose portion is so small
   Of present pain that with ambitious mind
35 Will covet more. With this advantage, then,
   To union, and firm faith, and firm accord,

5 Each is where he deserves to be on the chain of being. Satan
is at "the highest place" (27) of an inverted scale, furthest
from good. The doctrine of merit extends upwards to Christ,
"By merit more than birthright Son of God," iii, 309. Satan
has merely Oriental pomp, which "in the fifth line . . . is
pricked with the derisive collocation of sounds in 'Satan
exalted sat,' and all his gas escapes in sibilance and near-
rhyme" (J. B. Broadbent).   9 **Vain** same double meaning as in
i, 44 **by success untaught** i.e., not having learned by experience.
Success means *outcome,* good or bad.

More than can be in Heaven, we now return
To claim our just inheritance of old,
Surer to prosper than prosperity
Could have assured us, and by what best way,   40
Whether of open war or covert guile,
We now debate; who can advise, may speak.'
   He ceased; and next him Moloch, sceptred king,°
Stood up, the strongest and the fiercest Spirit
That fought in Heaven, now fiercer by despair.   45
His trust was with the Eternal to be deemed
Equal in strength, and rather than be less
Cared not to be at all; with that care lost
Went all his fear: of God, or Hell, or worse,
He recked not, and these words thereafter spake: 50
   'My sentence° is for open war. Of wiles,
More unexpert, I boast not: them let those
Contrive who need, or when they need, not now;
For, while they sit contriving, shall the rest—
Millions that stand in arms, and longing wait   55
The signal to ascend—sit lingering here,
Heaven's fugitives, and for their dwelling-place
Accept this dark opprobrious den of shame,
The prison of his tyranny who reigns
By our delay? No! let us rather choose,   60
Armed with Hell-flames and fury, all at once
O'er Heaven's high towers to force resistless way,
Turning our tortures into horrid arms
Against the Torturer; when, to meet the noise
Of his almighty engine, he shall hear   65
Infernal thunder, and, for lightning, see
Black fire and horror shot with equal rage
Among his Angels, and his throne itself
Mixed with Tartarean° sulphur and strange fire,
His own invented torments. But perhaps   70
The way seems difficult, and steep to scale
With upright wing against a higher foe.
Let such bethink them, if the sleepy drench
Of that forgetful lake benumb not still,

---

43 **Moloch, sceptred king** Milton keeps iterating the etymology
of Moloch.   51 **sentence** opinion (Latin *sententia*)   69 **Tartarean**
Tartarus was a place of punishment below Hades even.

75   That in our proper° motion we ascend
    Up to our native seat; descent and fall
    To us is adverse. Who but felt of late,
    When the fierce foe hung on our broken rear
    Insulting, and pursued us through the Deep,
80   With what compulsion and laborious flight
    We sunk thus low? The ascent is easy, then;°
    The event° is feared! Should we again provoke
    Our stronger, some worse way his wrath may find
    To our destruction, if there be in Hell
85   Fear to be worse destroyed! What can be worse
    Than to dwell here, driven out from bliss, condemned
    In this abhorrèd deep to utter woe,
    Where pain of unextinguishable fire
    Must exercise° us without hope of end°
90   The vassals of his anger, when the scourge
    Inexorably, and the torturing hour,
    Calls us to penance? More destroyed than thus,
    We should be quite abolished, and expire.
    What fear we then? what doubt we° to incense
95   His utmost ire? which, to the height enraged,
    Will either quite consume us, and reduce
    To nothing this essential°—happier far
    Than miserable to have eternal being—
    Or, if our substance be indeed divine,
100   And cannot cease to be, we are at worst
    On this side nothing; and by proof we feel
    Our power sufficient to disturb his Heaven,
    And with perpetual inroads to alarm,
    Though inaccessible, his fatal° throne:
105   Which, if not victory, is yet revenge.'
      He ended frowning, and his look denounced
    Desperate revenge and battle dangerous
    To less than gods. On the other side up rose

75 proper natural, characteristic   **81 The ascent is easy, then** opposite of the famous warning of the Sibyl, "The descent to Hell is easy" ("facilis descensus Averno") *Aeneid,* VI, 126. Cf. iii, 524   **82 event** same meaning as at i, 624   **89 exercise** has the Latin force of torture. **without hope of end** referring doubly to no end of pain and no end of existence   **94 what doubt we** Why do we hesitate?   **97 essential** essence   **104 fatal** fated

Belial, in act more graceful and humane;
A fairer person lost not Heaven; he seemed   *110*
For dignity composed, and high exploit,
But all was false and hollow, though his tongue
Dropped manna, and could make the worse appear
The better reason, to perplex and dash
Maturest counsels, for his thoughts were low,   *115*
To vice industrious, but to nobler deeds
Timorous and slothful; yet he pleased the ear,
And with persuasive accent thus began:
  'I should be much for open war, O Peers,
As not behind in hate, if what was urged   *120*
Main reason to persuade immediate war
Did not dissuade me most, and seem to cast
Ominous conjecture on the whole success;
When he who most excels in fact° of arms,
In what he counsels and in what excels   *125*
Mistrustful, grounds his courage on despair
And utter dissolution as the scope
Of all his aim, after some dire revenge.
First, what revenge? The towers of Heaven are filled
With armèd watch, that render all access   *130*
Impregnable: oft on the bordering Deep
Encamp their legions, or with obscure wing
Scout far and wide into the realm of Night,
Scorning surprise. Or could we break our way
By force, and at our heels all Hell should rise   *135*
With blackest insurrection, to confound
Heaven's purest light, yet our great Enemy,
All incorruptible, would on his throne
Sit unpolluted, and the ethereal mould,
Incapable of stain, would soon expel   *140*
Her mischief, and purge off the baser fire,
Victorious. Thus repulsed, our final hope
Is flat despair: we must exasperate
The Almighty Victor to spend all his rage,
And that must end us, that must be our cure,   *145*
To be no more°—sad cure, for who would lose,

124 **fact** feat   146 The clever arguer Belial poses as Hamlet,
though he is also Claudio (*Measure for Measure,* III, i, 116 ff.,
of which 120–21 connects with 600 below).

Though full of pain, this intellectual being,
Those thoughts that wander through eternity,
To perish rather, swallowed up and lost
150 In the wide womb of uncreated Night,
Devoid of sense and motion? And who knows,
Let this be good, whether our angry Foe
Can give it, or will ever? How he can
Is doubtful; that he never will is sure.
155 Will he, so wise, let loose at once his ire,
Belike° through impotence or unaware,
To give his enemies their wish, and end
Them in this anger whom his anger saves
To punish endless? "Wherefore cease we, then?"
160 Say they who counsel war; "we are decreed,
Reserved, and destined to eternal woe;
Whatever doing, what can we suffer more,
What can we suffer worse?" Is this, then, worst—
Thus sitting, thus consulting, thus in arms?
165 What when° we fled amain,° pursued and struck
With Heaven's afflicting thunder, and besought
The Deep to shelter us? this Hell then seemed
A refuge from those wounds. Or when we lay
Chained on the burning lake? that sure was worse.
170 What if the breath that kindled those grim fires,
Awaked, should blow them into sevenfold rage,
And plunge us in the flames, or from above
Should intermitted vengeance arm again
His red right hand° to plague us? What if all
175 Her stores were opened, and this firmament
Of Hell should spout her cataracts of fire,
Impendent horrors, threatening hideous fall
One day upon our heads, while we perhaps,
Designing or exhorting glorious war,
180 Caught in a fiery tempest, shall be hurled,
Each on his rock transfixed, the sport and prey
Of racking whirlwinds, or forever sunk
Under yon boiling ocean, wrapt in chains,

156 **Belike** in all likelihood   165 **What when** *what about when* is the modern idiom. **amain** under great force   174 **His red right hand** an expression first applied by Horace to Jupiter

There to converse with everlasting groans,
Unrespited, unpitied, unreprieved,   *185*
Ages of hopeless end? This would be worse.
War, therefore, open or concealed, alike
My voice dissuades; for what can force or guile°
With him, or who deceive his mind, whose eye
Views all things at one view? He from Heaven's height   *190*
All these our motions vain sees and derides,
Not more almighty to resist our might
Than wise to frustrate all our plots and wiles.
Shall we, then, live thus vile, the race of Heaven,
Thus trampled, thus expelled, to suffer here   *195*
Chains and these torments? Better these than worse,
By my advice; since fate inevitable
Subdues us, and omnipotent decree,
The Victor's will. To suffer, as to do,
Our strength is equal, nor the law unjust   *200*
That so ordains; this was at first resolved,
If we were wise, against so great a foe
Contending, and so doubtful what might fall.
I laugh when those who at the spear are bold
And venturous, if that fail them, shrink, and fear   *205*
What yet they know must follow—to endure
Exile, or ignominy, or bonds, or pain,
The sentence of their conqueror. This is now
Our doom, which if we can sustain and bear,
Our Súpreme Foe in time may much remit   *210*
His anger, and perhaps, thus far removed,
Not mind us not offending, satisfied
With what is punished; whence these raging fires
Will slacken, if his breath stir not their flames.
Our purer essence then will overcome   *215*
Their noxious vapour, or, inured, not feel;
Or, changed at length, and to the place conformed
In temper and in nature, will receive
Familiar the fierce heat, and void of pain;
This horror will grow mild, this darkness light;   *220*
Besides what hope the never-ending flight
Of future days may bring, what chance, what change
Worth waiting, since our present lot appears

188 **force or guile** cf. i, 121

For happy though but ill, for ill not worst,
225 If we procure not to ourselves more woe.'
    Thus Belial, with words clothed in reason's garb,
Counselled ignoble ease and peaceful sloth,
Not peace; and after him thus Mammon spake:
    'Either to disenthrone the King of Heaven
230 We war, if war be best, or to regain
Our own right lost. Him to unthrone we then
May hope when everlasting Fate shall yield
To fickle Chance, and Chaos judge the strife,
The former vain to hope argues as vain
235 The latter, for what place can be for us
Within Heaven's bound unless Heaven's Lord Supreme
We overpower? Suppose he should relent,
And publish grace to all, on promise made
Of new subjection; with what eyes could we
240 Stand in his presence humble and receive
Strict laws imposed, to celebrate his throne
With warbled hymns and to his Godhead sing
Forced Halleluiahs, while he lordly sits
Our envied sovran and his altar breathes
245 Ambrosial odours and ambrosial flowers,
Our servile offerings? This must be our task
In Heaven, this our delight. How wearisome
Eternity so spent in worship paid
To whom we hate! Let us not then pursue,
250 By force impossible, by leave obtained
Unacceptable, though in Heaven, our state
Of splendid vassalage, but rather seek°
Our own good from ourselves, and from our own
Live to ourselves, though in this vast recess,
255 Free and to none accountable, preferring
Hard liberty before the easy yoke
Of servile pomp. Our greatness will appear
Then most conspicuous when great things of small,
Useful of hurtful, prosperous of adverse,
260 We can create, and in what place soe'er
Thrive under evil, and work ease out of pain

249–52 The meaning is, Let us not seek to win a state
unattainable by force and unacceptable if given to us by
Heaven's permission, for it still means bondage.

Through labour and endurance. This deep world
Of darkness do we dread? How oft amidst
Thick clouds and dark doth Heaven's all-ruling Sire
Choose to reside, his glory unobscured, 265
And with the majesty of darkness round
Covers his throne, from whence deep thunders roar,
Mustering their rage, and Heaven resembles Hell!
As he our darkness, cannot we his light
Imitate when we please? This desert soil 270
Wants not her hidden lustre, gems and gold,°
Nor want we skill or art from whence to raise
Magnificence—and what can Heaven show more?
Our torments also may, in length of time,
Become our elements, these piercing fires 275
As soft as now severe, our temper changed
Into their temper; which must needs remove
The sensible° of pain. All things invite
To peaceful counsels, and the settled state
Of order, how in safety best we may 280
Compose our present evils, with regard
Of what we are and where,° dismissing quite
All thoughts of war. Ye have what I advise.'
  He scarce had finished when such murmur filled
The assembly as when hollow rocks retain 285
The sound of blustering winds, which all night long
Had roused the sea, now with hoarse cadence lull
Seafaring men o'erwatched,° whose bark by chance,
Or pinnace, anchors in a craggy bay
After the tempest. Such applause was heard 290
As Mammon ended, and his sentence pleased,
Advising peace, for such another field
They dreaded worse than Hell, so much the fear
Of thunder and the sword of Michael
Wrought still within them, and no less desire 295
To found this nether empire, which might rise,
By policy and long procéss of time,
In emulation opposite to Heaven.

---

271 **gems and gold** cf. i, 538 278 **sensible** sensibility,
sense 282 **where** 1674 reads *were*. 288 **o'erwatched** wearied
with watching ("overwatched and wearied out," *Samson
Agonistes,* 405)

　　　Which when Beëlzebub perceived—than whom,
300　Satan except, none higher sat—with grave
　　　Aspéct he rose, and in his rising seemed
　　　A pillar of state; deep on his front engraven
　　　Deliberation sat,° and public care,
　　　And princely counsel in his face yet shone,
305　Majestic, though in ruin; sage he stood,
　　　With Atlantean° shoulders, fit to bear
　　　The weight of mightiest monarchies; his look
　　　Drew audience and attention still as night
　　　Or summer's noontide air, while thus he spake:
310　　　'Thrones and Imperial Powers, Offspring of Heaven,
　　　Ethereal Virtues! or these titles now
　　　Must we renounce, and, changing style, be called
　　　Princes of Hell? for so the popular vote
　　　Inclines, here to continue, and build up here
315　A growing empire—doubtless! while we dream,
　　　And know not that the King of Heaven hath doomed
　　　This place our dungeon, not our safe retreat
　　　Beyond his potent arm, to live exempt
　　　From Heaven's high jurisdiction in new league
320　Banded against his throne, but to remain
　　　In strictest bondage, though thus far removed,°
　　　Under the inevitable curb, reserved
　　　His captive multitude. For he, be sure,
　　　In height or depth, still first and last will reign
325　Sole king, and of his kingdom lose no part
　　　By our revolt, but over Hell extend
　　　His empire, and with iron sceptre rule
　　　Us here, as with his golden those in Heaven.°
　　　What° sit we then projecting peace and war?
330　War hath determined us and foiled with loss
　　　Irreparable, terms of peace yet none
　　　Vouchsafed or sought; for what peace will be given
　　　To us enslaved, but custody severe,
　　　And stripes, and arbitrary punishment
335　Inflicted? and what peace can we return,

303 Cf. "care/ Sat on his faded cheek," i, 601 ff. 306
Atlantean Atlas the Titan bore up the heavens. 321 **thus far
removed** a contemptuous echo of Belial (211) 327–28 Cf.
"Lycidas," 111. 329 **What** why (Quid)

But, to our power, hostility and hate,
Untamed reluctance, and revenge, though slow,
Yet ever plotting how the Conqueror least
May reap his conquest, and may least rejoice
In doing what we most in suffering feel?   340
Nor will occasion want, nor shall we need
With dangerous expedition to invade
Heaven, whose high walls fear no assault or siege,
Or ambush from the Deep. What if we find
Some easier enterprise? There is a place   345
(If ancient and prophetic fame in Heaven
Err not), another World, the happy seat
Of some new race, called Man, about this time
To be created like to us, though less
In power and excellence, but favoured more   350
Of him who rules above; so was his will
Pronounced among the Gods, and by an oath
That shook Heaven's whole circumference confirmed.°
Thither let us bend all our thoughts, to learn
What creatures there inhabit, of what mould   355
Or substance, how endued, and what their power,
And where their weakness, how attempted best,
By force or subtlety. Though Heaven be shut,
And Heaven's high Arbitrator sit secure
In his own strength, this place may lie exposed,   360
The utmost border of his kingdom, left
To their defence who hold it; here, perhaps,
Some advantageous act may be achieved
By sudden onset, either with Hell-fire
To waste his whole creation, or possess   365
All as our own, and drive, as we were driven,
The puny° habitants, or, if not drive,
Seduce them to our party, that their God
May prove their foe, and with repenting hand
Abolish his own works. This would surpass   370
Common revenge, and interrupt his joy

352–53 The chief Olympian so swears in the *Aeneid* and the
Iliad, but this is biblical too, Genesis xxii, 16; Isaiah xlv, 23;
Hebrews vi, 13; etc. 367 **puny** Milton doubtless is
remembering the etymology *puis né,* later born.

In our confusion, and our joy upraise
In his disturbance, when his darling sons,
Hurled headlong° to partake with us, shall curse
375 Their frail originals,° and faded bliss,
Faded so soon! Advise if this be worth
Attempting, or to sit in darkness here
Hatching vain empires.' Thus Beëlzebub
Pleaded his devilish counsel, first devised
380 By Satan, and in part proposed—for whence
But from the author of all ill could spring
So deep a malice, to confound the race
Of mankind in one root, and Earth with Hell
To mingle and involve, done all to spite
385 The great Creator? But their spite still serves
His glory to augment. The bold design
Pleased highly those Infernal States, and joy
Sparkled in all their eyes: with full assent
They vote, whereat his speech he thus renews:
390   'Well have ye judged, well ended long debate,
Synod of Gods, and, like to what ye are,
Great things resolved, which from the lowest deep
Will once more lift us up, in spite of fate,
Nearer our ancient seat—perhaps in view
395 Of those bright confines, whence, with neighbouring arms,
And opportune excursion, we may chance
Re-enter Heaven, or else in some mild zone
Dwell, not unvisited of Heaven's fair light
Secure, and at the brightening orient beam
400 Purge off this gloom: the soft delicious air,
To heal the scar of those corrosive fires,
Shall breathe her balm. But, first, whom shall we send°
In search of this new world? whom shall we find
Sufficient? who shall tempt° with wandering feet
405 The dark, unbottomed, infinite abyss,
And through the palpable obscure find out
His uncouth° way, or spread his aery flight,

374 **Hurled headlong** cf. i, 45   375 **originals** 1674 has the
singular.   402 An ironic echo of Isaiah vi, 8: "Also I heard
the voice of the Lord, saying, Whom shall I send, and who
will go for us? Then said I, Here am I; send me."   404 **tempt**
attempt   407 **uncouth** unknown; cf. 827

Upborne with indefatigable wings
Over the vast abrupt, ere he arrive
The happy isle? What strength, what art, can then   410
Suffice, or what evasion bear him safe
Through the strict senteries and stations thick
Of Angels watching round? Here he had need
All circumspection,° and we now no less
Choice in our suffrage, for on whom we send   415
The weight of all, and our last hope, relies.'
    This said, he sat, and expectation held
His look suspense, awaiting who appeared
To second, or oppose, or undertake
The perilous attempt. But all sat mute,°   420
Pondering the danger with deep thoughts, and each
In other's countenance read his own dismay,
Astonished. None among the choice and prime
Of those Heaven-warring champions could be found
So hardy as to proffer or accept,   425
Alone, the dreadful voyage; till, at last,
Satan, whom now transcendent glory raised
Above his fellows, with monarchal pride
Conscious of highest worth, unmoved thus spake:
    'O Progeny of Heaven! Empyreal Thrones!   430
With reason hath deep silence and demur
Seized us, though undismayed: long is the way
And hard that out of Hell leads up to light;
Our prison strong, this huge convex of fire,
Outrageous to devour, immures us round   435
Ninefold; and gates of burning adamant,
Barred over us, prohibit all egress.
These passed, if any pass, the void profound
Of unessential° Night receives him next,
Wide-gaping, and with utter loss of being   440
Threatens him, plunged in that abortive° gulf.
If thence he 'scape, into whatever world,
Or unknown region, what remains him less

---

414 **circumspection** figurative and literal, *looking all
around*   420 ff. This is parallel to the embarrassing question
of who shall fight Hector, *Iliad,* VII, 92 ff. It is also parallel to
iii, 217 ff.   439 **unessential** uncreated (cf. 150)   441 **abortive**
from which arises nothing, or nothing but the monstrous

Than unknown dangers, and as hard escape?
445 But I should ill become this throne, O Peers,
    And this imperial sovranty, adorned
    With splendour, armed with power, if aught proposed
    And judged of public moment in the shape
    Of difficulty or danger could deter
450 Me from attempting. Wherefore do I assume
    These royalties, and not refuse to reign,
    Refusing to accept as great a share
    Of hazard as of honour, due alike
    To him who reigns, and so much to him due
455 Of hazard more as he above the rest
    High honoured sits? Go, therefore, mighty Powers,
    Terror of Heaven, though fallen; intend° at home,
    While here shall be our home, what best may ease
    The present misery, and render Hell
460 More tolerable, if there be cure or charm
    To respite, or deceive, or slack the pain
    Of this ill mansion; intermit no watch
    Against a wakeful foe, while I abroad
    Through all the coasts of dark destruction seek
465 Deliverance for us all: this enterprise
    None shall partake with me.' Thus saying, rose
    The Monarch, and prevented all reply;
    Prudent, lest, from his resolution raised,
    Others among the chief might offer now,
470 Certain to be refused, what erst they feared,
    And, so refused, might in opinion stand
    His rivals, winning cheap the high repute
    Which he through hazard huge must earn. But they
    Dreaded not more the adventure than his voice
475 Forbidding; and at once with him they rose.
    Their rising all at once was as the sound
    Of thunder heard remote. Towards him they bend
    With awful reverence prone, and as a God
    Extol him equal to the Highest in Heaven.
480 Nor failed they to express how much they praised
    That for the general safety he despised
    His own; for neither do the Spirits damned
    Lose all their virtue, lest bad men should boast

457 **intend** deliberate

Their specious deeds on earth, which glory excites,
Or close ambition varnished o'er with zeal. 485
Thus they their doubtful consultations dark
Ended, rejoicing in their matchless chief:
As when from mountain-tops the dusky clouds
Ascending, while the north wind sleeps, o'erspread
Heaven's cheerful face,° the louring element 490
Scowls o'er the darkened landscape snow, or shower,
If chance the radiant sun, with farewell sweet,
Extend his evening beam, the fields revive,
The birds their notes renew, and bleating herds
Attest their joy, that hill and valley rings. 495
O shame to men! Devil with devil damned
Firm concord holds; men only disagree
Of creatures rational, though under hope
Of heavenly grace, and, God proclaiming peace,
Yet live in hatred, enmity, and strife 500
Among themselves, and levy cruel wars,
Wasting the earth, each other to destroy—
As if (which might induce us to accord)
Man had not hellish foes enough besides,
That day and night for his destruction wait. 505
  The Stygian council thus dissolved, and forth
In order came the grand Infernal Peers;
Midst came their mighty Paramount,° and seemed
Alone the antagonist of Heaven, nor less
Than Hell's dread Emperor, with pomp supreme, 510
And godlike imitated state; him round
A globe of fiery Seraphim enclosed
With bright emblazonry and horrent° arms.
Then of their session ended they bid cry
With trumpet's regal sound the great result: 515
Toward the four winds four speedy Cherubim
Put to their mouths the sounding alchemy
By herald's voice explained; the hollow abyss
Heard far and wide, and all the host of Hell
With deafening shout returned them loud acclaim. 520
Thence more at ease their minds, and somewhat raised

490 **Heaven's cheerful face** a phrase from Spenser, *Faerie Queene*, II, xii, 34, 7   508 **Paramount** chief   513 **horrent** bristling (cf. i, 563)

By false presumptuous hope, the rangèd Powers
Disband, and, wandering, each his several way
Pursues, as inclination or sad choice
525 Leads him perplexed, where he may likeliest find
Truce to his restless thoughts, and entertain
The irksome hours till his great chief return.
Part on the plain, or in the air sublime,°
Upon the wing or in swift race contend,
530 As at the Olympian games or Pythian fields;°
Part curb their fiery steeds, or shun the goal
With rapid wheels, or fronted brígades form:
As when, to warn proud cities, war appears
Waged in the troubled sky, and armies rush
535 To battle in the clouds; before each van°
Prick forth the aery knights, and couch their spears,
Till thickest legions close; with feats of arms
From either end of heaven the welkin° burns.
Others, with vast Typhoean° rage, more fell,
540 Rend up both rocks and hills, and ride the air
In whirlwind; Hell scarce holds the wild uproar:
As when Alcides,° from Oechalia crowned
With conquest, felt the envenomed robe, and tore
Through pain up by the roots Thessalian pines,
545 And Lichas from the top of Oeta threw
Into the Euboic sea. Others, more mild,
Retreated in a silent valley, sing
With notes angelical to many a harp
Their own heroic deeds, and hapless fall
550 By doom of battle, and complain that Fate
Free Virtue should enthrall to Force or Chance.
Their song was partial;° but the harmony

528 **sublime** uplifted   530 **Pythian fields** south of Delphi,
where the Pythian Games were held   535 **van** vanguard   538
welkin sky   539 **Typhoean** Typhon (cf. i, 199), after his
defeat by Zeus, was placed under Mount Aetna, whence he
causes eruptions.   542 ff. Alcides is Hercules, who, after
defeating and slaying Eurytus the king of Oechalia in
Thessaly, became the victim of a deceit, a poisoned robe
innocently brought by an attendant, Lichas, whom the hero,
in his dying frenzy, hurled to destruction.   552 **partial**
prejudiced in their own favor, like the previous statements
of the fallen leaders

(What could it less when Spirits immortal° sing?)
Suspended Hell, and took with ravishment
The thronging audience. In discourse more sweet   555
(For Eloquence the Soul, Song charms the Sense)
Others apart sat on a hill retired,
In thoughts more elevate, and reasoned high
Of Providence, Foreknowledge, Will, and Fate—
Fixed fate, free will, foreknowledge absolute—   560
And found no end, in wandering mazes lost.
Of good and evil much they argued then,
Of happiness and final misery,
Passion and apathy, and glory and shame—
Vain wisdom all, and false philosophy!—   565
Yet, with a pleasing sorcery, could charm
Pain for a while or anguish, and excite
Fallacious hope, or arm the obdurèd breast
With stubborn patience as with triple steel.
Another part, in squadrons and gross° bands,   570
On bold adventure to discover wide°
That dismal world, if any clime perhaps
Might yield them easier habitation, bend
Four ways their flying march, along the banks
Of four infernal rivers, that disgorge   575
Into the burning lake° their baleful streams:
Abhorrèd Styx,° the flood of deadly hate;
Sad Acheron of sorrow, black and deep;
Cocytus, named of lamentation loud
Heard on the rueful stream; fierce Phlegethon,   580
Whose waves of torrent fire inflame with rage.
Far off from these, a slow and silent stream,
Lethe, the river of oblivion, rolls
Her watery labyrinth, whereof who drinks
Forthwith his former state and being forgets,   585
Forgets both joy and grief, pleasure and pain.
Beyond this flood a frozen continent
Lies dark and wild, beat with perpetual storms

---

553 **Spirits immortal** cf. "immortal Spirits," i, 622   570 **gross**
compact   571 **discover wide** i, 724 ends with the same
words.   576 **the burning lake** cf. "Chained on the burning
lake," i, 210; ii, 169   577–83 Each of the five names is followed
by its etymology—*hate, sorrow, lamentation, fire, oblivion.*

Of whirlwind and dire hail, which on firm land
590 Thaws not, but gathers heap, and ruin seems
Of ancient pile;° all else deep snow and ice,
A gulf profound as that Serbonian bog°
Betwixt Damiata and Mount Casius old,
Where armies whole have sunk: the parching air
595 Burns frore,° and cold performs the effect of fire.
Thither, by harpy-footed Furies haled,
At certain revolutions all the damned
Are brought, and feel by turns the bitter change
Of fierce extremes, extremes by change more fierce,
600 From beds of raging fire° to starve° in ice
Their soft ethereal warmth, and there to pine
Immovable, infixed, and frozen round
Periods of time, thence hurried back to fire.
They ferry over this Lethean sound
605 Both to and fro, their sorrow to augment,
And wish and struggle, as they pass, to reach
The tempting stream, with one small drop to lose
In sweet forgetfulness all pain and woe,
All in one moment, and so near the brink;
610 But Fate withstands, and, to oppose the attempt,
Medusa° with Gorgonian terror guards
The ford, and of itself the water flies
All taste of living wight, as once it fled
The lip of Tantalus.° Thus roving on
615 In cónfused march forlorn, the adventurous bands,
With shuddering horror pale and eyes aghast,

591 **pile** building   592 Referring to a treacherous mixture of
sand and water on the coast of Lower Egypt described by
Diodorus Siculus, who said, "many, unacquainted with the
nature of the place, by missing their way, have been there
swallowed up, together with whole armies."   595 **frore** frozen
(the old past participle; cf. German *gefroren*)   600 **raging fire**
plural at 213 **starve** The original meaning was perish.   611
Medusa one of three monstrous sisters, the Gorgons (cf. 628).
Odysseus feared on his visit to Hades she would turn him into
stone, as the mere sight of them was capable of doing.   614
Tantalus Having incurred the displeasure of Zeus, he received
in Hades the punishment that led to the word *tantalize;* cf.
Samson Agonistes, 496–501. Of course *once,* 613, is an
anachronism, like i, 550.

Viewed first their lamentable lot, and found
No rest. Through many a dark and dreary vale
They passed, and many a region dolorous,°
O'er many a frozen, many a fiery Alp,   620
Rocks, caves, lakes, fens, bogs, dens, and shades of
    death—
A universe of death, which God by curse
Created evil, for evil only good;
Where all life dies, death lives, and Nature breeds,
Perverse, all monstrous, all prodigious things,   625
Abominable, unutterable, and worse
Than fables yet have feigned or fear conceived,
Gorgons, and Hydras,° and Chimaeras° dire.
   Meanwhile the Adversary of God and Man,
Satan, with thoughts inflamed of highest design,   630
Puts on swift wings, and toward the gates of Hell
Explores his solitary flight: sometimes
He scours the right-hand coast, sometimes the left:
Now shares with level wing the deep, then soars
Up to the fiery concave towering high.   635
As when far off at sea a fleet descried
Hangs in the clouds, by equinoctial winds
Close sailing from Bengala,° or the isles
Of Ternate and Tidore,° whence merchants bring
Their spicy drugs; they on the trading flood,   640
Through the wide Ethiopian to the Cape,°
Ply stemming nightly toward the pole: so seemed
Far off° the flying Fiend. At last appear
Hell-bounds, high reaching to the horrid roof,
And thrice threefold the gates; three folds were brass, 645
Three iron, three of adamantine rock,
Impenetrable, impaled with circling fire

619 **region dolorous** a Dantean echo, "città dolente," *Inferno*,
III, i 628 **Hydras** many-headed snakes **Chimaeras** fire-
breathing monsters (given the same adjective at "Comus,"
517). The same list is in *Aeneid* VI, 287– 89. 638 **Bengala**
Bengal, in Milton's day part of the Mogul Empire 639
Ternate and Tidore "Spice Islands" in the East Indies in the
Molucca Sea 641 Through the Indian Ocean to the Cape of
Good Hope 643 **Far off** characteristic adverbial expression,
636, 582

Yet unconsumed. Before the gates there sat°
On either side a formidable Shape;
650 The one seemed woman to the waist, and fair,
But ended foul in many a scaly fold,
Voluminous° and vast, a serpent armed
With mortal sting. About her middle round
A cry° of Hell-hounds never-ceasing barked
655 With wide Cerberean° mouths full loud, and rung
A hideous peal, yet, when they list, would creep,
If aught disturbed their noise, into her womb,
And kennel there, yet there still barked and howled
Within unseen. Far less abhorred than these
660 Vexed Scylla, bathing in the sea that parts
Calabria from the hoarse Trinacrian shore,°
Nor uglier follow the night-hag, when, called
In secret, riding through the air she comes,
Lured with the smell of infant blood, to dance
665 With Lapland° witches, while the labouring moon
Eclipses at their charms. The other Shape—
If shape it might be called that shape had none
Distinguishable in member, joint, or limb,
Or substance might be called that shadow seemed,
670 For each seemed either—black it stood as Night,

648 ff. The prime impetus for the allegory of Sin and Death
comes from James i, 15: "Then when lust hath conceived, it
bringeth forth sin: and sin, when it is finished, bringeth forth
death." Further influences were the myth of Scylla (made a
symbol of sin by St. John Chrysostom), Pallas Athene's birth
from the head of Zeus (note 757–58), and Spenser's pic-
turizations of Error and Death (*F.Q.,* I, i, 14; VII, vii, 46).   652
Voluminous literally, in rolls (*volumina*)   654 **cry** means
pack.   655 Cerberus was the three-headed dog that guarded
the threshold of Hades. Milton is following Ovid's description
of Scylla (*Met.* XIV, 65).   660–61 Geographically, *Scylla* is a
rock on the Italian side of the Strait of Messina, opposite
Charybdis on the Sicilian side; once a lovely nymph whom
Circe, her rival for Glaucus's love, made a monster from the
waist down, beset by barking dogs.   665 Lapland, by which
"Russia is bounded on the north" (Milton's *History of
Muscovia*), surpassed "all nations in the world" for witches,
according to Hakluyt. They had magical power over the moon,
the very word "labouring" echoing Virgilian and Juvenalian
phrases meaning eclipse.

Fierce as ten Furies, terrible as Hell,
And shook a dreadful dart; what seemed his head
The likeness of a kingly crown had on.
Satan was now at hand, and from his seat
The monster moving onward came as fast   675
With horrid strides; Hell trembled as he strode.
The undaunted Fiend what this might be admired°—
Admired, not feared; God and his Son except,
Created thing naught valued he nor shunned;
And with disdainful look thus first began: 680
    'Whence and what art thou, execrable Shape,
That dar'st, though grim and terrible, advance
Thy miscreated front athwart my way
To yonder gates? Through them I mean to pass,
That be assured, without leave asked of thee.   685
Retire, or taste thy folly, and learn by proof,
Hell-born, not to contend with Spirits of Heaven.'
    To whom the Goblin, full of wrath, replied:
'Art thou that Traitor Angel, art thou he
Who first broke peace in Heaven and faith, till then   690
Unbroken,° and in proud rebellious arms
Drew after him the third part of Heaven's sons,
Conjured against the Highest, for which both thou
And they, outcast from God, are here condemned
To waste eternal days in woe and pain?   695
And reck'n'st thou thyself with Spirits of Heaven,
Hell-doomed,° and breath'st defiance here and scorn,
Where I reign king, and, to enrage thee more,
Thy king and lord? Back to thy punishment,
False fugitive, and to thy speed add wings,   700
Lest with a whip of scorpions I pursue
Thy lingering, or with one stroke of this dart
Strange horror seize thee, and pangs unfelt before.'
    So spake the grisly Terror, and in shape,
So speaking and so threatening, grew tenfold   705
More dreadful and deform. On the other side,
Incensed with indignation, Satan stood

---

677 **admired** wondered   691 **Unbroken** There is profit in the
ambiguity of this participle's reference—i.e., it fits "he"
almost as well as "peace . . . and faith."   697 **Hell-doomed**
a retort for "Hell-born," 687

Unterrified, and like a comet burned
That fires the length of Ophiuchus° huge
710 In the arctic sky, and from his horrid hair°
Shakes pestilence and war. Each at the head
Levelled his deadly aim; their fatal hands
No second stroke intend, and such a frown
Each cast at the other as when two black clouds,
715 With Heaven's artillery fraught, come rattling on
Over the Caspian, then stand front to front
Hovering a space, till winds the signal blow
To join their dark encounter in mid-air:°
So frowned the mighty combatants, that Hell
720 Grew darker at their frown; so matched they stood;
For never but once more was either like
To meet so great a foe:° and now great deeds
Had been achieved, whereof all Hell had rung,
Had not the snaky Sorceress that sat
725 Fast by Hell-gate and kept the fatal key
Risen, and with hideous outcry rushed between.
   'O Father, what intends thy hand,' she cried,
'Against thy only son? What fury, O son,
Possesses thee to bend that mortal dart
730 Against thy father's head? and know'st for whom?
For him who sits above, and laughs the while
At thee, ordained his drudge to execute
Whate'er his wrath, which he calls justice, bids,
His wrath, which one day will destroy ye both!'
735   She spake, and at her words the hellish Pest
Forbore, then these to her Satan returned:
   'So strange thy outcry, and thy words so strange
Thou interposest, that my sudden hand,
Prevented, spares to tell thee yet by deeds
740 What it intends, till first I know of thee

709 **Ophiuchus** "serpent-bearer," a big northern constellation
(evil, like barbaric invasion, comes from the north: cf. v,
689)   710 **hair** *Comet* derives from a Greek word meaning
long-haired, the reference being to its tail.   712–18 cf. vi,
310–18   721–22 1 Corinthians, xv, 25–26 explains that Christ
"must reign, till he hath put all enemies under his feet. The
last enemy that shall be destroyed is death;" cf. 734.   722 **so
great a foe** The opponent was so identified at 202 (and
compare i, 122).

What thing thou art, thus double-formed, and why,
In this infernal vale first met, thou call'st
Me father, and that phantasm call'st my son.
I know thee not, nor ever saw till now
Sight more detestable than him and thee.'   745
　　To whom thus the Portress of Hell-gate replied:
'Hast thou forgot me, then, and do I seem
Now in thine eye so foul, once deemed so fair
In Heaven, when at the assembly, and in sight
Of all the Seraphim with thee combined   750
In bold conspiracy against Heaven's King,
All on a sudden miserable pain
Surprised thee, dim thine eyes, and dizzy swum
In darkness, while thy head flames thick and fast
Threw forth, till on the left side opening wide,   755
Likest to thee in shape and countenance bright,
Then shining heavenly fair, a goddess armed,
Out of thy head I sprung. Amazement seized
All the host of Heaven; back they recoiled afraid
At first, and called me *Sin,* and for a sign   760
Portentous held me; but, familiar grown,
I pleased, and with attractive graces won
The most averse—thee chiefly, who, full oft
Thyself in me thy perfect image viewing,
Becam'st enamoured, and such joy thou took'st   765
With me in secret that my womb conceived
A growing burden. Meanwhile war arose
And fields were fought in Heaven,° wherein remained
(For what could else?) to our Almighty Foe
Clear victory, to our part loss and rout   770
Through all the Empyrean. Down they fell,
Driven headlong from the pitch of Heaven, down
Into this deep, and in the general fall
I also, at which time this powerful key
Into my hand was given, with charge to keep   775
These gates for ever shut, which none can pass
Without my opening. Pensive here I sat
Alone, but long I sat not, till my womb,
Pregnant by thee, and now excessive grown,
Prodigious motion felt and rueful throes.   780

768 **fought in Heaven** cf. 45

At last this odious offspring whom thou seest,
Thine own begotten, breaking violent way,
Tore through my entrails, that, with fear and pain
Distorted, all my nether shape thus grew
785 Transformed; but he my inbred enemy
Forth issued, brandishing his fatal dart,
Made to destroy. I fled, and cried out *Death!*
Hell trembled° at the hideous name, and sighed
From all her caves, and back resounded *Death!*
790 I fled; but he pursued (though more, it seems,
Inflamed with lust than rage), and, swifter far,
Me overtook, his mother, all dismayed,
And, in embraces forcible and foul
Engendering with me, of that rape begot
795 These yelling monsters, that with ceaseless cry
Surround me, as thou saw'st, hourly conceived
And hourly born, with sorrow infinite
To me, for, when they list, into the womb
That bred them they return, and howl, and gnaw
800 My bowels, their repast, then, bursting forth
Afresh, with conscious terrors vex me round,
That rest or intermission none I find.
Before mine eyes in opposition sits
Grim Death, my son and foe, who sets them on,
805 And me, his parent, would full soon devour
For want of other prey, but that he knows
His end with mine involved, and knows that I
Should prove a bitter morsel and his bane,
Whenever that shall be: so Fate pronounced.
810 But thou, O Father, I forewarn thee, shun
His deadly arrow; neither vainly hope
To be invulnerable in those bright arms,
Though tempered heavenly; for that mortal dint,°
Save he who reigns above, none can resist.'
815   She finished; and the subtle Fiend his lore
Soon learned, now milder, and thus answered smooth:
    'Dear daughter, since thou claim'st me for thy sire,
And my fair son here show'st me, the dear pledge

---

788 **Hell trembled** cf. 676   813 **mortal dint** deadly stroke
("dent" is another form of the same word)

Of dalliance had with thee in Heaven, and joys
Then sweet, now sad to mention, through dire change°   820
Befallen us unforeseen, unthought-of, know
I come no enemy, but to set free
From out this dark and dismal house of pain
Both him and thee, and all the heavenly host
Of Spirits that, in our just pretences armed,   825
Fell with us from on high. From them I go
This uncouth errand sole, and one for all
Myself expose, with lonely steps to tread
The unfounded deep, and through the void immense
To search, with wandering quest, a place foretold   830
Should be, and, by concurring signs, ere now
Created vast and round, a place of bliss
In the purlieus of Heaven, and therein placed
A race of upstart creatures, to supply
Perhaps our vacant room, though more removed,   835
Lest Heaven, surcharged with potent multitude,
Might hap to move new broils. Be this, or aught
Than this more secret, now designed, I haste
To know, and, this once known, shall soon return,
And bring ye to the place where thou and Death   840
Shall dwell at ease, and up and down unseen
Wing silently the buxom° air, embalmed
With odours. There ye shall be fed and filled
Immeasurably; all things shall be your prey.'
He ceased; for both seemed highly pleased, and Death   845
Grinned horrible° a ghastly smile to hear
His famine should be filled, and blessed his maw
Destined to that good hour. No less rejoiced
His mother bad, and thus bespake her sire:
    'The key of this infernal Pit, by due   850
And by command of Heaven's all-powerful King
I keep, by him forbidden to unlock
These adamantine gates; against all force
Death ready stands to interpose his dart,

---

820 **dire change** cf. i, 625   842 **buxom** yielding   846 **horrible**
adverb formed from the neuter singular accusative of the
adjective, as in Latin (*horribile*)

855 Fearless to be o'ermatched by living might.°
But what owe I to his commands above,
Who hates me and hath hither thrust me down
Into this gloom of Tartarus profound,
To sit in hateful office here confined,
860 Inhabitant of Heaven and heavenly-born,
Here in perpetual agony and pain,
With terrors and with clamours compassed round
Of mine own brood, that on my bowels feed?
Thou art my father, thou my author, thou
865 My being gav'st me; whom should I obey
But thee? whom follow? thou wilt bring me soon
To that new world of light and bliss, among
The gods who live at ease,° where I shall reign
At thy right hand voluptuous, as beseems
870 Thy daughter and thy darling, without end."°
    Thus saying, from her side the fatal key,°
Sad instrument of all our woe,° she took,
And, towards the gate rolling her bestial train,
Forthwith the huge portcullis high updrew,
875 Which, but herself, not all the Stygian Powers
Could once have moved; then in the key-hole turns
The intricate wards, and every bolt and bar
Of massy iron or solid rock with ease
Unfastens. On a sudden open fly,
880 With impetuous recoil and jarring sound,
The infernal doors, and on their hinges grate
Harsh thunder, that the lowest bottom shook
Of Erebus. She opened, but to shut
Excelled her power: the gates wide open stood,

855 **might** Third edition (1678) reads *wight*. 868 **The gods who live at ease** a literal translation of a Homeric expression 869–70 A blasphemous parody of the Nicene Creed: "And sitteth on the right hand of the Father: . . . whose Kingdom shall have no end." The poet has worked out in detail an Infernal Trinity as antithesis to the Heavenly Trinity. Note other correspondences between the first two books and the third, such as the two "consults" and the opposition between darkness and light. Compare the two references to "bliss," 867 and vi, 892. 871 **the fatal key** So ends l. 725. 872 **all our woe** cf. i, 3, where the phrase has greater relevance.

That with extended wings a bannered host,   885
Under spread ensigns marching, might pass through
With horse and chariots ranked in loose array;
So wide they stood, and like a furnace-mouth
Cast forth redounding smoke and ruddy flame.
Before their eyes in sudden view appear   890
The secrets of the hoary deep, a dark
Illimitable ocean, without bound,
Without dimension, where length, breadth, and height,
And time, and place, are lost, where eldest Night
And Chaos, ancestors of Nature, hold   895
Eternal anarchy, amidst the noise
Of endless wars, and by confusion stand.
For Hot, Cold, Moist, and Dry, four champions fierce,°
Strive here for mastery, and to battle bring
Their embryon atoms: they around the flag   900
Of each his faction, in their several clans,
Light-armed or heavy, sharp, smooth, swift, or slow,
Swarm populous, unnumbered as the sands
Of Barca or Cyrene's° torrid soil,
Levied to side with warring winds and poise   905
Their lighter wings. To whom these most adhere
He rules a moment; Chaos umpire sits,
And by decision more embroils the fray
By which he reigns: next him, high arbiter,
Chance governs all. Into this wild abyss,   910
The womb of Nature, and perhaps her grave,
Of neither sea, nor shore, nor air, nor fire,
But all these in their pregnant causes mixed
Confusedly, and which thus must ever fight,
Unless the Almighty Maker them ordain   915
His dark materials to create more worlds—
Into this wild abyss° the wary Fiend

898 The strife of the four elements—Fire, Air, Water, and
Earth—is a conception as old as Empedocles, the philosopher
named at iii, 471. The theme of evil as confusion and confusion
as evil is continuing. This is the "anarchy" outside the
cosmos.   904 **Barca, Cyrene** at present two towns in Cirenaica,
the part of "the Libyan sands" (i, 355) north of the Sahara
917 **Into this wild abyss** Here the poet catches a stitch in a
long sentence; cf. 910.

Stood on the brink of Hell and looked a while,
Pondering his voyage, for no narrow frith°
920 He had to cross. Nor was his ear less pealed
With noises loud and ruinous (to compare
Great things with small)° than when Bellona° storms
With all her battering engines bent to rase
Some capital city; or less than if this frame
925 Of Heaven were falling, and these elements
In mutiny had from her axle torn
The steadfast Earth. At last his sail-broad vans°
He spreads for flight, and, in the surging smoke
Uplifted, spurns the ground; thence many a league,
930 As in a cloudy chair, ascending rides
Audacious, but, that seat soon failing, meets
A vast vacuity. All unawares,
Fluttering his pennons° vain, plumb-down he drops
Ten thousand fathom° deep, and to this hour
935 Down had been falling, had not, by ill chance,
The strong rebuff of some tumultuous cloud,
Instinct with fire and nitre, hurried him
As many miles aloft; that fury stayed,
Quenched in a boggy Syrtis,° neither sea
940 Nor good dry land;° nigh foundered, on he fares,
Treading the crude consistence, half on foot,
Half flying; behooves him now both oar and sail.
As when a gryphon° through the wilderness
With winged course o'er hill or moory dale
945 Pursues the Arimaspian, who by stealth
Had from his wakeful custody purloined
The guarded gold, so eagerly the Fiend

919 **frith** firth, estuary   921–22 This parenthesis is a Virgilian
formula; repeated at vi, 310–11; x, 306.   922 **Bellona** goddess
of war   927 **vans** wings   933 **pennons** pinions   934 **fathom**
The original text has *fadom*.   939 **Syrtis** the Greek name for
each of two great ship-swallowing gulfs on the north coast of
Africa; generically quicksands (cf. Acts xxvii, 17—where the
name occurs in the Greek).   939–40 cf. 912   943 **gryphon** The
griffin was a fabulous eagle-headed winged lion, with a
penchant for hoarding gold. According to Herodotus: "The
story runs, that the one-eyed Arimaspi purloin it from the
griffins," in the region of the Urals.

O'er bog or steep, through strait, rough, dense, or rare,
With head, hands, wings, or feet, pursues his way,
And swims, or sinks, or wades, or creeps, or flies.   950
At length a universal hubbub wild
Of stunning sounds, and voices all confused,
Borne through the hollow dark, assaults his ear
With loudest vehemence; thither he plies,
Undaunted, to meet there whatever Power   955
Or Spirit of the nethermost abyss
Might in that noise reside, of whom to ask
Which way the nearest coast of darkness lies
Bordering on light; when straight behold the throne
Of Chaos, and his dark pavilion spread   960
Wide on the wasteful deep; with him enthroned
Sat sable-vested Night, eldest of things,
The consort of his reign, and by them stood
Orcus and Ades,° and the dreaded name
Of Demogorgon,° Rumour next, and Chance,   965
And Tumult, and Confusion, all embroiled,
And Discord with a thousand various mouths.
    To whom Satan, turning boldly, thus: 'Ye Powers
And Spirits of this nethermost abyss,°
Chaos and ancient Night, I come no spy   970
With purpose to explore or to disturb
The secrets of your realm, but, by constraint
Wandering this darksome desert, as my way
Lies through your spacious empire up to light,
Alone and without guide, half lost, I seek   975
What readiest path leads where your gloomy bounds
Confine with° Heaven; or, if some other place,
From your dominion won, the Ethereal King
Possesses lately, thither to arrive
I travel this profound. Direct my course: 980

964 Orcus and Ades Roman and Greek forms of Hades, god
of the underworld   **965 Demogorgon** "ancestor of all the
gods . . . also called Chaos by the ancients . . . begot the
Earth among many other children," observed Milton in his
Cambridge First Prolusion. The idea of the "dreaded" or
forbidden name comes from Lactantius on Statius. Demogorgon figures in Shelley's *Prometheus Unbound.*   **969** cf.
956   **977 Confine with** border on

Directed, no mean recompense it brings
To your behoof, if I that region lost,
All usurpation thence expelled, reduce
To her original darkness and your sway
985 (Which is my present journey), and once more
Erect the standard there of ancient Night;°
Yours be the advantage all, mine the revenge!'
 Thus Satan; and him thus the Anarch old,
With faltering speech and visage incomposed,°
990 Answered: 'I know thee, stranger, who thou art—
That mighty leading Angel, who of late
Made head against Heaven's King, though overthrown.
I saw and heard, for such a numerous host
Fled not in silence through the frighted deep,
995 With ruin upon ruin, rout on rout,
Confusion worse confounded, and Heaven-gates°
Poured out by millions her victorious bands,
Pursuing. I upon my frontiers here
Keep residence; if all I can will serve
1000 That little which is left so to defend,
Encroached on still through our intestine broils
Weakening the sceptre of old Night: first, Hell,
Your dungeon, stretching far and wide beneath;
Now lately Heaven° and Earth, another world
1005 Hung o'er my realm, linked in a golden chain
To that side Heaven° from whence your legions fell;
If that way be your walk, you have not far—
So much the nearer danger. Go, and speed;
Havoc, and spoil, and ruin, are my gain.'
1010 He ceased, and Satan stayed not to reply,
But, glad that now his sea should find a shore,
With fresh alacrity and force renewed
Springs upward, like a pyramid of fire,
Into the wild expanse, and through the shock
1015 Of fighting elements on all sides round
Environed, wins his way, harder beset

986 **ancient Night** cf. 970; also 1002 and i, 543. 989
incomposed not composed   996 **Heaven-gates** cf. i, 326   1004,
1006 The poet has been criticized for using "Heaven" in one
sentence in two different senses.

And more endangered than when Argo° passed
Through Bosporus betwixt the justling rocks,
Or when Ulysses on the larboard shunned
Charybdis, and by the other whirlpool° steered.   1020
So he with difficulty and labour hard
Moved on, with difficulty and labour he;
But, he once passed, soon after, when Man fell,
Strange alteration! Sin and Death amain,°
Following his track (such was the will of Heaven),   1025
Paved after him a broad and beaten way
Over the dark abyss, whose boiling gulf
Tamely endured a bridge of wondrous length,
From Hell continued, reaching the utmost orb
Of this frail world, by which the Spirits perverse   1030
With easy intercourse pass to and fro
To tempt or punish mortals, except whom
God and good Angels guard by special grace.
    But now at last the sacred influence
Of light appears, and from the walls of Heaven   1035
Shoots far into the bosom of dim Night
A glimmering dawn. Here Nature first begins
Her farthest verge, and Chaos to retire,
As from her outmost works, a broken foe,
With tumult less and with less hostile din,   1040
That Satan with less toil, and now with ease
Wafts on the calmer wave by dubious light,
And, like a weather-beaten vessel, holds
Gladly the port, though shrouds° and tackle torn,
Or in the emptier waste, resembling air,   1045
Weighs his spread wings, at leisure to behold
Far off the empyreal Heaven, extended wide
In circuit, undetermined square or round,°
With opal towers and battlements adorned
Of living sapphire,° once his native seat,   1050

1017 ff. **Argo** The ship that carried Jason in quest of the
Golden Fleece had to maneuver through "the justling rocks,"
the Sympleglades, at the entrance to the Black Sea from the
Sea of Marmora.   1020 **the other whirlpool** Scylla (see note
on 660–61)   1024 **amain** cf. 165   1044 **shrouds** the ropes of a
ship's rigging   1048 The "circuit" was so wide that its shape
could not be determined by the eye.   1050 **sapphire** on the
authority of Revelation xxi, 19

And, fast by, hanging in a golden chain,°
This pendent World,° in bigness as a star
Of smallest magnitude close by the moon.
Thither, full fraught with mischievous revenge
1055 Accursed, and in a cursèd hour, he hies.

1051 **hanging in a golden chain** cf. 1005   1052 **This pendent World** not "the pendulous round Earth" (iv, 1000) but the universe, the cosmos inside its shell unpenetrated as yet by Satan. He alights on "the utmost orb," 1029, the outside shell of the tenth sphere, the Primum Mobile "that first moved" (iii, 483) the concentric other nine which, according to the Ptolemaic astronomy, spin around the fixed earth—the Crystalline Sphere, the Sphere of the Fixed Stars, and the spheres of "the planets seven" (iii, 481): Saturn, Jupiter, Mars, the Sun, Venus, Mercury, and the Moon.

BOOK III

THE ARGUMENT

God, sitting on his throne, sees Satan flying towards this World, then newly created; shows him to the Son, who sat at his right hand; foretells the success of Satan in perverting mankind; clears his own justice and wisdom from all imputation, having created Man free and able enough to have withstood his Tempter; yet declares his purpose of grace towards him, in regard he fell not of his own malice, as did Satan, but by him seduced. The Son of God renders praises to his Father for the manifestation of his gracious purpose towards Man; but God again declares that grace cannot be extended towards Man without the satisfaction of Divine Justice; Man hath offended the majesty of God by aspiring to Godhead, and therefore, with all his progeny, devoted to death, must die, unless someone can be found sufficient to answer for his offence, and undergo his punishment. The Son of God freely offers himself a ransom for Man; the Father accepts him, ordains his incarnation, pronounces his exaltation above all names in Heaven and Earth, commands all the Angels to adore him; they obey, and, hymning to their harps in full choir, celebrate the Father and the Son. Meanwhile, Satan alights upon the bare convex of this World's outermost orb; where wandering he first finds a place since called the Limbo of Vanity; what persons and things fly up thither; thence comes to the gate of Heaven, described ascending by stairs, and the waters above the firmament that flow about it. His passage thence to the orb of the Sun; he finds there Uriel, the regent of that orb, but first changes himself into the shape of a meaner Angel, and, pretending a zealous desire to behold the new Creation, and Man whom God had placed here, inquires of him the place of his habitation, and is directed; alights first on Mount Niphates.

HAIL, holy Light, offspring of Heaven first-born!°
Or of the Eternal coeternal beam
May I express thee unblamed? since God is light,°
And never but in unapproachèd light
5 Dwelt from eternity, dwelt then in thee,
Bright effluence of bright essence increate!
Or hear'st thou rather pure ethereal stream,
Whose fountain who shall tell? before the Sun,
Before the Heavens, thou wert,° and at the voice
10 Of God, as with a mantle, didst invest
The rising world of waters dark and deep,
Won from the void and formless Infinite.
Thee I revisit now with bolder wing,
Escaped the Stygian Pool, though long detained
15 In that obscure sojourn, while in my flight,
Through utter and through middle darkness° borne,
With other notes than to the Orphean lyre°
I sung of Chaos and eternal Night,
Taught by the Heavenly Muse° to venture down
20 The dark descent, and up to reascend,
Though hard and rare—thee I revisit safe,°
And feel thy sovran vital lamp, but thou
Revisit'st not these eyes, that roll in vain
To find thy piercing ray, and find no dawn,
25 So thick a drop serene hath quenched their orbs,
Or dim suffusion veiled.° Yet not the more
Cease I to wander where the Muses haunt
Clear spring, or shady grove, or sunny hill,
Smit with the love of sacred song; but chief
30 Thee, Sion, and the flowery brooks beneath,°
That wash thy hallowed feet, and warbling flow,
Nightly I visit, nor sometimes forget

1 cf. i, 510   3 **God is light** 1 John i, 5   8–9 cf. Genesis i, 3,
16   16 Hell and Chaos are meant, respectively.   17 Again
Milton stresses that his is not the pagan inspiration, such as
that of the legendary Orpheus, on whom see "Lycidas,"
58.   19 **Heavenly Muse** as mentioned in the first invocation,
i, 6. "The precincts of light" (88) are the occasion for a fresh
and poignantly personal ceremonious beginning.   21 cf. 13
25–26 Milton did not know—nor do modern authorities
agree on—the nature and cause of the poet's blindness.   30
cf. i, 11

Those other two equalled with me in fate,
So were I equalled with them in renown,
Blind Thamyris° and blind Maeonides,°   *35*
And Tiresias° and Phineus,° prophets old,
Then feed on thoughts that voluntary move
Harmonious numbers,° as the wakeful bird°
Sings darkling,° and, in shadiest covert hid,
Tunes her nocturnal note. Thus with the year°   *40*
Seasons return, but not to me returns
Day, or the sweet approach of even or morn,
Or sight of vernal bloom, or summer's rose,
Or flocks, or herds, or human face divine,
But cloud instead and ever-during dark   *45*
Surrounds me, from the cheerful ways of men
Cut off, and, for the book of knowledge fair,
Presented with a universal blank
Of Nature's works, to me expunged and rased,
And wisdom at one entrance quite shut out.   *50*
So much the rather thou, Celestial Light,°
Shine inward, and the mind through all her powers
Irradiate; there plant eyes; all mist from thence
Purge and disperse, that I may see and tell
Of things invisible to mortal sight.   *55*
  Now had the Almighty Father from above,
From the pure empyrean where he sits
High throned above all height, bent down his eye,
His own works and their works at once to view;
About him all the Sanctities of Heaven   *60*
Stood thick as stars, and from his sight received
Beatitude past utterance; on his right
The radiant image of his glory sat,
His only Son; on Earth he first beheld
Our two first parents, yet the only two   *65*

35 **Thamyris** bard who, for his audacity in challenging the
Muses to a test of skill, was deprived by them of his sight
Maeonides Homer   36 **Tiresias** the blind soothsayer renowned
from Sophocles' *Oedipus Rex* to Eliot's *The Wasteland* **Phineus**
like Thamyris was from Thrace.   38 **numbers** verse **the
wakeful bird** the nightingale   39 **darkling** in the dark   40–50
cf. *Samson Agonistes*, 67–109   51 **Celestial Light** cf. i, 245

Of mankind, in the happy garden placed,
Reaping immortal fruits of joy and love,
Uninterrupted joy, unrivalled love,
In blissful solitude; he then surveyed
70 Hell and the gulf between, and Satan there
Coasting the wall of Heaven on this side Night,
In the dun air sublime, and ready now
To stoop, with wearied wings and willing feet,
On the bare outside of this World, that seemed
75 Firm land° imbosomed without firmament,
Uncertain which, in ocean or in air.
Him God beholding from his prospect high,
Wherein past, present, future, he beholds,
Thus to his only Son foreseeing spake:
80   'Only-begotten Son, seest thou what rage
Transports our Adversary? whom no bounds
Prescribed, no bars of Hell, nor all the chains
Heaped on him there, nor yet the main abyss
Wide interrupt,° can hold, so bent he seems
85 On desperate revenge° that shall redound
Upon his own rebellious head. And now,
Through all restraint broke loose, he wings his way
Not far off Heaven, in the precincts of light,
Directly towards the new-created World,
90 And Man there placed, with purpose to assay
If him by force he can destroy, or worse,
By some false guile pervert—and shall pervert;°
For Man will hearken to his glozing lies,
And easily transgress the sole command,
95 Sole pledge of his obedience:° so will fall
He and his faithless progeny. Whose fault?
Whose but his own? Ingrate, he had of me

75 **Firm land** cf. ii, 589 (*terra firma*)   84 **Wide interrupt**
referring to the wide division between Hell and Heaven   85
desperate revenge a phrase from ii, 107   92 **and shall pervert**
God foreknows the future, but this foreknowledge is not to be
interpreted as an interference with the creatures' free will;
God's foreknowledge is of the wrong choice that Man will
make. Cf. 117–18.   94–95 The forbidden tree had to be in the
garden or Man would have had nothing important on which
to exercise his free will. If he had had no opportunity to
disobey he would have been in effect a puppet; cf. 103 ff.

All he could have; I made him just and right,
Sufficient to have stood, though free to fall.
Such I created all the Ethereal Powers   *100*
And Spirits, both them who stood and them who failed;
Freely they stood who stood, and fell who fell.
Not free, what proof could they have given sincere
Of true allegiance, constant faith, or love,
Where only what they needs must do appeared,   *105*
Not what they would? What praise could they receive,
What pleasure I, from such obedience paid,
When Will and Reason (Reason also is Choice),°
Useless and vain, of freedom both despoiled,
Made passive both, had served Necessity,   *110*
Not me? They, therefore, as to right belonged,
So were created, nor can justly accuse
Their Maker, or their making, or their fate,
As if Predestination overruled
Their will, disposed by absolute decree   *115*
Or high foreknowledge; they themselves decreed
Their own revolt, not I: if I foreknew,
Foreknowledge had no influence on their fault,
Which had no less proved certain unforeknown.
So without least impulse or shadow of fate,   *120*
Or aught by me immutably foreseen,
They trespass, authors to themselves in all,
Both what they judge and what they choose; for so
I formed them free, and free they must remain
Till they enthrall themselves: I else must change   *125*
Their nature, and revoke the high decree
Unchangeable, eternal, which ordained
Their freedom; they themselves ordained their fall.
The first sort by their own suggestion fell,
Self-tempted, self-depraved; Man falls, deceived   *130*
By the other first: Man, therefore, shall find grace,
The other, none; in mercy and justice both,
Through Heaven and Earth, so shall my glory excel,
But mercy, first and last, shall brightest shine.'

108 "Many there be that complain of Divine Providence for
suffering Adam to transgress. Foolish tongues! When God gave
him reason, he gave him freedom to choose; for *reason* is but
choosing." *Areopagitica.*

135   Thus while God spake, ambrosial fragrance filled
       All Heaven, and in the blessed Spirits elect
       Sense of new joy ineffable diffused.
       Beyond compare the Son of God was seen
       Most glorious; in him all his Father shone
140   Substantially expressed; and in his face
       Divine compassion visibly appeared,
       Love without end, and without measure grace;
       Which uttering, thus he to his Father spake:
         'O Father, gracious was that word° which closed
145   Thy sovran sentence, that Man should find grace;
       For which both Heaven and Earth shall high extol
       Thy praises, with the innumerable sound
       Of hymns and sacred songs, wherewith thy throne
       Encompassed shall resound thee ever blest.
150   For should Man finally be lost, should man,
       Thy creature late so loved, thy youngest son,
       Fall circumvented thus by fraud, though joined
       With his own folly? That be from thee far,
       That far be from thee, Father, who art judge
155   Of all things made, and judgest only right.
       Or shall the Adversary thus obtain
       His end, and frustrate thine? shall he fulfil
       His malice, and thy goodness bring to naught,
       Or proud return, though to his heavier doom,
160   Yet with revenge accomplished, and to Hell
       Draw after him the whole race of mankind,
       By him corrupted? Or wilt thou thyself
       Abolish thy creation, and unmake,
       For him, what for thy glory thou hast made?
165   So should thy goodness and thy greatness both
       Be questioned and blasphemed without defence.'
         To whom the great Creator° thus replied:
       'O Son, in whom my soul hath chief delight,
       Son of my bosom, Son who art alone
170   My word, my wisdom, and effectual might,
       All hast thou spoken as my thoughts are, all

144 **gracious . . . word** a bit of a pun in so far as it echoes 131,
a subject repeated at 145 and 227   167 **the great Creator** a
phrase applied both to the Father and to the Son: ii, 385; iii,
673; vii, 567 ("their great Creator," iv, 684)

As my eternal purpose hath decreed.
Man shall not quite be lost, but saved who will,
Yet not of will in him, but grace in me
Freely vouchsafed. Once more I will renew   175
His lapsèd powers, though forfeit, and enthralled
By sin to foul exorbitant desires:
Upheld by me, yet once more he shall stand
On even ground against his mortal foe,
By me upheld, that he may know how frail   180
His fallen condition is, and to me owe
All his deliverance, and to none but me.
Some I have chosen of peculiar grace,
Elect above the rest; so is my will:
The rest shall hear me call, and oft be warned   185
Their sinful state, and to appease betimes
The incensèd Deity, while offered grace
Invites; for I will clear their senses dark
What may suffice, and soften stony hearts
To pray, repent, and bring obedience due.   190
To prayer, repentance, and obedience due,
Though but endeavoured with sincere intent,
Mine ear shall not be slow, mine eye not shut.
And I will place within them as a guide
My umpire Conscience, whom if they will hear   195
Light after light well used they shall attain,
And to the end persisting safe arrive.
This my long sufferance and my day of grace
They who neglect and scorn shall never taste;
But hard be hardened, blind be blinded more,   200
That they may stumble on, and deeper fall,
And none but such from mercy I exclude.
But yet all is not done. Man disobeying,
Disloyal, breaks his fealty, and sins
Against the high supremacy° of Heaven.   205
Affecting Godhead, and, so losing all,
To expiate his treason hath naught left,
But, to destruction sacred and devote,°

205 **high supremacy** cf. i, 132 208 **sacred and devote**
synonymous Latin expressions for doomed

He with his whole posterity must die—
210 Die he or Justice must, unless for him°
Some other, able, and as willing, pay
The rigid satisfaction, death for death.
Say, Heavenly Powers, where shall we find such love?
Which of ye will be mortal, to redeem
215 Man's mortal crime, and just the unjust to save?

210 ff. In theology the Ransom Theory (cf. xii, 424) was succeeded by the less crude Satisfaction Theory, set forth by Anselm in *Cur Deus Homo?*: "The problem is, how can God forgive man's sin? To clear our thoughts let us first consider what sin is, and what satisfaction for sin is. . . . *To sin* is to fail to render to God His due. What is due to God? Righteousness, or rectitude of will. He who fails to render this honor to God, robs God of that which belongs to Him, and dishonors God. This is *sin*. . . . And what is satisfaction? It is not enough simply to restore what has been taken away; but, in consideration of the insult offered, more than what was taken away must be rendered back.

"Let us consider whether God could properly remit sin by mercy alone without satisfaction. So to remit sin would be simply to abstain from punishing it. And since the only possible way of correcting sin for which no satisfaction has been made is to punish it, not to punish it, is to remit it uncorrected. But God cannot properly leave anything uncorrected in His Kingdom. Moreover, so to remit sin unpunished would be treating the sinful and the sinless alike, which would be incongruous to God's nature. And incongruity is injustice.

"It is necessary, therefore, that either the honor taken away should be repaid, or punishment should be inflicted. Otherwise one of two things follows—either God is not just to Himself, or He is powerless to do what He ought to do. A blasphemous supposition.

"The satisfaction ought to be in proportion to the sin.

"Satisfaction cannot be made unless there be some One able to pay to God for man's sin something greater than all that is beside God. . . . Now nothing is greater than all that is not God, except God Himself. None therefore can make this satisfaction except God. And none ought to make it except man. . . . If, then, it be necessary that the kingdom of heaven be completed by man's admission, and if man cannot be admitted unless the aforesaid satisfaction for sin be first made, and if God only *can*, and man only *ought* to make this satisfaction, then necessarily One must make it who is both God and man." Cf. iii, 238 and 282 ff.

Dwells in all Heaven charity° so dear?'
  He asked, but all the Heavenly choir stood mute,°
And silence was in Heaven: on Man's behalf
Patron or intercessor none appeared,
Much less that durst upon his own head draw   220
The deadly forfeiture and ransom set.
And now without redemption all mankind
Must have been lost, adjudged to Death and Hell
By doom severe, had not the Son of God,
In whom the fulness dwells of love divine,   225
His dearest mediation thus renewed:
  'Father, thy word is passed, Man shall find grace;
And shall grace not find means, that finds her way,
The speediest of thy wingèd messengers,
To visit all thy creatures, and to all   230
Comes unprevented, unimplored, unsought?
Happy for Man, so coming! He her aid
Can never seek, once dead in sins and lost;
Atonement for himself, or offering meet,
Indebted and undone, hath none to bring.   235
Behold me, then: me for him, life for life,
I offer; on me let thine anger fall;
Account me Man: I for his sake will leave
Thy bosom, and this glory next to thee
Freely put off, and for him lastly die   240
Well pleased;° on me let Death wreak all his rage.
Under his gloomy power I shall not long
Lie vanquished. Thou hast given me to possess
Life in myself forever; by thee I live;
Though now to Death I yield, and am his due,   245
All that of me can die, yet, that debt paid,
Thou wilt not leave me in the loathsome grave
His prey, nor suffer my unspotted soul
Forever with corruption there to dwell,
But I shall rise victorious, and subdue   250
My vanquisher, spoiled of his vaunted spoil.

216 **charity** love, as in the Anglican Version of St. Paul's
epistles   217 cf. ii, 417 ff.   241 **Well pleased** a characteristic
phrase; cf. x, 71 and *Paradise Regained*, i, 286 (quoting the
recurring Gospel sentence, Matt. iii, 17, etc.). Cf. 257 and 276
("complacence" means pleasure).

Death his death's wound shall then receive, and stoop
Inglorious, of his mortal sting° disarmed;
I through the ample air in triumph high
255 Shall lead Hell captive maugre Hell, and show
The powers of darkness bound. Thou, at the sight
Pleased, out of Heaven shalt look down and smile,
While, by thee raised, I ruin all my foes,
Death last, and with his carcase glut the grave;
260 Then, with the multitude of my redeemed,
Shall enter Heaven, long absent, and return,
Father, to see thy face, wherein no cloud
Of anger shall remain, but peace assured
And reconcilement: wrath shall be no more
265 Thenceforth, but in thy presence joy entire.'
    His words here ended; but his meek aspect
Silent yet spake, and breathed immortal love
To mortal men, above which only shone
Filial obedience; as a sacrifice
270 Glad to be offered, he attends the will
Of his great Father. Admiration° seized
All Heaven what this might mean and whither tend,
Wondering, but soon the Almighty thus replied:
    'O thou in Heaven and Earth the only peace
275 Found out for mankind under wrath, O thou
My sole complacence! well thou know'st how dear
To me are all my works, nor Man the least,
Though last created, that for him I spare
Thee from my bosom and right hand, to save,
280 By losing thee a while, the whole race lost.
Thou, therefore, whom thou only canst redeem,
Their nature also to thy nature join,
And be thyself Man among men on Earth,
Made flesh, when time shall be, of virgin seed,
285 By wondrous birth; be thou in Adam's room
The head of all mankind, though Adam's son.
As in him perish all men, so in thee,

253 **mortal sting** as in ii, 653. Cf. 1 Corinthians, xv, 55: "O death, where is thy sting? O grave, where is thy victory?" Compare with 252 the last line of John Donne's Holy Sonnet 10: "And Death shall be no more; Death, thou shalt die."   271 **Admiration** wonder, as with the verb at ii, 677, 678

As from a second root, shall be restored
As many as are restored; without thee, none.
His crime makes guilty all his sons; thy merit,   *290*
Imputed,° shall absolve them who renounce
Their own both righteous and unrighteous deeds,
And live in thee transplanted, and from thee
Receive new life. So Man, as is most just,
Shall satisfy for Man, be judged and die,   *295*
And dying rise, and, rising, with him raise
His brethren, ransomed with his own dear life.
So Heavenly love shall outdo hellish hate,
Giving to death, and dying to redeem,
So dearly to redeem what hellish hate   *300*
So easily destroyed, and still destroys
In those who, when they may, accept not grace.
Nor shalt thou, by descending to assume
Man's nature, lessen or degrade thine own.
Because thou hast, though throned in highest bliss   *305*
Equal to God, and equally enjoying
Godlike fruition, quitted all to save
A world from utter loss, and hast been found
By merit more than birthright Son of God,
Found worthiest to be so by being good,   *310*
Far more than great or high; because in thee
Love hath abounded more than glory abounds,
Therefore thy humiliation shall exalt
With thee thy manhood also to this throne:
Here shalt thou sit incarnate, here shalt reign   *315*
Both God and Man, Son both of God and Man,
Anointed universal King. All power
I give thee; reign forever, and assume
Thy merits; under thee, as Head Supreme,
Thrones, Princedoms, Powers, Dominions, I reduce: *320*
All knees to thee shall bow of them that bide
In Heaven, or Earth, or, under Earth, in Hell.
When thou, attended gloriously from Heaven,
Shalt in the sky appear, and from thee send

291 **Imputed** "As therefore our sins are imputed to Christ, so
the merits or righteousness of Christ are imputed to us through
faith." Milton's *De Doctrina Christiana*, I, 22. Cf. below, xii,
407–10.

325 The summoning Archangels to proclaim
     Thy dread tribunal, forthwith from all winds
     The living, and forthwith the cited dead
     Of all past ages, to the general doom
     Shall hasten; such a peal shall rouse their sleep.
330 Then, all thy Saints assembled, thou shalt judge
     Bad men and Angels; they arraigned shall sink
     Beneath thy sentence; Hell, her numbers full,
     Thenceforth shall be forever shut.° Meanwhile
     The World shall burn, and from her ashes spring
335 New Heaven and Earth, wherein the just shall dwell,
     And, after all their tribulations long,
     See golden days, fruitful of golden deeds,
     With Joy and Love triúmphing, and fair Truth.
     Then thou thy regal sceptre shalt lay by;
340 For regal sceptre then no more shall need;
     God shall be all in all. But all ye Gods,°
     Adore him who, to compass all this, dies;
     Adore the Son, and honour him as me.'
          No sooner had the Almighty ceased, but all
345 The multitude of Angels, with a shout
     Loud as from numbers without number, sweet
     As from blest voices, uttering joy, Heaven rung
     With jubilee, and loud hosannas filled
     The eternal regions. Lowly reverent
350 Towards either throne they bow, and to the ground
     With solemn adoration down they cast
     Their crowns, inwove with amaranth° and gold—
     Immortal amaranth, a flower which once
     In Paradise, fast by the Tree of Life,
355 Began to bloom, but soon for Man's offence
     To Heaven removed, where first it grew, there grows,
     And flowers aloft, shading the Fount of Life,
     And where the River of Bliss through midst of Heaven
     Rolls o'er Elysian flowers her amber stream;

333 **forever shut** cf. ii, 776   341 **Gods** a usage already
common in the poem, i, 116, 138, 240, 629; ii, 352, 391. "The
name of God is not infrequently ascribed, by the will and
concession of God the Father, even to angels and men." *De
Doctrina Christiana*, I, 6 (Columbia Milton, XIV, 245).
352–53 **amaranth** means *immortal* and reappears as an
adjective xi, 78.

With these, that never fade, the Spirits elect° 360
Bind their resplendent locks, inwreathed with beams,
Now in loose garlands thick thrown off, the bright
Pavement, that like a sea of jasper shone,
Impurpled with celestial roses smiled.
Then, crowned again, their golden harps they took, 365
Harps ever tuned, that glittering by their side
Like quivers hung, and with preamble sweet
Of charming symphony they introduce
Their sacred song,° and waken raptures high:
No voice exempt, no voice but well could join 370
Melodious part; such concord° is in Heaven.
    Thee, Father, first they sung, Omnipotent,
Immutable, Immortal, Infinite,°
Eternal King; thee, Author of all being,
Fountain of Light, thyself invisible 375
Amidst the glorious brightness where thou sitt'st
Throned inaccessible, but when thou shad'st
The full blaze of thy beams, and through a cloud
Drawn round about thee like a radiant shrine,
Dark with excessive bright thy skirts appear, 380
Yet dazzle Heaven, that brightest Seraphim
Approach not, but with both wings veil their eyes.
Thee next they sang, of all creation first,
Begotten Son, Divine Similitude,
In whose conspicuous countenance, without cloud 385
Made visible, the Almighty Father shines,
Whom else no creature can behold: on thee
Impressed the effulgence of his glory abides;
Transfused on thee his ample Spirit rests.
He Heaven of Heavens, and all the Powers therein, 390
By thee created; and by thee threw down
The aspiring Dominations; thou that day
Thy Father's dreadful thunder didst not spare,
Nor stop thy flaming chariot-wheels, that shook
Heaven's everlasting frame, while o'er the necks 395

---

360 **Spirits elect** The same words ended line 136. 369 **sacred
song** cf. 29, 148 371 **concord** a pun, of course. "Men only
disagree" (ii, 497). 373 The same line occurs in Milton's
popular predecessor, Joshua Sylvester, *Du Bartas, His Divine
Weeks* (1608).

Thou drov'st of warring Angels disarrayed.
Back from pursuit, thy Powers with loud acclaim°
Thee only extolled, Son of thy Father's might,
To execute fierce vengeance on his foes.
400 Not so on Man: him, through their malice fallen,
Father of mercy and grace, thou didst not doom
So strictly, but much more to pity incline.
No sooner did thy dear and only Son
Perceive thee purposed not to doom frail Man
405 So strictly, but much more to pity inclined,
He, to appease thy wrath, and end the strife
Of mercy and justice in thy face discerned,
Regardless of the bliss wherein he sat
Second to thee, offered himself to die
410 For Man's offence.° O unexampled love,
Love nowhere to be found less than Divine!
Hail, Son of God, Saviour of men; Thy name
Shall be the copious matter of my song
Henceforth, and never shall my harp thy praise
415 Forget, nor from thy Father's praise disjoin!
    Thus they in Heaven, above the starry sphere,
Their happy hours in joy and hymning spent.
Meanwhile, upon the firm opacous° globe
Of this round World, whose first convex divides
420 The luminous inferior orbs,° enclosed
From Chaos and the inroad of Darkness old,
Satan alighted walks. A globe far off
It seemed, now seems a boundless continent,
Dark, waste, and wild, under the frown of Night
425 Starless exposed, and ever-threatening storms
Of Chaos blustering round, inclement sky,
Save on that side which from the wall of Heaven,
Though distant far, some small reflection gains
Of glimmering air less vexed with tempest loud;
430 Here walked the Fiend at large in spacious field.
As when a vulture, on Imaus° bred,

397 **loud acclaim** parallel with ii, 520   410 Note the repetitions
for emphasis in this area—402, 405; "For Man's offence"
echoes 355.   418 **opacous** dark   419–20 cf. ii, 1052, note   431
Imaus the Himalayas (from Sanskrit Himava, "snowy," leading
to "snowy ridge," 432)

Whose snowy ridge the roving Tartar° bounds,
Dislodging from a region scarce of prey
To gorge the flesh of lambs or yeanling kids
On hills where flocks are fed, flies toward the springs　*435*
Of Ganges or Hydaspes, Indian streams,
But in his way lights on the barren plains
Of Sericana,° where Chineses° drive
With sails and wind their cany waggons light,
So on this windy sea of land the Fiend　*440*
Walked up and down alone, bent on his prey—
Alone, for other creature in this place,
Living or lifeless, to be found was none;
None yet, but store hereafter from the Earth
Up hither like aerial vapours flew　*445*
Of all things transitory and vain, when sin
With vanity had filled the works of men:
Both all things vain, and all who in vain things
Built their fond° hopes of glory or lasting fame,
Or happiness in this or the other life;　*450*
All who have their reward on earth, the fruits
Of painful superstition and blind zeal,
Naught seeking but the praise of men, here find
Fit retribution, empty as their deeds;
All the unaccomplished works of Nature's hand,　*455*
Abortive, monstrous, or unkindly mixed,
Dissolved on Earth, fleet hither, and in vain,
Till final dissolution, wander here,
Not in the neighbouring Moon, as some° have dreamed:

432 **Tartar** These invaders from east central Asia overran parts
of Asia and Europe under Mongol leadership in the thirteenth
century, and continued to trouble nearly all of Russia and
Siberia, as x, 431 indicates, "gorging" where they might.
437–38 **the barren plains/ Of Sericana** the Gobi desert **Chineses**
a plural in regular use in the seventeenth century. The story
of the Chinese wind-wagons was vouched for by several
geographers, though one of them, the Spanish Jesuit Mendoza,
bore a name that encouraged suspicion of mendacity.　449 **fond**
The modern meaning combines with the old of "foolish."　459
some Ariosto placed his "paradise of fools" in the moon:
with mock seriousness Milton relocates it, in this the
second—and last—large allegory of his poem (Sin and Death
being the first).

460 Those argent fields more likely habitants,°
    Translated Saints, or middle Spirits hold,
    Betwixt the angelical and human kind:
    Hither, of ill-joined sons and daughters born,
    First from the ancient world those Giants came,
465 With many a vain exploit, though then renowned:
    The builders next of Babel on the plain
    Of Sennaar,° and still with vain design
    New Babels, had they wherewithal, would build:
    Others came single; he who, to be deemed
470 A god, leaped fondly into Aetna flames,
    Empedocles;° and he who, to enjoy
    Plato's Elysium, leaped into the sea,
    Cleombrotus;° and many more, too long,
    Embryos and idiots, eremites and friars,
475 White, black, and grey,° with all their trumpery.
    Here pilgrims roam, that strayed so far to seek
    In Golgotha him dead who lives in Heaven;°
    And they who, to be sure of Paradise,
    Dying put on the weeds of Dominic,
480 Or in Franciscan think to pass disguised.
    They pass the planets seven, and pass the fixed,°
    And that crystálline sphere whose balance weighs
    The trepidation talked,° and that first moved;°

460 ff. The moon is reserved for such as Enoch and Elijah and
such "middle spirits" as the products of miscegenation between
angels and mortals or the giants of Genesis vi, 4. 467 **Sennaar**
Shinar (Gen. x, 10; xi, 2), but Milton avoids the "sh" sound,
as at i, 413. 471 **Empedocles** pre-Socratic philosopher who
professed miraculous and prophetic powers and hurled himself
into the crater (cf. i, 233) in order that he might be thought a
god from his sudden and total disappearance. *fondly* (470) may
refer in part to the tradition that the volcano threw up one of
his sandals and so betrayed him. 473 **Cleombrotus** young
Epirot who, according to Lactantius, was so eager to taste the
immortality of the soul after reading the *Phaedo* that he
drowned himself. 475 **White, black, and grey** Carmelites,
Dominicans, and Franciscans 476–77 Protestant that he
was, Milton waxes sarcastic on those who went on pilgrimage
to Mount Calvary; the futility of their quest is summed up
in *Golgotha,* "the place of the skull." 481 **fixed** i.e., stars
482–83 **whose balance weighs/ The trepidation talked** (of) Libra
the Scales weighs or calculates the alleged libration of the
eighth (Starry) sphere, this trepidation having been added to

And now Saint Peter at Heaven's wicket seems
To wait them with his keys, and now at foot   *485*
Of Heaven's ascent they lift their feet, when, lo!
A violent cross-wind from either coast
Blows them transverse,° ten thousand leagues awry,
Into the devious air: then might ye see
Cowls, hoods, and habits, with their wearers, tossed   *490*
And fluttered into rags; then relics, beads,
Indulgences, dispenses, pardons, bulls,
The sport of winds: all these, upwhirled aloft,
Fly o'er the backside of the World far off
Into a Limbo° large and broad, since called   *495*
The Paradise of Fools, to few unknown
Long after, now unpeopled and untrod.
All this dark globe the Fiend found as he passed,
And long he wandered, till at last a gleam
Of dawning light turned thitherward in haste   *500*
His travelled° steps. Far distant he descries,
Ascending by degrees magnificent
Up to the wall of Heaven,° a structure high,
At top whereof, but far more rich, appeared
The work as of a kingly palace-gate,   *505*
With frontispiece of diamond and gold
Embellished; thick with sparkling orient gems
The portal shone, inimitable on Earth
By model, or by shading pencil drawn.
The stairs were such as whereon Jacob saw°   *510*
Angels ascending and descending, bands
Of guardians bright, when he from Esau fled
To Padan-Aram,° in the field of Luz,°
Dreaming by night under the open sky,
And waking cried, *This is the gate of Heaven.*   *515*

---

the Ptolemaic system in the tenth century "to account for
certain phenomena . . . really due to the rotation of the earth's
axis" (*Oxford English Dictionary*). Another double reference
to the constellation Libra occurs at iv, 997 ff. **that first moved**
"That high first-moving sphere" ("Death of a Fair Infant," 39),
the Primum Mobile 488 **transverse** crosswise; cf. *Samson
Agonistes,* 209. 495 **Limbo** literally, edge 501 **travelled** play
on travailed, tired 503 **the wall of Heaven** cf. 71, 427 510 ff.
Genesis xxviii, 1–2, 11–17 513 **Padan-Aram** city to the east,
in Mesopotamia **Luz** twelve miles north of Jerusalem

Each stair mysteriously° was meant, nor stood
There always, but drawn up to Heaven sometimes
Viewless, and underneath a bright sea flowed
Of jasper, or of liquid pearl, whereon
520 Who after came from Earth sailing arrived
Wafted by Angels, or flew o'er the lake
Rapt in a chariot drawn by fiery steeds.°
The stairs were then let down, whether to dare
The Fiend by easy ascent,° or aggravate
525 His sad exclusion from the doors of bliss;
Direct against which opened from beneath,
Just o'er the blissful seat° of Paradise,
A passage down to the Earth, a passage wide,
Wider by far than that of after-times
530 Over Mount Sion, and, though that were large,
Over the Promised Land to God so dear,
By which, to visit oft those happy tribes,
On high behests his Angels to and fro
Passed frequent, and his eye with choice regard°
535 From Paneas, the fount of Jordan's flood,
To Beërsaba, where the Holy Land
Borders on Egypt and the Arabian shore.
So wide the opening seemed, where bounds were set
To darkness, such as bound the ocean wave.
540 Satan from hence, now on the lower stair,
That scaled by steps of gold to Heaven-gate,
Looks down with wonder at the sudden view°
Of all this World at once. As when a scout,
Through dark and desert ways with peril gone
545 All night, at last by break of cheerful dawn
Obtains the brow of some high-climbing hill,
Which to his eye discovers unaware
The goodly prospect of some foreign land
First seen, or some renowned metropolis
550 With glistering spires and pinnacles adorned,
Which now the rising sun gilds with his beams—
Such wonder seized, though after Heaven seen,

516 **mysteriously** allegorically 522 like Elijah 524 **easy ascent** cf. ii, 81 527 **blissful seat** cf. i, 5 534 **choice regard** The same phrase, so galling to Satan, ended line 653 of i. 542 **sudden view** cf. ii, 890

The Spirit malign, but much more envy seized,
At sight of all this World beheld so fair.
Round he surveys (and well might, where he stood   *555*
So high above the circling canopy
Of Night's extended shade) from eastern point
Of Libra to the fleecy star that bears
Andromeda far off Atlantic seas°
Beyond the horizon; then from pole to pole   *560*
He views in breadth, and, without longer pause,
Down right into the World's first region throws
His flight precipitant, and winds with ease
Through the pure marble° air his oblique way
Amongst innumerable stars, that shone   *565*
Stars distant, but nigh-hand seemed other worlds,
Or other worlds they seemed, or happy isles,
Like those Hesperian Gardens° famed of old,
Fortunate fields, and groves, and flowery vales,
Thrice happy isles, but who dwelt happy there   *570*
He stayed not to inquire: above them all
The golden Sun, in splendour likest Heaven,
Allured his eye. Thither his course he bends,
Through the calm firmament—but up or down,
By centre or eccentric,° hard to tell,   *575*
Or longitude—where the great luminary,
Aloof ° the vulgar constellations thick,
That from his lordly eye keep distance due,
Dispenses light from far. They, as they move
Their starry dance in numbers° that compute   *580*
Days, months, and years, towards his all-cheering lamp
Turn swift their various motions, or are turned
By his magnetic beam, that gently warms
The Universe, and to each inward part
With gentle penetration, though unseen,   *585*

558–59 Milton represents the constellation Andromeda as
borne by the fleecy star Aries, the Ram, inasmuch as the
former lies above the latter constellation in the sky, though
somewhat to the west.   564 **marble** bright as marble, which in
Greek means *shining*   568 **Hesperian Gardens** had been
referred to in a "Comus" variant after line 4—a pagan paradise
in the West, the isles (570) of the Blest.   575 **eccentric** away
from the center   577 **Aloof** preposition, apart from   580
numbers measures

Shoots invisible virtue even to the deep,°
So wondrously was set his station bright.
There lands the Fiend, a spot like which perhaps
Astronomer in the Sun's lucent orb
590 Through his glazed optic tube yet never saw.
The place he found beyond expression bright,
Compared with aught on Earth, metal° or stone;
Not all parts like, but all alike informed
With radiant light, as glowing iron with fire.
595 If metal, part seemed gold, part silver clear;
If stone, carbuncle most or chrysolite,
Ruby or topaz, to the twelve that shone
In Aaron's breastplate,° and a stone besides,
Imagined rather oft than elsewhere seen,
600 That stone, or like to that, which here below°
Philosophers in vain so long have sought,
In vain, though by their powerful art they bind
Volatile Hermes,° and call up unbound
In various shapes old Proteus° from the sea,
605 Drained through a limbec to his native form.
What wonder then if fields and regions here
Breathe forth elixir pure, and rivers run
Potable gold, when, with one virtuous touch,
The arch-chemic Sun, so far from us remote,
610 Produces, with terrestrial humour mixed,
Here in the dark so many precious things

583–86 The sexual aspect of the solar energy. Cf. 608–11 and
Diodorus Siculus: "Truly it is very apparent that colors, odors,
fruits, different savors, greatness of creatures, forms of things,
and variety of kinds produced by the earth—are made and
procreated by the heat of the Sun, which, warming the
moisture of the earth, is the true and only cause of those
productions." 592 **metal** 1667 and 1674 read *Medal*. 598 See
Exodus xxviii, 15 ff. for the description of the jeweled
breastplate of the elder brother of Moses who became high
priest. 600 ff. The proverbial quest of the alchemists or
philosophers was the stone that would turn baser metals into
gold. 603 **Volatile Hermes** mythological-alchemical wordplay.
The messenger god was winged, but the other reference is
to the tendency of quicksilver or mercury to evaporate. 604
Proteus the sea divinity who shepherded seals and who would
"take all manner of shapes" when seized (*Od.* IV, 417 ff.): an
apt metaphor for the transmuting elixir (607) of the alchemists.

Of colour glorious and effect so rare?
Here matter new to gaze the Devil met
Undazzled. Far and wide his eye commands,
For sight no obstacle found here, nor shade,   615
But all sunshine, as when his beams at noon
Culminate from the equator, as they now
Shot upward still direct, whence no way round
Shadow from body opaque can fall, and the air,
Nowhere so clear, sharpened his visual ray   620
To objects distant far, whereby he soon
Saw within ken a glorious Angel stand,
The same whom John saw also in the Sun.°
His back was turned, but not his brightness hid:
Of beaming sunny rays a golden tiar°   625
Circled his head, nor less his locks behind
Illustrious° on his shoulders fledge with wings
Lay waving round; on some great charge employed
He seemed, or fixed in cogitation deep.
Glad was the Spirit impure, as now in hope   630
To find who might direct his wandering flight
To Paradise, the happy seat of Man,
His journey's end, and our beginning woe.
But first he casts to change his proper shape,
Which else might work him danger or delay,   635
And now a stripling Cherub he appears,
Not of the prime, yet such as in his face
Youth smiled celestial, and to every limb
Suitable grace diffused; so well he feigned.
Under a coronet his flowing hair   640
In curls on either cheek played; wings he wore
Of many a coloured plume sprinkled with gold,
His habit° fit for speed succinct,° and held
Before his decent° steps a silver wand.
He drew not nigh unheard; the Angel bright,   645
Ere he drew nigh, his radiant visage turned,
Admonished by his ear, and straight was known
The Archangel Uriel,° one of the seven

---

623 "And I saw an angel standing in the sun." Revelations xix,
17   625 **tiar** tiara   627 **Illustrious** Latin *illustris,* gleaming   643
habit dress **succinct** girt up   644 **decent** graceful   648 **Uriel**
"Light of God"

Who in God's presence, nearest to his throne,
650 Stand ready at command, and are his eyes
That run through all the Heavens, or down to the Earth°
Bear his swift errands over moist and dry,°
O'er sea and land; him Satan thus accosts:
      'Uriel! for thou of those seven Spirits that stand
655 In sight of God's high throne, gloriously bright,
The first art wont his great authentic will
Interpreter through highest Heaven to bring,
Where all his Sons thy embassy attend,
And here art likeliest by supreme decree
660 Like honour to obtain, and as his eye
To visit oft this new Creation round—
Unspeakable desire to see and know
All these his wonderous works, but chiefly Man,
His chief delight and favour, him for whom
665 All these his works so wondrous he ordained,
Hath brought me from the choirs of Cherubim
Alone thus wandering. Brightest Seraph, tell
In which of all these shining orbs hath Man
His fixèd seat—or fixèd seat hath none,
670 But all these shining orbs his choice to dwell—
That I may find him, and with secret gaze
Or open admiration him behold
On whom the great Creator hath bestowed
Worlds, and on whom hath all these graces poured,
675 That both in him and all things, as is meet
The Universal Maker we may praise;
Who justly hath driven out his rebel foes
To deepest Hell, and, to repair that loss,
Created this new happy race of Men
680 To serve him better: wise are all his ways!'
      So spake the false dissembler unperceived,
For neither man nor angel can discern
Hypocrisy, the only evil that walks
Invisible, except to God alone,
685 By his permissive will, through Heaven and Earth;
And oft, though Wisdom wake, Suspicion sleeps
At Wisdom's gate, and to Simplicity
Resigns her charge, while Goodness thinks no ill

651 **down to the Earth** cf. 528   652 **moist and dry** cf. ii, 898

Where no ill seems: which now for once beguiled
Uriel, though Regent of the Sun, and held   *690*
The sharpest-sighted Spirit of all in Heaven,
Who to the fraudulent impostor foul,
In his uprightness, answer thus returned:
  'Fair Angel, thy desire, which tends to know
The works of God, thereby to glorify   *695*
The great Work-master, leads to no excess
That reaches blame, but rather merits praise
The more it seems excess, that led thee hither
From thy empyreal° mansion thus alone,
To witness with thine eyes what some perhaps,   *700*
Contented with report, hear only in Heaven—
For wonderful indeed are all his works,
Pleasant to know, and worthiest to be all
Had in remembrance always with delight;
But what created mind can comprehend   *705*
Their number, or the wisdom infinite
That brought them forth, but hid their causes deep?
I saw when, at his word, the formless mass,
This World's material mould, came to a heap;
Confusion heard his voice, and wild Uproar°   *710*
Stood ruled, stood vast Infinitude confined,
Till, at his second bidding,° Darkness fled,
Light shone, and order from disorder sprung.
Swift to their several quarters hasted then
The cumbrous elements, Earth, Flood, Air, Fire,   *715*
And this ethereal quintessence° of Heaven
Flew upward, spirited with various forms,
That rolled orbicular, and turned to stars
Numberless, as thou seest, and how they move:
Each had his place appointed, each his course;   *720*

699 **empyreal** In the midst of the irony of this extremely
inapposite word the reader may hear one that does fit:
imperial. 710 **wild Uproar** Chaos becomes linked with Hell
(Satan and Chaos are allies) by the previous appearance of
this phrase, ii, 541. 712 **at his second bidding,** which was "Let
there be light." 716 **ethereal quintessence** Ether and
quintessence are the same, in Aristotelian theory the highest
and last or celestial essence over and above the four
"cumbrous elements" (715); the constituent of the celestial
bodies.

The rest in circuit walls this Universe.
Look downward on that globe, whose hither side
With light from hence, though but reflected, shines:
That place is Earth, the seat of Man; that light
725 His day, which else, as the other hemisphere,
Night would invade; but there the neighbouring Moon
(So call that opposite fair star) her aid
Timely interposes, and, her monthly round
Still ending, still renewing, through mid-heaven,
730 With borrowed light her countenance triform°
Hence fills and empties to enlighten the Earth,
And in her pale dominion checks the night.
That spot to which I point is Paradise,
Adam's abode, those lofty shades his bower.
735 Thy way thou canst not miss; me mine requires.'
　　Thus said, he turned, and Satan, bowing low,
As to superior Spirits is wont in Heaven,
Where honour due and reverence none neglects,
Took leave, and toward the coast of Earth beneath,
740 Down from the ecliptic, sped with hoped success,
Throws his steep flight in many an aery wheel,°
Nor stayed, till on Niphates'° top he lights.

730 **triform** three-phased (cf. 731)—and the triple goddess,
Luna, Diana, Hecate.   740–41 The rhythm imitates the flight
or descent.   742 **Niphates** "Snow mountain," called "the
Assyrian mount," iv, 126 (cf. *ib*. 569), actually part of the
Taurus range in Armenia.

BOOK IV

THE ARGUMENT

Satan, now in prospect of Eden, and nigh the place where he must now attempt the bold enterprise which he undertook alone against God and Man, falls into many doubts with himself, and many passions, fear, envy, and despair; but at length confirms himself in evil; journeys on to Paradise, whose outward prospect and situation is described; overleaps the bounds; sits, in the shape of a cormorant, on the Tree of Life, as highest in the Garden, to look about him. The Garden described; Satan's first sight of Adam and Eve; his wonder at their excellent form and happy state, but with resolution to work their fall; overhears their discourse; thence gathers that the Tree of Knowledge was forbidden them to eat of under penalty of death, and thereon intends to found his temptation by seducing them to transgress; then leaves them a while, to know further of their state by some other means. Meanwhile Uriel, descending on a sunbeam, warns Gabriel, who had in charge the gate of Paradise, that some evil Spirit had escaped the Deep, and passed at noon by his Sphere, in the shape of a good Angel, down to Paradise, discovered after by his furious gestures in the mount. Gabriel promises to find him ere morning. Night coming on, Adam and Eve discourse of going to their rest: their bower described; their evening worship. Gabriel, drawing forth his bands of night-watch to walk the round of Paradise, appoints two strong Angels to Adam's bower, lest the evil Spirit should be there doing some harm to Adam or Eve sleeping: there they find him at the ear of Eve, tempting her in a dream, and bring him, though unwilling, to Gabriel: by whom questioned, he scornfully answers; prepares resistance; but, hindered by a sign from Heaven, flies out of Paradise.

O FOR that warning voice, which he° who saw
The Apocalypse heard cry in Heaven aloud,
Then when the dragon, put to second rout,
Came furious down to be revenged on men,
5   *Woe to the inhabitants on Earth!* that now,
While time was, our first parents° had been warned
The coming of their secret foe, and 'scaped,
Haply so 'scaped, his mortal snare; for now
Satan, now first inflamed with rage,° came down,
10   The tempter, ere the accuser,° of mankind,
To wreak° on innocent frail Man his loss
Of that first battle, and his flight to Hell—
Yet not rejoicing in his speed, though bold
Far off and fearless, nor with cause to boast,
15   Begins his dire attempt; which, nigh the birth
Now rolling, boils in his tumultuous breast
And like a devilish engine back recoils
Upon himself; horror and doubt distract
His troubled thoughts,° and from the bottom stir
20   The Hell within him, for within him Hell
He brings, and round about him, nor from Hell
One step, no more than from himself, can fly
By change of place. Now conscience wakes despair
That slumbered, wakes the bitter memory
25   Of what he was, what is, and what must be
Worse; of worse deeds worse sufferings must ensue.
Sometimes towards Eden, which now in his view
Lay pleasant, his grieved look he fixes sad,
Sometimes towards Heaven and the full-blazing Sun
30   Which now sat high in his meridian tower;
Then, much revolving,° thus in sighs began:

1 **he** St. John. See Revelation, xii, 12.   6 **our first parents** cf.
iii, 65   9 **inflamed with rage** Note the passage from the literal
to the figurative in the repeated use of this phrase: ii, 581,
791.   10 **accuser** "The accuser of our brethren is cast down,
which accused them before our God day and night" (Rev. xii,
10).   11 **To wreak** Anglo-Saxon *wrecan*, to avenge   19 **troubled
thoughts** cf. i, 557   31 **much revolving** a small instance of Milton's
profitably ambiguous syntax: "much" can be an adverb, or, Latin
multa volvens, it can be a noun, the object of "revolving." Satan
twists and turns (inwardly as outwardly), and he ponders many
things.

'O thou that, with surpassing glory crowned,°
Look'st from thy sole dominion like the god
Of this new World, at whose sight all the stars
Hide their diminished heads, to thee I call,   35
But with no friendly voice, and add thy name,
O Sun, to tell thee how I hate thy beams,
That bring to my remembrance from what state
I fell, how glorious once above thy sphere,
Till pride and worse ambition threw me down,   40
Warring in Heaven against Heaven's matchless King—
Ah wherefore? he deserved no such return
From me, whom he created what I was
In that bright eminence, and with his good
Upbraided none, nor was his service hard.   45
What could be less than to afford him praise,
The easiest recompense, and pay him thanks,
How due! Yet all his good proved ill in me,
And wrought but malice; lifted up so high,
I 'sdained subjection, and thought one step higher   50
Would set me highest, and in a moment quit
The debt immense of endless gratitude,
So burdensome, still paying, still to owe,
Forgetful what from him I still received,
And understood not that a grateful mind   55
By owing owes not, but still pays, at once
Indebted and discharged; what burden then?
Oh, had his powerful destiny ordained
Me some inferior Angel, I had stood
Then happy; no unbounded hope had raised   60
Ambition. Yet why not? some other Power
As great might have aspired, and me, though mean,
Drawn to his part; but other Powers as great
Fell not, but stand unshaken, from within
Or from without, to all temptations armed.   65
Hadst thou the same free will and power to stand?
Thou hadst. Whom hast thou then, or what, to accuse,

32–41 Milton's nephew said he saw this speech to the Sun early
in the 1640s in what was then planned as a drama. C. S. Lewis
observes of "and add thy name," 36: "On the stage Satan
would have had to do this in order to let the audience know
whom he was addressing."

But Heaven's free love dealt equally to all?
Be then his love accursed, since, love or hate,
70 To me alike it deals eternal woe.°
Nay, cursed be thou, since against his thy will
Chose freely what it now so justly rues.
Me miserable!° which way shall I fly
Infinite wrath and infinite despair?
75 Which way I fly is Hell; myself am Hell;°
And, in the lowest deep,° a lower deep
Still threatening to devour me opens wide,
To which the Hell I suffer seems a Heaven.
O, then, at last relent; is there no place
80 Left for repentance, none for pardon left?
None left but by submission; and that word
Disdain forbids me, and my dread of shame
Among the Spirits beneath, whom I seduced
With other promises and other vaunts
85 Than to submit, boasting I could subdue
The Omnipotent. Ay me! they little know
How dearly I abide° that boast so vain,
Under what torments inwardly I groan;
While they adore me on the throne of Hell,
90 With diadem and sceptre high advanced,
The lower still I fall, only supreme
In misery—such joy ambition finds!
But say I could repent, and could obtain,
By act of grace, my former state; how soon
95 Would height recall high thoughts, how soon unsay
What feigned submission swore; ease would recant
Vows made in pain, as violent and void—
For never can true reconcilement grow
Where wounds of deadly hate° have pierced so deep—
100 Which would but lead me to a worse relapse
And heavier fall; so should I purchase dear
Short intermission, bought with double smart.
This knows my Punisher; therefore as far
From granting he, as I from begging, peace.

70 **eternal woe** cf. ii, 161, 695   73 **Me miserable!** Latin
exclamatory accusative: *me miserum!*   75 cf. 20–21; i, 254–55   76
the lowest deep cf. ii, 392   87 **abide** suffer for   99 **deadly hate**
cf. ii, 577

All hope excluded thus, behold, instead   105
Of us, outcast, exiled, his new delight,
Mankind, created, and for him this World.
So farewell hope, and with hope, farewell fear,
Farewell remorse! All good to me is lost;
Evil, be thou my Good: by thee at least   110
Divided empire with Heaven's King I hold,
By thee, and more than half perhaps will reign;°
As Man erelong, and this new World, shall know.'
    Thus while he spake, each passion dimmed his face,
Thrice changed with pale ire, envy, and despair,   115
Which marred his borrowed visage, and betrayed
Him counterfeit, if any eye beheld,
For Heavenly minds from such distempers foul
Are ever clear. Whereof he soon aware
Each perturbation smoothed with outward calm,   120
Artificer of fraud, and was the first
That practised falsehood under saintly show,
Deep malice to conceal, couched with revenge;
Yet not enough had practised to deceive
Uriel, once warned, whose eye pursued him down   125
The way he went, and on the Assyrian mount°
Saw him disfigured, more than could befall
Spirit of happy sort: his gestures fierce
He marked and mad demeanor, then alone,
As he supposed, all unobserved, unseen.   130
So on he fares,° and to the border comes
Of Eden, where delicious Paradise,°
Now nearer, crowns with her enclosure green,
As with a rural mound, the champaign° head

---

112 If God rules Heaven and Satan Hell, he who holds earth "will
reign" over "more than half" of the universe.   126 **the Assyrian
mount** see iii, 742   131 **on he fares** as in ii, 940   132 **Paradise** is the
"eastward" (Gen. ii, 8) part of the tract of *Eden*. Cf. 209–10. Thus
at the end of the poem Adam and Eve leave Paradise but are still
in Eden (xii, 648–49).   134 **champaign** open, flat country. Lewis
comments on 134–37: "The Freudian idea that the happy garden is
an image of the human body would not have frightened Milton in
the least." It did not frighten Spenser in the Bower of Bliss (*Faerie
Queene* II, xii, 43 ff.) and the House of Temperance (II, ix, 22 and
32), but before concluding with a scene from the now familiar *Lady
Chatterley's Lover* it should be noticed that Milton remains
ambivalent in his combination of the inviting and the forbidden.

135 Of a steep wilderness, whose hairy sides
With thicket overgrown, grotesque° and wild,
Access denied; and overhead upgrew
Insuperable height of loftiest shade,
Cedar, and pine, and fir, and branching palm,
140 A sylvan scene, and, as the ranks ascend
Shade above shade, a woody theatre
Of stateliest view. Yet higher than their tops
The verdurous wall of Paradise upsprung,
Which to our general sire° gave prospect large
145 Into his nether empire° neighbouring round.
And higher than that wall a circling row
Of goodliest trees, loaden with fairest fruit,
Blossoms and fruits at once of golden hue,
Appeared, with gay enamelled° colours mixed,
150 On which the sun more glad impressed his beams
Than in fair evening cloud, or humid bow,
When God hath showered the earth: so lovely seemed
That landscape; and of pure, now purer air
Meets his approach, and to the heart inspires
155 Vernal delight and joy, able to drive
All sadness but despair. Now gentle gales,
Fanning their odoriferous wings, dispense
Native perfumes, and whisper whence they stole
Those balmy spoils. As when to them who sail
160 Beyond the Cape of Hope, and now are past
Mozambic,° off at sea north-east winds blow
Sabean° odours from the spicy shore
Of Araby the Blest, with such delay
Well pleased they slack their course, and many a league
165 Cheered with the grateful smell old Ocean smiles;
So entertained those odorous sweets the Fiend
Who came their bane, though with them better pleased
Than Asmodëus with the fishy fume°

136 **grotesque** connected with grotto 144 **our general sire** as
founder of the *genus humanum* 145 **nether empire** contrast
ii, 296 149 **enamelled** see "Lycidas," 139 161 **Mozambic** a
renowned harbor, Portuguese East Africa opposite Mad-
agascar. 162 **Sabean** Saba or Sheba was southern Arabia,
called *Araby the Blest,* 163, for being the fertile portion. 168 ff.
Milton emphasizes by this curious reference ("a remarkable
association of fallen and unfallen odours"—F. Kermode) the
foulness of the intruder, who, however, has not yet completely

That drove him, though enamoured, from the spouse
Of Tobit's son, and with a vengeance sent   *170*
From Media post to Egypt, there fast bound.
   Now to the ascent of that steep savage hill
Satan had journeyed on, pensive and slow,
But further way found none, so thick entwined,
As one continued brake, the undergrowth   *175*
Of shrubs and tangling bushes had perplexed°
All path of man or beast that passed that way.
One gate there only was, and that looked east
On the other side: which when the Arch-felon saw,
Due entrance he disdained, and, in contempt,   *180*
At one slight bound high overleaped all bound
Of hill or highest wall and sheer within
Lights on his feet. As when a prowling wolf,
Whom hunger drives to seek new haunt for prey,
Watching where shepherds pen their flocks at eve,   *185*
In hurdled cotes and amid the field secure,
Leaps o'er the fence with ease into the fold;
Or as a thief, bent to unhoard the cash
Of some rich burgher, whose substantial doors,
Cross-barred and bolted fast, fear no assault,°   *190*
In at the window climbs, or o'er the tiles;
So clomb this first grand Thief into God's fold:
So since into his Church lewd hirelings climb.
Thence up he flew, and on the Tree of Life,°
The middle tree and highest there that grew,   *195*

---

realized his own foulness and still remembers the time when
as the Talmudic "king of the demons" he would have slain
Sara's eighth husband (as he had slain the previous seven),
Tobias, "Tobit's son," if, by Raphael's advice, the latter had
not burned the heart and liver of a fish on his wedding night,
"the which smell when the evil spirit had smelled, he fled into
the utmost parts of Egypt, and the angel bound him" (the
Apocryphal Book of Tobit, viii, 3). **176 perplexed** literally,
entangled **190 fear no assault** cf. ii, 343. The likely association
is with the burgher in *Areopagitica* who searches out a minister
"to whose care and credit he may commit the whole managing
of his religious affairs. . . . To him he adheres, resigns the
whole warehouse of his religion with all the locks and keys
into his custody" (Columbia Milton, 333–34). **194 the Tree of
Life** Genesis ii, 9

Sat like a cormorant,° yet not true life
Thereby regained, but sat devising death
To them who lived, nor on the virtue thought
Of that life-giving plant, but only used
200 For prospect what, well used, had been the pledge°
Of immortality. So little knows
Any but God alone to value right
The good before him, but perverts best things
To worst abuse, or to their meanest use.
205 Beneath him with new wonder now he views,
To all delight of human sense exposed,
In narrow room Nature's whole wealth, yea more—
A Heaven on Earth: for blissful Paradise
Of God the garden was, by him in the east
210 Of Eden planted; Eden stretched her line
From Auran° eastward to the royal towers
Of great Seleucia,° built by Grecian kings,
Or where the sons of Eden long before
Dwelt in Telassar.° In this pleasant soil
215 His far more pleasant garden God ordained.
Out of the fertile ground he caused to grow
All trees of noblest kind for sight, smell, taste;
And all amid them stood the Tree of Life,
High eminent, blooming ambrosial fruit
220 Of vegetable gold, and, next to life,
Our death, the Tree of Knowledge, grew fast by,
Knowledge of good, bought dear by knowing ill.
Southward through Eden went a river large,
Nor changed his course, but through the shaggy hill
225 Passed underneath ingulfed, for God had thrown

196 **cormorant** literally, "sea-raven," like the vulture (iii, 431)
an established symbol of voraciousness   200 ff. Milton draws
a lesson out of the puzzling other tree, later the cause of an
embarrassed qualification, xi, 95–96.   211 **Auran** Vulgate form
of Haran, in Mesopotamia, the place whither Abraham
migrated (Gen. xi, 31)   212 **great Seleucia** The adjective is Pliny's
to distinguish this city on the Tigris, southeast of Baghdad, from
lesser cities of the same name. Its builder was Seleucus I Nicator,
a general of Alexander the Great's.   214 **Telassar** mentioned in
2 Kings xix, 12 and Isaiah, xxxvii, 12 as a city inhabited by
"the children of Eden" and associated with places in Western
Mesopotamia.

That mountain, as his garden-mould, high raised
Upon the rapid current, which through veins
Of porous earth with kindly° thirst updrawn
Rose a fresh fountain, and with many a rill
Watered the garden, thence united fell   230
Down the steep glade, and met the nether flood,
Which from his darksome passage now appears,
And now, divided into four main streams,
Runs diverse, wandering many a famous realm
And country whereof here needs no account,   235
But rather to tell how, if Art could tell
How, from that sapphire fount the crispèd° brooks,
Rolling on orient pearl and sands of gold,
With mazy error° under pendent shades
Ran nectar, visiting each plant, and fed   240
Flowers worthy of Paradise, which not nice Art
In beds and curious knots,° but Nature boon°
Poured forth profuse on hill, and dale, and plain,
Both where the morning sun first warmly smote
The open field, and where the unpierced shade   245
Embrowned the noontide bowers. Thus was this place,
A happy rural seat of various view:
Groves whose rich trees wept° odorous gums and balm;
Others whose fruit, burnished with golden rind,
Hung amiable, Hesperian° fables true,   250
If true, here only, and of delicious taste.
Betwixt them lawns, or level downs, and flocks
Grazing the tender herb, were interposed,
Or palmy hillock or the flowery lap
Of some irriguous valley spread her store,   255
Flowers of all hue, and without thorn the rose.°
Another side, umbrageous grots and caves
Of cool recess, o'er which the mantling vine°

228 **kindly** natural, as at 668   237 **crispèd** rippling   239 **error**
the literal Latin sense of *wandering*   242 **curious knots** elaborate
flower beds **boon** bounteous   248 **wept** "The melancholy of our
feeling that Eden must be lost so soon, once attached to its
vegetation, makes us feel that it is inherently melancholy"
(William Empson).   250 **Hesperian** see iii, 568   256 **without
thorn the rose** "Before man's fall, the rose was born,/ St.
Ambrose says, without the thorn." Robert Herrick, "The
Rose."   258 **mantling vine** had appeared in "Comus," 294.

Lays forth her purple grape and gently creeps
260   Luxuriant; meanwhile murmuring waters fall
Down the slope hills, dispersed, or in a lake,
That to the fringèd bank with myrtle crowned
Her crystal mirror holds, unite their streams.
The birds their choir apply; airs,° vernal airs,
265   Breathing the smell of field and grove, attune
The trembling leaves, while universal° Pan,
Knit with the Graces and the Hours in dance,
Led on the eternal Spring. Not that fair field
Of Enna,° where Proserpin gathering flowers,
270   Herself a fairer flower, by gloomy Dis
Was gathered, which cost Ceres all that pain
To seek her through the world, nor that sweet grove
Of Daphne,° by Orontes and the inspired
Castalian spring, might with this Paradise
275   Of Eden strive; nor that Nyseian isle,°
Girt with the river Triton, where old Cham,°
Whom Gentiles Ammon call, and Libyan Jove,
Hid Amalthea, and her florid son,
Young Bacchus, from his stepdame Rhea's eye;
280   Nor, where Abassin kings their issue guard,
Mount Amara (though this by some supposed
True Paradise) under the Ethiop line°
By Nilus' head, enclosed with shining rock,
A whole day's journey high, but wide remote
285   From this Assyrian garden, where the Fiend

264 **airs** in context a double meaning   266 **universal** "for *Pan*
signifieth all" (E. K.'s gloss to Spenser's *Shephards Calender*).
269 **Enna** This celebrated grove in Sicily, according to Ovid,
was the site of the abduction of Proserpina, daughter of Ceres
the Roman goddess of agriculture. Dis or Pluto took her to be
Queen of the Lower World. The connection with Eve, who is
also to be snatched by Death and Hell, operates powerfully in
the first part of a characteristic multiple simile.   273 **Daphne**
the name of a grove by the Orontes river in Syria, not far from
Antioch, where Apollo had a temple   275 **Nyseian isle** Nysa
(from which Dionysus, nurtured there, derived his name) was
near Tunis in North Africa (cf. "Libyan," 277).   276 **Cham**
Vulgate for Ham, Noah's son   281–82 Samuel Purchas wrote
of *Mount Amara:* "This hill is situate as the navel of that
Ethiopian body, and center of their empire, under the
equinoctial line."

Saw undelighted all delight, all kind
Of living creatures, new to sight and strange.
Two of far nobler shape, erect and tall,
Godlike erect, with native honour clad
In naked majesty, seemed lords of all,   290
And worthy seemed, for in their looks divine
The image of their glorious Maker shone,
Truth, wisdom, sanctitude severe and pure—
Severe, but in true filial freedom placed,
Whence true authority in men: though both   295
Not equal, as their sex not equal seemed;°
For contemplation he and valour formed,
For softness she and sweet attractive grace;°
He for God only, she for God in him.°
His fair large front and eye sublime declared   300
Absolute rule, and hyacinthine° locks
Round from his parted forelock manly hung
Clustering, but not beneath his shoulders broad:°
She, as a veil down to the slender waist,
Her unadorned golden tresses wore   305
Dishevelled, but in wanton ringlets waved
As the vine curls her tendrils, which implied
Subjection, but required with gentle sway,
And by her yielded, by him best received,
Yielded with coy° submission, modest pride,   310
And sweet, reluctant, amorous delay.
Nor those mysterious parts were then concealed;
Then was not guilty shame—dishonest° Shame

296 ff. The sentiments expressed here, on the differences
between the sexes, outrageous to some modern readers, were
commonplace in the Renaissance.   298 **attractive grace** cf. ii,
762   299 "He not for her, but she for him" *Tetrachordon*
(Columbia Milton, p. 76). These are versions of St. Paul's
"Neither was the man created for the woman, but the woman
for the man." 1 Corinthians, xi, 9.   301 **hyacinthine** perhaps, as
beautiful as Hyacinth, whom Apollo loved; or dark (maybe
specifically deep red—cf. "sanguine flower," "Lycidas," 106) and
curly like the flower; or flowing. See *Odyssey* VI, 231.   303 **but not
beneath his shoulders broad** a hit at the Cavaliers, possibly; cf. 1
Corinthians xi, 14–15. A 1654 publication by the preacher Thomas
Hall was *Loathsomeness of Long Hair*.   310 **coy** The word has
degenerated; it meant *shy*.   313 **dishonest** loose, unchaste

Of Nature's works, Honour dishonourable,
315 Sin-bred, how have ye troubled all mankind
With shows instead, mere shows of seeming pure,
And banished from man's life his happiest life,
Simplicity and spotless innocence.
So passed they naked on, nor shunned the sight
320 Of God or Angel, for they thought no ill;
So hand in hand° they passed, the loveliest pair
That ever since in love's embraces met—
Adam, the goodliest man of men since born
His sons; the fairest of her daughters Eve.°
325 Under a tuft of shade that on a green
Stood whispering soft, by a fresh fountain-side,
They sat them down, and, after no more toil
Of their sweet gardening labour than sufficed
To recommend cool Zephyr,° and made ease
330 More easy, wholesome thirst and appetite
More grateful, to their supper-fruits they fell,
Nectarine fruits, which the compliant° boughs
Yielded them, sidelong as they sat recline
On the soft downy bank damasked with flowers.
335 The savoury pulp they chew, and in the rind,
Still as they thirsted, scoop the brimming stream;
Nor gentle purpose, nor endearing smiles
Wanted, nor youthful dalliance, as beseems
Fair couple linked in happy nuptial league,
340 Alone as they. About them frisking played
All beasts of the earth, since wild, and of all chase
In wood or wilderness, forest or den;
Sporting the lion ramped, and in his paw
Dandled the kid; bears, tigers, ounces, pards,
345 Gambolled before them; the unwieldy elephant,
To make them mirth, used all his might, and wreathed
His lithe proboscis; close the serpent sly,

321 **hand in hand** cf. 689 and xii, 647 323, 324 The superlatives
represent a Greek construction that includes the comparative. 329 **Zephyr** the west (spring) wind; compare the
"General Prologue" to Chaucer's *Canterbury Tales,* 5 ff. 332
compliant in the literal sense of *bending,* in addition to the
figurative

Insinuating,° wove with Gordian twine°
His braided train, and of his fatal guile
Gave proof unheeded. Others on the grass 350
Couched, and, now filled with pasture, gazing sat,
Or bedward ruminating; for the sun,
Declined, was hasting now with prone career
To the Ocean Isles, and in the ascending scale
Of Heaven the stars that usher evening rose; 355
When Satan still in gaze, as first he stood,
Scarce thus at length failed speech recovered sad:
    'O Hell! what do mine eyes with grief behold?
Into our room of bliss thus high advanced
Creatures of other mould—Earth-born perhaps, 360
Not Spirits, yet to Heavenly Spirits bright
Little inferior°—whom my thoughts pursue
With wonder, and could love, so lively shines
In them divine resemblance, and such grace
The hand that formed them on their shape hath poured. 365
Ah! gentle pair, ye little think how nigh
Your change approaches, when all these delights
Will vanish, and deliver ye to woe,
More woe, the more your taste is now of joy:
Happy, but for so happy ill secured 370
Long to continue, and this high seat, your Heaven,
Ill fenced for Heaven to keep out such a foe
As now is entered; yet no purposed foe
To you whom I could pity thus forlorn,
Though I unpitied. League with you I seek 375
And mutual amity, so strait, so close,
That I with you must dwell, or you with me,
Henceforth. My dwelling, haply, may not please,
Like this fair Paradise, your sense; yet such
Accept your Maker's work; he gave it me, 380
Which I as freely give. Hell shall unfold,
To entertain you two, her widest gates,
And send forth all her kings; there will be room,
Not like these narrow limits, to receive

348 **Insinuating** moving sinuously (Latin *sinus*, folds) **Gordian twine** intricate tangle, like the Gordian knot that Alexander the Great cut with his sword. 362 **Little inferior** "A little lower than the angels." Psalms viii, 5

385 Your numerous offspring; if no better place,
Thank him who puts me, loath, to this revenge
On you, who wrong me not, for him who wronged.
And, should I at your harmless innocence
Melt, as I do, yet public reason just,
390 Honour and empire with revenge enlarged
By conquering this new world, compels me now
To do what else, though damned, I should abhor.'
    So spake the Fiend, and with necessity,
The tyrant's plea, excused his devilish deeds.
395 Then from his lofty stand on that high tree
Down he alights among the sportful herd
Of those four-footed kinds, himself now one,
Now other, as their shape served best his end
Nearer to view his prey, and, unespied,
400 To mark what of their state he more might learn
By word or action marked. About them round
A lion now he stalks with fiery glare;
Then as a tiger, who by chance hath spied
In some purlieu° two gentle fawns at play,
405 Straight couches; then, rising, changes oft
His couchant watch, as one who chose his ground,
Whence rushing he might surest seize them both
Gripped in each paw: when Adam, first of men,
To first of women, Eve, thus moving speech,
410 Turned him all ear to hear new utterance flow:
    'Sole partner and sole part of all these joys,
Dearer thyself than all, needs must the Power
That made us, and for us this ample World,
Be infinitely good, and of his good
415 As liberal and free as infinite,
That raised us from the dust, and placed us here
In all this happiness, who at his hand
Have nothing merited, nor can perform
Aught whereof he hath need; he who requires
420 From us no other service than to keep°

---

404 purlieu a tract of land on the fringe of a forest   **420 ff.** It is unfortunate, and perhaps psychologically significant (of awe, or of temptation, or of Adam's didactic tendency?), and certainly dramatically convenient that the first words to come from Adam should deal with the forbidden tree.

This one, this easy charge, of all the trees
In Paradise that bear delicious fruit
So various, not to taste that only Tree
Of Knowledge, planted by the Tree of Life;
So near grows Death to Life, whate'er Death is—   425
Some dreadful thing no doubt; for well thou know'st
God hath pronounced it Death to taste that Tree:
The only sign of our obedience left
Among so many signs of power and rule
Conferred upon us, and dominion given   430
Over all other creatures that possess
Earth, Air, and Sea. Then let us not think hard
One easy prohibition, who enjoy
Free leave so large to all things else, and choice
Unlimited of manifold delights,   435
But let us ever praise him, and extol
His bounty, following our delightful task,
To prune these growing plants, and tend these flowers;°
Which, were it toilsome, yet with thee were sweet.'

   To whom thus Eve replied: 'O thou for whom   440
And from whom I was formed flesh of thy flesh,
And without whom am to no end, my guide
And head, what thou hast said is just and right.°
For we to him, indeed, all praises owe,
And daily thanks—I chiefly, who enjoy   445
So far the happier lot, enjoying thee
Pre-eminent by so much odds, while thou
Like consort to thyself canst nowhere find.
That day I oft remember, when from sleep
I first awaked, and found myself reposed,   450
Under a shade, on° flowers, much wondering where
And what I was, whence thither brought, and how.
Not distant far from thence a murmuring sound
Of waters issued from a cave, and spread
Into a liquid plain; then stood unmoved,   455
Pure as the expanse of Heaven. I thither went
With unexperienced thought, and laid me down
On the green bank, to look into the clear

438 The origin of this occupation is in Genesis ii, 15. Cf. 618
ff.   443 **just and right** key words, ii, 18; iii, 98   451 **on** 1674
has *of*.

Smooth lake, that to me seemed another sky.
460 As I bent down to look, just opposite,°
A shape within the watery gleam appeared,
Bending to look on me. I started back,
It started back; but pleased I soon returned,
Pleased it returned as soon with answering looks
465 Of sympathy and love; there I had fixed
Mine eyes till now, and pined with vain desire,
Had not a voice thus warned me: "What thou seest,
What there thou seest, fair creature, is thyself;
With thee it came and goes; but follow me,
470 And I will bring thee where no shadow stays
Thy coming, and thy soft embraces, he
Whose image thou art, him thou shalt enjoy
Inseparably thine, to him shalt bear
Multitudes like thyself, and thence be called
475 Mother of human race." What could I do,
But follow straight, invisibly thus led?
Till I espied thee, fair, indeed, and tall,
Under a platan;° yet methought less fair,
Less winning soft, less amiably mild,
480 Than that smooth watery image. Back I turned;
Thou, following, cried'st aloud, "Return, fair Eve;
Whom fliest thou? Whom thou fliest, of him thou art,
His flesh, his bone; to give thee being I lent
Out of my side to thee, nearest my heart,
485 Substantial life, to have thee by my side
Henceforth an individual° solace dear:
Part of my soul I seek thee, and the claim
My other half." With that thy gentle hand
Seized mine; I yielded, and from that time see
490 How beauty is excelled by manly grace
And wisdom, which alone is truly fair.'
    So spake our general mother,° and, with eyes
Of conjugal attraction unreproved,
And meek surrender, half-embracing leaned

460 ff. This Narcissus-like recollection, with its implication of
vanity, is meant to put the reader in mind that self-love in that
case was death ("pined with vain desire," 466).   478 **platan**
the Oriental plane tree   486 **individual** undividable, inseparable
492 our general mother cf. 144

On our first father; half her swelling breast   495
Naked met his, under the flowing gold
Of her loose tresses hid. He, in delight
Both of her beauty and submissive charms,
Smiled with superior love, as Jupiter
On Juno smiles when he impregns° the clouds   500
That shed May flowers, and pressed her matron lip
With kisses pure. Aside the Devil turned
For envy, yet with jealous leer malign
Eyed them askance, and to himself thus 'plained:
    'Sight hateful, sight tormenting! Thus these two,°   505
Imparadised in one another's arms,
The happier Eden, shall enjoy their fill
Of bliss on bliss, while I to Hell am thrust,
Where neither joy nor love,° but fierce desire,
Among our other torments not the least,   510
Still unfulfilled, with pain of longing pines!
Yet let me not forget what I have gained
From their own mouths. All is not theirs, it seems;
One fatal tree there stands, of Knowledge called,
Forbidden them to taste. Knowledge forbidden?   515
Suspicious, reasonless. Why should their Lord
Envy them that? Can it be sin to know?°
Can it be death? And do they only stand
By ignorance? Is that their happy state,
The proof of their obedience and their faith?   520
O fair foundation laid whereon to build
Their ruin! Hence I will excite their minds
With more desire to know, and to reject
Envious commands, invented with design

---

500 **impregns** impregnates 505 ff. The distinguished
authority on Puritanism, William Haller, observes that
marriage "is the consummation of God's plan of creation on
earth. It is the projection of the divine order, of the order
of nature and of the soul, into human society. It is the whole
of human society in germ, the living microcosm, truly, of
family, church, and state. It is, in consequence, the prime
object of Satan's envy, and its disruption the first task to
which he addressed himself on this earth." " 'Hail Wedded
Love'," *ELH,* XIII (1946), 97.   509 **neither joy nor love** cf.
iii, 67, 338   517 ff. A corrupt version of the attitude made
famous in *Areopagitica*.

525 To keep them low, whom knowledge might exalt
Equal with gods. Aspiring° to be such,
They taste and die: what likelier can ensue?
But first with narrow search I must walk round
This garden, and no corner leave unspied;
530 A chance but chance may lead where I may meet
Some wandering Spirit of Heaven, by fountain-side,
Or in thick shade retired, from him to draw
What further would be learned. Live while ye may,
Yet happy pair; enjoy, till I return,
535 Short pleasures, for long woes are to succeed!'
     So saying, his proud step he scornful turned,
But with sly circumspection,° and began
Through wood, through waste, o'er hill, o'er dale, his roam.
Meanwhile in utmost longitude, where Heaven
540 With Earth and Ocean meets, the setting Sun
Slowly descended, and with right aspect°
Against the eastern° gate of Paradise
Levelled his evening rays. It was a rock
Of alabaster, piled up to the clouds,
545 Conspicuous far, winding with one ascent
Accessible from Earth, one entrance high;
The rest was craggy cliff, that overhung
Still as it rose, impossible to climb.
Betwixt these rocky pillars Gabriel sat,
550 Chief of the angelic guards, awaiting night;
About him exercised heroic games
The unarmed youth of Heaven; but nigh at hand
Celestial armoury, shields, helms, and spears,
Hung high, with diamond flaming and with gold.
555 Thither came Uriel, gliding through the even
On a sunbeam, swift as a shooting star
In autumn thwarts° the night, when vapours fired
Impress the air, and shows the mariner
From what point of his compass to beware

526 **Aspiring** cf. the first use of this word, i, 38 537
circumspection cf. ii, 414 541 **right aspect** direct view 542
eastern Keightley thought this a slip for "western," but it may
be that the setting sun is directing its rays against the inner
side of the "alabaster" (but later called "ivory," 778)
gate. 557 **thwarts** literally, *crosses*

Impetuous winds. He thus began in haste: 560
  'Gabriel, to thee thy course by lot hath given
Charge and strict watch that to this happy place
No evil thing approach or enter in.
This day at height of noon came to my sphere
A Spirit, zealous, as he seemed, to know   565
More of the Almighty's works, and chiefly Man,°
God's latest image. I described his way
Bent all on speed, and marked his aery gait,
But in the mount that lies from Eden north,
Where he first lighted, soon discerned his looks   570
Alien from Heaven, with passions foul obscured.
Mine eye pursued him still, but under shade
Lost sight of him. One of the banished crew,
I fear, hath ventured from the deep, to raise
New troubles; him thy care must be to find.'   575
  To whom the wingèd Warrior thus returned:
'Uriel, no wonder if thy perfect sight,
Amid the Sun's bright circle where thou sitt'st,
See far and wide. In at this gate none pass
The vigilance° here placed but such as come   580
Well known from Heaven, and since meridian hour
No creature thence. If Spirit of other sort,
So minded, have o'erleaped these earthly bounds
On purpose, hard thou know'st it to exclude
Spiritual substance with corporeal bar.   585
But if within the circuit of these walks,
In whatsoever shape, he lurk of whom
Thou tell'st, by morrow dawning I shall know.'
  So promised he, and Uriel to his charge
Returned on that bright beam, whose point now raised 590
Bore him slope downward to the Sun, now fallen
Beneath the Azores, whither° the prime orb,
Incredible how swift, had thither rolled
Diurnal, or this less voluble Earth,°

566 **chiefly Man** This connects with iii, 663, as iii, 664, "chief
delight," contrasts with iii, 168. 580 **vigilance** an abstract for
a concrete, the angelic watch or guard 592 **whither** Some
editors read *whether.* 594 Milton keeps his poem open to both
the Ptolemaic (fixed earth) and Copernican explanations; cf.
viii.

595 By shorter flight to the east, had left him there
     Arraying with reflected purple and gold
     The clouds that on his western throne attend.
     Now came still Evening on, and Twilight grey
     Had in her sober livery all things clad;
600 Silence accompanied; for beast and bird,
     They to their grassy couch, these to their nests
     Were slunk, all but the wakeful nightingale;
     She all night long her amorous descant sung;
     Silence was pleased: now glowed the firmament
605 With living sapphires; Hesperus, that led
     The starry host, rode brightest, till the Moon,
     Rising in clouded majesty, at length
     Apparent queen, unveiled her peerless light,
     And o'er the dark her silver mantle threw.
610   When Adam thus to Eve: 'Fair consort, the hour
     Of night, and all things now retired to rest,
     Mind us of like repose; since God hath set
     Labour and rest, as day and night, to men
     Successive, and the timely dew of sleep,
615 Now falling with soft slumberous weight, inclines
     Our eyelids. Other creatures all day long
     Rove idle, unemployed, and less need rest;
     Man hath his daily work of body or mind
     Appointed, which declares his dignity,
620 And the regard of Heaven on all his ways;
     While other animals unactive range,
     And of their doings God takes no account.
     To-morrow, ere fresh morning streak the east
     With first approach of light, we must be risen,
625 And at our pleasant labour, to reform
     Yon flowery arbours, yonder alleys green,
     Our walks at noon° with branches overgrown,
     That mock our scant manuring° and require
     More hands than ours to lop their wanton growth.
630 Those blossoms also, and those dropping gums,
     That lie bestrewn, unsightly and unsmooth,

627 **walks at noon** in consideration of the first pair's brevity of
existence so far, changed to the singular in 1674; cf. the
rhyming phrase at 655 628 **manuring** cultivating (with the
hands, Latin)

Ask riddance, if we mean to tread with ease.
Meanwhile, as Nature wills, Night bids us rest.'
    To whom thus Eve, with perfect beauty adorned:
'My author and disposer, what thou bidd'st   635
Unargued I obey; so God ordains:
God is thy law, thou mine: to know no more
Is woman's happiest knowledge, and her praise.
With thee conversing, I forget all time,
All seasons, and their change; all please alike.   640
Sweet is the breath of Morn, her rising sweet,°
With charm° of earliest birds; pleasant the Sun,
When first on this delightful land he spreads
His orient beams, on herb, tree, fruit, and flower,
Glistering with dew; fragrant the fertile Earth   645
After soft showers, and sweet the coming-on
Of grateful Evening mild; then silent Night,
With this her solemn bird, and this fair Moon,
And these the gems of Heaven, her starry train;
But neither breath of Morn, when she ascends   650
With charm of earliest birds, nor rising Sun°
On this delightful land, nor herb, fruit, flower,
Glistering with dew, nor fragrance after shower,
Nor grateful Evening mild, nor silent Night,
With this her solemn bird, nor walk by moon,   655
Or glittering starlight, without thee is sweet.
But wherefore all night long shine these? for whom
This glorious sight, when sleep hath shut all eyes?'
    To whom our general ancestor replied:
'Daughter of God and Man, accomplished Eve,   660
Those have their course to finish round the Earth
By morrow evening, and from land to land
In order, though to nations yet unborn,
Ministering light prepared, they set and rise,
Lest total darkness should by night regain   665
Her old possession, and extinguish life

641–56 The most brilliant example in English of the figure of
repetition known as epanadiplosis or "the recapitulator": a
series returning to the word with which it began, an exquisite
weaving and unweaving, the negatives marking the principal
points of detachment as the shuttle, going now in reverse
direction, unravels the fabric. 642 **charm** song (Latin
carmen)   651 **rising Sun** mentioned at iii, 551

In nature and all things, which these soft fires
Not only enlighten, but with kindly heat
Of various influence foment and warm,
670 Temper or nourish, or in part shed down
Their stellar virtue on all kinds that grow
On Earth, made hereby apter to receive
Perfection from the Sun's more potent ray.
These, then, though unbeheld in deep of night,
675 Shine not in vain. Nor think, though men were none,
That Heaven would want spectators, God want praise.
Millions of spiritual creatures walk the Earth
Unseen, both when we wake and when we sleep;°
All these with ceaseless praise his works behold
680 Both day and night. How often, from the steep
Of echoing hill or thicket, have we heard
Celestial voices to the midnight air,
Sole, or responsive each to other's note,
Singing their great Creator; oft in bands
685 While they keep watch, or nightly rounding walk,
With heavenly touch of instrumental sounds
In full harmonic number joined, their songs
Divide the night, and lift our thoughts to Heaven.'
      Thus talking, hand in hand alone they passed
690 On to their blissful bower. It was a place
Chosen by the sovran Planter, when he framed
All things to Man's delightful use; the roof
Of thickest covert was inwoven shade,
Laurel and myrtle, and what higher grew
695 Of firm and fragrant leaf; on either side
Acanthus,° and each odorous bushy shrub,
Fenced up the verdant wall; each beauteous flower,
Iris all hues, roses, and jessamine,

677–78 Compare "Sonnet on His Blindness": ". . . thousands
at His bidding speed,/ And post o'er land and ocean without
rest."   696 **Acanthus** species of plants native to the warmer
regions of the Old World, having large, deeply cut, shining
leaves that, models for decoration in Greek and Roman
architecture, in particular the Corinthian column, perhaps
contributed to Milton's train of thought—"Fenced up the
verdant wall," 697

Reared high their flourished° heads between, and wrought
Mosaic; under foot the violet,   700
Crocus, and hyacinth, with rich inlay
Broidered the ground, more coloured than with stone°
Of costliest emblem; other creature here,
Beast, bird, insect, or worm, durst enter none,
Such was their awe of Man. In shadier° bower   705
More sacred and sequestered, though but feigned,
Pan or Sylvanus never slept, nor Nymph,
Nor Faunus° haunted. Here, in close recess,
With flowers, garlands, and sweet-smelling herbs,
Espousèd Eve decked first her nuptial bed,   710
And heavenly choirs the hymenean sung,
What day the genial Angel to our sire
Brought her, in naked beauty more adorned,
More lovely, than Pandora, whom the gods
Endowed with all their gifts; and, O! too like°   715
In sad event, when, to the unwiser son
Of Japhet brought by Hermes, she ensnared
Mankind with her fair looks, to be avenged
On him who had stole° Jove's authentic fire.

Thus at their shady lodge arrived, both stood,   720
Both turned, and under open sky adored
The God that made both Sky, Air, Earth, and Heaven,
Which they beheld, the Moon's resplendent globe,
And starry Pole: 'Thou also mad'st the Night,
Maker Omnipotent, and thou the Day   725
Which we, in our appointed work employed,
Have finished, happy in our mutual help
And mutual love, the crown of all our bliss
Ordained by thee; and this delicious place,

699 **flourished** growing luxuriantly, with some play on *flowers*
700–02 This is very close to *Iliad* XIV, 347–49; cf. ix, 1027
ff.   705 **shadier** the *r* that made it comparative is not in the
1674 text. 707–08 All are wood deities. 714–15 Milton
translates the name *Pandora,* "all . . . gifts." She was brought
"to the unwiser son/ Of Japhet" (716–17), Epimetheus, as the
gods' revenge for Prometheus's theft of fire for man, for there
came with her a box containing all human ills, upon the
opening of which all escaped and spread over the earth, Hope
alone remaining.   719 **stole** perhaps a misprint for *stolen,* used
elsewhere, x, 20

730 For us too large, where thy abundance wants
     Partakers, and uncropped falls to the ground.
     But thou hast promised from us two a race
     To fill the Earth, who shall with us extol
     Thy goodness infinite, both when we wake,
735 And when we seek, as now, thy gift of sleep.'
         This said unanimous, and other rites
     Observing none, but adoration pure,°
     Which God likes best, into their inmost bower
     Handed they went, and, eased the putting-off
740 These troublesome disguises which we wear,
     Straight side by side were laid, nor turned, I ween,
     Adam from his fair spouse, nor Eve the rites
     Mysterious of connubial love refused:
     Whatever hypocrites austerely talk
745 Of purity, and place, and innocence,
     Defaming as impure what God declares
     Pure, and commands to some, leaves free to all.
     Our Maker bids increase; who bids abstain
     But our destroyer, foe to God and Man?
750 Hail, wedded Love, mysterious law, true source
     Of human offspring, sole propriety°
     In Paradise of all things common else!
     By thee adulterous lust was driven from men
     Among the bestial herds to range; by thee,
755 Founded in reason, loyal, just, and pure,
     Relations dear, and all the charities
     Of father, son, and brother, first were known.
     Far be it that I should write thee sin or blame,
     Or think thee unbefitting holiest place,
760 Perpetual fountain of domestic sweets,
     Whose bed is undefiled and chaste pronounced,
     Present, or past, as saints and patriarchs used.
     Here Love his golden shafts° employs, here lights
     His constant lamp, and waves his purple wings,
765 Reigns here and revels; not in the bought smile

736–37 Adam and Eve are Puritans, in the sense that they
worship simply and spontaneously, without rituals or prayer
books. Cf. xii, 534.   751 **sole propriety** sole exclusiveness of
possession (property)   763 **golden shafts** According to Ovid,
Metamorphoses I, 468, Cupid also possessed leaden arrows that
repelled love.

Of harlots, loveless, joyless, unendeared,
Casual fruition; nor in court amours,
Mixed dance, or wanton mask, or midnight ball,
Or serenade, which the starved lover sings
To his proud fair, best quitted with disdain.   770
These, lulled by nightingales, embracing slept,
And on their naked limbs the flowery roof
Showered roses, which the morn repaired. Sleep on,
Blest pair, and, O! yet happiest, if ye seek
No happier state,° and know to know no more.   775
    Now had Night measured with her shadowy cone
Halfway uphill this vast sublunar vault,
And from their ivory port the Cherubim
Forth issuing at the accustomed hour stood armed
To their night-watches in warlike parade,   780
When Gabriel to his next in power thus spake:
'Uzziel,° half these draw off, and coast the south
With strictest watch; these other wheel the north;
Our circuit meets full west.' As flame they part,
Half wheeling to the shield, half to the spear.   785
From these, two strong and subtle Spirits he called
That near him stood, and gave them thus in charge:
'Ithuriel and Zephon,° with winged speed
Search through this Garden; leave unsearched no nook,
But chiefly where those two fair creatures lodge,   790
Now laid perhaps asleep, secure° of harm.
This evening from the Sun's decline arrived
Who tells of some infernal Spirit seen
Hitherward bent (who could have thought?), escaped
The bars of Hell,° on errand bad, no doubt;   795
Such, where ye find, seize fast, and hither bring.'
    So saying, on he led his radiant files,
Dazzling the Moon; these° to the bower direct°
In search of whom they sought. Him there they found
Squat like a toad, close at the ear of Eve,°   800
Assaying by his devilish art to reach

775 **happier state** cf. ii, 24   782 **Uzziel** "Strength of God"   788
Ithuriel and Zephon appropriately, "Search of God" and
"Searcher"; cf. 789   791 **secure** Latin, without worry,
unsuspicious   795 **bars of Hell** cf. iii, 82   798 **these** i.e., Ithuriel
and Zephon **direct** straightway   800 A most deliberate reduction
of Satan's glamour

The organs of her fancy, and with them forge
Illusions as he list, phantasms and dreams;
Or if, inspiring venom, he might taint
805 The animal spirits,° that from pure blood arise
Like gentle breaths from rivers pure, thence raise,
At least distempered, discontented thoughts,
Vain hopes, vain aims, inordinate desires,
Blown up with high conceits engendering pride.
810 Him thus intent Ithuriel with his spear
Touched lightly, for no falsehood can endure
Touch of celestial temper, but returns
Of force to its own likeness. Up he starts,
Discovered and surprised. As, when a spark
815 Lights on a heap of nitrous powder° laid
Fit for the tun,° some magazine to store
Against a rumoured war, the smutty grain,
With sudden blaze diffused, inflames the air,
So started up, in his own shape, the Fiend.
820 Back stepped those two fair Angels, half amazed
So sudden to behold the grisly King;
Yet thus, unmoved with fear, accost him soon:
 'Which of those rebel Spirits adjudged to Hell
Com'st thou, escaped thy prison? and, transformed,
825 Why satt'st thou like an enemy in wait,
Here watching at the head of these that sleep?'
 'Know ye not, then,' said Satan, filled with scorn,
'Know ye not me? Ye knew me once no mate
For you, there sitting where ye durst not soar!
830 Not to know me argues° yourselves unknown,
The lowest of your throng; or, if ye know,
Why ask ye, and superfluous begin
Your message, like to end as much in vain?'
 To whom thus Zephon, answering scorn with scorn:
835 'Think not, revolted Spirit, thy shape the same,
Or undiminished brightness, to be known
As when thou stood'st in Heaven upright and pure.

---

805 **The animal spirits** (the adjective comes from Latin animal
soul—*inspiring venom* [804] is *Aeneid* VIII, 351, "*vipeream
inspirans animam*") went to the brain. 815 **nitrous powder**
gunpowder 816 **tun** storage barrel 830 **argues** proves; cf.
Samson Agonistes, 1081–82.

That glory then, when thou no more wast good,
Departed from thee; and thou resemblest now
Thy sin and place of doom obscure and foul.   *840*
But come; for thou, be sure, shalt give account
To him who sent us, whose charge is to keep
This place inviolable, and these from harm.'
    So spake the Cherub, and his grave rebuke,
Severe in youthful beauty, added grace   *845*
Invincible. Abashed the Devil stood,
And felt how awful goodness is, and saw
Virtue in her shape how lovely, saw, and pined
His loss, but chiefly to find here observed
His lustre visibly impaired, yet seemed   *850*
Undaunted. 'If I must contend,' said he,
'Best with the best, the sender, not the sent,
Or all at once: more glory will be won,
Or less be lost.' 'Thy fear,' said Zephon bold,
'Will save us trial what the least can do   *855*
Single against thee wicked, and thence weak.'
    The Fiend replied not, overcome with rage,
But, like a proud steed reined, went haughty on,
Champing his iron curb. To strive or fly
He held it vain; awe from above had quelled   *860*
His heart, not else dismayed. Now drew they nigh
The western point, where those half-rounding guards
Just met, and, closing, stood in squadron joined,
Awaiting next command. To whom their chief,
Gabriel, from the front thus called aloud: *865*
    'O friends, I hear the tread of nimble feet°
Hasting this way, and now by glimpse discern
Ithuriel and Zephon through the shade,
And with them comes a third, of regal port
But faded splendour wan, who by his gait   *870*
And fierce demeanour seems the Prince of Hell—
Not likely to part hence without contést;°
Stand firm, for in his look defiance lours.'
    He scarce had ended when those two approached,
And brief related whom they brought, where found,   *875*

866–73 A speech that is probably a remnant of the days when
Paradise Lost was a drama.   872 **contést** accented on the
second syllable

How busied, in what form and posture couched.
　　To whom, with stern regard, thus Gabriel spake:
'Why hast thou, Satan, broke the bounds prescribed
To thy transgressions, and disturbed the charge
880 Of others, who approve not to transgress
By thy example, but have power and right
To question thy bold entrance on this place;
Employed, it seems, to violate sleep, and those
Whose dwelling God hath planted here in bliss?'
885 　　To whom thus Satan, with contemptuous brow:
'Gabriel, thou hadst in Heaven the esteem of wise,
And such I held thee, but this question asked
Puts me in doubt. Lives there who loves his pain?
Who would not, finding way, break loose from Hell,
890 Though thither doomed? Thou wouldst thyself, no doubt,
And boldly venture to whatever place
Farthest from pain, where thou mightst hope to change
Torment with ease, and soonest recompense
Dole with delight;° which in this place I sought:
895 To thee no reason, who know'st only good,
But evil hast not tried. And wilt object
His will who bound us? Let him surer bar
His iron gates, if he intends our stay
In that dark durance. Thus much what was asked;
900 The rest is true: they found me where they say,
But that implies not violence or harm.'
　　Thus he in scorn. The warlike Angel moved,
Disdainfully half smiling, thus replied:
'O loss of one in Heaven to judge of wise,
905 Since Satan fell, whom folly overthrew,
And now returns him from his prison 'scaped,
Gravely in doubt whether to hold them wise
Or not, who ask what boldness brought him hither
Unlicensed from his bounds in Hell prescribed!
910 So wise he judges it to fly from pain,
However, and to 'scape his punishment.
So judge thou still, presumptuous till the wrath,
Which thou incurr'st by flying, meet thy flight
Sevenfold, and scourge that wisdom back to Hell

---

894 **Dole with delight** cf. *Hamlet,* I, ii, 13: "In equal scale
weighing delight and dole" (Claudius)

Which taught thee yet no better that no pain 915
Can equal anger infinite provoked.
But wherefore thou alone? Wherefore with thee
Came not all Hell broke loose?° Is pain to them
Less pain, less to be fled? or thou than they
Less hardy to endure? Courageous chief, 920
The first in flight from pain, hadst thou alleged
To thy deserted host this cause of flight,
Thou surely hadst not come sole fugitive.'
    To which the Fiend thus answered, frowning stern:
'Not that I less endure, or shrink from pain, 925
Insulting Angel; well thou know'st I stood
Thy fiercest, when in battle to thy aid
The° blasting volleyed thunder made all speed
And seconded thy else not dreaded spear.
But still thy words at random, as before 930
Argue thy inexperience what behooves,
From hard assays and ill successes past,
A faithful leader—not to hazard all
Through ways of danger by himself untried.
I, therefore, I alone, first undertook 935
To wing the desolate abyss, and spy
This new-created World, whereof in Hell
Fame is not silent, here in hope to find
Better abode, and my afflicted Powers
To settle here on Earth, or in mid Air; 940
Though for possession put to try once more
What thou and thy gay legions dare against,
Whose easier business were to serve their Lord
High up in Heaven, with songs to hymn his throne,
And° practised distances to cringe, not fight.' 945
    To whom the Warrior-Angel soon replied:
'To say and straight unsay, pretending first

918 **all Hell broke loose** Although another Puritan, John
Bastwick, used a similar expression in his *Litany,* 1637, Milton
was the first to say this memorably (cf. iii, 87). It was taken
up popularly and degenerated, like "Something is rotten in
the state of Denmark" (*Hamlet,* I, iv, 90).   928 **The** 1674 has
Thy   945 **And** Add *with* for the meaning. The sentiment of
943–45 is similar to Prometheus's "So worship, flatter, adore
the ruler of the day; but I have no thought in my heart for
Zeus." Aeschylus, *Prometheus Bound,* 937–38.

Wise to fly pain, professing next the spy,
Argues no leader, but a liar traced,
950 Satan; and couldst thou "faithful" add? O name,°
O sacred name of faithfulness profaned!
Faithful to whom? to thy rebellious crew?
Army of fiends, fit body to fit head;
Was this your discipline and faith engaged,
955 Your military obedience, to dissolve
Allegiance to the acknowledged Power Supreme?
And thou, sly hypocrite, who now wouldst seem
Patron of liberty, who more than thou
Once fawned, and cringed, and servilely adored
960 Heaven's awful Monarch? wherefore, but in hope
To dispossess him, and thyself to reign?
But mark what I arede° thee now: Avaunt!
Fly thither whence thou fledd'st. If from this hour
Within these hallowed limits thou appear,
965 Back to the Infernal Pit I drag thee chained,
And seal thee so as henceforth not to scorn°
The facile gates of Hell too slightly barred.'
    So threatened he; but Satan to no threats
Gave heed, but waxing more in rage, replied:
970   'Then when I am thy captive talk of chains,
Proud limitary° Cherub, but ere then
Far heavier load thyself expect to feel
From my prevailing arm, though Heaven's King°
Ride on thy wings, and thou with thy compeers,
975 Used to the yoke, draw'st his triumphant wheels
In progress through the road of Heaven star-paved.'
    While thus he spake, the angelic squadron bright
Turned fiery red, sharpening in moonèd horns
Their phalanx, and began to hem him round
980 With ported° spears, as thick as when a field
Of Ceres, ripe for harvest waving, bends
Her bearded grove of ears which way the wind
Sways them; the careful ploughman doubting stands,

950 cf. 933   962 **arede** counsel   966 Revelation, xx, 3   971
limitary play on (1) guarding the limits (cf. 964) and (2)
prescribing limits   973 **Heaven's King** a favorite fixed epithet,
ii, 751, 992; iv, 111 (also found in *Paradise Regained* i, 421); in
other places with an intervening adjective i, 131; ii, 851; v, 220;
x, 387   980 **ported** carried aslant across the breast

Lest on the threshing-floor his hopeful sheaves
Prove chaff. On the other side, Satan, alarmed,°   985
Collecting all his might, dilated stood,
Like Tenerife° or Atlas° unremoved;°
His stature reached the sky, and on his crest
Sat Horror plumed, nor wanted in his grasp
What seemed both spear and shield. Now dreadful deeds°   990
Might have ensued, nor only Paradise,
In this commotion, but the starry cope°
Of Heaven perhaps, or all the elements
At least, had gone to wrack, disturbed and torn
With violence of this conflict, had not soon   995
The Eternal, to prevent such horrid fray,
Hung forth in Heaven his golden scales, yet seen°
Betwixt Astraea° and the Scorpion° sign,
Wherein all things created first he weighed,
The pendulous round Earth with balanced air   1000
In counterpoise, now ponders all events,
Battles and realms. In these he put two weights,
The sequel each of parting and of fight;
The latter quick up flew, and kicked the beam,
Which Gabriel spying thus bespake the Fiend: 1005
   'Satan, I know thy strength, and thou know'st mine,
Neither our own, but given; what folly then
To boast what arms can do, since thine no more
Than Heaven permits, nor mine, though doubled now

---

985 **alarmed** not fearful, but ready for battle   987 **Tenerife** A
celebrated peak in the Canary Islands, of which John Donne wrote:
"Doth not a Tenerife or higher hill/ Rise so high like a rock, that
one might think/ The floating moon would shipwreck there and
sink?" (*First Anniversary*, 286–88). **Atlas** the mountain in Libya, so
high that it seemed "to bear up Heaven," *Samson Agonistes,* 150
unremoved unremovable   990 **dreadful deeds** cf. i, 130   992 **cope**
mantel or roof   997 ff. Besides literally referring to Libra the
constellation, the poet combines classical precedent for the scales—
they are like those in which the chief Olympian weighed issues
(*Iliad* VII, 69; XXII, 209; *Aeneid* XII, 725–27)—with Biblical moral:
"God hath numbered thy kingdom, and finished it. . . . Thou art
weighed in the balances, and art found wanting" (Daniel, v, 26–27).
Cf. 1012.   998 **Astraea** Justice, the constellation Virgo, who fled
the earth at the end of the Golden Age. **Scorpion** has its symbolic
value too.

1010 To trample thee as mire.° For proof look up,
     And read thy lot in yon celestial sign,
     Where thou art weighed, and shown how light, how weak,
     If thou resist.' The Fiend looked up, and knew
     His mounted scale aloft; nor° more, but fled
1015 Murmuring, and with him fled the shades of Night.°

BOOK V

THE ARGUMENT

Morning approached, Eve relates to Adam her trouble-some dream; he likes it not, yet comforts her; they come forth to their day labours; their morning hymn at the door of their bower. God, to render Man inexcusable, sends Raphael to admonish him of his obedience, of his free estate, of his enemy near at hand, who he is, and why his enemy, and whatever else may avail Adam to know. Raphael comes down to Paradise; his appearance described; his coming discerned by Adam afar off, sitting at the door of his bower; he goes out to meet him, brings him to his lodge, entertains him with the choicest fruits of Paradise, got together by Eve; their discourse at table. Raphael performs his message, minds Adam of his state and of his enemy; relates, at Adam's request, who that enemy is, and how he came to be so, beginning from his first revolt in Heaven, and the occasion thereof; how he drew his legions after him to the parts of the North, and there incited them to rebel with him, persuading all but only Abdiel, a seraph, who in argument dissuades and opposes him, then forsakes him.

Now Morn, her rosy steps in the eastern clime
Advancing, sowed the earth with orient pearl,°
When Adam waked, so customed, for his sleep
Was aery light, from pure digestion bred,
And temperate vapours bland, which° the only° sound   5
Of leaves and fuming° rills, Aurora's fan,

1–2 Compare the embellishment of another poet: "But look, the morn in russet mantle clad,/ Walks o'er the dew of yon high eastern hill." *Hamlet,* I, i, 166–67. Cf. "Lycidas," 187.   2 **orient pearl** dewdrops; cf. iv, 238   5 **which** i.e., sleep **only** sole   6 **fuming** referring to the early-morning mist or steam, as *Aurora's fan* is the leaves in the breeze

Lightly dispersed, and the shrill matin song
Of birds on every bough. So much the more
His wonder was to find unwakened Eve,
10   With tresses discomposed, and glowing cheek,°
As through unquiet rest. He, on his side
Leaning half raised, with looks of cordial° love
Hung over her enamoured, and beheld
Beauty which, whether waking or asleep,
15   Shot forth peculiar° graces; then, with voice
Mild as when Zephyrus on Flora breathes,
Her hand soft touching, whispered thus: 'Awake,°
My fairest, my espoused, my latest found,
Heaven's last, best gift, my ever-new delight,
20   Awake, the morning shines, and the fresh field
Calls us; we lose the prime, to mark how spring
Our tended plants, how blows° the citron grove,
What drops the myrrh, and what the balmy reed,
How Nature paints her colours, how the bee
25   Sits on the bloom extracting liquid sweet.'
      Such whispering waked her, but with startled eye
On Adam, whom embracing, thus she spake:
'O sole in whom my thoughts find all repose,
My glory, my perfection, glad I see
30   Thy face, and morn returned; for I this night
(Such night till this I never passed) have dreamed,
If dreamed, not, as I oft am wont, of thee,
Works of day past, or morrow's next design,
But of offence and trouble, which my mind
35   Knew never till this irksome night. Methought
Close at mine ear one called me forth to walk
With gentle voice; I thought it thine: it said,
"Why sleep'st thou,° Eve? now is the pleasant time,
The cool, the silent, save where silence yields

10 **glowing cheek** a bad sign; cf. 384–85; ix, 887   12 **cordial** Milton
never forgets the derivation from *cor,* heart.   15 **peculiar** unique;
cf. the theological use of the phrase, iii, 183   17–25 An aubade
or morning serenade, with parallels in Milton's earlier Latin, in
Herrick's "Corinna's Going A-Maying" ("Get up, get up, for
shame, the blooming morn . . ."), in the Song of Songs (ii, 10),
"My beloved spake, and said unto me, Rise up, my love, my fair
one, and come away."   22 **blows** blooms   38 **Why sleep'st thou**
cf. 673

To the night-warbling bird, that now awake°   40
Tunes sweetest his love-laboured song; now reigns
Full-orbed the moon, and, with more pleasing light,
Shadowy sets off the face of things—in vain,
If none regard; Heaven wakes with all his eyes;
Whom to behold but thee, Nature's desire,°   45
In whose sight all things joy, with ravishment
Attracted by thy beauty still to gaze?"
I rose as at thy call, but found thee not:
To find thee I directed then my walk,
And on, methought, alone I passed through ways   50
That brought me on a sudden to the tree
Of interdicted Knowledge. Fair it seemed,
Much fairer to my fancy than by day,
And, as I wondering looked, beside it stood
One shaped and winged like one of those from Heaven   55
By us oft seen: his dewy locks distilled
Ambrosia. On that tree he also gazed,
And, "O fair plant," said he, "with fruit surcharged,
Deigns none to ease thy load, and taste thy sweet,
Nor God, nor Man? Is knowledge so despised?°   60
Or envy, or what reserve forbids to taste?
Forbid who will, none shall from me withhold
Longer thy offered good, why else set here?"
This said, he paused not, but with venturous arm
He plucked, he tasted. Me damp horror chilled   65
At such bold words° vouched° with a deed so bold;
But he° thus, overjoyed: "O fruit divine,
Sweet of thyself, but much more sweet thus cropped,
Forbidden here, it seems, as only fit
For gods, yet able to make gods of men!   70
And why not gods of men, since good, the more
Communicated, more abundant grows,
The author not impaired, but honoured more?
Here, happy creature, fair angelic Eve,
Partake thou also: happy though thou art,   75

40 cf. Sonnet 1: "O Nightingale that on yon bloomy spray/
Warbl'st at eve . . ." 45 **Nature's desire** nature's object of
desire. As Book IX tragically shows, it will be the flatterer
versus the true lover. 60 ff. Looking back to iv, 515 ff. and
ahead to ix, 727 ff. 66 **bold words** cf. i, 82 **vouched**
reinforced 67 **he** supply *spoke*

Happier thou may'st be, worthier canst not be.
Taste this, and be henceforth among the gods
Thyself a goddess; not to Earth confined,
But sometimes in the Air, as we; sometimes
80 Ascend to Heaven, by merit thine, and see
What life the gods live there, and such live thou."
So saying, he drew nigh, and to me held,
Even to my mouth, of that same fruit held part
Which he had plucked: the pleasant savoury smell
85 So quickened appetite that I, methought,
Could not but taste. Forthwith up to the clouds
With him I flew, and underneath beheld
The Earth outstretched immense, a prospect wide
And various; wondering° at my flight and change
90 To this high exaltation, suddenly
My guide was gone, and I, methought, sunk down,
And fell asleep, but oh, how glad I waked
To find this but a dream!' Thus Eve her night
Related, and thus Adam answered sad:°
95   'Best image of myself, and dearer half,
The trouble of thy thoughts this night in sleep
Affects me equally; nor can I like
This uncouth dream, of evil sprung, I fear;
Yet evil whence? in thee can harbour none,
100 Created pure. But know that in the soul
Are many lesser faculties, that serve
Reason as chief. Among these Fancy next
Her office holds; of all external things,
Which the five watchful senses represent,
105 She forms imaginations, aery shapes,
Which Reason, joining or disjoining, frames
All what we affirm or what deny, and call
Our knowledge or opinion; then retires
Into her private cell when Nature rests.
110 Oft, in her absence, mimic Fancy wakes
To imitate her, but, misjoining shapes,
Wild work produces oft, and most in dreams,
Ill matching words and deeds long past or late.
Some such resemblances, methinks, I find

89 **wondering** a somewhat dangling participle going with I,
91   94 **sad** in all seriousness

Of our last evening's talk° in this thy dream,   *115*
But with addition strange. Yet be not sad:
Evil into the mind of God° or Man
May come and go, so unapproved, and leave
No spot or blame behind; which gives me hope
That what in sleep thou didst abhor to dream   *120*
Waking thou never wilt consent to do.
Be not disheartened, then, nor cloud those looks,
That wont to be more cheerful and serene
Than when fair Morning first smiles on the world;
And let us to our fresh employments rise   *125*
Among the groves, the fountains, and the flowers,
That open now their choicest blossomed smells
Reserved from night, and kept for thee in store.'
    So cheered he his fair spouse,° and she was cheered,
But silently a gentle tear let fall   *130*
From either eye, and wiped them with her hair;
Two other precious drops that ready stood,
Each in their crystal sluice, he, ere they fell,
Kissed as the gracious signs of sweet remorse
And pious awe, that feared to have offended.   *135*
    So all was cleared, and to the field they haste.
But first, from under shady arborous roof
Soon as they forth were come to open sight
Of day-spring,° and the Sun, who, scarce uprisen,
With wheels yet hovering o'er the ocean brim,   *140*
Shot parallel to the Earth his dewy ray,
Discovering in wide landscape all the east
Of Paradise and Eden's happy plains,
Lowly they bowed, adoring, and began
Their orisons, each morning duly paid   *145*
In various style; for neither various style
Nor holy rapture wanted they to praise
Their Maker, in fit strains pronounced, or sung
Unmeditated;° such prompt eloquence
Flowed from their lips, in prose or numerous verse,   *150*

115 **our last evening's talk** cf. iv, 420 ff 117 **God** may mean
angel, as in other places (see note to iii, 341), and if it does
not the statement is not so unorthodox as Saurat in his *Milton:
Man and Thinker* thought. See Titus, i, 15. 129 **his fair spouse**
as in iv, 742 139 **day-spring** the dawning 149 **Unmeditated**
cf. iv, 736–37 and note

More tuneable than needed lute or harp
To add more sweetness: and they thus began:
  'These are thy glorious works, Parent of good,°
Almighty, thine this universal frame,
155 Thus wondrous fair; thyself how wondrous then!
Unspeakable, who sitt'st above these heavens
To us invisible, or dimly seen
In these thy lowest works, yet these declare
Thy goodness beyond thought, and power divine.
160 Speak, ye who best can tell, ye sons of Light,
Angels, for ye behold him, and with songs
And choral symphonies, day without night,°
Circle his throne rejoicing, ye in Heaven,
On Earth join, all ye creatures, to extol
165 Him first, him last, him midst, and without end.°
Fairest of Stars,° last in the train of Night,
If better thou belong not to the Dawn,
Sure pledge of day, that crown'st the smiling morn
With thy bright circlet, praise him in thy sphere
170 While day arises, that sweet hour of prime.
Thou Sun, of this great World both eye and soul,°
Acknowledge him thy greater; sound his praise
In thy eternal course, both when thou climb'st
And when high noon has gained, and when thou fall'st.
175 Moon, that now meet'st the orient Sun, now fliest,
With the fixed Stars, fixed in their orb that flies;
And ye five other wandering Fires, that move
In mystic dance, not without song,° resound
His praise who out of Darkness called up Light.
180 Air, and ye Elements, the eldest birth
Of Nature's womb, that in quaternion° run

153–205 This Benedicite is to be compared with Psalm
cxlviii. 162 **day without night** "for there shall be no night
there" (Rev. xxi, 25) 165 "I am Alpha and Omega, the
beginning and the end, and the first and the last" (Rev. xxii,
13). 166 **Fairest of Stars** Venus (the superlative is from *Iliad*
XXII, 318), both Morning Star (Phosphorus, Lucifer) and
Evening Star (Hesperus, Vesper) 171 **of this great World
both eye and soul** The former designation is from Ovid, the
latter from Pliny. 178 **song** the music of the spheres, audible
to Man only before the fall. 181 **quaternion** combination of
the four elements

Perpetual circle, multiform, and mix
And nourish all things, let your ceaseless change
Vary to our great Maker still new praise.
Ye Mists and Exhalations, that now rise   185
From hill or steaming lake, dusky or grey,
Till the sun paint your fleecy skirts with gold,
In honour to the World's great Author rise,
Whether to deck with clouds the uncoloured° sky,
Or wet the thirsty earth with falling showers,   190
Rising or falling, still advance his praise.
His praise, ye Winds, that from four quarters blow,
Breathe soft or loud, and wave your tops, ye Pines,
With every Plant, in sign of worship wave.
Fountains, and ye that warble as ye flow°   195
Melodious murmurs, warbling tune his praise.
Join voices, all ye living Souls; ye Birds,
That, singing, up to Heaven-gate ascend,°
Bear on your wings and in your notes his praise.
Ye that in waters glide, and ye that walk   200
The earth, and stately tread, or lowly creep,
Witness if I be silent, morn or even,
To hill or valley, fountain, or fresh shade,
Made vocal by my song, and taught his praise.
Hail, universal Lord, be bounteous still   205
To give us only good, and, if the night
Have gathered aught of evil, or concealed,
Disperse it, as now light dispels the dark.'
     So prayed they innocent, and to their thoughts
Firm peace recovered soon, and wonted calm.   210
On to their morning's rural work they haste,
Among sweet dews and flowers,° where any row
Of fruit-trees, overwoody, reached too far
Their pampered boughs, and needed hands to check
Fruitless embraces: or they led the vine   215
To wed her elm; she, spoused, about him twines
Her marriageable arms, and with her brings

189 **uncoloured** unvariegated, having only one color   195 **that
warble as ye flow** cf. iii, 31   198 Reminiscent of Shakespeare's
"Hark, hark! the lark at heaven's gate sings" (*Cymbeline,* II, iii, 21)
and "Like to the lark at break of day arising/ From sullen earth,
sings hymns at heaven's gate" (Sonnet 29).   212 **Among ... dews
and flowers** cf. i, 771

Her dower, the adopted clusters, to adorn
His barren leaves. Them thus employed beheld
220 With pity Heaven's high King, and to him called
Raphael,° the sociable Spirit, that deigned
To travel with Tobias, and secured
His marriage with seven-times-wedded maid.°
  'Raphael,' said he, 'thou hear'st what stir on Earth
225 Satan, from Hell 'scaped through the darksome gulf,
Hath raised in Paradise, and how disturbed
This night the human pair; how he designs
In them at once to ruin all mankind.
Go, therefore; half this day, as friend with friend°
230 Converse with Adam, in what bower or shade
Thou find'st him from the heat of noon retired
To respite his day-labour with repast
Or with repose; and such discourse bring on
As may advise him of his happy state—
235 Happiness in his power left free to will,
Left to his own free will, his will though free
Yet mutable. Whence warn him to beware
He swerve not, too secure; tell him withal
His danger, and from whom, what enemy,
240 Late fallen himself from Heaven, is plotting now
The fall of others from like state of bliss.
By violence? no, for that shall be withstood;
But by deceit and lies. This let him know,
Lest, wilfully transgressing, he pretend
245 Surprisal, unadmonished, unforewarned.'
  So spake the Eternal Father, and fulfilled
All justice. Nor delayed the wingèd Saint
After his charge received, but from among
Thousand celestial Ardours° where he stood
250 Veiled with his gorgeous wings upspringing light
Flew through the midst of Heaven. The angelic choirs,
On each hand parting, to his speed gave way
Through all the empyreal road, till, at the gate
Of Heaven arrived, the gate self-opened wide,

221 **Raphael** "Divine healer"   222–23 see iv, 168 ff.   229 "And
the Lord spake unto Moses face to face, as a man speaketh
unto his friend" (Ex. xxxiii, 11).   249 **Ardours** a translation of
Hebrew *Seraphim*, which is from a verb meaning *to burn*

On golden hinges turning, as by work 255
Divine the sovran Architect had framed.
   From hence no cloud, or, to obstruct his sight,
Star interposed, however small, he sees,
Not unconform to other shining globes,
Earth, and the Garden of God, with cedars crowned 260
Above all hills. As when by night the glass
Of Galileo, less assured, observes
Imagined lands and regions in the Moon,
Or pilot from amidst the Cyclades
Delos or Samos first appearing kens, 265
A cloudy spot. Down thither prone in flight
He speeds, and through the vast ethereal sky°
Sails between worlds and worlds, with steady wing
Now on the polar winds; then with quick fan
Winnows the buxom air,° till, within soar 270
Of towering eagles, to all the fowls he seems
A phoenix,° gazed by all, as that sole bird,
When, to enshrine his relics in the Sun's
Bright temple, to Egyptian Thebes he flies.
At once on the eastern cliff of Paradise 275
He lights and to his proper shape° returns,
A Seraph winged. Six wings° he wore, to shade
His lineaments° divine: the pair that clad
Each shoulder broad came mantling° o'er his breast
With regal ornament; the middle pair 280
Girt like a starry zone his waist, and round
Skirted his loins and thighs with downy gold
And colours dipped in Heaven; the third his feet
Shadowed from either heel with feathered mail,
Sky-tinctured grain. Like Maia's son° he stood, 285
And shook his plumes, that heavenly fragrance filled
The circuit wide. Straight knew him all the bands
Of Angels under watch, and to his state°
And to his message high in honour rise,

267 **the . . . ethereal sky** cf. i, 45   270 **the buxom air** as at ii,
842 272 **phoenix** the "self-begotten bird" of *Samson
Agonistes,* 1699 276 **his proper shape** cf. iii, 634 277 **Six
wings** as in Isaiah, vi, 2 278 **lineaments** body's lines, as at vii,
477 279 **mantling** using the wings like a mantle, by raising
them so that they meet (compare the swan at vii, 439) 285
Maia's son Hermes or Mercury 288 **state** stateliness

290 For on some message high they guessed him bound.
      Their glittering tents he passed, and now is come
      Into the blissful field, through groves of myrrh,
      And flowering odours, cassia, nard, and balm,
      A wilderness of sweets, for Nature here
295 Wantoned as in her prime, and played at will
      Her virgin fancies, pouring forth more sweet,
      Wild above rule or art,° enormous bliss.
      Him, through the spicy forest onward come,
      Adam discerned, as in the door he sat°
300 Of his cool bower, while now the mounted Sun
      Shot down direct his fervid rays, to warm
      Earth's inmost womb, more warmth than Adam needs;°
      And Eve, within, due° at her hour, prepared
      For dinner savoury fruits, of taste to please
305 True appetite, and not disrelish thirst
      Of nectarous draughts between, from milky stream,
      Berry or grape: to whom thus Adam called:
        'Haste hither, Eve, and, worth thy sight, behold
      Eastward among those trees what glorious Shape
310 Comes this way moving; seems another morn
      Risen on mid-noon. Some great behest from Heaven
      To us perhaps he brings, and will vouchsafe
      This day to be our guest. But go with speed,
      And what thy stores contain bring forth, and pour
315 Abundance, fit to honour and receive
      Our heavenly stranger; well we may afford
      Our givers their own gifts, and large bestow
      From large bestowed, where Nature multiplies
      Her fertile growth, and by disburdening grows
320 More fruitful; which instructs us not to spare.'
        To whom thus Eve: 'Adam,° Earth's hallowed mould,
      Of God inspired, small store will serve where store,
      All seasons, ripe for use hangs on the stalk;
      Save what, by frugal storing, firmness gains
325 To nourish, and superfluous moist consumes.

297 1667 has a semicolon instead of a comma, making *pouring*
(296) intransitive and *enormous bliss* appositional.   299 "And
the Lord appeared unto him [Abraham] in the plains of
Mamre: and he sat in the tent door in the heat of the day"
(Gen. xviii, 1).   301–302 cf. iii, 583–86   303 **due** an adverb
321 **Adam** means *earth*

But I will haste, and from each bough and brake,
Each plant and juiciest gourd, will pluck such choice
To entertain our Angel-guest as he,
Beholding, shall confess that here on Earth
God hath dispensed his bounties as in Heaven.'   330
   So saying, with dispatchful looks in haste
She turns, on hospitable thoughts intent
What choice to choose for delicacy best,°
What order so contrived as not to mix
Tastes, not well joined, inelegant, but bring   335
Taste after taste upheld with kindliest change.
Bestirs her then, and from each tender stalk
Whatever Earth, all-bearing mother, yields
In India East or West, or middle shore°
In Pontus or the Punic coast, or where   340
Alcinous° reigned, fruit of all kinds, in coat
Rough or smooth rind,° or bearded husk, or shell,
She gathers, tribute large, and on the board
Heaps with unsparing hand. For drink the grape
She crushes, inoffensive must,° and meaths°   345
From many a berry, and from sweet kernels pressed
She tempers dulcet creams, nor these to hold
Wants her fit vessels pure; then strews the ground
With rose and odours from the shrub unfumed.°
   Meanwhile our primitive great Sire, to meet   350
His godlike guest walks forth, without more train
Accompanied than with his own complete

---

333 ff. This was not an indifferent subject to the poet, as is
further illustrated by his remark to his third wife: "God have
mercy, Betty, I see thou wilt perform according to thy promise
in providing me such dishes as I think fit whilst I live; and,
when I die, thou knowest that I have left thee all"; cf. ix,
232–33.   339 **middle shore** an etymological reference to the
lands bordering the Mediterranean, as *Pontus* (340) is the
Black Sea (*Pontus Euxinus*) or its southern shore, and *Punic
coast* is probably guided by the thought of African figs   341
Alcinous the happy ruler of the Phaeacians, who entertained
Odysseus. Homer describes his gardens about the palace as
paradisial.   342 **rind** in the earliest editions a participle,
rin'd   345 **inoffensive must** unintoxicating grape juice **meaths**
a honey drink   349 **unfumed** unburned (not in the form of
incense but from the fresh plant)

Perfections; in himself was all his state,
More solemn than the tedious pomp that waits
355　On princes, when their rich retinue long
Of horses led and grooms besmeared with gold
Dazzles the crowd and sets them all agape.
Nearer his presence, Adam, though not awed,
Yet with submiss approach and reverence meek,
360　As to a superior nature, bowing low,°
Thus said: 'Native of Heaven, for other place
None can than Heaven such glorious shape° contain,
Since, by descending from the thrones above,
Those happy places thou hast deigned a while
365　To want,° and honour these, vouchsafe with us,
Two only, who° yet by sovran gift possess
This spacious ground, in yonder shady bower
To rest, and what the garden choicest bears
To sit and taste, till this meridian° heat
370　Be over, and the sun more cool decline.'
　　　Whom thus the angelic Virtue answered mild:
'Adam, I therefore came; nor art thou such
Created, or such place hast here to dwell,
As may not oft invite, though Spirits of Heaven,
375　To visit thee. Lead on, then, where thy bower
O'ershades, for these mid-hours, till evening rise,
I have at will.' So to the sylvan lodge
They came, that like Pomona's° arbour smiled
With flowerets decked and fragrant smells. But Eve,
380　Undecked, save with herself, more lovely fair
Than wood-nymph, or the fairest goddess° feigned
Of three that in Mount Ida naked strove,
Stood to entertain her guest from Heaven; no veil
She needed, virtue-proof; no thought infirm
385　Altered her cheek. On whom the Angel 'Hail!'

360 **bowing low** cf. iii, 736 (also i, 434)　362 **glorious shape** cf.
309　365 **To want** to be without　366 **only, who** by elision
the three syllables become two, as *No ingrateful food* (407)
is *N'ingrateful food*　369 **meridian** noonday　378 **Pomona** the
Roman goddess of flowers and fruits　381–82 Aphrodite won
from Paris the award "to the fairest" over Hera and Pallas
Athene in the celebrated beauty contest held before the
shepherd in Mysia, Asia Minor. That was strife over a
mischievous apple too and led directly to the Trojan War.

Bestowed, the holy salutation used
Long after to blest Mary, second Eve:
   'Hail! Mother of mankind, whose fruitful womb°
Shall fill the world more numerous with thy sons
Than with these various fruits the trees of God   390
Have heaped this table!' Raised of grassy turf
Their table was, and mossy seats had round,
And on her° ample square, from side to side,
All Autumn piled, though Spring and Autumn here
Danced hand in hand. A while discourse they hold, 395
No fear lest dinner cool;° when thus began
Our Author: 'Heavenly stranger,° please to taste
These bounties, which our Nourisher, from whom
All perfect good, unmeasured out, descends,°
To us for food and for delight hath caused   400
The Earth to yield: unsavoury food, perhaps,
To spiritual natures; only this I know,
That one Celestial Father gives to all.'
   To whom the Angel: 'Therefore, what he gives
(Whose praise be ever sung) to Man, in part   405
Spiritual, may of purest Spirits be found
No ingrateful food—and food alike those pure°
Intelligential substances require
As doth your rational, and both contain
Within them every lower faculty   410
Of sense, whereby they hear, see, smell, touch, taste,

388 ff. The garden is overabundant in preparation for this
posterity. 393 **her** its 396 **No fear lest dinner cool** "A
terrible bathos after the beautiful imagery, but shows Milton's
simplicity" (Tennyson)—and illuminates the question of his
sense of humor. 397 **Heavenly stranger** as at 316 399 "Every
good gift and every perfect gift is from above, and cometh
down from the Father of lights" (James, i, 17). 407 ff.
Regardless of how uncomfortable the angelic digestion (and
further on the angelic bodily love and armored war) makes
the modern reader, Milton is metaphysically a materialist—he
believes in the goodness and unity of matter ("one first matter
all," 472), and he insists on a solid presentment of beings that
look as if they differ from unfallen man in degree rather than
in kind (490). There is "angels' food" in Psalm lxxviii, 25 and
in this book of *Paradise Lost,* 633. Spirit and matter are
connected, 469 ff. This view fits well with the poet's necessity
of making the abstract concrete (571 ff.)

Tasting concoct,° digest,° assimilate,
And corporeal to incorporeal turn.
For know, whatever was created needs
415 To be sustained and fed. Of elements
The grosser feeds the purer: Earth the Sea;
Earth and the Sea feed Air; the Air those Fires
Ethereal, and, as lowest, first the Moon,
Whence in her visage round those spots, unpurged
420 Vapours not yet into her substance turned.
Nor doth the Moon no nourishment exhale
From her moist continent to higher orbs.
The Sun, that light imparts to all, receives
From all his alimental recompense
425 In humid exhalations, and at even
Sups with the Ocean; though in Heaven the trees
Of life ambrosial fruitage bear, and vines
Yield nectar, though from off the boughs each morn
We brush mellifluous dews, and find the ground
430 Covered with pearly grain, yet God hath here
Varied his bounty so with new delights°
As may compare with Heaven; and to taste
Think not I shall be nice.' So down they sat,
And to their viands fell; nor seemingly
435 The Angel, nor in mist (the common gloss
Of theologians) but with keen dispatch
Of real hunger and concoctive heat
To transubstantiate: what redounds transpires
Through Spirits with ease, nor wonder, if by fire
440 Of sooty coal the empiric alchemist°
Can turn, or holds it possible to turn,
Metals of drossiest ore to perfect gold,
As from the mine. Meanwhile at table Eve
Ministered naked, and their flowing cups
445 With pleasant liquors crowned: O innocence
Deserving Paradise! If ever, then,
Then had the Sons of God excuse to have been
Enamoured at that sight. But in those hearts
Love unlibidinous reigned, nor jealousy°
450 Was understood, the injured lover's hell.

412 **concoct, digest** synonyms   431 **new delights** cf. 19   440 ff.
cf. iii, 600 ff   449 **nor jealousy** It comes with ix, 827–30.

Thus when with meats and drinks they had sufficed,
Not burdened, nature, sudden mind arose
In Adam not to let the occasion pass,
Given him by this great conference, to know
Of things above his world, and of their being   455
Who dwell in Heaven, whose excellence he saw
Transcend his own so far, whose radiant forms,
Divine effulgence, whose high power so far
Exceeded human, and his wary speech
Thus to the empyreal minister he framed: 460
'Inhabitant with God, now know I well
Thy favour in this honour done to Man,
Under whose lowly roof thou hast vouchsafed
To enter, and these earthly fruits to taste,
Food not of Angels, yet accepted so   465
As that more willingly thou couldst not seem
At Heaven's high feasts to have fed, yet what compare!'
To whom the wingèd Hierarch replied:
'O Adam, one Almighty is, from whom
All things proceed, and up to him return,   470
If not depraved from good, created all
Such to perfection; one first matter all,
Endued with various forms,° various degrees
Of substance, and, in things that live, of life,
But more refined, more spirituous and pure,   475
As nearer to him placed or nearer tending
Each in their several active spheres assigned,
Till body up to spirit work, in bounds
Proportioned to each kind. So from the root
Springs lighter the green stalk, from thence the leaves   480
More aery, last the bright consummate flower
Spirits odorous breathes: flowers and their fruit,
Man's nourishment, by gradual scale sublimed,
To vital spirits aspire, to animal,
To intellectual, give both life and sense,   485
Fancy and understanding, whence the Soul
Reason receives, and Reason is her being,
Discursive, or intuitive: discourse
Is oftest yours, the latter most is ours,
Differing but in degree, of kind the same.   490

473 **various forms** cf. iii, 717

Wonder not, then, what God for you saw good
If I refuse not, but convert, as you,
To proper° substance. Time may come when Men
With Angels may participate, and find
495 No inconvenient diet, nor too light fare,
And from these corporal nutriments, perhaps,
Your bodies may at last turn all to spirit,
Improved by tract of time, and winged ascend
Ethereal, as we, or may at choice
500 Here or in heavenly paradises dwell,
If ye be found obedient, and retain
Unalterably firm his love entire
Whose progeny you are.° Meanwhile enjoy
Your fill° what happiness this happy state
505 Can comprehend, incapable of more.'
      To whom the Patriarch of Mankind replied:
'O favourable Spirit, propitious guest,
Well hast thou taught the way that might direct
Our knowledge, and the scale of Nature set
510 From centre to circumference, whereon,
In contemplation of created things,
By steps we may ascend to God. But say,
What meant that caution joined, *If ye be found
Obedient?* Can we want obedience, then,
515 To him, or possibly his love desert,
Who formed us from the dust, and placed us here
Full to the utmost measure of what bliss
Human desires can seek or apprehend?'
      To whom the Angel: 'Son of Heaven and Earth,
520 Attend: That thou art happy, owe to God;
That thou continuest such, owe to thyself,
That is, to thy obedience; therein stand.
This was that caution given thee; be advised.
God made thee perfect, not immutable,
525 And good he made thee, but to persevere
He left it in thy power, ordained thy will
By nature free, not overruled by fate
Inextricable, or strict necessity.

493 **proper** (my) own (Latin *proprius*)   503 **Whose progeny
you are** This derives from St. Paul, quoting Aratus (Acts, xvii,
28).   503–04 **enjoy . . . fill** cf. iv, 507

Our voluntary service he requires,
Not our necessitated. Such with him   530
Finds no acceptance, nor can find; for how
Can hearts not free be tried whether they serve
Willing or no, who will but what they must
By destiny, and can no other choose?
Myself, and all the Angelic Host, that stand   535
In sight of God enthroned, our happy state
Hold, as you yours, while our obedience holds;
On other surety none: freely we serve
Because we freely love, as in our will
To love or not; in this we stand or fall: 540
And some are fallen, to disobedience fallen,
And so from Heaven to deepest Hell.° O fall
From what high state of bliss° into what woe!'
    To whom our great Progenitor: 'Thy words
Attentive and with more delighted ear,   545
Divine instructor, I have heard, than when
Cherubic songs by night from neighbouring hills
Aerial music send. Nor knew I not
To be, both will and deed, created free.
Yet that we never shall forget to love   550
Our Maker, and obey him whose command
Single is yet so just, my constant thoughts
Assured me, and still assure; though what thou tell'st
Hath passed in Heaven, some doubt within me move,
But more desire to hear, if thou consent,   555
The full relation, which must needs be strange,
Worthy of sacred silence° to be heard.
And we have yet large day, for scarce the Sun
Hath finished half his journey, and scarce begins
His other half in the great zone of Heaven.'   560
    Thus Adam made request; and Raphael,
After short pause assenting, thus began:
    'High matter thou enjoin'st me, O prime of Men,
Sad task and hard, for how shall I relate
To human sense the invisible exploits   565
Of warring Spirits? how, without remorse,

542 **to deepest Hell** as at iii, 678   543 **state of bliss** cf. 241   557
Worthy of sacred silence Horace's *sacro digna silentio* (*Carm.*
II, xiii, 29).

The ruin of so many, glorious once
And perfect while they stood? how, last, unfold
The secrets of another world, perhaps
570 Not lawful to reveal? Yet for thy good
This is dispensed, and what surmounts the reach
Of human sense I shall delineate so,
By likening spiritual to corpóral forms,
As may express them best—though what if Earth
575 Be but the shadow of Heaven, and things therein
Each to other like, more than on Earth is thought?
 'As yet this World was not, and Chaos wild
Reigned where these Heavens now roll, where Earth
  now rests
Upon her centre poised, when on a day
580 (For Time, though in Eternity, applied
To motion, measures all things durable
By present, past, and future), on such day
As Heaven's great year brings forth, the empyreal host
Of Angels, by imperial summons called,
585 Innumerable before the Almighty's throne
Forthwith from all the ends of Heaven appeared
Under their hierarchs in orders bright.°
Ten thousand thousand ensigns high advanced,°
Standards and gonfalons,° 'twixt van and rear,
590 Stream in the air, and for distinction serve
Of hierarchies, of orders, and degrees,
Or in their glittering tissues bear emblazed
Holy memorials, acts of zeal and love
Recorded eminent. Thus when in orbs
595 Of circuit inexpressible they stood,
Orb within orb, the Father Infinite,
By whom in bliss embosomed sat the Son,
Amidst as from a flaming mount, whose top
Brightness had made invisible, thus spake:°
600 ' "Hear, all ye Angels, Progeny of Light,°
Thrones, Dominations, Princedoms, Virtues, Powers,°

587 **orders bright** cf. i, 737   588 **high advanced** cf. iv, 90, 359
589 **gonfalons** banners usually of two or three streamers   599
cf. iii, 380   600 **Light** God (iii, 3)   601 This grand nominative
of address, employed twice more in the fifth book, 772, 840,
and again in the tenth, 460, refers to different ranks in the
celestial hierarchy.

Hear my decree, which unrevoked shall stand.
This day I have begot° whom I declare
My only Son, and on this holy hill
Him have anointed,° whom ye now behold   605
At my right hand. Your head I him appoint,
And by myself have sworn to him shall bow
All knees in Heaven, and shall confess him Lord:
Under his great vicegerent reign abide,
United as one individual soul,   610
Forever happy; him who disobeys,
Me disobeys, breaks union, and, that day,
Cast out from God and blesséd vision, falls
Into utter darkness,° deep engulfed, his place
Ordained without redemption, without end."°   615
  'So spake the Omnipotent, and with his words
All seemed well pleased; all seemed, but were not all.
That day, as other solemn days, they spent
In song and dance about the sacred hill—
Mystical dance,° which yonder starry sphere   620
Of planets and of fixed in all her wheels
Resembles nearest; mazes intricate,
Eccentric, intervolved, yet regular
Then most when most irregular they seem,
And in their motions harmony divine   625
So smooths her charming tones that God's own ear
Listens delighted. Evening now approached
(For we have also our evening and our morn,
We ours for change delectable, not need),
Forthwith from dance to sweet repast they turn 630
Desirous; all in circles as they stood,
Tables are set, and on a sudden piled

603 **begot** used metaphorically to denote not the production or
creation of the Son, but his exaltation, as explained in *Christian
Doctrine* (I, 5): "it will be apparent from the second Psalm
that God has begotten the Son, that is, has made him a king."
Cf. 663, and for the prior existence of the son, 835 ff.; iii,
390–91. 605 **anointed** which is what *Messiah* means
(664) 614 **utter darkness** prophetic and a pun, since *utter*,
besides meaning *outer* (as in the same phrase at i, 72), also
has its modern coloration 615 **without end** a standard phrase,
both for damnation and for salvation (i, 67; ii, 870; iii, 142; v,
165; vi, 137; vii, 161, 542; x, 797) 620 **Mystical dance** cf. 178

With Angels' food, and rubied nectar flows:
In pearl, in diamond, and massy gold,
635 Fruit of delicious vines, the growth of Heaven.
On flowers reposed, and with fresh flowerets crowned,°
They eat, they drink, and in communion sweet°
Quaff immortality and joy, secure
Of surfeit where full measure only bounds
640 Excess, before the all-bounteous King, who showered
With copious hand, rejoicing in their joy.
Now when ambrosial Night,° with clouds exhaled
From that high mount of God whence light and shade
Spring both, the face of brightest Heaven had changed
645 To grateful twilight (for Night comes not there
In darker veil), and roseate dews disposed
All but the unsleeping eyes of God to rest,
Wide over all the plain, and wider far
Than all this globous Earth in plain outspread
650 (Such are the courts of God), the Angelic throng,
Dispersed in bands and files, their camp extend
By living streams among the trees of life—
Pavilions numberless and sudden reared,
Celestial tabernacles, where they slept,
655 Fanned with cool winds, save those who, in their course,
Melodious hymns about the sovran throne
Alternate all night long. But not so waked
Satan—so call him now; his former name
Is heard no more in Heaven: he, of the first,
660 If not the first Archangel, great in power,
In favour, and pre-eminence, yet fraught
With envy against the Son of God that day
Honoured by his great Father and proclaimed
Messiah, King Anointed, could not bear,
665 Through pride, that sight, and thought himself impaired.
Deep malice° thence conceiving and disdain,
Soon as midnight brought on the dusky hour
Friendliest to sleep and silence, he resolved

636 This line is not in the first edition.   637 ff. 1667 reads:
"They eat, they drink, and with reflection sweet/ Are filled,
before th'all bounteous King, who showered, etc."   642
ambrosial Night a Homeric expression (*Il*. II, 57)   666 **Deep
malice** cf. ii, 382; iv, 123

With all his legions to dislodge, and leave
Unworshipped, unobeyed, the Throne supreme,   670
Contemptuous, and, his next subordinate°
Awakening, thus to him in secret spake:
  ' "Sleep'st thou, companion dear? what sleep can close
Thy eyelids? and rememberest what decree
Of yesterday, so late hath passed the lips   675
Of Heaven's Almighty? Thou to me thy thoughts
Wast wont, I mine to thee was wont, to impart;
Both waking we were one; how then can now
Thy sleep dissent? New laws thou seest imposed;
New laws from him who reigns, new minds may raise   680
In us who serve, new counsels, to debate
What doubtful may ensue. More in this place
To utter is not safe. Assemble thou
Of all those myriads which we lead the chief;
Tell them that, by command, ere yet dim Night   685
Her shadowy cloud withdraws, I am to haste,
And all who under me their banners wave,
Homeward with flying march° where we possess
The quarters of the North, there to prepare
Fit entertainment to receive our King,°   690
The great Messiah, and his new commands,
Who speedily through all the hierarchies
Intends to pass triumphant, and give laws."
  'So spake the false° Archangel, and infused
Bad influence into the unwary breast   695
Of his associate; he° together calls,
Or several one by one, the regent Powers,
Under him regent; tells, as he was taught,
That, the Most High commanding, now ere Night
Now ere dim Night° had disencumbered Heaven,   700
The great hierarchal standard was to move,
Tells the suggested cause, and casts between
Ambiguous words and jealousies to sound
Or taint integrity. But all obeyed
The wonted signal and superior voice   705

---

671 **his next subordinate** presumably Beelzebub 688 **flying
march** cf. ii, 574 690 The devil's first sarcasm or "Ambiguous
words" (703) 694 **So spake the false** cf. iii, 681 696 **he** i.e.,
his associate. 700 **dim Night** cf. 685 and ii, 1036

Of their great Potentate, for great indeed
His name and high was his degree in Heaven:
His countenance, as the morning-star° that guides
The starry flock, allured them, and with lies
710 Drew after him the third part of Heaven's host.°
Meanwhile, the Eternal Eye, whose sight discerns
Abstrusest thoughts, from forth his holy mount,
And from within the golden lamps that burn
Nightly before him, saw without their light°
715 Rebellion rising, saw in whom, how spread
Among the Sons of Morn,° what multitudes
Were banded to oppose his high decree,°
And, smiling, to his only Son thus said:
    ' "Son, thou in whom my glory I behold
720 In full resplendence, Heir of all my might,
Nearly it now concerns us to be sure
Of our omnipotence,° and with what arms
We mean to hold what anciently we claim
Of deity or empire: such a foe
725 Is rising who intends to erect his throne
Equal to ours, throughout the spacious North,
Nor, so content, hath in his thought to try
In battle what our power is or our right.
Let us advise, and to this hazard draw
730 With speed what force is left, and all employ
In our defence, lest unawares we lose
This our high place, our sanctuary, our hill."
    'To whom the Son, with calm aspèct and clear
Light'ning divine, ineffable, serene,
735 Made answer: "Mighty Father, thou thy foes
Justly hast in derision, and secure°
Laugh'st at their vain designs° and tumults vain,
Matter to me of glory, whom their hate
Illústrates,° when they see all regal power
740 Given me to quell their pride, and in event
Know whether I be dextrous to subdue

708 **as the morning-star** i.e., Lucifer   710 ii, 692 is identical except
for the last word. 713–14 cf. Revelation, iv, 5   716 **Sons of
Morn** cf. Isaiah, xiv, 12   717 **high decree** cf. iii, 126; x,
953   721–22 God is amused; cf. 735–37 and Psalms ii, 4.   736
Psalms lix, 8   737 **vain designs** cf. iii, 467   739 **Illústrates**
makes illustrious

Thy rebels, or be found the worst in Heaven."
  'So spake the Son; but Satan with his Powers
Far was advanced on wingèd speed,° an host
Innumerable as the stars at night,   745
Or stars of morning, dewdrops which the sun
Impearls on every leaf and every flower.
Regions they passed, the mighty regencies
Of Seraphim and Potentates and Thrones
In their triple degrees, regions to which   750
All thy dominion, Adam, is no more
Than what this garden is to all the earth
And all the sea, from one entire globose°
Stretched into longitude; which having passed,
At length into the limits of the North   755
They came, and Satan to his royal seat
High on a hill, far-blazing, as a mount
Raised on a mount, with pyramids and towers
From diamond quarries hewn and rocks of gold,
The palace of great Lucifer (so call   760
That structure, in the dialect of men
Interpreted) which, not long after, he,
Affecting all equality with God,
In imitation° of that mount whereon
Messiah was declared in sight of Heaven,   765
The Mountain of the Congregation called;
For thither he assembled all his train,
Pretending so commanded to consult
About the great reception of their King
Thither to come, and with calumnious art   770
Of counterfeited truth thus held their ears:
  ' "Thrones, Dominations, Princedoms, Virtues, Powers,
If these magnific titles yet remain
Not merely titular, since by decree
Another now hath to himself engrossed   775
All power, and us eclipsed under the name
Of King Anointed;° for whom all this haste
Of midnight march, and hurried meeting here,

---

744 **wingèd speed** cf. i, 674; iv, 788; also ii, 700   753 **globose**
a noun, *sphere* 764 **In imitation** The poem continually
illustrates the old view that the devil is the ape of God (*simia
Dei*).   777 **King Anointed** cf. 664; 870; vi, 718; xii, 359

This only to consult, how we may best,
780 With what may be devised of honours new,
Receive him coming to receive from us
Knee-tribute yet unpaid, prostration vile,
Too much to one, but double how endured,
To one and to his image now proclaimed?
785 But what if better counsels might erect
Our minds, and teach us to cast off this yoke?
Will ye submit your necks and choose to bend
The supple knee? ye will not, if I trust°
To know ye right, or if ye know yourselves
790 Natives and Sons of Heaven° possessed before
By none, and, if not equal all, yet free,
Equally free; for orders and degrees°
Jar not with liberty, but well consist.
Who can in reason, then, or right, assume
795 Monarchy over such as live by right
His equals—if in power and splendour less,
In freedom equal? or can introduce
Law and edíct on us, who without law
Err not? much less for this to be our Lord,
800 And look for adoration, to the abuse
Of those imperial titles which assert
Our being ordained to govern, not to serve!"
  'Thus far his bold discourse without control
Had audience, when, among the Seraphim,
805 Abdiel,° than whom none with more zeal adored
The Deity, and divine commands obeyed,
Stood up, and in a flame of zeal severe
The current of his fury thus opposed:
  ' "O argument blasphémous, false, and proud!
810 Words which no ear ever to hear in Heaven
Expected, least of all from thee, ingrate,
In place thyself so high above thy peers.
Canst thou with impious obloquy condemn

787–88 Compare the similar expression, i, 111–12.   790 **Sons of Heaven** cf. i, 654   792 **orders and degrees** cf. 591   805 **Abdiel** "Servant of God" (vi, 29), in the Bible a human name only (1 Chron. v, 15). There is reason to suspect that Milton when he created Abdiel was thinking of himself and his own lonely and perilous defiance, "Among the faithless, faithful only he" (897), when his countrymen backslid; cf. with 876; vii, 27.

The just decree of God, pronounced and sworn,
That to his only Son, by right endued   *815*
With regal sceptre,° every soul in Heaven
Shall bend the knee, and in that honour due°
Confess him rightful King? Unjust, thou say'st,
Flatly unjust, to bind with laws the free,
And equal over equals to let reign,   *820*
One over all with unsucceeded power.
Shalt thou give law to God? shalt thou dispute
With him the points of liberty who made
Thee what thou art, and formed the Powers of Heaven
Such as he pleased, and circumscribed their being?   *825*
Yet, by experience taught, we know how good,
And of our good and of our dignity
How provident he is, how far from thought
To make us less, bent rather to exalt
Our happy state, under one head more near   *830*
United. But, to grant it thee unjust
That equal over equals monarch reign,°
Thyself, though great and glorious, dost thou count,
Or all angelic nature joined in one,
Equal to him, begotten Son, by whom,   *835*
As by his Word, the mighty Father made
All things, even thee, and all the Spirits of Heaven
By him created in their bright degrees,
Crowned them with glory, and to their glory named
Thrones, Dominations, Princedoms, Virtues, Powers,°   *840*
Essential Powers, nor by his reign obscured,
But more illustrious made, since he, the head,
One of our number thus reduced becomes,
His laws our laws, all honour to him done
Returns our own. Cease, then, this impious rage,   *845*
And tempt not these; but hasten to appease
The incensèd Father and the incensèd Son
While pardon may be found, in time besought."
  'So spake the fervent Angel, but his zeal
None seconded, as out of season judged,   *850*
Or singular and rash: whereat rejoiced
The Apostate, and, more haughty, thus replied:

816 **regal sceptre** cf. iii, 339, 340 817 **honour due** cf. iii,
738 832 cf. 820 840 cf. Col. i, 16

' "That we were formed, then, say'st thou? and the work°
Of secondary hands, by task transferred
855 From Father to his Son? Strange point and new!
Doctrine which we would know whence learnt; who saw
When this creation was? rememberest thou
Thy making, while the Maker gave thee being?°
We know no time when we were not as now,
860 Know none before us, self-begot, self-raised
By our own quickening power when fatal course
Had circled his full orb, the birth mature
Of this our native Heaven, Ethereal Sons.
Our puissance is our own; our own right hand
865 Shall teach us highest deeds, by proof to try°
Who is our equal: then thou shalt behold
Whether by supplication we intend
Address, and to begirt the Almighty Throne
Beseeching or besieging.° This report,
870 These tidings, carry to the anointed King,
And fly, ere evil intercept thy flight."
  'He said, and, as the sound of waters, deep,°
Hoarse murmur echoed to his words applause
Through the infinite host, nor less for that
875 The flaming Seraph, fearless, though alone,
Encompassed round with foes, thus answered bold:
  ' "O alienate from God, O Spirit accursed,
Forsaken of all good! I see thy fall
Determined, and thy hapless crew involved
880 In this perfidious fraud, contagion spread°
Both of thy crime and punishment; henceforth
No more be troubled how to quit the yoke
Of God's Messiah: those indulgent laws
Will not now be vouchsafed; other decrees

853 ff. Beatrice explained that the unfallen angels "were
modest to acknowledge themselves derived from that same
Excellence which made them swift to so great understanding."
Paradiso, xxix, 58–60.   857–58 A silly argument, since, as Adam
says, "for who himself beginning knew?" (viii, 251). Cf. Job,
xxxviii, 4. The Apostate is already weaker in his faculties (from
overweening pride), but his audience corresponds.   864–65
"Thy right hand shall teach thee terrible things" (Ps. xlv,
4).   869 **Beseeching or besieging** contemptuous wordplay   872
cf. Revelation, xix, 6   880 **contagion spread** cf. "Lycidas," 127

Against thee are gone forth without recall;   885
That golden sceptre which thou didst reject
Is now an iron rod to bruise and break°
Thy disobedience. Well thou didst advise,
Yet not for thy advice or threats I fly
These wicked tents devoted, lest the wrath   890
Impendent, raging into sudden flame,
Distinguish not, for soon expect to feel°
His thunder on thy head, devouring fire.
Then who created thee lamenting learn
When who can uncreate thee thou shalt know."   895
  'So spake the Seraph Abdiel, faithful found,
Among the faithless, faithful only he;
Among innumerable false unmoved,
Unshaken, unseduced, unterrified,
His loyalty he kept, his love, his zeal,   900
Nor number nor example with him wrought
To swerve from truth, or change his constant mind,
Though single. From amidst them forth he passed,
Long way through hostile scorn, which he sustained
Superior, nor of violence feared aught;   905
And with retorted° scorn his back he turned
On those proud towers, to swift destruction° doomed.'

886–87 cf. ii, 327–28 and "Lycidas," 111.   892 **expect to feel**
cf. iv, 972   906 **retorted** literally, *turned back*   907 **swift
destruction** a phrase from 2 Peter, ii, 1

BOOK VI

THE ARGUMENT

Raphael continues to relate how Michael and Gabriel were sent forth to battle against Satan and his angels. The first fight described: Satan and his Powers retire under night. He calls a council; invents devilish engines, which, in the second day's fight, put Michael and his Angels to some disorder, but they at length, pulling up mountains, overwhelmed both the force and machines of Satan. Yet, the tumult not so ending, God, on the third day, sends Messiah his Son, for whom he had reserved the glory of that victory. He, in the power of his Father, coming to the place, and causing all his legions to stand still on either side, with his chariot and thunder driving into the midst of his enemies, pursues them, unable to resist, towards the wall of Heaven, which opening, they leap down with horror and confusion into the place of punishment prepared for them in the Deep. Messiah returns with triumph to his Father.

'ALL night the dreadless Angel, unpursued,
Through Heaven's wide champaign° held his way, till
    Morn,
Waked by the circling Hours, with rosy hand°
Unbarred the gates of Light. There is a cave
5 Within the Mount of God, fast by his throne,
Where Light and Darkness in perpetual round
Lodge and dislodge by turns, which makes through
    Heaven
Grateful vicissitude, like day and night;
Light issues forth, and at the other door
10 Obsequious° Darkness enters, till her hour
To veil the heaven, though darkness there might well
Seem twilight here. And now went forth the Morn

2 **champaign** plains (cf. 15) 3 **with rosy hand** suggested by Homer's "rosy-fingered Dawn" 10 **Obsequious** obedient, as at 783

146

Such as in highest heaven, arrayed in gold
Empyreal; from before her vanished Night,
Shot through with orient beams,° when all the plain   15
Covered with thick embattled squadrons bright,
Chariots, and flaming arms, and fiery steeds,
Reflecting blaze on blaze, first met his view.
War he perceived, war in procinct,° and found
Already known what he for news had thought   20
To have reported. Gladly then he mixed
Among those friendly Powers, who him received
With joy and acclamations loud, that one,
That of so many myriads fallen, yet one
Returned not lost. On to the sacred hill°   25
They led him, high applauded, and present
Before the seat supreme; from whence a voice,
From midst a golden cloud, thus mild was heard:
   ' "Servant of God, well done! Well hast thou fought
The better fight, who single hast maintained°   30
Against revolted multitudes the cause
Of truth, in word mightier than they in arms,°
And for the testimony of truth hast borne
Universal reproach, far worse to bear
Than violence; for this was all thy care—   35
To stand approved in sight of God, though worlds
Judged thee perverse. The easier conquest now
Remains thee, aided by this host of friends,
Back on thy foes more glorious to return
Than scorned thou didst depart, and to subdue   40
By force who reason for their law refuse,
Right reason for their law, and for their King
Messiah, who by right of merit reigns.
Go, Michael, of celestial armies prince,
And thou, in military prowess next,   45
Gabriel; lead forth to battle these my sons
Invincible; lead forth my armèd Saints,
By thousands and by millions ranged for fight,

---

15 **orient beams** cf. iv, 644   19 **in procinct** in readiness   25 **the sacred hill** cf. v, 619   29–30 A combination of "Well done, thou good and faithful servant" (Matt. xxv, 21) and "I have fought a good fight" (2 Tim. iv, 7).   32 Interpretable as a boost for the mightier pen.

Equal in number to that godless crew
50   Rebellious.° Them with fire and hostile arms
Fearless assault, and, to the brow of Heaven
Pursuing, drive them out from God and bliss
Into their place of punishment, the gulf
Of Tartarus, which ready opens wide
55   His fiery chaos to receive their fall."
     'So spake the Sovran Voice, and clouds began
To darken all the hill, and smoke to roll
In dusky wreaths reluctant° flames, the sign
Of wrath awaked, nor with less dread the loud
60   Ethereal trumpet from on high 'gan blow.°
At which command the Powers Militant
That stood for Heaven, in mighty quadrate° joined
Of union irresistible, moved on
In silence their bright legions to° the sound
65   Of instrumental harmony, that breathed
Heroic ardour to adventurous deeds
Under their godlike leaders, in the cause
Of God and his Messiah. On they move,
Indissolubly firm; nor obvious° hill,
70   Nor straitening vale, nor wood, nor stream divides
Their perfect ranks, for high above the ground
Their march was, and the passive air upbore
Their nimble tread;° as when the total kind
Of birds, in orderly array on wing,
75   Came summoned over Eden to receive
Their names of thee, so over many a tract
Of Heaven they marched, and many a province wide,
Tenfold the length of this terrene. At last,
Far in the horizon to the north, appeared
80   From skirt to skirt a fiery region, stretched
In battailous aspéct, and, nearer view,
Bristled with upright beams innumerable
Of rigid spears, and helmets thronged, and shields

49–50 **crew/Rebellious** cf. iv, 952   56–60 Such were the signs of
God on Sinai, Exodus, xix, 16, 18–19.   58 **reluctant** struggling
(against   the   smoke)   62   **quadrate**   in   "square"   formation   63–64 **moved on/In silence . . . to** cf. i, 561   69
obvious Latin *obvius,* lying in the way   73 **nimble tread** cf.
"tread of nimble feet," iv, 866

Various, with boastful arguments° portrayed,
The banded Powers of Satan hasting on   85
With furious expedition:° for they weened
That selfsame day, by fight or by surprise,
To win the Mount of God, and on his throne
To set the envier of his state, the proud
Aspirer, but their thoughts proved fond° and vain   90
In the mid-way, though strange to us it seemed
At first that Angel should with Angel war,
And in fierce hosting meet, who wont to meet
So oft in festivals of joy and love
Unanimous as sons of one great Sire,   95
Hymning the Eternal Father. But the shout
Of battle now began, and rushing sound
Of onset ended soon each milder thought.
High in the midst, exalted as a God,
The Apostate in his sun-bright chariot sat,   100
Idol of majesty divine, enclosed
With flaming Cherubim and golden shields,
Then lighted from his gorgeous throne, for now
'Twixt host and host but narrow space was left,
A dreadful interval, and front to front   105
Presented stood, in terrible array
Of hideous length. Before the cloudy van,
On the rough edge of battle° ere it joined,
Satan, with vast and haughty strides advanced,
Come towering, armed in adamant and gold.°   110
Abdiel that sight endured not,° where he stood
Among the mightiest, bent on highest deeds,°
And thus his own undaunted heart explores:
  ' "O Heaven! that such resemblance of the Highest°
Should yet remain, where faith and realty°   115
Remain not; wherefore should not strength and might
There fail where virtue fails, or weakest prove

84 **arguments** mottoes   86 **expedition** a pun, since the Latin
meaning is haste   90 **fond** foolish   108 **edge of battle** cf. i,
276–77 and note   109–110 Compare Achilles: "Then to the
city, terrible and strong,/ With high and haughty steps he
tower'd along." Pope's translation of *Iliad*, XXII, 21–22.   111
that sight endured not Virgil's "*Non tulit hanc speciem*,"
Aeneid II, 407   112 **highest deeds** cf. v, 865   114–26 not
spoken   115 **realty** reality (if not a misprint for lealty or fealty)

Where boldest, though to sight unconquerable?
His puissance, trusting in the Almighty's aid,
120 I mean to try, whose reason I have tried
Unsound and false, nor is it aught but just
That he who in debate of truth hath won
Should win in arms, in both disputes alike
Victor. Though brutish that contést and foul,
125 When reason hath to deal with force, yet so
Most reason is that reason overcome."
  'So pondering, and from his armèd peers
Forth-stepping opposite, halfway he met
His daring foe, at this prevention more
130 Incensed, and thus securely° him defied:
  ' "Proud, art thou met? Thy hope was to have reached
The height of thy aspiring unopposed,
The throne of God unguarded, and his side
Abandoned at the terror of thy power
135 Or potent tongue. Fool! not to think how vain
Against the Omnipotent to rise in arms,
Who out of smallest things could without end
Have raised incessant armies to defeat
Thy folly, or, with solitary hand
140 Reaching beyond all limit, at one blow
Unaided could have finished thee and whelmed
Thy legions under darkness; but thou seest
All are not of thy train; there be who° faith
Prefer, and piety to God, though then
145 To thee not visible when I alone
Seemed in thy world erroneous to dissent
From all: my sect° thou seest; now learn too late
How few sometimes may know when thousands err."
  'Whom the grand Foe, with scornful eye askance,
150 Thus answered: "Ill for thee, but in wished hour
Of my revenge first sought for thou return'st
From flight, seditious Angel, to receive
Thy merited reward, the first assay
Of this right hand provoked, since first that tongue,
155 Inspired with contradiction, durst oppose

130 **securely** fearlessly   143 **there be who** there are some
who   147 **sect** a word used with seventeenth-century flavor
and fervor

A third part of the gods, in synod met
Their deities to assert, who, while they feel
Vigour divine within them, can allow
Omnipotence to none. But well thou com'st
Before thy fellows, ambitious to win   160
From me some plume, that thy success may show
Destruction to the rest. This pause between
(Unanswered lest thou boast) to let thee know;
At first I thought that Liberty and Heaven
To heavenly souls had been all one, but now   165
I see that most through sloth had rather serve,
Ministering Spirits, trained up in feast and song:
Such hast thou armed, the minstrelsy of Heaven,
Servility with freedom to contend,
As both their deeds compared this day shall prove." 170
   'To whom, in brief, thus Abdiel stern replied:
   "Apostate, still thou err'st, nor end wilt find
Of erring, from the path of truth remote;
Unjustly thou deprav'st it with the name
Of servitude, to serve whom God ordains,°   175
Or Nature: God and Nature bid the same,
When he who rules is worthiest and excels
Them whom he governs. This is servitude,
To serve the unwise, or him who hath rebelled
Against his worthier, as thine now serve thee   180
Thyself not free, but to thyself enthralled;
Yet lewdly° dar'st our ministering upbraid.
Reign thou in Hell, thy kingdom; let me serve
In Heaven God ever blest, and his divine°
Behests obey, worthiest to be obeyed.   185
Yet chains in Hell, not realms, expect; meanwhile,
From me returned, as erst thou saidst, from flight,
This greeting on thy impious crest receive."
   'So saying, a noble stroke he lifted high,
Which hung not, but so swift with tempest fell   190
On the proud crest of Satan that no sight,
Nor motion of swift thought, less could his shield,
Such ruin intercept. Ten paces huge
He back recoiled;° the tenth on bended knee

175 **God ordains** as at iv, 636   182 **lewdly** basely   183–84 cf. i,
263   194 **He back recoiled** cf. ii, 759. Similarly "Amazement
seized" is common to 198 and ii, 758.

195 His massy spear upstayed, as if, on earth,
Winds under ground, or waters forcing way,
Sidelong had pushed a mountain from his seat,
Half-sunk with all his pines. Amazement seized
The rebel Thrones, but greater rage, to see
200 Thus foiled their mightiest; ours joy filled, and shout,
Presage of victory, and fierce desire°
Of battle: whereat Michael bid sound
The Archangel trumpet. Through the vast of Heaven
It sounded, and the faithful armies rung
205 Hosanna to the Highest; nor stood at gaze
The adverse legions, nor less hideous joined
The horrid shock. Now storming fury rose,
And clamour such as heard in Heaven till now
Was never; arms on armour clashing brayed
210 Horrible discord, and the madding° wheels
Of brazen chariots raged; dire was the noise
Of conflict; overhead the dismal hiss
Of fiery darts in flaming volleys flew,
And, flying, vaulted either host with fire.°
215 So under fiery cope together rushed
Both battles° main, with ruinous assault
And inextinguishable rage. All Heaven
Resounded, and, had Earth been then, all Earth
Had to her centre shook. What wonder, when
220 Millions of fierce encountering Angels fought
On either side, the least of whom could wield
These elements, and arm him with the force
Of all their regions? How much more of power
Army against army numberless to raise
225 Dreadful combustion warring, and disturb,
Though not destroy, their happy native seat;
Had not the Eternal King° Omnipotent
From his strong hold of Heaven high overruled
And limited their might; though numbered such
230 As each divided legion might have seemed
A numerous host; in strength each armèd hand

201 **fierce desire** cf. iv, 509 210 **madding** whirling 214
vaulted . . . with fire This phrase links war with hell, i,
298. 216 **battles** armies (cf. battalions) 227 **Eternal King** cf.
iii, 374

A legion; led in fight, yet leader seemed
Each warrior single as in chief, expert
When to advance, or stand, or turn the sway
Of battle, open when, and when to close   235
The ridges of grim war; no thought of flight,
None of retreat, no unbecoming deed
That argued fear; each on himself relied
As only in his arm the moment lay
Of victory. Deeds of eternal fame   240
Were done, but infinite, for wide was spread
That war, and various: sometimes here on firm ground
A standing fight, then, soaring on main wing,
Tormented all the air; all air seemed then
Conflicting fire. Long time in even scale   245
The battle hung, till Satan, who that day
Prodigious power had shown, and met in arms
No equal, ranging through the dire attack
Of fighting Seraphim confused, at length
Saw where the sword of Michael smote, and felled   250
Squadrons at once: with huge two-handed sway
Brandished aloft, the horrid edge came down
Wide-wasting. Such destruction to withstand
He hasted, and opposed the rocky orb
Of tenfold adamant, his ample shield,   255
A vast circumference. At his approach
The great Archangel from his warlike toil
Surceased, and, glad, as hoping here to end
Intestine war° in Heaven, the Arch-foe subdued,
Or captive dragged in chains, with hostile frown   260
And visage all inflamed, first thus began:
    ' "Author of Evil, unknown till thy revolt,
Unnamed in Heaven, now plenteous, as thou seest,
These acts of hateful strife—hateful to all,
Though heaviest, by just measure, on thyself   265
And thy adherents—how hast thou disturbed
Heaven's blessed peace, and into Nature brought
Misery, uncreated till the crime
Of thy rebellion! how hast thou instilled
Thy malice into thousands, once upright   270
And faithful, now proved false! But think not here

259 **Intestine war** civil war

To trouble holy rest; Heaven casts thee out
From all her confines; Heaven, the seat of bliss,
Brooks not the works of violence and war.
275 Hence, then, and Evil go with thee along,
Thy offspring, to the place of Evil, Hell,
Thou and thy wicked crew; there mingle broils,
Ere this avenging sword begin thy doom,
Or some more sudden vengeance, winged from God,
280 Precipitate thee with augmented pain."
    'So spake the Prince of Angels; to whom thus
The Adversary: "Nor think thou with wind
Of airy threats to awe whom yet with deeds
Thou canst not. Hast thou turned the least of these
285 To flight—or, if to fall, but that they rise
Unvanquished—easier to transact with me
That thou shouldst hope, imperious, and with threats
To chase me hence? Err not that° so shall end
The strife which thou call'st evil, but we style
290 The strife of glory—which we mean to win,
Or turn this Heaven itself into the Hell
Thou fablest; here, however, to dwell free,
If not to reign. Meanwhile thy utmost force,
And join him named Almighty to thy aid,
295 I fly not, but have sought thee far and nigh."
    'They ended parle,° and both addressed for fight
Unspeakable; for who, though with the tongue
Of Angels, can relate, or to what things
Liken on Earth conspicuous, that may lift
300 Human imagination to such height
Of godlike power? for likest gods they seemed,
Stood they or moved, in stature, motion, arms,
Fit to decide the empire of great Heaven.
Now waved their fiery swords, and in the air
305 Made horrid circles; two broad suns their shields
Blazed opposite, while Expectation stood
In horror; from each hand with speed retired,
Where erst was thickest fight, the Angelic throng,°
And left large field, unsafe within the wind

288 **Err not that** do not wrongly think that   296 **They ended
parle** The parley between warriors has been after the Homeric
fashion.   308 **the Angelic throng** cf. v, 650

Of such commotion: such as (to set forth   310
Great things by small) if, Nature's concord broke,
Among the constellations war were sprung,
Two planets, rushing from aspect malign
Of fiercest opposition, in mid sky
Should combat, and their jarring spheres confound.   315
Together both, with next to almighty arm
Uplifted imminent, one stroke they aimed°
That might determine, and not need repeat,
As not of power, at once; nor odds appeared
In might or swift prevention. But the sword   320
Of Michael° from the armoury of God
Was given him tempered so that neither keen
Nor solid might resist that edge; it met
The sword of Satan, with steep force to smite
Descending, and in half cut sheer, nor stayed,   325
But, with swift wheel reverse, deep entering, sheared
All his right side. Then Satan first knew pain,°
And writhed him to and fro convolved; so sore
The griding° sword with discontinuous wound
Passed through him—but the ethereal substance closed, 330
Not long divisible, and from the gash
A stream of nectarous humour issuing flowed
Sanguine, such as celestial Spirits may bleed,
And all his armour stained, erewhile so bright.
Forthwith, on all sides, to his aid was run°   335
By Angels many and strong, who interposed
Defence, while others bore him on their shields
Back to his chariot, where it stood retired°
From off the files of war;° there they him laid
Gnashing for anguish, and despite, and shame   340
To find himself not matchless, and his pride
Humbled by such rebuke, so far beneath
His confidence to equal God in power.

317 Sound and rhythm echo sense. 320–21 **the sword/Of Michael** mentioned at 250 and ii, 294. The "armoury of God" derives from Jeremiah, 1 (50), 25. 327 **Then Satan first knew pain** at odds, perhaps, with ii, 752 329 **griding** cutting with a grating sound 335 **was run** the Latin impersonal passive 336–38 Modeled on the rescue of the wounded Hector, *Iliad*, XIV, 427–30. 339 **the files of war** "the armèd files," i, 567, or ranks

Yet soon he healed; for Spirits that live throughout
345 Vital in every part, not, as frail Man,
In entrails, heart or head, liver or reins,°
Cannot but by annihilating die;
Nor in their liquid texture mortal wound
Receive, no more than can the fluid air;
350 All heart they live, all head, all eye, all ear,
All intellect, all sense, and as they please
They limb themselves, and colour, shape, or size
Assume, as like them best, condense or rare.
  'Meanwhile, in other parts, like deeds deserved
355 Memorial, where the might of Gabriel° fought,
And with fierce ensigns pierced the deep array
Of Moloch, furious king, who him defied,
And at his chariot-wheels to drag him bound
Threatened, nor from the Holy One of Heaven
360 Refrained his tongue blasphémous, but anon,
Down cloven to the waist, with shattered arms
And uncouth° pain fled bellowing. On each wing
Uriel and Raphael his vaunting foe,°
Though huge and in a rock of diamond armed,
365 Vanquished Adramelech° and Asmadai,°
Two potent Thrones, that to be less than Gods
Disdained, but meaner thoughts learned in the flight,
Mangled with ghastly wounds through plate and mail.
Nor stood unmindful Abdiel to annoy
370 The atheist crew, but with redoubled blow
Ariel,° and Arioch,° and the violence
Of Ramiel,° scorched and blasted, overthrew.

346 **reins** kidneys   355 **the might of Gabriel** Homerism for
"the mighty Gabriel"   362 **uncouth** strange, hitherto unknown   363 As a relater whose name Adam does not know,
and in modesty, Raphael speaks of himself in the third
person.   365 **Adramelech** originally an idol of the Sepharvites,
who burned their children to him (the first part of his name
probably means fire) 2 Kings, xvii, 31. **Asmadai** same as
Asmodeus, iv, 168; by medieval tradition chief of the fourth
order of the fallen angels.   371 **Ariel** Sometimes translated as
"lionlike," thus his fierceness, but also doubtless associated
with Ares. **Arioch** known to demonologists as the spirit of
revenge.   372 **Ramiel** "Thunder of God." The name occurs in
the Book of Enoch and Cabalistic demonologies.

I might relate of thousands, and their names
Eternize here on Earth, but those elect
Angels, contented with their fame in Heaven,   375
Seek not the praise of men: the other sort,
In might though wondrous and in acts of war,
Nor of renown less eager, yet by doom
Cancelled from Heaven and sacred memory,
Nameless in dark oblivion let them dwell.   380
For strength from truth divided, and from just,
Illaudable,° naught merits but dispraise
And ignominy, yet to glory aspires,
Vain-glorious, and through infamy seeks fame:
Therefore eternal silence be their doom!   385
    'And now, their mightiest quelled, the battle swerved,
With many an inroad gored; deformèd rout
Entered, and foul disorder; all the ground
With shivered armour strown, and on a heap
Chariot and charioteer lay overturned,   390
And fiery foaming steeds;° what stood, recoiled
O'erwearied, through the faint Satanic host,
Defensive scarce, or with pale fear surprised—
Then first with fear surprised and sense of pain—
Fled ignominious, to such evil brought   395
By sin of disobedience, till that hour
Not liable to fear, or flight, or pain.
Far otherwise the inviolable Saints
In cubic phalanx firm advanced entire,
Invulnerable, impenetrably armed;   400
Such high advantages their innocence
Gave them above their foes, not to have sinned,
Not to have disobeyed; in fight they stood
Unwearied, unobnoxious to be pained°
By wound, though from their place by violence moved.   405
    'Now Night her course began, and, over Heaven
Inducing° darkness, grateful° truce imposed
And silence on the odious din of war.°

382 **Illaudable** unworthy of praise   391 **foaming steeds**
anticipating xi, 643, while *fiery* looks back: 17; ii, 531; iii,
522   404 **unobnoxious to be pained** unliable to harm   407
Inducing bringing on **grateful** pleasing, as at iv, 331   408 **din
of war** cf. i, 668

Under her cloudy covert both retired,
410 Victor and vanquished; on the foughten field
Michaël and his Angels prevalent
Encamping, placed in guard their watches round,
Cherubic waving fires;° on the other part,
Satan with his rebellious disappeared,
415 Far in the dark dislodged, and, void of rest,
His potentates to council called by night,
And in the midst thus undismayed began:
       ' "O now in danger tried, now known in arms
Not to be overpowered, companions dear,°
420 Found worthy not of liberty alone,
Too mean pretence, but, what we more affect,
Honour, dominion, glory, and renown;
Who have sustained one day in doubtful fight
(And, if one day, why not eternal days?)
425 What Heaven's Lord had powerfulest to send
Against us from about his throne, and judged
Sufficient to subdue us to his will,
But proves not so, then fallible, it seems,
Of future we may deem him, though till now
430 Omniscient thought. True is, less firmly armed,
Some disadvantage we endured, and pain,
Till now not known, but, known, as soon contemned;
Since now we find this our empyreal form
Incapable of mortal injury,
435 Imperishable, and, though pierced with wound,
Soon closing, and by native vigour healed.
Of evil, then, so small as easy think
The remedy; perhaps more valid arms,
Weapons more violent, when next we meet,
440 May serve to better us and worse our foes,
Or equal what between us made the odds,
In nature none. If other hidden cause
Left them superior, while we can preserve
Unhurt our minds, and understanding sound,
445 Due search and consultation will disclose."
       'He sat; and in the assembly next upstood

---

413 The "flaming Cherubim" (102) were, as usual, employed
as sentinels.   419 **companions dear** cf. v, 673

Nisroch,° of Principalities the prime:
As one he stood escaped from cruel fight,
Sore toiled, his riven arms to havoc hewn,
And, cloudy in aspect, thus answering spake: 450
  ' "Deliverer from new Lords, leader to free
Enjoyment of our right as Gods; yet hard
For Gods, and too unequal work, we find
Against unequal arms to fight in pain,
Against unpained, impassive°—from which evil   455
Ruin must needs ensue. For what avails
Valour or strength, though matchless, quelled with pain,
Which all subdues, and makes remiss the hands
Of mightiest? Sense of pleasure we may well
Spare out of life perhaps, and not repine,   460
But live content, which is the calmest life;
But pain is perfect misery, the worst
Of evils, and, excessive, overturns
All patience. He who, therefore, can invent
With what more forcible we may offend   465
Our yet unwounded enemies, or arm
Ourselves with like defence, to me deserves
No less than for deliverance what we owe."°
  'Whereto, with look composed, Satan replied:
"Not uninvented that, which thou aright   470
Believ'st so main to our success, I bring.
Which of us who beholds the bright surface
Of this ethereous mould whereon we stand,
This continent of spacious Heaven, adorned
With plant, fruit, flower ambrosial, gems and gold,   475
Whose eye so superficially surveys
These things as not to mind from whence they grow
Deep under ground: materials dark and crude,
Of spiritous and fiery spume, till, touched
With Heaven's ray, and tempered, they shoot forth   480
So beauteous, opening to the ambient light?
These in their dark nativity the Deep

447 **Nisroch** the name of an idol of Nineveh in whose temple
the Assyrian king Sennacherib was worshiping when assassinated by his sons   455 Only the sinful, rebellious angels
suffer pain.   467–68 **to me deserves,** etc. In my opinion
deserves no less than what we owe (to Satan) for our
deliverance (from the tyranny of heaven).

Shall yield us, pregnant with infernal flame,
Which, into hollow engines long and round
485 Thick-rammed, at the other bore with touch of fire
Dilated and infuriate, shall send forth
From far, with thundering noise, among our foes
Such implements of mischief as shall dash
To pieces and o'erwhelm whatever stands
490 Adverse, that they shall fear we have disarmed
The Thunderer of his only dreaded bolt.
Nor long shall be our labour, yet ere dawn
Effect shall end our wish. Meanwhile revive,
Abandon fear; to strength and counsel joined
495 Think nothing hard, much less to be despaired."
    'He ended; and his words their drooping cheer
Enlightened, and their languished hope revived,
The invention all admired, and each how he
To be the inventor missed, so easy it seemed
500 Once found, which yet unfound most would have thought
Impossible; yet, haply, of thy race,
In future days, if malice should abound,
Someone, intent on mischief or inspired
With devilish machination,° might devise
505 Like instrument to plague the sons of men
For sin, on war and mutual slaughter bent.
Forthwith from council to the work they flew;
None arguing stood; innumerable hands
Were ready; in a moment up they turned
510 Wide the celestial soil, and saw beneath
The originals of Nature in their crude
Conception; sulphurous and nitrous foam
They found, they mingled, and, with subtle art,
Concocted and adusted,° they reduced
515 To blackest grain, and into store conveyed.

504 **devilish machination** Spenser, following Renaissance
tradition, spoke of "that devilish iron engine"—it is Milton's
"devilish engine" of iv, 17—"wrought/ In deepest hell, and fram'd
by furies' skill,/ With windy nitre and quick sulphur fraught,/ And
ramm'd with bullet round, ordained to kill." *Faerie Queene*, I,
vii, 13, 1–4. Voltaire in *Candide* complained that Milton "imitates
seriously Ariosto's comical invention of firearms by making the
devils fire a cannon in Heaven."   514 **Concocted and adusted**
baked and burned to ashes

Part hidden veins digged up (nor hath this Earth
Entrails unlike) of mineral and stone,
Whereof to found their engines and their balls
Of missive ruin;° part incentive reed°
Provide, pernicious with one touch to fire.   520
So all ere day-spring, under conscious Night,
Secret they finished, and in order set,
With silent circumspection, unespied.
      'Now, when fair Morn orient in Heaven appeared,
Up rose the victor Angels, and to arms   525
The matin triumpet sung. In arms they stood
Of golden panoply, refulgent host,
Soon banded; others from the dawning hills
Looked round, and scouts each coast light-armèd scour
Each quarter to descry the distant foe,   530
Where lodged, or whither fled, or if for fight,
In motion or in halt. Him soon they met
Under spread ensigns° moving nigh, in slow
But firm battalion; back with speediest sail
Zophiel,° of Cherubim the swiftest wing,   535
Came flying, and in mid-air aloud thus cried:
      ' "Arm, Warriors, arm for fight, the foe at hand,
Whom fled we thought, will save us long pursuit
This day; fear not his flight—so thick a cloud
He comes, and settled in his face I see   540
Sad resolution and secure. Let each
His adamantine coat gird well, and each
Fit well his helm, grip fast his orbèd shield,
Borne even or high, for this day will pour down
If I conjecture aught, no drizzling shower,   545
But rattling storm of arrows barbed with fire."
      'So warned he them, aware themselves, and soon
In order, quit of all impediment,
Instant, without disturb, they took alarm,
And onward move embattled: when, behold,   550
Not distant far, with heavy pace the foe
Approaching gross and huge, in hollow cube
Training his devilish enginery,° impaled

---

519 **missive ruin** missile destruction **incentive reed** Miltonic
diction for the gunner's match; cf. 579–80   533 **Under spread
ensigns** cf. ii, 886   535 **Zophiel** "Spy of God" or "Scout"   553
devilish enginery see note to 504

On every side with shadowing squadrons deep,
555 To hide the fraud. At interview both stood
A while but suddenly at head appeared
Satan, and thus was heard commanding loud:
' "Vanguard, to right and left the front unfold,
That all may see who hate us how we seek
560 Peace and composure,° and with open breast
Stand ready to receive them, if they like
Our overture, and turn not back perverse—
But that I doubt. However, witness Heaven,
Heaven, witness thou anon, while we discharge
565 Freely our part. Ye, who appointed stand,
Do as you have in charge, and briefly touch
What we propound, and loud that all may hear."
'So scoffing in ambiguous words° he scarce
Had ended, when to right and left the front°
570 Divided, and to either flank retired,
Which to our eyes discovered, new and strange,
A triple-mounted row of pillars laid
On wheels (for like to pillars most they seemed,
Or hollowed bodies made of oak or fir,
575 With branches lopped, in wood or mountain felled),
Brass, iron, stony mould, had not their mouths
With hideous orifice gaped on us wide,
Portending hollow° truce. At each, behind,
A Seraph stood, and in his hand a reed
580 Stood waving, tipped with fire, while we, suspense,
Collected stood within our thoughts amused,°
Not long, for sudden all at once their reeds
Put forth, and to a narrow vent applied
With nicest touch. Immediate in a flame,
585 But soon obscured with smoke, all Heaven appeared,
From those deep-throated engines belched, whose roar

---

560 **composure** agreement, but also anticipatory of the pun in 612–13   568 **ambiguous words** cf. v, 703   569 **to right and left the front** as above, 558   578 **hollow** literal and figurative. The Sonnet to Vane has a comparable pun about the treacherous Hollanders—"hollow states." 579–81. *Stood* three times in three lines has been criticized. Some such word as "held" has been conjectured for "stood" in 580. *Suspense* is an adjective meaning full of suspense; *amused* means wondering, in a muse.

Embowelled° with outrageous noise the air,
And all her entrails tore, disgorging foul
Their devilish glut, chained thunderbolts and hail
Of iron globes, which, on the victor host   590
Levelled, with such impetuous fury smote
That whom they hit none on their feet might stand,
Though standing else as rocks, but down they fell°
By thousands, Angel on Archangel rolled,
The sooner for their arms; unarmed, they might   595
Have easily, as Spirits, evaded swift
By quick contraction or remove; but now
Foul dissipation° followed, and forced rout,
Nor served it to relax their serried files.
What should they do? If on they rushed, repulse   600
Repeated and indecent° overthrow
Doubled would render them yet more despised,
And to their foes a laughter, for in view
Stood ranked of Seraphim another row,
In posture to displode° their second tire°   605
Of thunder; back defeated to return
They worse abhorred. Satan beheld their plight,
And to his mates thus in derision called:
  ' "O friends, why come not on these victors proud?
Erewhile they fierce were coming, and, when we   610
To entertain them fair with open front
And breast° (what could we more?) propounded terms
Of composition,° straight they changed their minds,
Flew off, and into strange vagaries fell,
As they would dance, yet for a dance they seemed°   615
Somewhat extravagant and wild; perhaps
For joy of offered peace. But I suppose,
If our proposals once again were heard,°

587 **Embowelled** filled   593 **down they fell** cf. ii, 771   598
dissipation scattering, rout   601 **indecent** disgraceful   605
displode explode   **tire** battery   611–12 **with open . . . breast** cf.
560   613 In the fiendish series of puns (611–27), *composition*
is being used in both its figurative and its chemical (513–15)
sense.   615 Doubtless in reminiscence of two grim jests in
Book XVI of the *Iliad*: Aeneas calls Meriones an excellent
dancer for dodging his spear, and Patroclus mocks Hector's
charioteer, Cebriones, who has plunged to his death from the
chariot, as a nimble diver.   618 **heard** still punning

We should compel them to a quick result."°
620   'To whom thus Belial, in like gamesome mood:
"Leader, the terms we sent were terms of weight,
Of hard contents, and full of force urged home,
Such as we might perceive amused° them all,
And stumbled many. Who receives them right
625   Had need from head to foot well understand;°
Not understood, this gift they have besides,
They show us when our foes walk not upright."
'So they among themselves in pleasant vein
Stood scoffing, heightened in their thoughts beyond
630   All doubt of victory; Eternal Might
To match with their inventions they presumed
So easy, and of his thunder made a scorn
And all his host derided, while they stood
A while in trouble. But they stood not long;
635   Rage prompted them at length, and found them arms°
Against such hellish mischief fit to oppose.
Forthwith (behold the excellence, the power,
Which God hath in his mighty Angels placed)
Their arms away they threw, and to the hills
640   (For Earth hath this variety from Heaven
Of pleasure situate in hill and dale°)
Light as the lightning-glimpse they ran, they flew;°
From their foundations, loosening to and fro,
They plucked the seated hills, with all their load,°
645   Rocks, waters, woods, and, by the shaggy tops
Uplifting, bore them in their hands. Amaze,
Be sure, and terror seized the rebel host,
When coming towards them so dread they saw
The bottom of the mountains upward turned,
650   Till on those cursed engines' triple row

619 **result** remembering the Latin meaning, *resultare,* to spring
back.   623 **amused** i.e., stunned   625 **understand** stand under,
a Shakespearean quibble; see *Two Gentlemen of Verona,* II, v,
23 ff.   635 **Rage . . . found them arms** *furor arma ministrat*
(*Aen.* I, 150)   641 **hill and dale** a familiar combination, iv, 243;
cf. ii, 944; iv, 538; viii, 262   642 "And the living creatures ran
and returned as the appearance of a flash of lightning" (Ezek.
i, 14).   644 The Giants against the Titans resorted to similar
tactics, and Otus and Ephialtes in an assault on the gods of
Olympus piled Mount Pelion on Mount Ossa.

They saw them whelmed, and all their confidence
Under the weight of mountains buried deep;
Themselves invaded next, and on their heads
Main promontories flung, which in the air
Came shadowing, and oppressed whole legions armed.   655
Their armour helped their harm,° crushed in and bruised,
Into their substance pent, which wrought them pain
Implacable, and many a dolorous groan,
Long struggling underneath ere they could wind
Out of such prison, though Spirits of purest light,   660
Purest at first, now gross by sinning grown.
The rest, in imitation, to like arms
Betook them, and the neighbouring hills uptore;
So hills amid the air encountered hills,
Hurled to and fro with jaculation° dire   665
That under ground they fought in dismal shade:°
Infernal noise! war seemed a civil game
To this uproar; horrid confusion heaped
Upon confusion rose. And now all Heaven
Had gone to wrack,° with ruin overspread,   670
Had not the Almighty Father, where he sits
Shrined in his sanctuary of Heaven secure,
Consulting on the sum of things, foreseen
This tumult and permitted all, advised,
That his great purpose he might so fulfill   675
To honour his anointed Son, avenged
Upon his enemies, and to declare
All power on him transferred: whence to his Son,
The assessor° of his throne, he thus began:
' "Effulgence of my glory,° Son beloved,   680
Son in whose face invisible is beheld
Visibly what by Deity I am

656 **Their armour helped their harm** an encapsulation of like
sounds   665 **jaculation** throwing   666 A Spartan at Thermopylae,
told that "Such was the number of the barbarians, that when
they shot forth their arrows the sun would be darkened by their
multitude," answered: "If the Medes darken the sun, we shall
have our fight in the shade."   670 **Had gone to wrack** cf. iv,
994   679 **assessor** sharer (literally, co-sitter). "So the Son is
called by some of the Fathers, thus expressing in one word the
doctrine of the Creed, 'sitteth at the right hand of the Father' "
(R. C. Browne).   680 **Effulgence of my glory** cf. iii, 388

And in whose hand what by decree I do,
Second Omnipotence, two days are passed,
685 Two days, as we compute the days of Heaven,
Since Michael and his Powers went forth to tame
These disobedient; sore hath been their fight,
As likeliest was when two such foes met armed,
For to themselves I left them, and thou know'st
690 Equal in their creation they were formed,
Save what sin hath impaired,° which yet hath wrought
Insensibly, for I suspend their doom;
Whence in perpetual fight they needs must last
Endless, and no solution will be found.
695 War wearied hath performed what war can do,
And to disordered rage let loose the reins,
With mountains, as with weapons, armed, which makes
Wild work° in Heaven, and dangerous to the main.°
Two days are, therefore, passed, the third is thine:
700 For thee I have ordained it, and thus far
Have suffered that the glory may be thine
Of ending this great war, since none but thou
Can end it. Into thee such virtue and grace
Immense I have transfused, that all may know
705 In Heaven and Hell thy power above compare,
And this perverse commotion governed thus,
To manifest thee worthiest to be Heir
Of all things, to be Heir, and to be King
By sacred unction,° thy deservèd right.
710 Go, then, thou Mightiest, in thy Father's might;
Ascend my chariot; guide the rapid wheels
That shake Heaven's basis; bring forth all my war;
My bow and thunder, my almighty arms,
Gird on, and sword upon thy puissant thigh;°
715 Pursue these Sons of Darkness,° drive them out
From all Heaven's bounds into the utter Deep;
There let them learn, as likes them, to despise
God, and Messiah his anointed King."

691 **impaired** remembering the literal sense of *unequaled* 698
Wild work differently applied at v, 112 **the main** the
universe. 709 **By sacred unction** cf. Psalm xlv, 7 714 "Gird
thy sword upon thy thigh, O Most Mighty" (Ps. xlv, 3). 715
Sons of Darkness in contrast to "the Sons of Morn," v, 716

'He said, and on his Son with rays direct
Shone full, he all his Father full expressed   720
Ineffably into his face received;
And thus the Filial Godhead answering spake:
' "O Father, O Supreme of Heavenly Thrones,
First, Highest, Holiest, Best, thou always seek'st
To glorify thy Son; I always thee,   725
As is most just. This I my glory account,
My exaltation and my whole delight,
That thou in me well pleased declar'st thy will
Fulfilled, which to fulfill is all my bliss.
Sceptre and power, thy giving, I assume,   730
And gladlier shall resign when in the end
Thou shalt be all in all, and I in thee°
Forever, and in me all whom thou lov'st.
But whom thou hat'st I hate,° and can put on
Thy terrors as I put thy mildness on,   735
Image of thee in all things; and shall soon,
Armed with thy might, rid Heaven of these rebelled,
To their prepared ill mansion° driven down
To chains of darkness and the undying worm,°
That from thy just obedience could revolt,   740
Whom to obey is happiness entire.
Then shall thy Saints, unmixed, and from the impure
Far separate, circling thy holy mount,
Unfeignèd halleluiahs to thee sing,
Hymns of high praise, and I among them chief."   745
'So said, he, o'er his sceptre bowing, rose
From the right hand of Glory where he sat,
And the third sacred morn began to shine,
Dawning through Heaven. Forth rushed with
　　whirlwind sound°
The chariot of Paternal Deity,   750
Flashing thick flames, wheel within wheel indrawn,
Itself instinct with spirit, but convoyed
By four cherubic Shapes. Four faces each

732 cf. iii, 341   734 "Do not I hate them, O Lord, that hate
thee?" (Ps. cxxxix, 21).   738 **ill mansion** cf. ii, 462   739
undying worm Isaiah, lxvi, 24; Mark, ix, 44   749–59 Modeled
on Ezekiel's vision (ch. i) of four cherubim and four wheels.
As Broadbent observes, "It was a convention in hexemeral
epics to use Ezekiel's chariot to end the angelomachia."

Had wondrous; as with stars, their bodies all
755 And wings were set with eyes, with eyes the wheels
Of beryl, and careering fires between;
Over their heads a crystal firmament,
Whereon a sapphire throne, inlaid with pure
Amber and colours of the showery arch.
760 He, in celestial panoply all armed
Of radiant Urim,° work divinely wrought,
Ascended; at his right hand Victory
Sat eagle-winged; beside him hung his bow
And quiver with three-bolted thunder stored;
765 And from about him fierce effusion rolled
Of smoke and bickering° flame and sparkles dire.
Attended with ten thousand thousand Saints°
He onward came; far off his coming shone,
And twenty thousand (I their number heard)
770 Chariots of God, half on each hand, were seen.°
He on the wings of Cherub rode sublime
On the crystálline sky, in sapphire throned.
Illustrious far and wide, but by his own
First seen, them unexpected joy surprised
775 When the great ensign of Messiah blazed
Aloft, by Angels borne, his sign in Heaven,
Under whose conduct Michael soon reduced°
His army, circumfused° on either wing,
Under their Head embodied all in one.
780 Before him Power Divine his way prepared;
At his command the uprooted hills retired
Each to his place; they heard his voice, and went
Obsequious; Heaven his wonted face renewed,
And with fresh flowerets° hill and valley smiled.
785 This saw his hapless foes, but stood obdured,
And to rebellious fight rallied their Powers,
Insensate, hope conceiving from despair.

761 **Urim** first mentioned in the Bible as Aaron's "breastplate
of judgment," Exodus xxviii, 30. Probably a traditional survival
of lots used in divination. Roman Version has "Lights" for
Urim: compare "radiant" here. 766 **bickering** flickering 767
cf. Jude, xiv; Revelation, v, 11 769–70 Psalm lxviii, 17 777
reduced led back 778 **circumfused** spread about 784 **with
fresh flowerets** cf. v, 636

In Heavenly Spirits could such perverseness dwell?°
But to convince the proud what signs avail,
Or wonders move the obdúrate to relent?   790
They, hardened more by what might most reclaim,
Grieving to see his glory, at the sight
Took envy, and, aspiring to his height,
Stood re-embattled fierce, by force or fraud
Weening to prosper, and at length prevail   795
Against God and Messiah, or to fall
In universal ruin last; and now
To final battle drew, disdaining flight
Or faint retreat; when the great Son of God
To all his host on either hand thus spake: 800
    ' "Stand still in bright array, ye Saints; here stand,
Ye angels armed; this day from battle rest.
Faithful hath been your warfare, and of God
Accepted, fearless in his righteous cause;
And, as ye have received, so have ye done,   805
Invincibly; but of this cursed crew
The punishment to other hand belongs;
Vengeance is his, or whose he sole appoints.°
Number to this day's work is not ordained,
Nor multitude; stand only and behold   810
God's indignation on these godless poured
By me; not you, but me, they have despised,
Yet envied; against me is all their rage,
Because the Father, to whom in Heaven supreme
Kingdom and power and glory appertains,   815
Hath honoured me, according to his will.
Therefore to me their doom he hath assigned,
That they may have their wish, to try with me
In battle which the stronger proves, they all,
Or I alone against them, since by strength   820
They measure all, of other excellence
Not emulous, nor care who them excels;
Nor other strife with them do I vouchsafe."
    'So spake the Son, and into terror changed
His countenance, too severe to be beheld,   825

788 an imitation of Virgil's well-known "tantaene animis
caelestibus irae?" (*Aen.* I, 11) 808 Romans, xii, 19

And full of wrath bent on his enemies.°
At once the Four spread out their starry wings
With dreadful shade contiguous, and the orbs
Of his fierce chariot rolled, as with the sound
830 Of torrent floods, or of a numerous host.°
He on his impious foes right onward drove,
Gloomy as Night. Under his burning wheels
The steadfast empyrean shook throughout,°
All but the throne itself of God. Full soon
835 Among them he arrived, in his right hand
Grasping ten thousand thunders, which he sent
Before him, such as in their souls infixed
Plagues.° They, astonished, all resistance lost,
All courage; down their idle weapons dropped;
840 O'er shields, and helms, and helmèd heads he rode
Of Thrones and mighty Seraphim prostrate,
That wished the mountains now might be again
Thrown on them as a shelter from his ire.°
Nor less on either side tempestuous fell
845 His arrows, from the fourfold-visaged Four,
Distinct with eyes, and from the living wheels,
Distinct alike with multitude of eyes;
One spirit in them ruled, and every eye
Glared lightning and shot forth pernicious fire
850 Among the accurs'd, that withered all their strength
And of their wonted vigour left them drained,
Exhausted, spiritless, afflicted, fallen.
Yet half his strength he put not forth, but checked
His thunder in mid-volley, for he meant
855 Not to destroy but root them out of Heaven.
The overthrown he raised, and, as a herd
Of goats or timorous flock together thronged,
Drove them before him thunderstruck, pursued
With terrors and with furies to the bounds
860 And crystal wall of Heaven, which, opening wide,
Rolled inward, and a spacious gap disclosed
Into the wasteful Deep.° The monstrous sight

825–26 excommunication   830 **a numerous host** as at 231; ii,
993   833 cf. 712   838 **Plagues** in the Greek sense of *stroke,
blow*   842–43 cf. Revelation, vi, 16   862 **the wasteful Deep** cf.
ii, 961

Struck them with horror backward, but far worse
Urged them behind: headlong themselves they threw
Down from the verge of Heaven; eternal wrath   *865*
Burnt after them to the bottomless pit.
  'Hell heard the unsufferable noise; Hell saw
Heaven ruining° from Heaven, and would have fled
Affrighted; but strict Fate had cast too deep
Her° dark foundations, and too fast had bound.   *870*
Nine days° they fell; confounded Chaos roared,
And felt tenfold confusion in their fall
Through his wild anarchy, so huge a rout
Encumbered him with ruin. Hell at last,
Yawning, received them whole, and on them closed°—   *875*
Hell, their fit habitation, fraught with fire
Unquenchable, the house of woe and pain.
Disburdened Heaven rejoiced, and soon repaired
Her mural breach,° returning whence it rolled.
Sole victor, from the expulsion of his foes   *880*
Messiah his triumphal chariot turned.
To meet him all his Saints, who silent stood
Eye-witness of his almighty acts,
With jubilee advance, and, as they went,
Shaded with branching palm,° each order bright   *885*
Sung triumph, and him sung victorious King,
Son, Heir, and Lord, to him dominion given,
Worthiest to reign. He celebrated rode
Triumphant through mid Heaven, into the courts
And temple of his mighty Father° throned   *890*
Oh high, who into glory him received,
Where now he sits at the right hand of bliss.
  'Thus, measuring things in Heaven by things on Earth,
At thy request, and that thou may'st beware
By what is past, to thee I have revealed   *895*
What might have else to human race been hid:
The discord which befell, and war in Heaven°
Among the Angelic Powers, and the deep fall

868 **ruining** falling in ruins   870 **Her** Hell's   871 **Nine days** cf.
i, 50   874–75 Isaiah, v, 14   879 **Her mural breach** breach in
the walls   885 **branching palm** as in iv, 139 and *Samson
Agonistes*, 1735   890 **mighty Father** cf. v, 735, 836   897 **war in
Heaven** cf. i, 43

Of those too high aspiring who rebelled
900 With Satan; he who envies now thy state,
Who now is plotting how he may seduce
Thee also from obedience, that, with him
Bereaved of happiness, thou may'st partake
His punishment, eternal misery,
905 Which would be all his solace and revenge,
As a despite done against the Most High,
Thee once to gain companion of his woe.°
But listen not to his temptations; warn
Thy weaker,° let it profit thee to have heard,
910 By terrible example, the reward
Of disobedience; firm they might have stood,
Yet fell; remember, and fear to transgress.'

---

907 This "misery loves company" idea has its similarly phrased
exposition from the Tempter in *Paradise Regained* (i, 398–99);
Envy, they say, excites me, thus to gain/ Companions of my
misery and woe!   909 **Thy weaker** Eve is "the weaker vessel,"
1 Peter, iii, 7.

BOOK VII

THE ARGUMENT

Raphael, at the request of Adam, relates how and where-
fore this world was first created: that God, after the expel-
ling of Satan and his Angels out of Heaven, declared his
pleasure to create another world, and other creatures to
dwell therein; sends his Son with glory, and attendance of
Angels, to perform the work of creation in six days; the
Angels celebrate with hymns the performance thereof, and
his reascension into Heaven.

DESCEND from Heaven, Urania,° by that name
If rightly thou art called, whose voice divine
Following, above the Olympian hill I soar,
Above the flight of Pegasean° wing.
The meaning, not the name, I call; for thou   5
Nor of the Muses nine, nor on the top
Of old Olympus dwell'st, but, heavenly-born,
Before the hills appeared or fountain flowed,
Thou with eternal wisdom didst converse,
Wisdom thy sister, and with her didst play   10
In presence of the Almighty Father,° pleased
With thy celestial song.° Up led by thee,
Into the Heaven of Heavens I have presumed,
An earthly guest, and drawn empyreal air,

---

1 **Urania** At first Milton invokes an unnamed "Heavenly
Muse" (i, 6; iii, 19); here he uses the name of the Muse of
astronomy among the ancients, but denies a link with the
pagan Nine. In Du Bartas's *La Muse Chrétienne*, Urania is the
celestial patroness of divine poetry.   4 **Pegasean** Pegasus was
the immortal "flying steed" (17) of Bellerophon (18), whose
hoofprint made the spring of Hippocrene (sacred to the
Muses), which gave the gift of song to those who drank of
it.   11 **the Almighty Father** cf. iii, 56, 386; vi, 671   8–12 see
Proverbs, viii, 23–30

15   Thy tempering. With like safety guided down,
     Return me to my native element,°
     Lest, from this flying steed unreined (as once
     Bellerophon,° though from a lower clime)
     Dismounted, on the Aleian field° I fall,
20   Erroneous° there to wander and forlorn.
     Half yet remains unsung, but narrower bound
     Within the visible diurnal sphere;
     Standing on Earth, not rapt above the pole,
     More safe I sing with mortal voice, unchanged
25   To hoarse or mute, though fallen on evil days,
     On evil days though fallen, and evil tongues;
     In darkness, and with dangers compassed round,
     And solitude; yet not alone, while thou
     Visit'st my slumbers nightly, or when Morn
30   Purples the East. Still govern thou my song,
     Urania, and fit audience find, though few.°
     But drive far off the barbarous dissonance
     Of Bacchus and his revellers,° the race
     Of that wild rout that tore the Thracian bard°
35   In Rhodope, where woods and rocks had ears
     To rapture till the savage clamour drowned
     Both harp and voice, nor could the Muse defend
     Her son. So fail not thou who thee implores,
     For thou art heavenly, she an empty dream.
40   Say, Goddess, what ensued when Raphael,
     The affable Archangel, had forewarned
     Adam, by dire example, to beware
     Apostasy, by what befell in Heaven

16 **my native element** earth; cf. 23   18 **Bellerophon** who dared many things on his "flying steed"; when he presumed too far by attempting to mount to Olympus, or Heaven, he was thrown; "hated of all the gods, then verily he wandered alone over the Aleian plain, devouring his own soul, and shunning the paths of men" (*Iliad*, VI, 200 ff.) 19 **Aleian field** near Ale (= wandering; cf. 20) in Lycia, Asia Minor 20 **Erroneous** in the Latin sense of straying 31 Horace's "content with few readers" (*Sat.* I, x, 74) 32–33 a reference to the court of Charles II; cf. i, 498–502 34 **Thracian bard** Orpheus; see "Lycidas," 58 ff. A proffered masque subject in *A Midsummer Night's Dream* (V, i, 48–49) was: "The riot of the tipsy Bacchanals,/Tearing the Thracian singer in their rage."

To those apostates, lest the like befall
In Paradise to Adam or his race,   45
Charged not to touch the interdicted tree,
If they transgress, and slight that sole command,
So easily obeyed amid the choice
Of all tastes else to please their appetite,
Though wandering. He, with his consorted Eve,   50
The story heard attentive, and was filled
With admiration° and deep muse, to hear
Of things so high and strange, things to their thought
So unimaginable as hate in Heaven,
And war so near the peace of God in bliss,   55
With such confusion; but the evil, soon
Driven back, redounded as a flood on those
From whom it sprung, impossible to mix
With blessedness. Whence Adam soon repealed°
The doubts that in his heart arose; and, now   60
Led on, yet sinless, with desire to know
What nearer might concern him—how this World
Of heaven and earth conspicuous first began;
When, and whereof, created; for what cause;
What within Eden, or without, was done   65
Before his memory—as one whose drought,
Yet scarce allayed, still eyes the current stream,
Whose liquid murmur heard new thirst excites,
Proceeded thus to ask his heavenly guest:
    'Great things, and full of wonder in our ears,   70
Far differing from this World, thou hast revealed,
Divine interpreter, by favour sent
Down from the empyrean to forewarn
Us timely of what might else have been our loss,
Unknown, which human knowledge could not reach;   75
For which to the infinitely Good° we owe
Immortal thanks, and his admonishment
Receive with solemn purpose to observe
Immutably his sovran will, the end
Of what we are. But, since thou hast vouchsafed   80
Gently for our instruction to impart

52 **admiration** wonder   59 **repealed** called back. The further
predicate in the long sentence that begins here is *Proceeded*,
69.   76 **infinitely Good** a tribute paid before, iv, 414

Things above earthly thought, which yet concerned
Our knowing as to highest wisdom seemed,
Deign to descend now lower and relate
85   What may no less perhaps avail us known—
How first began this Heaven which we behold
Distant so high, with moving fires adorned
Innumerable, and this which yields or fills
All space, the ambient air, wide interfused,
90   Embracing round this florid Earth; what cause
Moved the Creator, in his holy rest°
Through all eternity, so late to build
In Chaos, and, the work begun, how soon
Absolved:° if unforbid thou may'st unfold
95   What we not to explore the secrets ask
Of his eternal empire, but the more
To magnify his works° the more we know.
And the great light of day yet wants to run
Much of his race, though steep; suspense° in Heaven,
100 Held by thy voice, thy potent voice, he hears,
And longer will delay, to hear thee tell
His generation, and the rising birth
Of Nature from the unapparent deep,°
Or, if the Star of Evening and the Moon
105 Haste to thy audience, Night with her will bring
Silence, and Sleep listening to thee will watch,
Or we can bid his absence till thy song
End, and dismiss thee ere the morning shine.'°
Thus Adam his illustrious guest besought,
110 And thus the godlike Angel answered mild:
    'This also thy request, with caution asked,
Obtain; though to recount almighty works
What words or tongue of Seraph can suffice,
Or heart of man suffice to comprehend?
115 Yet what thou canst attain, which best may serve
To glorify the Maker, and infer°
Thee also happier, shall not be withheld

---

91 **holy rest** cf. vi, 272   94 **Absolved** finished   97 **magnify his
works** another biblical echo, Job, xxxvi, 24   99 **suspense**
suspended, as at ii, 418; vi, 580   103 **unapparent deep** compare
233–34   108 **the morning shine** cf. v, 20   116 **infer** dem-
onstrate, imply

Thy hearing, such commission from above
I have received, to answer thy desire
Of knowledge within bounds; beyond abstain   120
To ask, nor let thine own inventions hope
Things not revealed, which the invisible King,°
Only omniscient, hath suppressed in night,
To none communicable in Earth or Heaven.
Enough is left besides to search and know;   125
But Knowledge is as food, and needs no less
Her temperance over appetite to know
In measure what the mind may well contain,
Oppresses else with surfeit, and soon turns
Wisdom to folly, as nourishment to wind.   130
    'Know then, that after Lucifer from Heaven°
(So call him, brighter once amidst the host
Of Angels than that star the stars among)
Fell with his flaming legions through the Deep
Into his place, and the great Son returned   135
Victorious with his Saints,° the Omnipotent
Eternal Father from his throne beheld
Their multitude, and to his Son thus spake:
    ' "At least° our envious foe hath failed, who thought
All like himself rebellious, by whose aid   140
This inaccessible high strength, the seat
Of Deity supreme, us dispossessed,
He trusted to have seized, and into fraud
Drew many whom their place knows here no more.°
Yet far the greater part have kept, I see,   145
Their station;° Heaven, yet populous, retains
Number sufficient to possess her realms,
Though wide, and this high temple to frequent
With ministeries due and solemn rites.
But, lest his heart exalt him in the harm   150
Already done, to have dispeopled Heaven—
My damage fondly° deemed—I can repair
That detriment, if such it be to lose

122 **the invisible King** "the King . . . invisible," 1 Timothy, i,
17 131 ff. "How art thou fallen from Heaven, O Lucifer, son
of the morning!" (Is. xiv, 12) 136 **Saints** loyal angels 139 **At
least** at last(?) 144 Job, vii, 10 145–46 **kept . . . Their station**
"And the angels which kept not their first estate, but left their
own habitation . . ." (Jude, 6) 152 **fondly** foolishly, deludedly

Self-lost, and in a moment will create
155 Another world; out of one man a race
Of men innumerable, there to dwell,
Not here, till, by degrees of merit raised,
They open to themselves at length the way
Up hither, under long obedience tried,
160 And Earth be changed to Heaven, and Heaven to Earth,
One kingdom, joy and union without end.
Meanwhile inhabit lax,° ye Powers of Heaven,
And thou, my Word, begotten Son,° by thee
This I perform: speak thou, and be it done:
165 My overshadowing Spirit and might with thee°
I send along; ride forth, and bid the Deep
Within appointed bounds be heaven and earth;
Boundless the deep, because I am who fill
Infinitude, nor vacuous the space,
170 Though I, uncircumscribed, myself retire,
And put not forth my goodness, which is free
To act or not, Necessity and Chance
Approach not me, and what I will is Fate."
   'So spake the Almighty, and to what he spake
175 His Word, the Filial Godhead,° gave effect.
Immediate are the acts of God, more swift
Than time or motion, but to human ears
Cannot without procéss of speech be told,
So told as earthly notion can receive.
180 Great triumph and rejoicing was in Heaven
When such was heard declared the Almighty's will.
Glory they sung to the Most High, good-will
To future men, and in their dwellings, peace,
Glory to him whose just avenging ire
185 Had driven out the ungodly from his sight
And the habitations of the just; to him
Glory and praise whose wisdom had ordained
Good out of evil° to create, instead
Of Spirits malign, a better race to bring

162 **inhabit lax** spread out widely, dwell at ease (in area one third less populous because of the revolt)   163 **begotten Son** cf. iii, 80, 384; v, 835.   165 "The Holy Ghost shall come upon thee, and the power of the Highest shall overshadow thee" (Luke, i, 35).   175 **the Filial Godhead** cf. vi, 722   188 **Good out of evil** cf. i, 163; xii, 470

Into their vacant room° and thence diffuse   190
His good to worlds and ages infinite.
    'So sang the Hierarchies. Meanwhile the Son
On his great expedition now appeared,
Girt with omnipotence, with radiance crowned
Of majesty divine, sapience and love   195
Immense, and all his Father in him shone.°
About his chariot numberless were poured
Cherub and Seraph,° Potentates and Thrones,
And Virtues, wingèd Spirits, and chariots winged
From the armoury of God,° where stand of old   200
Myriads, between two brazen mountains lodged
Against° a solemn day, harnessed at hand,
Celestial equipage, and now came forth
Spontaneous, for within them Spirit lived,
Attendant on their Lord. Heaven opened wide   205
Her ever-during gates, harmonious sound
On golden hinges moving,° to let forth
The King of Glory,° in his powerful Word
And Spirit coming to create new worlds.
On heavenly ground they stood, and from the shore   210
They viewed the vast immeasurable abyss,
Outrageous as a sea, dark, wasteful, wild,°
Up from the bottom turned by furious winds
And surging waves, as mountains to assault
Heaven's height, and with the centre mix the pole.   215
    ' "Silence, ye troubled waves, and thou keep peace!"
Said then the omnific° Word: "your discord end!"
Nor stayed, but, on the wings of Cherubim
Uplifted, in paternal glory rode
Far into Chaos and the World unborn,   220
For Chaos heard his voice; him all his train
Followed in bright procession, to behold

190 **vacant room** cf. ii, 835   196 cf. iii, 139.   198 **Cherub and
Seraph** cf. i, 324   200 **From the armoury of God** cf. vi,
321   202 **Against** in readiness for   207 **moving** "might be a
transitive participle agreeing with *gates* and governing *sound*;
or again the whole phrase from *harmonious* to *moving* might
be an ablative absolute," observes C. S. Lewis, finding the
syntactic ambiguity characteristic and profitable; cf. v, 253–55.
208 **King of Glory** Psalm xxiv, 8   212 **dark, wasteful, wild** cf.
i, 60; ii, 588; iii, 424   217 **omnific** all-creating (Latin)

Creation, and the wonders of his might.
Then stayed the fervid° wheels, and in his hand
225 He took the golden compasses, prepared°
In God's eternal store, to circumscribe
This Universe, and all created things.
One foot he centred and the other turned
Round through the vast profundity obscure,
230 And said, "Thus far extend, thus far thy bounds;
This be thy just circumference, O World."
Thus God the Heaven created, thus the Earth,
Matter unformed and void. Darkness profound
Covered the abyss, but on the watery calm°
235 His brooding wings the Spirit of God outspread,
And vital virtue infused, and vital warmth,
Throughout the fluid mass, but downward purged
The black, tartareous, cold, infernal dregs,
Adverse to life; then founded, then conglobed
240 Like things to like, the rest to several place
Disparted, and between spun out the air,
And Earth, self-balanced, on her centre hung.
    ' "Let there be light," said God, and forthwith light
Ethereal, first of things, quintessence pure,
245 Sprung from the deep, and from her native East
To journey through the aery gloom began,
Sphered in a radiant cloud, for yet the Sun
Was not; she in a cloudy tabernacle°
Sojourned the while. God saw the light was good,
250 And light from darkness by the hemisphere
Divided: light the Day, and darkness Night,
He named. Thus was the first day even and morn;
Nor passed uncelebrated, nor unsung
By the celestial choirs, when orient light
255 Exhaling first from darkness they beheld,
Birth-day of Heaven and Earth. With joy and shout°
The hollow universal orb they filled,

224 **fervid** glowing ("*fervidis . . . rotis*" being found in
Horace) 225 ff. see Proverbs, viii, 27 and Dante's *Paradiso,*
XIX, 40–42 234–37 cf. i, 19–22 248 **cloudy tabernacle** cf.
Psalm xix, 4, and "cloudy shrine," 360 256 "When the
morning stars sang together, and all the sons of God shouted
for joy?" (Job, xxxviii, 7)

And touched their golden harps,° and hymning praised
God and his works; Creator him they sung,
Both when first evening was, and when first morn.   260
   'Again God said, "Let there be firmament
Amid the waters, and let it divide
The waters from the waters." And God made
The firmament, expanse of liquid, pure,
Transparent, elemental air, diffused   265
In circuit to the uttermost convex
Of this great round: partition firm and sure,
The waters underneath from those above
Dividing, for, as Earth, so he the World
Built on circumfluous waters calm, in wide   270
Crystàlline ocean, and the loud misrule
Of Chaos far removed, lest fierce extremes°
Contiguous might distemper the whole frame,
And Heaven he named the Firmament. So even
And morning chorus sung the second day.   275
   'The Earth was formed, but, in the womb as yet
Of waters, embryon immature, involved,°
Appeared not; over all the face of Earth
Main ocean flowed, not idle, but, with warm
Prolific humour softening all her globe,   280
Fermented the great mother° to conceive,
Satiate with genial° moisture; when God said,
"Be gathered now, ye waters under Heaven,
Into one place, and let dry land appear."
Immediately the mountains huge appear   285
Emergent, and their broad bare backs upheave
Into the clouds; their tops ascend the sky.°
So high as heaved the tumid hills, so low
Down sunk a hollow bottom° broad and deep,
Capacious bed of waters: thither they   290
Hasted with glad precipitance, unrolled,
As drops on dust conglobing, from the dry;
Part rise in crystal wall, or ridge direct,

258 **their golden harps** cf. iii, 365   272 **fierce extremes** cf. ii,
599   277 **involved** wrapped   281 **the great mother** earth   282
genial procreative   285–87 Compare the animation in Milton's
translation (at age fifteen) of Psalm cxiv: "The high, huge-
bellied mountains skip like rams."   289 **bottom** valley

For haste, such flight the great command impressed
295 On the swift floods. As armies at the call
Of trumpet (for of armies thou hast heard)
Troop to their standard, so the watery throng,
Wave rolling after wave, where way they found—
If steep, with torrent rapture, if through plain,
300 Soft-ebbing; nor withstood them rock or hill;
But they, or underground or circuit wide
With serpent° error° wandering, found their way,
And on the washy ooze deep channels wore:
Easy, ere God had bid the ground be dry,
305 All but within those banks where rivers now
Stream, and perpetual draw their humid train.°
The dry land Earth, and the great receptacle
Of congregated waters he called Seas:
And saw that it was good, and said "Let the Earth
310 Put forth the verdant grass, herb yielding seed,
And fruit-tree yielding fruit after her kind,
Whose seed is in herself upon the Earth."
He scarce had said when the bare Earth, till then
Desert and bare, unsightly, unadorned,
315 Brought forth the tender grass, whose verdure clad
Her universal face with pleasant green;
Then herbs of every leaf, that sudden flowered,
Opening their various colours, and made gay
Her bosom, smelling sweet; and, these scarce blown,
320 Forth flourished thick the clustering vine, forth crept
The smelling° gourd, up stood the corn reed
Embattled in her field; add° the humble° shrub,
And bush with frizzled hair implicit;° last
Rose, as in dance, the stately trees and spread
325 Their branches, hung with copious fruit, or gemmed°
Their blossoms; with high woods the hills were crowned,

302 **serpent** serpentine   **error** again the Latin use, as at 20 and
iv, 239   306 The line itself illustrates the slow process.   321
smelling Emended by Bentley to swelling, but "smelling sweet"
occurs two lines above, and G. McColley notes, "We have . . .
a pungently smelling gourd in the East Indian pepper of Du
Bartas."   322 **add** *and,* 1674   **humble** Latin *humilis,* low
(-growing).   323 **frizzled hair implicit** curled foliage (Latin
coma=both hair of the head and leaves) entangled.   325
gemmed inspired by Latin *gemma,* a bud

With tufts the valleys and each fountain-side,
With borders long the rivers; that Earth now
Seemed like to Heaven, a seat where gods might dwell,
Or wander with delight, and love to haunt   330
Her sacred shades; though God had yet not rained
Upon the Earth, and man to till the ground
None was, but from the Earth a dewy mist
Went up and watered all the ground, and each
Plant of the field, which ere it was in the Earth   335
God made, and every herb before it grew
On the green stem. God saw that it was good;
So even and morn recorded the third day.

   'Again the Almighty spake, "Let there be lights
High in the expanse of Heaven, to divide   340
The day from night; and let them be for signs,
For seasons, and for days, and circling years;
And let them be for lights, as I ordain
Their office in the firmament of Heaven,
To give light on the Earth," and it was so.   345
And God made two great lights,° great for their use
To man, the greater to have rule by day,
The less by night, altern; and made the Stars,
And set them in the firmament of Heaven
To illuminate the Earth, and rule the day   350
In their vicissitude, and rule the night,
And light from darkness° to divide. God saw,
Surveying his great work, that it was good,°
For, of celestial bodies, first the Sun
A mighty sphere he framed, unlightsome first,   355
Though of ethereal mould;° then formed the Moon
Globose, and every magnitude of Stars,
And sowed with stars the Heaven thick as a field.
Of light by far the greater part he took,
Transplanted from her cloudy shrine, and placed   360
In the Sun's orb, made porous to receive
And drink the liquid light, firm to retain

346 **And God made two great lights** Milton, of course, is
following the Bible closely; this, for instance, is literally the
King James Version, Genesis i, 16. 352 **And light from
darkness** Line 250 starts the same way. 352–53 **God saw . . .
that it was good** cf. 337; also 249, 395 356 **ethereal mould** cf.
ii, 139; vi, 473

Her gathered beams, great palace now of light
Hither, as to their fountain, other stars
365 Repairing, in their golden urns draw light,
And hence the morning planet° gilds her° horns;
By tincture or reflection they augment
Their small peculiar,° though, from human sight
So far remote, with diminution seen.
370 First in his east the glorious lamp was seen,
Regent of day, and all the horizon round
Invested with bright rays, jocund to run
His longitude through Heaven's high road; the grey
Dawn, and the Pleiades,° before him danced,
375 Shedding sweet influence. Less bright the Moon
But opposite in levelled° west was set
His mirror, with full face borrowing her light°
From him, for other light she needed none
In that aspéct, and still that distance keeps
380 Till night; then in the east her turn she shines,
Revolved on Heaven's great axle, and her reign
With thousand lesser lights dividual° holds,
With thousand thousand° stars, that then appeared
Spangling the hemisphere; then first adorned
385 With their bright luminaries, that set and rose,
Glad evening and glad morn crowned the fourth day.
  'And God said, "Let the waters generate
Reptile° with spawn abundant, living soul;
And let Fowl fly above the earth, with wings
390 Displayed on the open firmament of Heaven."°
And God created the great whales, and each
Soul living, each that crept, which plenteously
The waters generated by their kinds,

366 **the morning planet** Venus, which, as Hesperus, is "the Star of Evening" (104) **her** is superior to the 1667 reading, *his*. 368 **peculiar** store 374 **Pleiades** the seven daughters of Atlas transformed into a group of stars, in the constellation Taurus. 374–75 echo "the sweet influences of Pleiades" (Job, xxxviii, 31). 376 **levelled** due 377 **borrowing her light** cf. iii, 730 382 **dividual** shared in common (modifies "reign," 381) 383 **thousand thousand** cf. v, 588 388 **Reptile** whatever creeps (cf. 392), reptilia, including fishes. Notice how much more Milton is interested in the birds than in the fishes. 390 cf. 344, 349

And every bird of wing after his kind,
And saw that it was good, and blessed them, saying,   *395*
"Be fruitful, multiply, and, in the seas,
And lakes, and running streams, the waters fill;
And let the fowl be multiplied on the earth."
Forthwith the sounds and seas, each creek and bay,
With fry innumerable swarm, and shoals   *400*
Of fish that, with their fins and shining scales,
Glide under the green wave in schools° that oft
Bank the mid-sea. Part, single or with mate,
Graze the sea-weed, their pasture, and through groves
Of coral stray, or, sporting with quick glance,   *405*
Show to the sun their waved coats dropped with gold,
Or, in their pearly shells at ease, attend
Moist nutriment, or under rocks their food
In jointed armour watch; on smooth° the seal
And bended dolphins° play, part, huge of bulk,   *410*
Wallowing unwieldy, enormous in their gait,
Tempest the ocean. There leviathan,°
Hugest of living creatures, on the deep
Stretched like a promontory, sleeps or swims,
And seems a moving land, and at his gills   *415*
Draws in, and at his trunk spouts out, a sea.
Meanwhile the tepid caves, and fens, and shores,
Their brood as numerous hatch, from the egg that soon,
Bursting with kindly rupture, forth disclosed
Their callow young; but feathered soon and fledge,   *420*
They summed their pens,° and, soaring the air sublime,°
With clang° despised the ground, under a cloud
In prospect. There the eagle and the stork
On cliffs and cedar-tops their eyries build.
Part loosely° wing the region; part, more wise,   *425*
In common, ranged in figure, wedge their way,
Intelligent of seasons, and set forth
Their aery caravan, high over seas
Flying, and over lands with mutual wing

402 **schools** printed *sculls* 409 **smooth** i.e., sea (Latin
aequor) 410 **bended dolphins** The adjective was suggested by
Ovid (*Fasti*, II, 113); the fish meant is the porpoise. 412
leviathan the whale, as at i, 201 421 **summed their pens**
developed to full growth the wings **the air sublime** as at ii,
528; iii, 72 422 **clang** cf. xi, 835 425 **loosely** separately

430 Easing their flight; so steers the prudent crane
Her annual voyage, borne on winds; the air
Floats as they pass, fanned with unnumbered plumes.
From branch to branch the smaller birds with song
Solaced the woods, and spread their painted wings,
435 Till even; nor then the solemn nightingale
Ceased warbling, but all night tuned her soft lays.
Others on silver lakes and rivers bathed
Their downy breast; the swan, with arched neck
Between her white wings mantling° proudly, rows
440 Her state with oary feet; yet oft they quit
The dank,° and, rising on stiff pennons,° tower
The mid aerial sky. Others on ground
Walked firm°—the crested cock, whose clarion sounds
The silent hours, and the other, whose gay train
445 Adorns him, coloured with the florid hue
Of rainbows and starry eyes. The waters thus
With Fish replenish, and the air with Fowl,
Evening and morn solemnized the fifth day.
      'The sixth, and of Creation last, arose
450 With evening harps and matin; when God said,
"Let the Earth bring forth soul° living in her kind,
Cattle, and creeping things, and beast of the earth,
Each in their kind." The Earth obeyed, and, straight
Opening her fertile womb, teemed at a birth
455 Innumerous living creatures, perfect forms,
Limbed and full grown. Out of the ground uprose,
As from his lair, the wild beast, where he wons°
In forest wild, in thicket, brake, or den—
Among the trees in pairs they rose, they walked;
460 The cattle in the fields and meadows green:
Those rare and solitary, these in flocks
Pasturing at once, and in broad herds,° upsprung.
The grassy clods now calved; now half appeared
The tawny lion, pawing to get free
465 His hinder parts, then springs, as broke from bonds,

---

439 **mantling** see above, v, 279 441 **dank** water **pennons**
pinions 442–43 **ground . . . firm** terra firma, vi, 242, though
the first thought is the adverbial sense 451 **soul** Bentley's
emendation of *Fowle* 457 **wons** dwells (German *wohnen*)
462 **broad herds** from *Iliad*, XI, 679

And rampant° shakes his brinded° mane; the ounce,°
The libbard,° and the tiger, as the mole
Rising, the crumbled earth above them threw
In hillocks; the swift stag from underground
Bore up his branching head; scarce from his mould   470
Behemoth,° biggest born of earth, upheaved
His vastness; fleeced the flocks and bleating rose,
As plants; ambiguous between sea and land,
The river-horse° and scaly crocodile.
At once came forth whatever creeps the ground,   475
Insect or worm.° Those waved their limber fans°
For wings, and smallest lineaments° exact
In all the liveries decked of summer's pride,
With spots of gold and purple, azure and green;
These as a line their long dimension drew°   480
Streaking the ground with sinuous trace; not all
Minims° of nature; some of serpent kind,
Wondrous in length and corpulence, involved°
Their snaky folds, and added wings. First crept
The parsimonious emmet,° provident   485
Of future, in small room large heart enclosed—
Pattern of just equality perhaps
Hereafter—joined in her popular tribes
Of commonalty. Swarming next appeared
The female bee, that feeds her husband drone°   490
Deliciously, and builds her waxen cells
With honey stored. The rest are numberless,
And thou their natures know'st, and gav'st them names,
Needless to thee repeated; nor unknown
The serpent, subtlest beast of all the field,   495
Of huge extent sometimes, with brazen eyes
And hairy mane° terrific, though to thee

466 **rampant** rearing **brinded** streaked **ounce** lynx 467 **libbard**
leopard 471 **Behemoth** the elephant 474 **The river-horse** Milton
translates Greek *hippopotamus* into English. 476 **Insect or worm**
cf. iv, 704; *worm* includes serpents **limber fans** flexible wings 477
lineaments cf. v, 278 480 This even sounds like a line about
snakes. 482 **Minims** tiniest creatures 483 **involved** wound 485
emmet ant 490 The poet, perhaps thinking of wifely duties, has
neglected the fact that the working bees are *males*; the "husband
drone" is the queen bee. 497 Right down to the *mane* or crest
Milton would seem to be thinking of the species that crushed
Laocoön and his sons (*Aen.* II, 203 ff.).

Not noxious, but obedient at thy call.°
   'Now Heaven in all her glory shone, and rolled
500 Her motions, as the great First Mover's hand
First wheeled their course; Earth, in her rich attire
Consummate lovely smiled; air, water, earth,
By fowl, fish, beast, was flown, was swum, was walked,
Frequent;° and of the sixth day yet remained;
505 There wanted yet the master-work, the end°
Of all yet done—a creature who, not prone
And brute as other creatures, but endued
With sanctity of reason, might erect
His stature, and upright with front° serene
510 Govern the rest, self-knowing, and from thence
Magnanimous° to correspond with Heaven,
But grateful to acknowledge whence his good
Descends; thither with heart, and voice, and eyes
Directed in devotion, to adore
515 And worship God Supreme, who made him chief
Of all his works. Therefore the Omnipotent
Eternal Father° (for where is not he
Present?) thus to his Son audibly spake:
   "Let us make now Man in our image, Man
520 In our similitude, and let them rule
Over the fish and fowl of sea and air,
Beast of the field, and over all the earth,
And every creeping thing° that creeps the ground."
This said, he formed thee, Adam, thee, O Man,
525 Dust of the ground, and in thy nostrils breathed
The breath of life; in his own image he
Created thee, in the image of God
Express,° and thou becam'st a living soul.
Male he created thee, but thy consort
530 Female, for race; then blessed mankind, and said:
   "Be fruitful, multiply, and fill the Earth;°
Subdue it, and throughout dominion hold
Over fish of the sea, and fowl of the air,

497–98 constitute dramatic irony. 504 **Frequent** thronged
505 **end** in the sense of both object and conclusion 509 **front**
brow 511 **Magnanimous** great-minded 516–17 **the Omni-
potent/Eternal Father** as at 136–37 523 **creeping thing** cf.
452 528 **Express** "the express image of his person," Hebrews,
i, 3 531 Partly echoing 396, partly iv, 733.

And every living thing that moves on the Earth."
Wherever thus created—for no place   *535*
Is yet distinct by name—thence, as thou know'st,
He brought thee into this delicious grove,
This garden, planted with the trees of God,
Delectable both to behold and taste,
And freely all their pleasant fruit for food   *540*
Gave thee. All sorts are here that all the earth yields,
Variety without end; but of the tree
Which, tasted, works knowledge of good and evil
Thou may'st not; in the day thou eat'st thou diest.
Death is the penalty imposed; beware,   *545*
And govern well thy appetite, lest Sin
Surprise thee, and her black attendant, Death.
  'Here finished he, and all that he had made
Viewed, and, behold! all was entirely good.
So even and morn° accomplished the sixth day;   *550*
Yet not till the Creator, from his work
Desisting, though unwearied, up returned,
Up to the Heaven of Heavens,° his high abode,
Thence to behold this new-created World,
The addition of his empire, how it showed   *555*
In prospect from his throne, how good, how fair,
Answering his great idea.° Up he rode,
Followed with acclamation, and the sound
Symphonious of ten thousand harps that tuned
Angelic harmonies: the earth, the air   *560*
Resounded (thou remember'st, for thou heard'st),
The Heavens and all the constellations rung,
The planets in their stations listening stood
While the bright pomp ascended jubilant.
"Open, ye everlasting gates," they sung;   *565*
"Open, ye Heavens, your living doors; let in
The great Creator,° from his work returned
Magnificent, his six days' work, a World;
Open, and henceforth oft, for God will deign
To visit oft the dwellings of just men   *570*

550 **even and morn** as at 252, 338   553 **to the Heaven of Heavens** cf. 13   557 **idea** conception   567 Doubling back on 551–52. *The great Creator* is one of the poem's fixed epithets—ii, 385; iii, 167, 673; iv, 684.

Delighted, and with frequent intercourse
Thither will send his wingèd messengers
On errands of supernal grace." So sung
The glorious train ascending; he through Heaven,
575 That opened wide her blazing portals, led
To God's eternal house direct the way,
A broad and ample road, whose dust is gold,
And pavement stars, as stars to thee appear
Seen in the galaxy, that milky way
580 Which nightly as a circling zone thou seest
Powdered with stars. And now on Earth the seventh
Evening arose in Eden, for the sun
Was set, and twilight from the east came on,
Forerunning night, when at the holy mount°
585 Of Heaven's high-seated top, the imperial throne
Of Godhead, fixed forever firm and sure,
The Filial Power arrived, and sat him down
With his great Father; for he also went
Invisible, yet stayed (such privilege
590 Hath Omnipresence) and the work ordained,
Author and end of all things, and, from work
Now resting, blessed and hallowed the seventh day,
As resting on that day from all his work;
But not in silence holy kept; the harp
595 Had work, and rested not; the solemn pipe
And dulcimer,° all organs of sweet stop,
All sounds on fret by string or golden wire,
Tempered soft tunings, intermixed with voice
Choral or unison;° of incense clouds,
600 Fuming from golden censers, hid the Mount.°
Creation and the six days' acts they sung:
"Great are thy works, Jehovah, infinite
Thy power; what thought can measure thee, or tongue
Relate thee; greater now in thy return
605 Than from the giant-angels; thee that day
Thy thunders magnified; but to create

584 **holy mount** cf. v, 712; vi, 743   596 **dulcimer** stringed
instrument mentioned in Daniel, iii, 5, 10, 15   599 **unison**
solo   599–600 Revelation viii, 3–4

Is greater than created° to destroy.
Who can impair thee, mighty King, or bound
Thy empire? easily the proud attempt
Of Spirits apostate and their counsels vain   610
Thou hast repelled, while impiously they thought
Thee to diminish, and from thee withdraw
The number of thy worshippers. Who seeks
To lessen thee against his purpose serves
To manifest the more thy might; his evil   615
Thou usest, and from thence creat'st more good.
Witness this new-made World, another Heaven
From Heaven-gate not far, founded in view
On the clear hyaline,° the glassy sea;
Of amplitude almost immense, with stars   620
Numerous, and every star perhaps a world
Of destined habitation; but thou know'st°
Their seasons; among these the seat of men,°
Earth, with her nether ocean circumfused,
Their pleasant dwelling-place. Thrice happy men,   625
And sons of men, whom God hath thus advanced,
Created in his image, there to dwell
And worship him, and in reward to rule
Over his works, on earth, in sea, or air,
And multiply a race of worshippers   630
Holy and just; thrice happy, if they know
Their happiness, and persevere upright."
    'So sung they, and the Empyrean rung
With halleluiahs: thus was Sabbath kept.
And thy request think now fulfilled, that asked   635
How first this World and face of things began,
And what before thy memory was done
From the beginning, that posterity,
Informed by thee, might know; if else thou seek'st
Aught, not surpassing human measure, say.'   640

---

607 **created** object of *to destroy*   619 **hyaline** "the glassy sea"
(cf. Rev. iv, 6; xv, 2)   621–22 It is apparent that the theory
of the plurality of worlds was not thought incompatible with
Christianity; cf. viii, 145, 153–58.   623 **the seat of men** cf. iii,
724

BOOK VIII

THE ARGUMENT

Adam inquires concerning celestial motions, is doubtfully answered, and exhorted to search rather things more worthy of knowledge. Adam assents, and, still desirous to detain Raphael, relates to him what he remembered since his own creation: his placing in Paradise; his talk with God concerning solitude and fit society; his first meeting and nuptials with Eve. His discourse with the Angel thereupon; who, after admonitions repeated, departs.

    THE Angel ended, and in Adam's ear
So charming left his voice that he a while
Thought him still speaking, still stood fixed to hear;
Then, as new-waked, thus gratefully replied:°
5   'What thanks sufficient, or what recompense
Equal, have I to render thee, divine
Historian, who thus largely hast allayed
The thirst I had of knowledge, and vouchsafed
This friendly condescension to relate
10 Things else by me unsearchable, now heard
With wonder, but delight, and, as is due,
With glory áttribúted to the high
Creator? Something yet of doubt remains,
Which only thy solution can resolve.
15 When I behold this goodly frame,° this World,
Of Heaven and Earth consisting, and compute
Their magnitudes—this Earth, a spot, a grain,
An atom, with the firmament compared
And all her numbered stars, that seem to roll°
20 Spaces incomprehensible (for such

1–4 Added in second edition, 1674, when Books VII and X of 1667 were split to increase the poem from ten books to twelve. 15 **this goodly frame** a phrase of Hamlet's (II, ii, 316) 19–38 cf. ix, 103-07

Their distance argues, and their swift return
Diurnal) merely to officiate° light
Round this opacous° Earth, this punctual° spot,
One day and night, in all their vast survey
Useless besides, reasoning, I oft admire°   25
How Nature, wise and frugal, could commit
Such disproportions, with superfluous hand
So many nobler bodies to create,
Greater so manifold, to this one use,
For aught appears, and on their orbs impose   30
Such restless revolution day by day
Repeated, while the sedentary° Earth,
That better might with far less compass move,
Served by more noble than herself, attains
Her end without least motion, and receives,   35
As tribute, such a sumless journey brought
Of incorporeal speed, her warmth and light—
Speed, to describe whose swiftness number fails.'
    So spake our Sire, and by his countenance seemed
Entering on studious thoughts abstruse; which Eve   40
Perceiving, where she sat retired in sight,
With lowliness majestic from her seat,
And grace that won who saw to wish her stay,
Rose, and went forth among her fruits and flowers,
To visit how they prospered, bud and bloom,   45
Her nursery; they at her coming sprung,
And, touched by her fair tendance, gladlier grew.
Yet went she not as not with such discourse
Delighted, or not capable her ear
Of what was high; such pleasure she reserved,   50
Adam relating, she sole auditress;
Her husband the relater she preferred
Before the Angel, and of him to ask
Chose rather; he, she knew, would intermix
Grateful digressions, and solve high dispute   55
With conjugal caresses: from his lip

22 **officiate** supply 23 **opacous** dark, as at iii, 418 **punctual**
like a point 25 **admire** wonder 32 **the sedentary** the
stationary earth of the Ptolemaic system. Milton is bringing his
poem (which touches on all major knowledge) up to date by
leaving room for the possibility that the Copernican theory
is right.

Not words alone pleased her. Oh, when meet now
Such pairs, in love and mutual honour joined?
With goddesslike demeanour forth she went,
60 Not unattended for on her as queen
A pomp° of winning Graces waited still,
And from about her shot darts of desire
Into all eyes, to wish her still in sight.
And Raphael now to Adam's doubt proposed
65 Benevolent and facile thus replied:
     'To ask or search I blame thee not; for Heaven
Is as the Book of God before thee set,
Wherein to read his wondrous works,° and learn
His seasons, hours, or days, or months, or years.
70 This to attain, whether Heaven move or Earth
Imports not, if thou reckon right; the rest
From Man or Angel the great Architect
Did wisely to conceal, and not divulge
His secrets, to be scanned by them who ought
75 Rather admire. Or, if they list to try
Conjecture, he his fabric of the Heavens
Hath left to their disputes, perhaps to move
His laughter at their quaint opinions wide°
Hereafter, when they come to model Heaven,
80 And calculate the stars; how they will wield
The mighty frame; how build, unbuild, contrive
To save appearances; how gird the sphere
With centric and eccentric scribbled o'er,
Cycle and epicycle,° orb in orb.
85 Already by thy reasoning this I guess,
Who art to lead thy offspring, and supposest
That bodies bright and greater should not serve
The less not bright, nor Heaven such journeys run,

61 **pomp** train or procession, as at vii, 564.   68 **his wondrous works** cf. iii, 663, 665   78 **wide** (of the mark)   84 **epicycle** a small circle with its center on the circumference of a greater circle. Ptolemaic "theories set out from the simple conception of a planet uniformly describing a circle with the Earth at the center, and then refined upon it by displacing the center of the circle from the Earth, referring the uniform motion to an arbitrarily chosen point within the circle, regarding the moving point on the circle as merely the center of a smaller circle in which the planet actually revolved, and so forth" (A. Wolf).

Earth sitting still, when she alone receives
The benefit: consider, first, that great   90
Or bright infers not excellence: the Earth,
Though, in comparison of Heaven, so small,
Nor glistering, may of solid good contain
More plenty than the Sun that barren shines,
Whose virtue on itself works no effect,   95
But in the fruitful Earth; there first received,
His beams, unactive else, their vigour find.
Yet not to Earth are those bright luminaries°
Officious,° but to thee, Earth's habitant.
And, for the Heaven's wide circuit, let it speak   100
The Maker's high magnificence, who built
So spacious, and his line stretched out so far,°
That Man may know he dwells not in his own—
An edifice too large for him to fill,
Lodged in a small partition, and the rest   105
Ordained for uses to his Lord best known.
The swiftness of those circles áttribúte,
Though numberless, to his omnipotence,
That to corporeal substances could add
Speed almost spiritual. Me thou think'st not slow, 110
Who since the morning-hour set out from Heaven
Where God resides, and ere midday arrived
In Eden, distance inexpressible
By numbers that have name. But this I urge,
Admitting motion in the Heavens, to show   115
Invalid that which thee to doubt it moved;
Not that I so affirm, though so it seem
To thee who hast thy dwelling here on Earth.
God, to remove his ways from human sense,
Placed Heaven from Earth so far that earthly sight, 120
If it presume, might err in things too high,
And no advantage gain. What if the Sun°
Be centre to the World, and other stars,
By his attractive virtue° and their own
Incited, dance about him various rounds?   125

98 **bright luminaries** cf. vii, 385 99 **Officious** ministering 102
"Who hath laid the measures thereof, if thou knowest? or who
hath stretched the line upon it [the Earth]?" (Job, xxxviii,
5) 122–30 the Copernican theory 124 **attractive virtue** power
of attraction

Their wandering course, now high, now low, then hid,
Progressive, retrograde, or standing still,
In six° thou seest; and what if, seventh to these,
The planet Earth, so steadfast though she seem,
130 Insensibly three different motions move?
Which else° to several spheres thou must ascribe,
Moved contrary with thwart° obliquities,
Or save the Sun his labour, and that swift
Nocturnal and diurnal rhomb° supposed,
135 Invisible else above all stars, the wheel
Of Day and Night; which needs not thy belief,
If Earth, industrious of herself, fetch Day,°
Travelling east, and with her part averse
From the Sun's beam meet Night, her other part
140 Still luminous by his ray. What if that light,
Sent from her through the wide transpicuous air,
To the terrestrial Moon be as a star,
Enlightening her° by day, as she by night
This Earth—reciprocal,° if land be there,
145 Fields and inhabitants? Her spots thou seest
As clouds, and clouds may rain, and rain produce
Fruits in her softened soil, for some to eat
Allotted there; and other Suns, perhaps,
With their attendant Moons, thou wilt descry,
150 Communicating male and female light,
Which two great sexes animate the World,
Stored in each orb perhaps with some that live.
For such vast room in Nature unpossessed
By living soul,° desert and desolate,
155 Only to shine, yet scarce to cóntribute
Each orb a glimpse of light, conveyed so far
Down to this habitable,° which returns
Light back to them, is obvious° to dispute.
But whether thus these things, or whether not—

128 **six** planets. The "seventh" is the sun by the old system, the
Earth by the new.   131 **else** either   132 **thwart** transverse   134
Nocturnal and diurnal rhomb the night-and-day evolving wheel
(Greek *rombos*), the Primum Mobile   137 If the Earth, moving,
obtains light for herself (from the sun)—.   143 **her** the
moon   144 **reciprocal** i.e., service   154 **living soul** cf. v, 197;
vii, 388, 528   157 **this habitable** a Greek idiom for the
Earth   158 **obvious** open

Whether the Sun, predominant in heaven,   160
Rise on the Earth, or Earth rise on the Sun;
He from the east his flaming road begin,
Or she from west her silent course advance
With inoffensive° pace that spinning sleeps
On her soft axle, while she paces even,   165
And bears thee soft with the smooth air along—
Solicit not thy thoughts with matters hid:
Leave them to God above; him serve and fear.
Of other creatures as him pleases best,
Wherever placed, let him dispose; joy thou   170
In what he gives to thee, this Paradise
And thy fair Eve;° Heaven is for thee too high°
To know what passes there. Be lowly wise;
Think only what concerns thee and thy being;
Dream not of other worlds, what creatures there   175
Live, in what state, condition, or degree,
Contented that thus far hath been revealed
Not of Earth only, but of highest Heaven.'
　　To whom thus Adam, cleared of doubt, replied:
'How fully hast thou satisfied me, pure   180
Intelligence of Heaven, Angel serene,
And, freed from intricacies, taught to live
The easiest way, nor with perplexing thoughts°
To interrupt the sweet of life, from which
God hath bid dwell far off all anxious cares,   185
And not molest us, unless we ourselves
Seek them with wandering thoughts, and notions vain!
But apt the mind or fancy is to rove
Unchecked,° and of her roving is no end,
Till, warned, or by experience taught, she learn   190
That not to know at large of things remote
From use, obscure and subtle, but to know
That which before us lies in daily life,
Is the prime wisdom: what is more is fume,°
Or emptiness, or fond impertinence,°   195

164 **inoffensive** meeting with no obstacle, unimpeded   172 **fair
Eve** cf. iv, 481 **too high** a pun   183 cf. *Samson Agonistes,* 302–
06   188–89 Idle philosophizing was an occupation of the devils
in Hell, ii, 561.   194 **fume** vapor (whence vapid), smoke   195
fond impertinence foolish irrelevance

And renders us in things that most concern
Unpractised, unprepared, and still to seek.
Therefore from this high pitch let us descend
A lower flight, and speak of things at hand
200 Useful; whence, haply, mention may arise
Of something not unseasonable to ask,
By sufferance, and thy wonted favour, deigned.
Thee I have heard relating what was done
Ere my remembrance; now hear me relate
205 My story, which, perhaps, thou hast not heard;
And day is yet not spent; till then thou seest
How subtly to detain thee I devise,
Inviting thee to hear while I relate—
Fond, were it not in hope of thy reply.
210 For while I sit with thee I seem in Heaven,
And sweeter thy discourse is to my ear
Than fruits of palm-tree, pleasantest to thirst
And hunger both, from labour, at the hour
Of sweet repast; they satiate, and soon fill,
215 Though pleasant, but thy words, with grace divine
Imbued, bring to their sweetness no satiety.'
    To whom thus Raphael answered, heavenly meek:
'Nor are thy lips ungraceful,° Sire of Men,
Nor tongue ineloquent; for God on thee
220 Abundantly his gifts hath also poured,
Inward and outward both, his image fair:
Speaking or mute all comeliness and grace
Attends thee, and each word, each motion, forms.
Nor less think we in Heaven of thee on Earth
225 Than of our fellow-servant, and inquire
Gladly into the ways of God with Man;°
For God, we see, hath honoured thee, and set
On Man his equal love. Say therefore on,
For I that day was absent, as befell,
230 Bound on a voyage úncouth and obscure,
Far on excursion toward the gates of Hell,
Squared in full legion (such command we had),
To see that none thence issued forth a spy
Or enemy, while God was in his work,

218 "Full of grace are thy lips" (Ps. xlv, 2, Prayer Book
version).   226 cf. i, 26

Lest he, incensed at such eruption bold,   235
Destruction with Creation might have mixed.
Not that they durst without his leave attempt;
But us he sends upon his high behests°
For state, as sovran King, and to inure°
Our prompt obedience. Fast we found, fast shut,   240
The dismal gates, and barricadoed strong;
But, long ere our approaching, heard within
Noise, other than the sound of dance or song,
Torment, and loud lament, and furious rage.
Glad we returned up to the coasts of Light   245
Ere Sabbath-evening; so we had in charge.
But thy relation now; for I attend,
Pleased with thy words no less than thou with mine.'
    So spake the godlike Power, and thus our Sire:
'For Man to tell how human life began   250
Is hard: for who himself beginning knew?
Desire with thee still longer to converse
Induced me. As new-waked from soundest sleep,
Soft on the flowery herb I found me laid,
In balmy sweat, which with his beams the Sun   255
Soon dried, and on the reeking moisture fed.
Straight toward Heaven my wondering eyes I turned,
And gazed a while the ample sky, till, raised
By quick instinctive motion, up I sprung,
As thitherward endeavouring, and upright   260
Stood on my feet. About me round I saw
Hill, dale, and shady woods, and sunny plains,
And liquid lapse° of murmuring streams; by these,
Creatures that lived and moved, and walked or flew,
Birds on the branches warbling: all things smiled;   265
With fragrance and with joy my heart o'erflowed.
Myself I then perused, and limb by limb
Surveyed, and sometimes went,° and sometimes ran
With supple joints, as° lively vigour led;
But who I was, or where, or from what cause,   270
Knew not. To speak I tried, and forthwith spake;
My tongue obeyed, and readily could name
Whate'er I saw. "Thou Sun," said I, "fair light,

238 **high behests** cf. iii, 533   239 **inure** accustom   263 **lapse**
pun on (1) lappings and (2) Latin sense of slipping past, a
flowing   268 **went** walked   269 **as** *and*, 1674

And thou enlightened Earth,° so fresh and gay,
275 Ye hills and dales, ye rivers, woods, and plains,
And ye that live and move, fair creatures,° tell,
Tell, if ye saw, how came I thus, how here?
Not of myself; by some great Maker° then,
In goodness and in power pre-eminent.
280 Tell me, how may I know him, how adore,
From whom I have that thus I move and live,°
And feel that I am happier than I know?"
While thus I called, and strayed I knew not whither,
From where I first drew air, and first beheld
285 This happy light, when answer none returned,
On a green shady bank, profuse of flowers,
Pensive I sat me down. There gentle sleep
First found me, and with soft oppression seized
My drowsèd sense, untroubled, though I thought
290 I then was passing to my former state°
Insensible, and forthwith to dissolve,
When suddenly stood at my head a dream,
Whose inward apparition gently moved
My fancy to believe I yet had being,
295 And lived. One came, methought, of shape divine,
And said, "Thy mansion wants thee, Adam; rise,
First Man, of men innumerable ordained
First father, called by thee, I come thy guide
To the garden of bliss, thy seat prepared."
300 So saying, by the hand he took me, raised,
And over fields and waters, as in air
Smooth sliding° without step, last led me up
A woody mountain, whose high top was plain,
A circuit wide,° enclosed, with goodliest trees°
305 Planted, with walks, and bowers, that what I saw
Of Earth before scarce pleasant seemed. Each tree
Loaden with fairest fruit,° that hung to the eye
Tempting, stirred in me sudden appetite
To pluck and eat; whereat I waked, and found

274 **enlightened Earth** cf. iii, 731   276 **fair creatures** cf. iv,
790   278 **great Maker** cf. v, 184   281 "For in him we live and
move" (Acts, xvii, 28)   290 **former state** cf. ii, 585; iv, 94   302
Smooth sliding cf. "Lycidas," 86   304 **circuit wide** cf. vii, 301;
viii, 100   **goodliest trees** cf. iv, 147   307 **Loaden with fairest
fruit** cf. iv, 147

Before mine eyes all real, as the dream   *310*
Had lively shadowed. Here had new begun
My wandering, had not he who was my guide
Up hither from among the trees° appeared,
Presence Divine. Rejoicing, but with awe,
In adoration at his feet I fell   *315*
Submiss. He reared me, and, "Whom thou sought'st I am,"
Said mildly, "Author of all this thou seest
Above, or round about thee, or beneath.
This Paradise I give thee: count it thine
To till and keep, and of the fruit to eat: *320*
Of every tree that in the garden grows
Eat freely with glad heart—fear here no dearth;
But of the tree whose operation brings
Knowledge of good and ill, which I have set,
The pledge of thy obedience and thy faith,   *325*
Amid the garden by the Tree of Life,
Remember what I warn thee: shun to taste,
And shun the bitter consequence, for know,
The day thou eat'st thereof, my sole command°
Transgressed, inevitably thou shalt die,   *330*
From that day mortal, and this happy state
Shalt lose, expelled from hence into a world
Of woe and sorrow." Sternly he pronounced
The rigid interdiction, which resounds
Yet dreadful in mine ear,° though in my choice   *335*
Not to incur; but soon his clear aspéct
Returned, and gracious purpose° thus renewed:
"Not only these fair bounds, but all the Earth
To thee and to thy race I give; as lords
Possess it, and all things that therein live,   *340*
Or live in sea or air,° beast, fish, and fowl.
In sign whereof, each bird and beast behold
After their kinds; I bring them to receive
From thee their names, and pay thee fealty
With low subjection. Understand the same   *345*
Of fish within their watery residence,
Not hither summoned, since they cannot change
Their element to draw the thinner air."

313 **among the trees** cf. vii, 459   329 **sole command** cf. iii, 94;
vii, 47   335 cf. x, 779–80   337 **purpose** conversation, as at iv,
337 (French *propos*)   341 **in sea or air** cf. vii, 629

As thus he spake, each bird and beast behold
350 Approaching two and two, these° cowering low
With blandishment; each bird stooped on his wing.°
I named them as they passed, and understood
Their nature; with such knowledge God endued
My sudden apprehension. But in these
355 I found not what methought I wanted still,
And to the Heavenly Vision° thus presumed:
    ' "O, by what name—for thou above all these,
Above mankind, or aught than mankind higher,
Surpassest far my naming—how may I
360 Adore thee, Author of this Universe,
And all this good to Man, for whose well-being
So amply, and with hands so liberal,
Thou hast provided all things? But with me
I see not who partakes. In solitude
365 What happiness? who can enjoy alone,
Or, all enjoying, what contentment find?"
Thus I, presumptuous, and the Vision bright,
As with a smile more brightened, thus replied:
    ' "What call'st thus solitude? Is not the earth
370 With various living creatures, and the air,
Replenished, and all these at thy command
To come and play before thee? Know'st thou not
Their language and their ways? They also know,
And reason not contemptibly; with these
375 Find pastime, and bear rule; thy realm is large."
So spake the Universal Lord, and seemed
So ordering. I, with leave of speech implored,
And humble deprecation, thus replied:
    ' "Let not my words offend thee, Heavenly Power;°
380 My Maker, be propitious while I speak.
Hast thou not made me here thy substitute,
And these inferior far beneath me set?
Among unequals what society
Can sort, what harmony or true delight?
385 Which must be mutual, in proportion due

350 **these** the beasts 351 **each bird stooped on his wing** an odd anticipation of the salute (wing-dipping) of planes in formation 356 **the Heavenly Vision** an expression from Acts, xxvi, 19 379 Abraham said, "Oh let not the Lord be angry, and I will speak" (Gen. xviii, 30).

Given and received, but, in disparity,
The one intense,° the other still remiss,°
Cannot well suit with either, but soon prove
Tedious alike. Of fellowship I speak
Such as I seek, fit to participate   390
All rational delight, wherein the brute
Cannot be human consort. They rejoice
Each with their kind, lion with lioness;
So fitly them in pairs thou hast combined:
Much less can bird with beast, or fish with fowl,   395
So well converse,° nor with the ox the ape;
Worse, then, can man with beast, and least of all."
  'Whereto the Almighty answered, not displeased:
"A nice° and subtle happiness, I see,
Thou to thyself proposest, in the choice   400
Of thy associates, Adam, and wilt taste
No pleasure, though in pleasure,° solitary.
What think'st thou, then, of me, and this my state?
Seem I to thee sufficiently possessed
Of happiness, or not, who am alone   405
From all eternity? for none I know
Second to me or like, equal much less.°
How have I, then, with whom to hold converse,
Save with the creatures which I made, and those°
To me inferior, infinite descents   410
Beneath what other creatures are to thee?"
  'He ceased, I lowly answered: "To attain
The height and depth of thy eternal ways
All human thoughts come short, Supreme of Things;
Thou in thyself art perfect, and in thee   415
Is no deficience found; not so is Man,
But in degree, the cause of his desire
By conversation with his like to help
Or solace his defects. No need that thou
Should'st propagate, already infinite,   420
And through all numbers absolute,° though One;

387 **intense** high-strung **remiss** low, like a beast   396
converse have fellowship with   399 **nice** fastidious   402
though in pleasure pun on Eden, which in Hebrew means
pleasure; cf. iv, 27–28   407 Horace said this of Jove (*Carm.* I,
xii, 18).   409 **those** the angels   421 **through all numbers
absolute** in all respects perfect

But Man by number is to manifest
His single imperfection, and beget
Like of his like, his image multiplied,
425 In unity° defective, which requires
Collateral° love and dearest amity.
Thou, in thy secrecy although alone,
Best with thyself accompanied, seek'st not
Social communication, yet, so pleased,
430 Canst raise thy creature to what height thou wilt
Of union or communion, deified;
I, by conversing, cannot these erect
From prone, nor in their ways complacence find."
Thus I emboldened spake, and freedom used
435 Permissive, and acceptance found, which gained
This answer from the gracious Voice Divine:
' "Thus far to try thee, Adam, I was pleased,
And find thee knowing not of beasts alone,
Which thou hast rightly named, but of thyself,
440 Expressing well the spirit within thee free,
My image, not imparted to the brute,
Whose fellowship, therefore, unmeet, for thee,
Good reason was thou freely shouldst dislike,
And be so minded still; I, ere thou spak'st,
445 Knew it not good for Man to be alone,°
And no such company as then thou saw'st
Intended thee, for trial only brought,
To see how thou couldst judge of fit and meet.
What next I bring shall please thee, be assured,
450 Thy likeness, thy fit help, thy other self,
Thy wish exactly to thy heart's desire."
'He ended, or I heard no more; for now
My earthly, by his heavenly overpowered,°
Which it had long stood under, strained to the height
455 In that celestial colloquy sublime,
As with an object that excels the sense
Dazzled and spent, sunk down, and sought repair
Of sleep, which instantly fell on me, called
By Nature as in aid, and closed mine eyes.

425 **In unity** in the single state   426 **Collateral** with a glance
at the etymological meaning, "side by side"   445 Genesis, ii,
18   453 Daniel, x, 17

Mine eyes he closed, but open left the cell°   460
Of fancy, my internal sight; by which,
Abstract° as in a trance, methought I saw,
Though sleeping where I lay, and saw the Shape
Still glorious before whom awake I stood,
Who, stooping, opened my left side, and took°   465
From thence a rib, with cordial° spirits warm,
And life-blood streaming fresh; wide was the wound,
But suddenly with flesh filled up and healed.
The rib he formed and fashioned with his hands;
Under his forming hands a creature grew,   470
Manlike, but different sex, so lovely fair
That what seemed fair in all the world seemed now
Mean, or in her summed up, in her contained,
And in her looks, which from that time infused
Sweetness into my heart unfelt before,   475
And into all things from her air inspired
The spirit of love and amorous delight.
She disappeared, and left me dark; I waked
To find her, or forever to deplore°
Her loss and other pleasures all abjure;   480
When out of hope, behold her, not far off,
Such as I saw her in my dream, adorned
With what all Earth or Heaven could bestow
To make her amiable. On she came,
Led by her Heavenly Maker, though unseen,   485
And guided by his voice, nor uninformed
Of nuptial sanctity and marriage rites.
Grace was in all her steps, Heaven in her eye,
In every gesture dignity and love.
I, overjoyed, could not forbear aloud: 490
    ' "This turn° hath made amends; thou hast fulfilled
Thy words, Creator bounteous and benign,
Giver of all things fair, but fairest this
Of all thy gifts, nor enviest.° I now see

460 Numbers, xxiv, 4 462 **Abstract** withdrawn (for better
contemplation) 465–68 The reader who prefers the unclinical
brevity of Genesis, ii, 21 will perhaps be reminded of a
contemporary production, Rembrandt's "The Anatomy Lesson
of Dr. Tulp." 466 **cordial** pertaining to the heart (*cor*) 478–79
There are curious connections here and in the preceding four
lines with the last lines of Milton's sonnet "On his Deceased
Wife." 491 **This turn** good turn 494 **enviest** grudgest

495 Bone of my bone, flesh of my flesh, my self
Before me; Woman is her name, of Man
Extracted; for this cause he shall forgo
Father and mother, and to his wife adhere;°
And they shall be one flesh, one heart, one soul."
500 'She heard me thus, and, though divinely brought,
Yet innocence and virgin modesty,
Her virtue, and the conscience° of her worth,
That would be wooed, and not unsought be won,
Not obvious, not obtrusive, but retired,
505 The more desirable—or, to say all,
Nature herself, though pure of sinful thought,
Wrought in her so, that, seeing me, she turned.
I followed her; she what was honour knew,
And with obsequious majesty approved
510 My pleaded reason. To the nuptial bower
I led her blushing like the Morn; all Heaven
And happy constellations on that hour
Shed their selectest influence; the Earth
Gave sign of gratulation, and each hill;
515 Joyous the birds; fresh gales and gentle airs
Whispered it to the woods, and from their wings
Flung rose, flung odours from the spicy shrub,
Disporting, till the amorous bird of night°
Sung spousal, and bid haste the Evening-star
520 On his hill-top to light the bridal lamp.
'Thus I have told thee all my state, and brought
My story to the sum of earthly bliss
Which I enjoy, and must confess to find
In all things else delight indeed, but such
525 As, used or not, works in the mind no change,
Nor vehement desire—these delicacies
I mean of taste, sight, smell, herbs, fruits, and flowers,
Walks, and the melody of birds; but here,
Far otherwise, transported I behold,
530 Transported touch; here passion first I felt,
Commotion strange, in all enjoyments else
Superior and unmoved, here only weak

---

498 **to his wife adhere** *adhaerebit uxori suae,* read the Vulgate
and Junius versions (Gen. ii, 24). 502 **conscience** con-
sciousness 518 **the amorous bird of night** cf. v, 40

Against the charm of beauty's powerful glance.°
Or Nature failed in me, and left some part
Not proof enough such object to sustain,   535
Or, from my side subducting, took perhaps
More than enough—at least on her bestowed
Too much of ornament, in outward show
Elaborate, of inward less exact.°
For well I understand in the prime end   540
Of Nature her the inferior, in the mind
And inward faculties, which most excel;
In outward also her resembling less
His image who made both, and less expressing
The character of that dominion given   545
O'er other creatures. Yet when I approach
Her loveliness, so absolute° she seems
And in herself complete, so well to know
Her own, that what she wills to do or say
Seems wisest, virtuousest, discreetest, best.   550
All higher knowledge in her presence falls
Degraded; Wisdom in discourse with her
Loses, discountenanced, and like Folly shows;
Authority and Reason on her wait,
As one intended first, not after made   555
Occasionally; and, to consúmmate all,
Greatness of mind and nobleness their seat
Build in her loveliest, and create an awe
About her, as a guard angelic placed.'
    To whom the Angel, with contracted brow: 560
'Accuse not Nature, she hath done her part;
Do thou but thine, and be not diffident
Of Wisdom; she deserts thee not if thou
Dismiss not her, when most thou need'st her nigh,
By áttribúting overmuch to things   565
Less excellent, as thou thself perceiv'st.
For what admir'st thou, what transports thee so?
An outside; fair, no doubt, and worthy well
Thy cherishing, thy honouring, and thy love—
Not thy subjection, weigh with her thyself,   570
Then value: oft-times nothing profits more
Than self-esteem, grounded on just and right

532–33 cf. *Samson Agonistes*, 1003–07 538–39 *Samson
Agonistes*, 1025–26 547 **absolute** perfect, as at 421

Well managed. Of that skill, the more thou know'st,
The more she will acknowledge thee her head,
575 And to realities yield all her shows,
Made so adorn for thy delight the more,
So awful, that with honour thou may'st love
Thy mate, who sees when thou art seen least wise.
But, if the sense of touch, whereby mankind
580 Is propagated, seem such dear delight
Beyond all other, think the same vouchsafed
To cattle and each beast; which would not be
To them made common and divulged if aught
Therein enjoyed were worthy to subdue
585 The soul of Man or passion in him move.
What higher in her society thou find'st
Attractive, human, rational, love still:
In loving thou dost well, in passion not,
Wherein true love consists not. Love refines
590 The thoughts, and heart enlarges, hath his seat
In Reason, and is judicious, is the scale°
By which to heavenly love thou may'st ascend,
Not sunk in carnal pleasure, for which cause
Among the beasts no mate for thee was found.'
595   To whom thus, half abashed, Adam replied:
'Neither her outside formed so fair, nor aught
In procreation, common to all kinds
(Though higher of the genial° bed by far,
And with mysterious reverence, I deem),
600 So much delights me as those graceful acts,°
Those thousand decencies,° that daily flow
From all her words and actions, mixed with love
And sweet compliance, which declare unfeigned
Union of mind, or in us both one soul—
605 Harmony to behold in wedded pair
More grateful than harmonious sound to the ear.
Yet these subject not; I to thee disclose
What inward thence I feel, not therefore foiled,
Who meet with various objects, from the sense
610 Variously representing; yet, still free,

591 **scale** ladder   598 **genial** nuptial   600 **graceful acts** also
attributed to Belial, ii, 109   601 **decencies** graces, winsome
traits

Approve the best, and follow what I approve.°
To love thou blam'st me not, for Love, thou say'st,
Leads up to Heaven, is both the way and guide;
Bear with me, then, if lawful what I ask.
Love not the Heavenly Spirits,° and how their love   615
Express they, by looks only, or do they mix
Irradiance, virtual or immediate touch?'
    To whom the Angel, with a smile that glowed
Celestial rosy-red, Love's proper hue,
Answered: 'Let it suffice thee that thou know'st   620
Us happy, and without Love no happiness.
Whatever pure thou in the body enjoy'st
(And pure thou wert created) we enjoy
In eminence, and obstacle find none
Of membrane, joint, or limb, exclusive bars;   625
Easier than air with air, if Spirits embrace,
Total they mix, union of pure with pure
Desiring, nor restrained conveyance need
As flesh to mix with flesh, or soul with soul.
But I can now no more: the parting Sun   630
Beyond the Earth's green cape and verdant isles°
Hesperean sets, my signal to depart.
Be strong, live happy, and love! but first of all
Him whom to love is to obey,° and keep
His great command; take heed lest passion sway   635
Thy judgement to do aught which else free-will
Would not admit; thine and of all thy sons
The weal or woe in thee is placed; beware!
I in thy persevering shall rejoice,
And all the Blest. Stand fast; to stand or fall   640
Free in thine own arbitrament it lies.
Perfect within, no outward aid require;
And all temptation to transgress repel.'
    So saying, he arose, whom Adam thus
Followed with benediction: 'Since to part,   645

608–11 Adam gives reassurances that he is still making
reasonable choices. 615 **Heavenly Spirits** cf. iv, 361; vi, 788;
also ii, 824–25 631 **green cape and verdant isles** evidently a
reference to Cape Verde and the Cape Verde Islands on the
west (which is what *Hesperean* [632] means) coast of
Africa. 634 "For this is the love of God, that we keep his
commandments" (1 John, v, 3).

Go, Heavenly Guest,° Ethereal Messenger,
Sent from whose sovran goodness I adore.
Gentle to me and affable hath been
Thy condescension, and shall be honoured° ever
650 With grateful memory. Thou to Mankind
Be good° and friendly still, and oft return.'
  So parted they, the Angel up to Heaven
From the thick shade, and Adam to his bower.

BOOK IX

THE ARGUMENT

Satan having compassed the Earth, with meditated guile returns as a mist by night into Paradise; enters into the Serpent sleeping. Adam and Eve in the morning go forth to their labours, which Eve proposes to divide in several places, each labouring apart; Adam consents not, alleging the danger lest that enemy of whom they were forewarned should attempt her found alone. Eve, loth to be thought not circumspect or firm enough, urges her going apart, the rather desirous to make trial of her strength; Adam at last yields. The Serpent finds her alone: his subtle approach, first gazing, then speaking, with much flattery extolling Eve above all other creatures. Eve, wondering to hear the Serpent speak, asks how he attained to human speech and such understanding not till now; the Serpent answers that by tasting of a certain tree in the garden he attained both to speech and reason, till then void of both. Eve requires him to bring her to that tree, and finds it to be the Tree of Knowledge forbidden; the Serpent, now grown bolder, with many wiles and arguments induces her at length to eat. She, pleased with the taste, deliberates a while whether to impart thereof to Adam or not; at last brings him of the fruit; relates what persuaded her to eat thereof. Adam, at first amazed, but perceiving her lost, resolves, through vehemence of love, to perish with her, and, extenuating the trespass, eats also of the fruit. The effects thereof in them both; they seek to cover their nakedness; then fall to variance and accusation of one another.

No more of talk where God or Angel Guest°
With Man, as with his friend, familiar used
To sit indulgent, and with him partake

1 **Angel Guest** cf. v, 328

Rural repast, permitting him the while
5　Venial discourse unblamed. I now must change
Those notes to tragic, foul distrust, and breach
Disloyal on the part of man, revolt
And disobedience; on the part of Heaven,
Now alienated, distance and distaste,
10　Anger and just rebuke, and judgement given,
That brought into this World a world of woe,°
Sin and her shadow Death, and Misery,
Death's harbinger. Sad task,° yet argument°
Not less but more heroic than the wrath
15　Of stern Achilles on his foe° pursued
Thrice fugitive about Troy wall; or rage
Of Turnus for Lavinia disespoused;°
Or Neptune's ire, or Juno's, that so long
Perplexed the Greek° and Cytherea's son:°
20　If answerable style I can obtain
Of my celestial patroness, who deigns
Her nightly visitation unimplored,
And dictates to me slumbering, or inspires
Easy my unpremeditated verse;
25　Since first this subject for heroic song
Pleased me, long choosing and beginning late;
Not sedulous by nature to indite
Wars, hitherto the only argument
Heroic deemed, chief mastery to dissect
30　With long and tedious havoc fabled knights
In battles feigned (the better fortitude
Of patience° and heroic martyrdom
Unsung), or to describe races and games,
Or tilting furniture, emblazoned shields,
35　Impresses° quaint, caparisons° and steeds,

11　**a world of woe** cf. viii, 332–33　13　**Sad task** cf. v,
564　**argument** subject　15　**his foe** Hector in the *Iliad*　17
Lavinia disespoused As related in the latter part of the *Aeneid*,
the daughter of Latinus king of Latium had been betrothed to
Turnus but married Aeneas.　19　**the Greek** Ulysses **Cytherea's
son** Cytherea is Venus, mother of Aeneas.　31–32　**the better
fortitude/ Of patience** This also sounds personal.　35
Impresses emblems on knights' shields (Italian *imprese*—
something stamped on)　**caparisons** ornamental coverings for
horses

Bases° and tinsel trappings, gorgeous knights
At joust and tournament, then marshalled feast
Served up in hall with sewers and seneschals°—
The skill of artifice or office mean,
Not that which justly gives heroic name   40
To person or to poem. Me, of these
Nor skilled nor studious, higher argument
Remains, sufficient of itself to raise
That name, unless an age too late,° or cold
Climate,° or years, damp my intended wing   45
Depressed; and much they may if all be mine,
Not hers who brings it nightly to my ear.
    The sun was sunk, and after him the star
Of Hesperus, whose office is to bring
Twilight upon the Earth, short arbiter   50
'Twixt day and night, and now from end to end
Night's hemisphere had veiled the horizon round,
When Satan, who late fled before the threats
Of Gabriel out of Eden, now improved
In meditated fraud and malice, bent   55
On Man's destruction, maugre° what might hap
Of heavier on himself, fearless returned.
By night he fled, and at midnight returned
From compassing the Earth; cautious of day,°
Since Uriel, Regent of the Sun, descried   60
His entrance and forewarned the Cherubim
That kept their watch. Thence full of anguish driven,

---

36 **Bases** housings for horses. Or possibly the reference is to
a kilt which hung from the waists of knights on horseback to
about their knees. The word is also used of the lower part of
a shield. 38 **sewers and seneschals** waiters and house
stewards 44 **an age too late** for epic poetry 44–45 **cold/
Climate** a subject Milton kept returning to, as when, on the
last page of his *History of Britain,* he wrote, "the sun, which
we want, ripens wits as well as fruits." The last sentence of
the first paragraph of *Areopagitica* begins: "But if from the
industry of a life wholly dedicated to studious labors, and those
natural endowments haply not the worst for two and fifty
degrees of northern latitude . . ." 56 **maugre** in spite of, as
at iii, 255 58–59 "And the Lord said unto Satan, Whence
comest thou? Then Satan answered the Lord, and said, From
going to and fro in the earth, and from walking up and down
in it" (Job, i, 7).

The space of seven continued nights he rode
With darkness, thrice the equinoctial line
65 He circled, four times crossed the car of Night
From pole to pole,° traversing each colure,°
On the eighth returned, and on the coast averse
From entrance or cherubic watch by stealth
Found unsuspected way. There was a place
70 (Now not, though Sin, not Time, first wrought
    the change)
Where Tigris, at the foot of Paradise,
Into a gulf shot under ground, till part
Rose up a fountain by the Tree of Life;
In with the river sunk, and with it rose
75 Satan, involved in rising mist; then sought
Where to lie hid. Sea he had searched and land
From Eden over Pontus, and the Pool
Maeotis,° up beyond the river Ob;°
Downward as far antarctic; and, in length,
80 West from Orontes° to the ocean barred
At Darien,° thence to the land where flows
Ganges and Indus. Thus the orb he roamed
With narrow search, and with inspection deep
Considered every creature, which of all
85 Most opportune might serve his wiles, and found
The Serpent subtlest beast of all the field.°
Him, after long debate,° irresolute
Of thoughts revolved, his final sentence chose
Fit vessel, fittest imp of fraud, in whom

---

66 **From pole to pole** cf. iii, 560 **colure** defined by the *Oxford
English Dictionary* as "each of two great circles which intersect
each other at right angles at the poles, and divide the
equinoctial and the ecliptic into four equal parts. One passes
through the equinoctial, the other the solstitial, points of the
ecliptic." 77–78 **Pontus, and the Pool/ Maeotis** the Black Sea
and the Sea of Azov 78 **Ob** in Siberia 80 **Orontes** the river
in Syria 81 **Darien** the Isthmus of Panama, which "barred"
the way from the Atlantic to the Pacific 86 Compare the
almost punning return at 560, and the previous use of the line
at vii, 495. Without reference to the serpent, "beast of the
field" begins one line in the seventh book (522) and ends
another in the tenth (176). 87 **long debate** cf. ii, 390

To enter, and his dark suggestions° hide   90
From sharpest sight; for in the wily snake,
Whatever sleights, none would suspicious mark,
As from his wit and native subtlety
Proceeding, which, in other beasts observed,
Doubt might beget of diabolic power   95
Active within beyond the sense of brute.
Thus he resolved, but first from inward grief
His bursting passion into plaints thus poured:°
  'O Earth, how like to Heaven, if not preferred°
More justly, seat worthier of gods, as built   100
With second thoughts, reforming what was old!
For what God, after better, worse would build?
Terrestrial Heaven, danced round by other Heavens,
That shine, yet bear their bright officious° lamps,
Light above light, for thee alone, as seems,   105
In thee concentring all their precious beams
Of sacred influence:° As God in Heaven
Is centre, yet extends to all, so thou
Centring receiv'st from all those orbs; in thee,
Not in themselves, all their known virtue appears,°   110
Productive in herb, plant, and nobler birth
Of creatures animate with gradual life
Of growth, sense, reason, all summed up in Man.
With what delight could I have walked thee round,
If I could joy in aught—sweet interchange   115
Of hill and valley,° rivers, woods, and plains,°
Now land, now sea, and shores with forest crowned,
Rocks, dens, and caves;° but I in none of these
Find place or refuge, and the more I see
Pleasures about me, so much more I feel   120
Torment within me, as from the hateful siege
Of contraries; all good to me becomes
Bane,° and in Heaven much worse would be my state.
But neither here seek I, no, nor in Heaven,
To dwell, unless by mastering Heaven's Supreme,   125

90 **suggestions** temptations 98 Note the passionate alliteration. 99 cf. vii, 328–29 104 **officious** as at viii, 99 107 **sacred influence** cf. ii, 1034 110 **virtue appears** elide, for scansion 116 **hill and valley** cf. ii, 495; vi, 784 **rivers, woods, and plains** cf. viii, 275 118 **Rocks, dens, and caves** cf. ii, 621 122–23 cf. iv, 109

Nor hope to be myself less miserable
By what I seek, but others to make such
As I, though thereby worse to me redound.
For only in destroying I find ease
130 To my relentless thoughts; and him destroyed,
Or won to what may work his utter loss,°
For whom all this was made, all this will soon
Follow, as to him linked in weal or woe°—
In woe then, that destruction wide may range:
135 To me shall be the glory sole among
The Infernal Powers, in one day to have marred
What he, Almighty styled, six nights and days
Continued making, and who knows how long
Before had been contriving? though perhaps
140 Not longer than since I in one night freed
From servitude inglorious well-nigh half
The angelic name, and thinner left the throng
Of his adorers. He, to be avenged,
And to repair his numbers thus impaired—
145 Whether such virtue, spent of old, now failed
More Angels to create (if they at least
Are his created), or to spite us more—
Determined to advance into our room
A creature formed of earth, and him endow,
150 Exalted from so base original,°
With heavenly spoils, our spoils. What he decreed
He effected; Man he made, and for him built
Magnificent this World, and Earth his seat,
Him lord pronounced, and, O indignity!
155 Subjected to his service Angel-wings
And flaming ministers,° to watch and tend
Their earthy° charge. Of these the vigilance
I dread, and to elude, thus wrapped in mist
Of midnight vapour, glide obscure, and pry
160 In every bush and brake, where hap may find
The Serpent sleeping, in whose mazy folds
To hide me, and the dark intent I bring.
O foul descent! that I, who erst contended

131 **utter loss** cf. ii, 440; iii, 308   133 **weal or woe** cf. viii, 638
150 **original** origin   156 **flaming ministers** "who maketh his
angels spirits; his ministers a flaming fire" (Ps. civ, 4).   157 **earthy**
There is no textual authority for earthly.

With Gods to sit the highest, am now constrained
Into a beast, and, mixed with bestial slime, 165
This essence to incarnate and imbrute,
That to the height of deity aspired;
But what will not ambition and revenge
Descend to? who aspires must down as low
As high he soared, obnoxious,° first or last, 170
To basest things. Revenge, at first though sweet,
Bitter ere long back on itself recoils;°
Let it; I reck not, so it light well aimed,
Since higher I fall short, on him who next
Provokes my envy, this new favourite 175
Of Heaven, this man of clay, son of despite,
Whom, us the more to spite, his Maker raised
From dust: spite then with spite is best repaid.'°
    So saying, through each thicket, dank or dry,
Like a black mist low-creeping, he held on 180
His midnight search, where soonest he might find
The Serpent.° Him fast sleeping soon he found,
In labyrinth of many a round self-rolled,
His head the midst, well stored with subtle wiles;
Not yet in horrid shade or dismal den, 185
Nor° nocent yet, but on the grassy herb,
Fearless, unfeared, he slept. In at his mouth
The Devil entered, and his brutal sense,
In heart or head, possessing soon inspired
With act intelligential, but his sleep 190
Disturbed not, waiting close° the approach of morn.
Now, whenas sacred light began to dawn
In Eden on the humid flowers, that breathed
Their morning incense, when all things that breathe
From the Earth's great altar send up silent praise 195
To the Creator, and his nostrils fill
With grateful smell,° forth came the human pair
And joined their vocal worship to the choir
Of creatures wanting voice; that done, partake

170 **obnoxious** exposed (to)   172 **back on itself recoils** cf. ii, 759; vi,
194   178 So Prometheus says, "I but answered insult with insult"
(Aeschylus, *Prometheus Bound,* 970). 181–82 **might find/ The
Serpent** cf. 160–61   186 **Nor** *Not,* 1667   191 **close** hidden   196–97
"And the Lord smelled a sweet savour" (Gen. viii, 21).   197
grateful smell cf. iv, 165

200 The season, prime for sweetest scents and airs,
Then cómmune how that day they best may ply
Their growing work—for much their work outgrew
The hands' dispatch of two gardening so wide.
And Eve first to her husband thus began:
205   'Adam, well may we labour still to dress
This garden, still to tend plant, herb, and flower,
Our pleasant task enjoined; but, till more hands
Aid us, the work under our labour grows
Luxurious by restraint; what we by day
210 Lop overgrown, or prune, or prop, or bind,
One night or two with wanton growth° derides,
Tending to wild. Thou, therefore, now advise,
Or hear° what to my mind first thoughts present:
Let us divide our labours—thou where choice
215 Leads thee, or where most needs, whether to wind
The woodbine round this arbour, or direct
The clasping ivy where to climb, while I
In yonder spring° of roses intermixed
With myrtle find what to redress till noon.
220 For, while so near each other thus all day
Our task we choose, what wonder if so near
Looks intervene and smiles, or object new
Casual discourse draw on, which intermits
Our day's work, brought to little, though begun
225 Early, and the hour of supper comes unearned.'
  To whom mild answer Adam thus returned:
'Sole Eve, associate sole, to me beyond
Compare° above all living creatures° dear,
Well hast thou motioned, well thy thoughts employed
230 How we might best fulfil the work which here
God hath assigned us, nor of me shalt pass
Unpraised; for nothing lovelier can be found
In woman than to study household good,
And good works in her husband to promote.
235 Yet not so strictly hath our Lord imposed
Labour as to debar us when we need
Refreshment, whether food, or talk between,

211 **wanton growth** cf. iv, 629   213 **hear** *bear*, 1674   218 **spring**
thicket of young shrubs   227–28 **beyond/ Compare** cf. i, 587–88;
iii, 138   228 **living creatures** cf. iv, 287; vii, 413, 455; viii, 370

Food of the mind, or this sweet intercourse
Of looks and smiles; for smiles from reason flow,
To brute denied, and are of love the food— 240
Love, not the lowest end of human life.
For not to irksome toil but to delight
He made us, and delight to reason joined.
These paths and bowers doubt not but our joint hands
Will keep from wilderness with ease, as wide 245
As we need walk, till younger hands ere long°
Assist us. But, if much convérse perhaps
Thee satiate, to short absence I could yield,
For solitude sometimes is best society,°
And short retirement urges sweet return. 250
But other doubt possesses me, lest harm
Befall thee, severed from me, for thou know'st
What hath been warned us—what malicious foe,
Envying our happiness, and of his own
Despairing, seeks to work us woe and shame 255
By sly assault, and somewhere nigh at hand
Watches, no doubt, with greedy hope to find
His wish and best advantage, us asunder,
Hopeless to circumvent us joined, where each
To other speedy aid might lend at need; 260
Whether his first design be to withdraw
Our fealty from God, or to disturb
Conjugal love, than which perhaps no bliss
Enjoyed by us excites his envy more;
Or this, or worse, leave not the faithful side 265
That gave thee being, still shades thee and protects.
The wife, where danger or dishonour lurks,
Safest and seemliest by her husband stays,
Who guards her, or with her the worst endures.'
  To whom the virgin majesty of Eve, 270
As one who loves and some unkindness meets,
With sweet austere composure thus replied:
  'Offspring of Heaven° and Earth, and all Earth's lord,
That such an enemy we have, who seeks
Our ruin, both by thee informed I learn, 275

246 **ere long** cf. 172 249 a Ciceronian sentiment 273
Offspring of Heaven Compare other applications of this
phrase, ii, 310; iii, 1.

And from the parting Angel overheard,
As in a shady nook I stood behind,
Just then returned at shut of evening flowers.
But that thou shouldst my firmness therefore doubt
280 To God or thee, because we have a foe
May tempt it, I expected not to hear.
His violence thou fear'st not, being such
As we, not capable of death or pain,
Can either not receive, or can repel.
285 His fraud is, then, thy fear; which plain infers
Thy equal fear that my firm faith° and love
Can by his fraud be shaken or seduced—
Thoughts, which how found they harbour in thy breast,
Adam, misthought of her to thee so dear?'
290   To whom, with healing words,° Adam replied:
'Daughter of God and Man, immortal Eve,°
For such thou art, from sin and blame entire,°
Not diffident of thee do I dissuade
Thy absence from my sight, but to avoid
295 The attempt itself, intended by our foe.
For he who tempts, though in vain, at least asperses
The tempted with dishonour foul, supposed
Not incorruptible of faith, not proof
Against temptation. Thou thyself with scorn
300 And anger wouldst resent the offered wrong,
Though ineffectual found; misdeem not, then,
If such affront I labour to avert
From thee alone, which on us both at once
The enemy, though bold, will hardly dare;
305 Or, daring, first on me the assault shall light.
Nor thou his malice and false guile contemn;
Subtle he needs must be who could seduce
Angels, nor think superfluous others' aid.
I from the influence of thy looks receive
310 Access in every virtue—in thy sight
More wise, more watchful, stronger, if need were
Of outward strength; while shame, thou looking on,
Shame to be overcome or overreached,

286 **firm faith** cf. a Satanic phrase, ii, 36   290 **healing words**
cf. *Samson Agonistes,* 605   291 Identical, except for one word,
with iv, 660.   292 **entire** untouched, whole (integer)

Would utmost vigour raise, and raised unite.
Why shouldst not thou like sense within thee feel   *315*
When I am present, and thy trial choose
With me, best witness of thy virtue tried?'
  So spake domestic Adam in his care
And matrimonial love; but Eve, who thought
Less áttribúted to her faith sincere,   *320*
Thus her reply with accent sweet renewed:
'If this be our condition, thus to dwell
In narrow circuit straitened by a foe,
Subtle or violent, we not endued
Single with like defence wherever met,   *325*
How are we happy, still in fear of harm?
But harm precedes not sin; only our foe
Tempting affronts us with his foul esteem
Of our integrity; his foul esteem
Sticks no dishonour on our front,° but turns   *330*
Foul on himself—then wherefore shunned or feared
By us, who rather double honour gain
From his surmise proved false, find peace within,
Favour from Heaven, our witness, from the event?
And what is faith, love, virtue, unassayed   *335*
Alone, without exterior help sustained?°
Let us not then suspect our happy state
Left so imperfect by the Maker wise
As not secure to single or combined.
Frail is our happiness if this be so,   *340*
And Eden were no Eden, thus exposed.'
  To whom thus Adam fervently replied:°
'O Woman, best are all things as the will
Of God ordained them; his creating hand
Nothing imperfect or deficient left   *345*
Of all that he created, much less Man,
Or aught that might his happy state° secure,
Secure from outward force. Within himself

330 **front** brow, a pun with *affronts* (328)   335–36 Compare the
famous sentence in *Areopagitica* that begins, "I cannot praise a
fugitive and cloistered virtue, unexercised and unbreathed, that
never sallies out and sees her adversary. . . ."   342 One of the
many formula lines of speaking, here comparable to iv,
440.   347 **happy state** the last of many uses of this phrase, i,
29, 141; iv, 519; v, 234, 504, 536, 830; viii, 331; ix, 337

The danger lies, yet lies within his power;
350 Against his will he can receive no harm.
But God left free the Will; for what obeys
Reason is free, and Reason he made right,
But bid her well beware, and still erect,°
Lest, by some fair appearing good surprised,
355 She dictate false, and misinform the Will
To do what God expressly hath forbid.
Not then mistrust, but tender love, enjoins
That I should mind thee oft; and mind° thou me.
Firm we subsist, yet possible to swerve,
360 Since Reason not impossibly may meet
Some specious object by the foe suborned,
And fall into deception unaware,
Not keeping strictest watch,° as she was warned.
Seek not temptation, then, which to avoid
365 Were better, and most likely if from me
Thou sever not; trial will come unsought.
Wouldst thou approve thy constancy, approve
First thy obedience; the other who can know,
Not seeing thee attempted, who attest?
370 But if thou think trial unsought may find
Us both securer than thus warned thou seem'st,
Go; for thy stay, not free, absents thee more.
Go in thy native innocence; rely
On what thou hast of virtue; summon all;
375 For God towards thee hath done his part: do thine.'°
    So spake the Patriarch of Mankind, but Eve
Persisted; yet submiss, though last,° replied:
    'With thy permission, then, and thus forewarned,
Chiefly by what thy own last reasoning words
380 Touched only, that our trial, when least sought,
May find us both perhaps far less prepared,
The willinger I go, nor much expect
A foe so proud will first the weaker seek;°
So bent, the more shall shame him his repulse.'
385   Thus saying, from her husband's hand her hand

353 **still erect** always on guard   358 **mind** remind   363 **strictest
watch** cf. iv, 783   375 Adam passes on Raphael's admonition,
viii, 561–62.   377 **though last** i.e., determined to get in the last
word   383 The most foolish thought of all: cf. 421–24, 480–90

Soft° she withdrew, and, like a wood-nymph light,
Oread or Dryad,° or of Delia's° train,
Betook her to the groves, but Delia's self
In gait surpassed and goddesslike deport,
Though not as she with bow and quiver armed,°   390
But with such gardening tools as Art, yet rude,
Guiltless of fire, had formed, or Angels brought.
To Pales,° or Pomona,° thus adorned,
Likest° she seemed, Pomona when she fled
Vertumnus,° or to Ceres in her prime,   395
Yet virgin of Proserpina from Jove.°
Her long with ardent look his eye pursued°
Delighted, but desiring more her stay.
Oft he to her his charge of quick return
Repeated; she to him as oft engaged   400
To be returned by noon amid the bower,
And all things in best order to invite
Noontide repast, or afternoon's repose.
O much deceived, much failing, hapless Eve,
Of thy presumed return! event perverse!   405
Thou never from that hour in Paradise
Found'st either sweet repast° or sound repose;
Such ambush, hid among sweet flowers and shades,
Waited, with hellish rancour imminent,
To intercept thy way, or send thee back   410
Despoiled of innocence, of faith, of bliss.
For now, and since first break of dawn, the Fiend,
Mere serpent° in appearance, forth was come,

386 **Soft** It is profitably ambiguous whether this is an adjective
or an adverb; cf. v, 17.   387 **Oread or Dryad** mountain or
wood nymph   **Delia** Diana   389–90 "Sometimes Diana he her
takes to be,/ But misseth bow, and shafts, and buskins to her
knee" *Faerie Queene*, I, vi, 16.   393 **Pales** Roman protectress
of flocks and herds   **Pomona** as at v, 378; appropriately
assigned a pruning hook by Ovid (cf. 391)   394 **Likest**
Likeliest, 1674   395 **Vertumnus** the god of vegetative change
(verto)   395–96 cf. iv, 268 ff.   397 cf. iv, 125, 572   407 **sweet
repast** cf. v, 630; viii, 214   413 **Mere serpent** all serpent, in
contrast to Rabbinical glosses and some previous literature
(such as Andreini's play *L'Adamo,* 1613) and old illustrations
(e.g., Raphael's "Adam and Eve," 1510) that assigned a human
countenance to the tempting serpent

And on his quest where likeliest he might find
415 The only two of mankind, but in them
The whole included race, his purposed prey.
In bower and field he sought, where any tuft
Of grove or garden-plot more pleasant lay,
Their tendance or plantation for delight;
420 By fountain or by shady rivulet
He sought them both, but wished his hap might find
Eve separate; he wished, but not with hope
Of what so seldom chanced, when to his wish,
Beyond his hope, Eve separate he spies,°
425 Veiled in a cloud of fragrance, where she stood,
Half-spied, so thick the roses bushing round
About her glowed, oft stooping to support
Each flower of slender stalk, whose head, though gay
Carnation, purple, azure, or specked with gold,
430 Hung drooping unsustained. Them she upstays
Gently with myrtle band, mindless the while
Herself, though fairest unsupported flower,°
From her best prop so far, and storm so nigh.
Nearer he drew, and many a walk traversed
435 Of stateliest covert, cedar, pine, or palm;
Then voluble° and bold, now hid, now seen
Among thick-woven arborets and flowers
Imbordered on each bank, the hand° of Eve—
Spot more delicious than those gardens feigned
440 Or of revived Adonis,° or renowned
Alcinous,° host of old Laertes' son,
Or that, not mystic,° where the sapient king
Held dalliance with his fair Egyptian spouse.°
Much he the place admired, the person more.
445 As one who long in populous city pent,
Where houses thick and sewers annoy the air,

424 cf. 422   432 cf. iv, 270   436 **voluble** rolling   438 **hand**
handiwork   440 **revived Adonis** after being slain by the boar,
cf. i, 46 ff.   441 **Alcinous** see v, 341; whose gardens were
likewise paired by Pliny with the gardens of Adonis, *Natural
History*, XIX, iv, 19   442 **not mystic** It is disputed whether this
means (a) not mythical (unlike the garden of Adonis) or (b)
not symbolic or allegorical, contrary to common Biblical
interpretation.   442–43 a reference to the marriage of
Solomon with "Pharaoh's daughter" (1 Kings, iii, 1)

Forth issuing on a summer's morn to breathe
Among the pleasant villages and farms
Adjoined, from each thing met conceives delight,
The smell of grain, or tedded grass, or kine,   450
Or dairy, each rural sight, each rural sound;
If chance with nymphlike step fair virgin pass,
What pleasing seemed, for her° now pleases more,°
She most, and in her looks sums all delight:
Such pleasure took the Serpent to behold   455
This flowery plat,° the sweet recess of Eve
Thus early, thus alone; her heavenly form
Angelic, but more soft and feminine,
Her graceful innocence, her every air
Of gesture or least action, overawed   460
His malice, and with rapine sweet bereaved
His fierceness of the fierce intent it brought.
That space the Evil One abstracted stood
From his own evil, and for the time remained
Stupidly good, of enmity disarmed,   465
Of guile, of hate, of envy, of revenge.
But the hot hell that always in him burns,
Though in mid Heaven, soon ended his delight,
And tortures him now more the more he sees
Of pleasure not for him ordained: then soon   470
Fierce hate he recollects, and all his thoughts
Of mischief, gratulating, thus excites:
   'Thoughts, whither have ye led me? with what sweet
Compulsion thus transported to forget
What hither brought us? hate, not love, nor hope   475
Of Paradise for Hell, hope here to taste
Of pleasure, but all pleasure to destroy,
Save what is in destroying; other joy
To me is lost. Then let me not let pass
Occasion which now smiles: behold alone   480
The Woman, opportune to all attempts;
Her husband, for I view far round, not nigh,
Whose higher intellectual more I shun,
And strength, of courage haughty, and of limb

452–53 "And all, though pleasant, yet she made much more."
Faerie Queene, II, vi, 24, 5   453 **for her** on her account   456
plat plot

485 Heroic built, though of terrestrial mould;
    Foe not informidable, exempt from wound,
    I not; so much hath Hell debased and pain
    Enfeebled me to what I was in Heaven.
    She fair, divinely fair, fit love for gods,
490 Not terrible, though terror be in love,
    And beauty, not approached by stronger hate,
    Hate stronger under show of love well feigned,
    The way which to her ruin now I tend.'°
        So spake the Enemy of Mankind, enclosed
495 In serpent, inmate bad, and toward Eve
    Addressed his way; not with indented wave,
    Prone on the ground, as since, but on his rear,
    Circular base of rising folds, that towered
    Fold above fold, a surging maze; his head
500 Crested aloft, and carbuncle his eyes;
    With burnished neck of verdant gold, erect
    Amidst his circling spires, that on the grass
    Floated redundant. Pleasing was his shape
    And lovely; never since of serpent kind
505 Lovelier—not those that in Illyria changed°
    Hermione and Cadmus, or the god
    In Epidaurus;° nor to which transformed
    Ammonian Jove,° or Capitoline,° was seen,
    He with Olympias, this with her who bore
510 Scipio,° the height of Rome. With tract oblique
    At first, as one who sought access but feared
    To interrupt, sidelong he works his way.
    As when a ship, by skilful steersman wrought
    Nigh river's mouth or foreland, where the wind

493 This sounds like the end of a stage speech.   505 ff. After
founding Thebes, *Cadmus* retired to *Illyria,* north of the
Adriatic, where he prayed that he might be transformed to a
serpent, and the prayer was granted for both him and his wife
Hermione (or Harmonia).   506–07 **the god/ In Epidaurus** In
Argolis, the Peloponnesus, the deity of healing, Aesculapius,
was supposed to put in an oracular appearance as a serpent.
508 **Ammonian Jove** changed to a serpent to woo *Olympias,*
the mother of Alexander the Great   **Capitoline** Jove as
presider over the Roman Capitol   510 **Scipio** Africanus (the
Elder) (237–183 B.C.), Rome's greatest general up to the time
of Julius Caesar

Veers oft, as oft so steers and shifts her sail,   515
So varied he, and of his tortuous train
Curled many a wanton wreath in sight of Eve
To lure her eye; she, busied, heard the sound
Of rustling leaves but minded not, as used
To such disport before her through the field   520
From every beast, more duteous at her call
Than at Circean° call the herd disguised.
He, bolder now, uncalled before her stood,
But as in gaze admiring. Oft he bowed
His turret° crest and sleek enamelled° neck,   525
Fawning, and licked the ground whereon she trod.
His gentle dumb expression turned at length
The eye of Eve to mark his play; he, glad
Of her attention gained, with serpent-tongue
Organic, or impulse of vocal air,   530
His fraudulent temptation thus began:
   'Wonder not, sovran mistress, if perhaps
Thou canst who art sole wonder, much less arm
Thy looks, the heaven of mildness, with disdain,
Displeased that I approach thee thus, and gaze   535
Insatiate, I thus single, nor have feared
Thy awful brow, more awful thus retired.
Fairest resemblance of thy Maker fair,
Thee all things living gaze on, all things thine
By gift, and thy celestial beauty adore,   540
With ravishment beheld, there best beheld
Where universally admired. But here,
In this enclosure wild, these beasts among,
Beholders rude, and shallow to discern
Half what in thee is fair, one man except,   545
Who sees thee? (and what is one?) who shouldst be seen
A Goddess among Gods, adored and served
By Angels numberless, thy daily train?'
   So glozed° the Tempter, and his proem° tuned.
Into the heart of Eve his words made way,   550
Though at the voice much marvelling; at length,

---

522 In the *Odyssey* the enchantress Circe changed some of
Ulysses' men into swine—a myth that became the basis of
"Comus." 525 **turret** towering **enamelled** variegated 549
glozed flattered **proem** preliminary speech

Not unamazed, she thus in answer spake:
  'What may this mean? Language of Man pronounced
By tongue of brute, and human sense expressed?
555 The first at least of these I thought denied
To beasts, whom God on their creation-day
Created mute to all articulate sound;
The latter I demur,° for in their looks
Much reason, and in their actions, oft appears.
560 Thee, Serpent, subtlest beast of all the field°
I knew, but not with human voice endued;
Redouble, then, this miracle, and say,
How cam'st thou speakable of mute, and how
To me so friendly grown above the rest
565 Of brutal kind that daily are in sight:
Say, for such wonder claims attention due.'
  To whom the guileful Tempter thus replied:
'Empress of this fair World, resplendent Eve,
Easy to me it is to tell thee all
What thou command'st, and right thou shouldst be
570   obeyed.
I was at first as other beasts that graze
The trodden herb, of abject thoughts and low,
As was my food, nor aught but food discerned
Or sex, and apprehended nothing high,
575 Till on a day, roving the field, I chanced
A goodly tree far distant° to behold,
Loaden with fruit° of fairest colours mixed,
Ruddy and gold; I nearer drew to gaze,
When from the boughs a savoury odour blown,
580 Grateful to appetite, more pleased my sense
Than smell of sweetest fennel,° or the teats
Of ewe or goat dropping with milk at even,
Unsucked of lamb or kid, that tend their play.
To satisfy the sharp desire I had
585 Of tasting those fair apples, I resolved
Not to defer, hunger and thirst at once,

558 **The latter I demur** As for the question of beasts lacking
sense, I have my doubts. 560 cf. 86 576 **far distant** a
standard combination, iii, 428, 501, 621; iv, 453; vi, 551 576–77
tree . . . Loaden with fruit cf. iv, 147; viii, 306–07 581 **fennel**
This vegetable was supposed to be a favorite with snakes, as
helping them to shed their skins and to clear their sight.

Powerful persuaders, quickened at the scent
Of that alluring fruit, urged me so keen.
About the mossy trunk I wound me soon,
For, high from ground, the branches would require 590
Thy utmost reach, or Adam's: round the tree
All other beasts that saw, with like desire
Longing and envying stood, but could not reach.
Amid the tree now got, where plenty hung
Tempting so nigh, to pluck and eat° my fill 595
I spared not, for such pleasure till that hour
At feed or fountain never had I found.
Sated at length, ere long I might perceive
Strange alteration° in me, to degree
Of reason in my inward powers, and speech 600
Wanted not long, though to this shape retained.
Thenceforth to speculations high or deep
I turned my thoughts, and with capacious mind
Considered all things visible in Heaven,
Or Earth, or Middle,° all things fair and good. 605
But all that fair and good in thy divine
Semblance, and in thy beauty's heavenly ray,
United I beheld—no fair to thine
Equivalent or second, which compelled
Me thus, though importune perhaps, to come 610
And gaze, and worship thee of right declared
Sovran of creatures, universal Dame.'°
    So talked the spirited° sly Snake, and Eve,
Yet more amazed, unwary thus replied:
    'Serpent, thy overpraising leaves in doubt 615
The virtue of that fruit, in thee first proved.
But say, where grows the tree? from hence how far?
For many are the trees of God that grow
In Paradise, and various, yet unknown
To us; in such abundance lies our choice 620
As leaves a greater store of fruit untouched,
Still hanging incorruptible, till men
Grow up to their provision, and more hands

---

595 **to pluck and eat** cf. viii, 309   599 **Strange alteration** cf.
ii, 1024   605 **Middle** air   612 **universal Dame** Lady (Latin
domina) of the universe   613 **spirited** i.e., possessed by a
demon. Note the hissing sibilance.

Help to disburden Nature of her birth.'°
625   To whom the wily Adder, blithe and glad:
'Empress, the way is ready, and not long:
Beyond a row of myrtles, on a flat,
Fast by a fountain, one small thicket past
Of blowing° myrrh and balm;° if thou accept
630 My conduct, I can bring thee thither soon.'
    'Lead, then,' said Eve. He, leading, swiftly rolled
In tangles, and made intricate seem straight,
To mischief swift. Hope elevates, and joy
Brightens his crest, as when a wandering fire,°
635 Compact of° unctuous vapour, which the night
Condenses, and the cold environs round,
Kindled through agitation to a flame
(Which oft, they say, some evil spirit attends),
Hovering and blazing with delusive light,
640 Misleads the amazed night-wanderer from his way°
To bogs and mires, and oft through pond or pool,
There swallowed up and lost, from succour far,
So glistered the dire Snake, and into fraud
Led Eve, our credulous mother, to the Tree
645 Of Prohibition, root° of all our woe;
Which when she saw, thus to her guide she spake:
    'Serpent, we might have spared our coming hither,
Fruitless to me, though fruit be here to excess,
The credit of whose virtue rest with thee—
650 Wondrous, indeed, if cause of such effects.
But of this tree we may not taste nor touch;
God so commanded, and left that command
Sole daughter of his voice: the rest,° we live
Law to our selves; our reason is our law.'°
655   To whom the Tempter guilefully replied:
'Indeed? Hath God then said that of the fruit
Of all these garden-trees ye shall not eat,

624 **birth** in the original editions *bearth,* which shows the
meaning—what Nature bears, produce   629 **blowing** blooming
balm balsam tree   634 **wandering fire** will-o'-the-wisp   635
Compact of composed of   640 Puck in *A Midsummer-Night's
Dream* (II, i, 39) is said to "Mislead night-wanderers, laughing
at their harm."   645 **root** a pun (cf. 648)   653 **the rest** Latin
construction for "as to the rest"   654 "These are a law unto
themselves" (Rom. ii, 14).

Yet lords declared of all in earth or air?'
  To whom thus Eve, yet sinless: 'Of the fruit
Of each tree in the garden we may eat,   660
But of the fruit of this fair tree, amidst
The garden, God hath said, "Ye shall not eat
Thereof, nor shall ye touch it, lest ye die." '
  She scarce had said, though brief, when now more bold
The Tempter, but with show of zeal and love   665
To Man, and indignation at his wrong,
New part puts on, and, as to passion moved,
Fluctuates disturbed, yet comely, and in act
Raised as of some great matter to begin.
As when of old some orator renowned   670
In Athens or free Rome, where eloquence
Flourished, since mute, to some great cause addressed,
Stood in himself collected,° while each part,
Motion, each act, won audience ere the tongue
Sometimes in height began, as no delay   675
Of preface brooking through his zeal of right:
So standing, moving, or to height upgrown,
The Tempter, all impassioned, thus began:
  'O sacred, wise, and wisdom-giving Plant,
Mother of science,° now I feel thy power   680
Within me clear, not only to discern
Things in their causes,° but to trace the ways
Of highest agents, deemed however wise.
Queen of this Universe, do not believe
Those rigid threats of death; ye shall not die.°   685
How should ye? by the fruit? it gives you life
To knowledge; by the Threatener? look on me,
Me who have touched and tasted, yet both live
And life more perfect have attained than Fate
Meant me, by venturing higher than my lot.   690
Shall that be shut to Man which to the beast
Is open? or will God incense his ire
For such a petty trespass, and not praise

---

673 **Stood in himself collected** an Italian idiom indicating
complete self-possession 680 **science** knowledge 680–82
power . . . to discern/ Things in their causes a phrase based
on Virgil's *Georgics* (II, 490) 685 "And the serpent said unto
the woman, Ye shall not surely die" (Gen. iii, 4).

Rather your dauntless virtue, whom the pain
695 Of death denounced, whatever thing Death be,
Deterred not from achieving what might lead
To happier life, knowledge of good and evil?
Of good, how just? of evil, if what is evil
Be real, why not known, since easier shunned?
700 God, therefore, cannot hurt ye, and be just;
Not just, not God; not feared° then, nor obeyed:
Your fear itself of death removes the fear.°
Why, then, was this forbid? Why but to awe?
Why but to keep ye low and ignorant,
705 His worshippers? He knows that in the day
Ye eat thereof your eyes, that seem so clear
Yet are but dim, shall perfectly be then
Opened and cleared, and ye shall be as Gods,
Knowing both good and evil, as they know.
710 That ye should be as Gods, since I as Man,
Internal Man, is but proportion meet;
I, of brute, human; ye, of human, Gods.°
So ye shall die perhaps, by putting off
Human, to put on Gods—death to be wished,
715 Though threatened, which no worse than this can bring.
And what are Gods, that Man may not become
As they, participating godlike food?
The Gods are first, and that advantage use
On our belief, that all from them proceeds.
720 I question it, for this fair Earth I see,
Warmed by the Sun, producing every kind,
Them nothing. If they all things, who enclosed
Knowledge of good and evil° in this tree,
That whoso eats thereof forthwith attains
725 Wisdom without their leave? and wherein lies
The offence, that Man should thus attain to know?
What can your knowledge hurt him, or this tree
Impart against his will, if all be his?
Or is it envy? and can envy dwell

701 **not feared** not to be feared   701–02 The line of reasoning is that he who is not just is not God and consequently lacks the power to bring death to mankind.   710–12 An inference Adam repeats, 932–37.   723 **Knowledge of good and evil** cf. 697; vii, 543; also iv, 222; viii, 324; xi, 87

In heavenly breasts?° These, these and many more   730
Causes import your need of this fair fruit.
Goddess humane, reach, then, and freely taste.'
　　He ended, and his words, replete with guile,
Into her heart too easy entrance won:
Fixed on the fruit she gazed, which to behold   735
Might tempt alone, and in her ears the sound
Yet rung of his persuasive words, impregned°
With reason, to her seeming, and with truth.
Meanwhile the hour of noon drew on, and waked
An eager appetite, raised by the smell   740
So savory of that fruit, which with desire,°
Inclinable now grown to touch or taste,
Solicited her longing eye; yet first,
Pausing a while, thus to herself she mused:
　　'Great are thy virtues, doubtless, best of fruits,   745
Though kept from Man, and worthy to be admired,
Whose taste, too long forborne, at first assay
Gave elocution to the mute, and taught
The tongue not made for speech to speak thy praise.
Thy praise he also who forbids thy use   750
Conceals not from us, naming thee the Tree
Of Knowledge, knowledge both of good and evil;
Forbids us then to taste;° but his forbidding
Commends thee more, while it infers the good
By thee communicated, and our want;   755
For good unknown sure is not had, or, had
And yet unknown, is as not had at all.
In plain, then, what forbids he but to know,
Forbids us good, forbids us to be wise?
Such prohibitions bind not. But, if Death   760
Bind us with after-bands, what profits then
Our inward freedom? In the day we eat
Of this fair fruit, our doom is we shall die.
How dies the Serpent? He hath eaten, and lives,
And knows, and speaks, and reasons, and discerns,   765
Irrational till then. For us alone
Was death invented? or to us denied

729–30 cf. the note to vi, 788 737 **impregned** im-
pregnated 741 **with desire** "a tree to be desired" (Gen. iii, 6)
753 **Forbids . . . to taste** cf. v, 61

This intellectual food, for beasts reserved?
For beasts it seems, yet that one beast which first
770 Hath tasted envies not, but brings with joy
The good befallen him, author unsuspect,°
Friendly to Man, far from deceit or guile.
What fear I, then? rather, what know to fear
Under this ignorance of good and evil,
775 Of God or Death, of law or penalty?
Here grows the cure of all, this fruit divine,
Fair to the eye, inviting to the taste,
Of virtue to make wise. What hinders, then,
To reach, and feed at once both body and mind?'
780   So saying, her rash hand in evil hour
Forth-reaching to the fruit, she plucked, she eat;°
Earth felt the wound, and Nature from her seat,
Sighing through all her works, gave signs° of woe
That all was lost. Back to the thicket slunk
785 The guilty Serpent, and well might, for Eve,
Intent now wholly on her taste, naught else
Regarded; such delight till then, as seemed,
In fruit she never tasted, whether true
Or fancied so through expectation high
790 Of knowledge; nor was Godhead from her thought.
Greedily she engorged without restraint,°

771 **author unsuspect** authority not to be suspected   781 **eat** pronounced "ate" in Milton's day and rhyming with "seat" in the next line   783 **Sighing . . . signs** alliterative wordplay   791 It was Milton's view, which he demonstrated in his text, that the sin of eating of the fruit was "manifold" (x, 16), embraced all seven deadly sins: here for instance is gluttony. And when the concupiscent idlers lie down by "a shady bank," 1037 ff., they illustrate lust and sloth. Milton's words in I, xi, of his *Christian Doctrine* are: "at once distrust of the divine veracity, and a proportionate credulity in the assurances of Satan; unbelief; ingratitude; disobedience; gluttony; in the man excessive uxoriousness, in the woman a want of proper regard for her husband, in both an insensibility to the welfare of their offspring, and that offspring the whole human race; parricide, theft, invasion of the rights of others, sacrilege, deceit, presumption in aspiring to divine attributes, fraud in the means employed to attain the object, pride, and arrogance." To this indictment is to be added premeditated murder, 826 ff. The sprig that Eve brings to her husband is a poison, and a part of her knows it.

And knew not eating death. Satiate at length,
And heightened as with wine,° jocund and boon,°
Thus to herself she pleasingly began:
'O sovran, virtuous, precious of all trees   795
In Paradise, of operation blest
To sapience, hitherto obscured, infamed,
And thy fair fruit let hang, as to no end
Created, but henceforth my early care,
Not without song, each morning, and due praise,   800
Shall tend thee, and the fertile burden ease
Of thy full branches, offered free to all,
Till, dieted by thee, I grow mature
In knowledge, as the Gods who all things know,
Though others envy what they cannot give—   805
For, had the gift been theirs, it had not here
Thus grown. Experience,° next to thee I owe,
Best guide: not following thee, I had remained
In ignorance; thou open'st Wisdom's way,
And giv'st access, though secret she retire.   810
And I perhaps am secret:° Heaven is high—
High, and remote to see from thence distinct
Each thing on Earth; and other care perhaps
May have diverted from continual watch
Our great Forbidder, safe° with all his spies   815
About him. But to Adam in what sort
Shall I appear? Shall I to him make known
As yet my change, and give him to partake
Full happiness with me, or rather not,
But keep the odds of knowledge in my power   820
Without co-partner? so to add what wants
In female sex, the more to draw his love,
And render me more equal, and perhaps,
A thing not undesirable, sometime
Superior—for, inferior, who is free?   825
This may be well; but what if God have seen,
And death ensue? Then I shall be no more,
And Adam, wedded to another Eve,

793 The fruit in its effect on both Eve and Adam is as an
intoxicant; cf. 1008 (and incidentally an aphrodisiac). **boon**
gay, as in boon companion   807 **Experience** experiment   811
secret hidden   815 **safe** harmless

Shall live with her enjoying, I extinct—
830 A death to think. Confirmed, then, I resolve
Adam shall share with me in bliss or woe.
So dear I love him that with him all deaths
I could endure, without him live no life.'°
    So saying, from the tree her step she turned,
835 But first low reverence done, as to the Power
That dwelt within,° whose presence had infused
Into the plant sciential° sap, derived
From nectar, drink of Gods. Adam the while,
Waiting desirous her return, had wove°
840 Of choicest flowers a garland, to adorn
Her tresses and her rural labours crown,
As reapers oft are wont their harvest-queen.
Great joy he promised to his thoughts, and new
Solace in her return, so long delayed;
845 Yet oft his heart, divine of° something ill,
Misgave him. He the faltering measure felt,
And forth to meet her went, the way she took
That morn when first they parted; by the Tree
Of Knowledge he must pass; there he her met,
850 Scarce from the tree returning, in her hand
A bough of fairest fruit, that downy smiled,
New gathered, and ambrosial smell diffused.°
To him she hasted; in her face Excuse
Came prologue, and apology to prompt,
855 Which, with bland words at will, she thus addressed:
    'Hast thou not wondered, Adam, at my stay?
Thee I have missed, and thought it long, deprived
Thy presence, agony of love till now
Not felt, nor shall be twice, for never more
860 Mean I to try, what rash untried I sought,
The pain of absence from thy sight. But strange
Hath been the cause, and wonderful to hear:

832–33 This romantic sentiment actually comes from Horace
(*Carm.* III, ix, 24). 835 ff. Eve has fallen to tote-
mism. 835–36 **Power . . . within** cf. 95–96, 680–81 837
sciential yielding knowledge 839 ff. So Hector's wife, not
knowing that he had been slain, embroidered flowers while
waiting for his return, *Iliad*, XXII, 437 ff. 845 **divine of**
foreboding (like the verb) 852 **ambrosial smell diffused**
ambrosiae diffundit odorem (*Georg.*, IV, 415)

This tree is not, as we are told, a tree
Of danger tasted, nor to evil unknown
Opening the way, but of divine effect   865
To open eyes, and make them Gods who taste;
And hath been tasted such. The Serpent wise,
Or not restrained as we or not obeying,
Hath eaten of the fruit, and is become,
Not dead, as we are threatened, but thenceforth   870
Endued with human voice and human sense,
Reasoning to admiration, and with me
Persuasively hath so prevailed that I
Have also tasted, and have also found
The effects to correspond—opener mine eyes,   875
Dim erst, dilated spirits, ampler heart,
And growing up to Godhead; which for thee
Chiefly I sought, without thee can despise.
For bliss, as thou hast part, to me is bliss,
Tedious, unshared with thee, and odious soon.   880
Thou, therefore, also taste, that equal lot
May join us, equal joy, as equal love,
Lest, thou not tasting, different degree
Disjoin us, and I then too late renounce
Deity for thee, when Fate will not permit.'°   885
    Thus Eve, with countenance blithe, her story told,
But in her cheek distemper flushing glowed.
On the other side, Adam, soon as he heard
The fatal trespass done by Eve, amazed,
Astonied, stood and blank, while horror chill°   890
Ran through his veins, and all his joints relaxed.
From his slack hand the garland wreathed for Eve
Down dropped, and all the faded roses shed.
Speechless he stood and pale, till thus at length
First to himself he inward silence broke: 895
    'O fairest of creation, last and best
Of all God's works, creature in whom excelled
Whatever can to sight or thought be formed,
Holy, divine, good, amiable, or sweet!
How art thou lost, how on a sudden lost,   900
Defaced, deflowered, and now to death devote?°

883–85 deluding and deluded. 890 **horror chill** another
Virgilian phrase (*Aen.* III, 29), *frigidus horror* 901 **to death
devote** an Horatian Latinism

Rather, how hast thou yielded to transgress
The strict forbiddance, how to violate
The sacred fruit forbidden? Some cursèd fraud
905 Of enemy hath beguiled thee, yet unknown,
And me with thee hath ruined; for with thee
Certain my resolution is to die.
How can I live without thee? how forgo
Thy sweet converse and love so dearly joined,
910 To live again in these wild woods forlorn?
Should God create another Eve, and I
Another rib afford, yet loss of thee
Would never from my heart. No, no! I feel
The link of nature draw me: flesh of flesh,
915 Bone of my bone thou art,° and from thy state
Mine never shall be parted, bliss or woe.'
   So having said, as one from sad dismay
Recomforted, and, after thoughts disturbed,
Submitting to what seemed remediless,
920 Thus in calm mood his words to Eve he turned:
   'Bold deed thou hast presumed, adventurous Eve,
And peril great provoked, who thus hast dared,°
Had it been only coveting to eye
That sacred fruit,° sacred to abstinence,
925 Much more to taste it, under ban to touch.
But past who can recall, or done undo?
Not God Omnipotent, nor Fate; yet so
Perhaps° thou shalt not die; perhaps the fact°
Is not so heinous now, foretasted fruit,

914–15 cf. viii, 495. St. Augustine commented: "so we cannot
believe that Adam was deceived, and supposed the devil's
word to be truth, and therefore transgressed God's law, but
that he by the drawings of kindred yielded to the woman, the
husband to the wife, the one human being to the only other
human being . . . the man could not bear to be severed from
his only companion, even though this involved a partnership
in sin . . . he was possibly deceived in so far as he thought his
sin venial" (*City of God,* XIV, xi). 922 **hast dared** 1674 has
hath, and the early editions put a comma after *dared,* but the
infinitive construction—"to eye," etc.—is tighter. 924 **sacred
fruit** (in the Latin sense of having a curse on it: a repetition
from 904) 928 **Perhaps** a word, *forte,* from the Vulgate
version of Genesis, iii, 3 **fact** deed

Profaned first by the Serpent, by him first 930
Made common and unhallowed ere our taste,
Nor yet on him found deadly; he yet lives—
Lives, as thou saidst, and gains to live, as Man,
Higher degree of life: inducement strong
To us, as likely, tasting, to attain 935
Proportional ascent; which cannot be
But to be Gods, or Angels, demi-gods.
Nor can I think that God, Creator wise,
Though threatening, will in earnest so destroy
Us, his prime creatures, dignified so high, 940
Set over all his works; which, in our fall,
For us created, needs with us must fail,
Dependent made. So God shall uncreate,
Be frustrate, do, undo, and labour lose,
Not well conceived of God,° who, though his power 945
Creation could repeat, yet would be loth
Us to abolish, lest the Adversary
Triúmph and say: "Fickle their state whom God°
Most favours; who can please him long? Me first
He ruined, now Mankind; whom will he next?"— 950
Matter of scorn not to be given the Foe.
However, I with thee have fixed my lot,
Certain° to undergo like doom; if death
Consort with thee, death is to me as life,
So forcible within my heart I feel 955
The bond of Nature draw me to my own;°
My own in thee, for what thou art is mine.
Our state cannot be severed; we are one,
One flesh; to lose thee were to lose myself.'
      So Adam; and thus Eve to him replied: 960
'O glorious trial of exceeding love,
Illustrious evidence, example high!
Engaging me to emulate; but, short
Of thy perfection, how shall I attain,
Adam, from whose dear side I boast me sprung, 965

---

945 **Not well conceived of God** Adam, though technically not
fallen yet, is on the way; he is already a critic. 947–48 "Lest
their adversaries should judge amiss, lest they should say, 'Our
hand is triumphant'" (Deut. xxxii, 27, Revised Standard
Version). 953 **Certain** determined 956 cf. 914

And gladly of our union hear thee speak,
One heart, one soul° in both; whereof good proof
This day affords, declaring thee resolved,
Rather than death, or aught than death more dread,
970 Shall separate us, linked in love so dear,
To undergo with me one guilt, one crime,
If any be, of tasting this fair fruit,°
Whose virtue (for of good still good proceeds,
Direct, or by occasion) hath presented
975 This happy trial of thy love, which else
So eminently never had been known.
Were it I thought death menaced would ensue°
This my attempt, I would sustain alone
The worst, and not persuade thee—rather die
980 Deserted than oblige° thee with a fact
Pernicious to thy peace, chiefly assured
Remarkably so late of thy so true,
So faithful, love unequalled. But I feel
Far otherwise the event: not death, but life
985 Augmented, opened eyes, new hopes, new joys,
Taste so divine that what of sweet before
Hath touched my sense flat seems to this and harsh.
On my experience, Adam, freely taste,°
And fear of death deliver to the winds.'
990   So saying, she embraced him, and for joy
Tenderly wept, much won that he his love
Had so ennobled as of choice to incur
Divine displeasure for her sake, or death.
In recompense (for such compliance bad
995 Such recompense best merits), from the bough
She gave him of that fair enticing fruit
With liberal hand. He scrupled not to eat,
Against his better knowledge, not deceived,°
But fondly° overcome with female charm.
1000 Earth trembled from her entrails, as again
In pangs, and Nature gave a second groan;
Sky lowered, and, muttering thunder, some sad drops

967 **one soul** cf. viii, 604   972 **this fair fruit** cf. 731, 763   977–81
This assertion is belied by 826–33.   980 **oblige** entangle in
guilt   988 **freely taste** echoing the Serpent (732)   998 "Adam
was not deceived" (1 Tim. ii, 14).   999 **fondly** a pun—
affectionately and foolishly.

Wept at completing of the mortal sin
Original; while Adam took no thought,
Eating his fill, nor Eve to iterate 1005
Her former trespass feared, the more to soothe
Him with her loved society; that now,
As with new wine intoxicated both,
They swim in mirth, and fancy that they feel
Divinity within them breeding wings 1010
Wherewith to scorn the Earth: but that false fruit
Far other operations first displayed,
Carnal desire inflaming; he on Eve
Began to cast lascivious eyes; she him
As wantonly repaid; in lust they burn, 1015
Till Adam thus 'gan Eve to dalliance move:
    'Eve, now I see thou art exact of taste°
And elegant, of sapience no small part,
Since to each meaning savour we° apply,
And palate call judicious. I the praise 1020
Yield thee, so well this day thou hast purveyed.
Much pleasure we have lost while we abstained
From this delightful fruit, nor known till now
True relish, tasting. If such pleasure° be
In things to us forbidden, it might be wished 1025
For this one tree had been forbidden ten.
But come; so well refreshed, now let us play,°
As meet is, after such delicious fare;
For never did thy beauty, since the day
I saw thee first and wedded thee, adorned 1030
With all perfections, so inflame my sense
With ardour to enjoy thee, fairer now
Than ever, bounty of this virtuous tree.'
    So said he, and forbore not glance or toy°
Of amorous intent, well understood 1035
Of Eve, whose eye darted contagious fire.
Her hand he seized, and to a shady bank,°

1017 **taste** a pun   1019 **we** 1674 misprints *me*   1024 **such
pleasure** cf. 455, 596; viii, 50   1027 ff. There is an odd reminiscence
of the *Iliad* here (XIV, 292–353). Adam gazes on Eve as if she were
Hera equipped with Aphrodite's girdle, and he says to her what
Zeus said on that deceitful but sensually memorable occasion.
The hyacinth—1041—helped make up the flowery bed of both
couples.   1034 **toy** caress   1037 **shady bank** cf. viii, 286

Thick overhead with verdant roof embowered,
He led her, nothing loth; flowers were the couch,
1040 Pansies, and violets, and asphodel,
And hyacinth—Earth's freshest, softest lap.
There they their fill of love and love's disport°
Took largely, of their mutual guilt the seal,
The solace of their sin, till dewy sleep
1045 Oppressed them, wearied with their amorous play.
Soon as the force of that fallacious fruit,
That with exhilarating vapour bland
About their spirits had played, and inmost powers
Made err, was now exhaled, and grosser sleep,°
1050 Bred of unkindly° fumes, with conscious dreams
Encumbered, now had left them, up they rose
As from unrest, and, each the other viewing,
Soon found their eyes how opened, and their minds
How darkened; innocence, that as a veil
1055 Had shadowed them from knowing ill, was gone;
Just confidence, and native righteousness,
And honour, from about them, naked left
To guilty shame:° he covered, but his robe
Uncovered more. So rose the Danite strong,
1060 Herculean Samson, from the harlot-lap
Of Philistean Dalilah, and waked
Shorn of his strength; they destitute and bare
Of all their virtue. Silent, and in face
Confounded, long they sat, as stricken° mute;
1065 Till Adam, though not less than Eve abashed,
At length gave utterance to these words constrained:
    'O Eve, in evil hour° thou didst give ear
To that false Worm, of whomsoever taught
To counterfeit Man's voice—true in our fall,
1070 False in our promised rising; since our eyes
Opened we find indeed, and find we know

1042 "Come, let us take our fill of love until the morning; let
us solace ourselves with loves" (Prov. vii, 18).   1049 **grosser
sleep** contrast v, 3–5   1050 **unkindly** not natural   1058 **guilty
shame** cf. iv, 313 (the anatomical pun is familiar in
German)   1064 **stricken** *struck'n* in the original editions   1067
in evil hour a pun repeated from 780

Both good and evil,° good lost and evil got:
Bad fruit° of knowledge, if this be to know,
Which leaves us naked thus, of honour void,
Of innocence, of faith, of purity,   1075
Our wonted ornaments now soiled and stained,
And in our faces evident the signs
Of foul concupiscence, whence evil store,
Even shame, the last° of evils—of the first
Be sure then. How shall I behold the face   1080
Henceforth of God or Angel, erst with joy
And rapture so oft beheld? Those heavenly shapes
Will dazzle now this earthly with their blaze
Insufferably bright. Oh, might I here
In solitude live savage, in some glade   1085
Obscured, where highest woods, impenetrable
To star or sunlight, spread their umbrage broad,
And brown° as evening: Cover me, ye pines,
Ye cedars, with innumerable boughs
Hide me, where I may never see them more.   1090
But let us now, as in bad plight, devise
What best may, for the present, serve to hide
The parts of each from° other that seem most
To shame obnoxious, and unseemliest seen—
Some tree, whose broad smooth leaves, together sewed, 1095
And girded on our loins, may cover round
Those middle parts, that this new comer, Shame,
There sit not, and reproach us as unclean.'
     So counselled he, and both together went
Into the thickest wood; there soon they chose   1100
The fig-tree—not that kind for fruit renowned,°
But such as at this day, to Indians known,
In Malabar or Deccan spreads her arms
Branching so broad and long that in the ground
The bended twigs take root, and daughters grow   1105

1072 **good and evil** perhaps "an error of the scribe or the printer for *evil and good,* which gives a better verse" (Robert Bridges) 1073 **fruit** used with a double meaning, as at i, 1 1079 **the last** the most extreme 1088 **brown** dark, as in "Lycidas," 2. 1092–93 **for** *and* **from** were interchanged in 1674. 1101–1111 It has long been known that Milton based his description of the arched Indian fig tree on Gerard's *Herbal,* 1597, 1634.

About the mother tree, a pillared shade
High overarched,° and echoing walks between:
There oft the Indian herdsman, shunning heat,
Shelters in cool, and tends his pasturing herds
1110 At loop-holes cut through thickest shade:° Those leaves
They gathered, broad as Amazonian targe,°
And with what skill they had together sewed,°
To gird their waist—vain covering, if to hide
Their guilt and dreaded shame; O how unlike
1115 To that first naked glory. Such of late
Columbus found the American so girt
With feathered cincture,° naked else and wild
Among the trees on isles and woody shores.
Thus fenced, and, as they thought, their shame in part
1120 Covered, but not at rest or ease of mind,
They sat them down to weep. Nor only tears
Rained at their eyes, but high winds worse within
Began to rise, high passions—anger, hate,
Mistrust, suspicion, discord—and shook sore
1125 Their inward state of mind, calm region once
And full of peace, now tossed and turbulent:
For Understanding ruled not, and the Will°
Heard not her lore, but in subjection now
To sensual Appetite, who, from beneath
1130 Usurping over sovran Reason, claimed
Superior sway. From thus distempered breast
Adam, estranged in look and altered style,
Speech intermitted thus to Eve renewed:
    'Would thou hadst hearkened to my words, and stayed
1135 With me, as I besought thee, when that strange
Desire of wandering, this unhappy morn,
I know not whence possessed thee; we had then
Remained still happy, not, as now, despoiled
Of all our good, shamed, naked, miserable.

1107 **High overarched** cf. i, 304   1110 **thickest shade** cf. iv,
532; viii, 653   1111 **Amazonian targe** shield such as that carried
by one of the fabulous female warriors, the Amazons,
"crescent-shaped" in *Aeneid,* I, 490.   1112 **together sewed**
going back to 1095   1117 **With feathered cincture** This notion
that the Indians were so girt follows decorations and
illustrations in Renaissance geographies and maps, and
Spenser, *Faerie Queene,* III, xii, 8.   1127–31 cf. 351–56

Let none henceforth seek needless cause to approve *1140*
The faith they owe; when earnestly they seek
Such proof, conclude they then begin to fail.'
   To whom, soon moved with touch of blame, thus Eve:
'What words have passed thy lips, Adam severe,
Imput'st thou that to my default, or will *1145*
Of wandering, as thou call'st it, which who knows
But might as ill have happened thou being by,
Or to thyself perhaps: hadst thou been there,
Or here the attempt, thou couldst not have discerned
Fraud in the Serpent, speaking as he spake; *1150*
No ground of enmity between us known
Why he should mean me ill or seek to harm.
Was I to have never parted from thy side?
As good have grown there still, a lifeless rib.
Being as I am, why didst not thou, the head, *1155*
Command me absolutely not to go,
Going into such danger, as thou saidst?
Too facile then, thou didst not much gainsay,
Nay, didst permit, approve, and fair dismiss.
Hadst thou been firm and fixed in thy dissent, *1160*
Neither had I transgressed, nor thou with me.'
   To whom, then first incensed, Adam replied:
'Is this the love, is this the recompense
Of mine to thee, ingrateful Eve, expressed
Immutable when thou wert lost, not I, *1165*
Who might have lived, and joyed immortal bliss,
Yet willingly chose rather death with thee?
And am I now upbraided as the cause
Of thy transgressing? not enough severe,
It seems, in thy restraint. What could I more? *1170*
I warned thee, I admonished thee, foretold
The danger and the lurking enemy
That lay in wait; beyond this had been force,
And force upon free will hath here no place.
But confidence then bore thee on, secure *1175*
Either to meet no danger or to find
Matter of glorious trial;° and perhaps
I also erred in overmuch admiring
What seemed to thee so perfect that I thought

1177 **glorious trial** cf. 961

1180 No evil durst attempt thee—but I rue
That error now, which is become my crime,
And thou the accuser. Thus it shall befall
Him who, to worth in women° overtrusting,
Lets her will rule: restraint she will not brook,
1185 And, left to herself, if evil thence ensue,
She first his weak indulgence will accuse.'
    Thus they in mutual accusation spent
The fruitless hours, but neither self-condemning,
And of their vain contést appeared no end.

1183 **women** It has been conjectured that Milton dictated the
singular, but he may well have slipped into the plural since he
knew so many instances.

BOOK X

THE ARGUMENT

Man's transgression known, the guardian Angels forsake Paradise and return up to Heaven to approve their vigilance, and are approved, God declaring that the entrance of Satan could not be by them prevented. He sends his Son to judge the transgressors, who descends and gives sentence according-ly; then, in pity, clothes them both, and reascends. Sin and Death sitting till then at the gates of Hell, by wondrous sympathy feeling the success of Satan in this new World, and the sin by Man there committed, resolve to sit no longer confined in Hell, but to follow Satan, their sire, up to the place of Man; to make the way easier from Hell to this World to and fro, they pave a broad highway or bridge over Chaos, according to the track that Satan first made; then, preparing for Earth, they meet him, proud of his suc-cess, returning to Hell; their mutual gratulation. Satan ar-rives at Pandemonium, in full assembly relates with boasting his success against Man; instead of applause is entertained with a general hiss by all his audience, transformed, with himself also, suddenly into Serpents, according to his doom given in Paradise; then, deluded with a show of the Forbid-den Tree springing up before them, they, greedily reaching to take of the fruit, chew dust and bitter ashes. The proceed-ings of Sin and Death: God foretells the final victory of his Son over them, and the renewing of all things, but, for the present, commands his Angels to make several alterations in the Heavens and Elements. Adam, more and more per-ceiving his fallen condition, heavily bewails, rejects the con-dolement of Eve; she persists, and at length appeases him; then, to evade the curse likely to fall on their offspring, proposes to Adam violent ways; which he approves not, but, conceiving better hope, puts her in mind of the late promise made them that her seed should be revenged on the Serpent, and exhorts her, with him, to seek peace of the offended Deity by repentance and supplication.

MEANWHILE the heinous and despiteful act
Of Satan done in Paradise, and how
He, in the Serpent, had perverted Eve,
Her husband she, to taste the fatal fruit,
5   Was known in Heaven,° for what can 'scape the eye
Of God all-seeing or deceive his heart
Omniscient, who, in all things wise and just,
Hindered not Satan to attempt the mind
Of Man, with strength entire° and free will armed
10 Complete to have discovered and repulsed
Whatever wiles of foe or seeming friend.
For still they knew, and ought to have still remembered,
The high injunction not to taste that fruit,
Whoever tempted; which they not obeying
15 Incurred (what could they less?) the penalty,
And, manifold in sin, deserved to fall.
Up into Heaven from Paradise in haste
The Angelic guards° ascended, mute and sad
For Man, for of his state by this they knew,
20 Much wondering how the subtle Fiend° had stolen
Entrance unseen. Soon as the unwelcome news
From Earth arrived at Heaven-gate, displeased
All were who heard; dim sadness did not spare
That time celestial visages, yet, mixed
25 With pity, violated not their bliss.
About the new-arrived, in multitudes,
The ethereal people ran, to hear and know
How all befell. They towards the throne supreme,
Accountable, made haste to make appear,
30 With righteous plea, their utmost vigilance,
And easily approved; when the Most High
Eternal Father,° from his secret cloud
Amidst, in thunder uttered thus his voice:
   'Assembled Angels, and ye Powers returned
35 From unsuccessful charge, be not dismayed
Nor troubled at these tidings from the Earth
Which your sincerest care could not prevent,

5 **Was known in Heaven** cf. i, 732–33 9 **strength entire** cf. i,
146 18 **The Angelic guards** cf. iv, 550 20 **the subtle Fiend**
cf. ii, 815 32 **Eternal Father** cf. 68 and v, 246; vi, 96; vii,
137, 517

Foretold so lately what would come to pass,
When first this Tempter crossed the gulf from Hell.
I told ye then he should prevail, and speed   40
On his bad errand°—Man should be seduced
And flattered out of all, believing lies
Against his Maker, no decree of mine
Concurring to necessitate his fall,
Or touch with lightest moment° of impulse   45
His free will, to her own inclining left
In even scale. But fallen he is, and now
What rests° but that the mortal sentence pass
On his transgression, Death denounced that day,
Which he presumes already vain and void   50
Because not yet inflicted, as he feared,
By some immediate stroke, but soon shall find
Forbearance no acquittance ere day end.
Justice shall not return, as bounty, scorned.°
But whom send I to judge them? Whom but thee,   55
Vicegerent Son; to thee I have transferred
All judgement, whether in Heaven, or Earth, or Hell.°
Easy it may be seen that I intend
Mercy colléague with justice, sending thee,
Man's friend, his Mediator, his designed   60
Both ransom and Redeemer voluntary
And destined Man himself to judge Man fallen.'
   So spake the Father, and, unfolding bright
Toward the right hand his glory, on the Son
Blazed forth unclouded deity. He full   65
Resplendent all his Father manifest
Expressed, and thus divinely answered mild:
   'Father Eternal, thine is to decree,
Mine both in Heaven and Earth to do thy will
Supreme, that thou in me, thy Son beloved,°   70
May'st ever rest well pleased. I go to judge
On Earth these thy transgressors; but thou know'st,
Whoever judged, the worst on me must light,
When Time shall be; for so I undertook

41 **bad errand** cf. iv, 795   45 **moment** momentum   48 **rests**
remains   54 Justice shall not return scorned, as bounty has
been.   55–57 "For the Father judgeth no man, but hath
committed all judgment unto the Son" (John, v, 22).   70 **Son
beloved** cf. vi, 680

75 Before thee and,° not repenting, this obtain
     Of right, that I may mitigate their doom
     On me derived;° yet I shall temper so
     Justice with mercy as may illustrate most°
     Them° fully satisfied,° and thee appease.
80 Attendance none shall need, nor train, where none
     Are to behold the judgement but the judged,
     Those two; the third best absent is condemned,
     Convíct° by flight, and rebel to all law;
     Conviction to the Serpent none belongs.'°
85   Thus saying, from his radiant seat he rose
     Of high collateral° glory. Him° Thrones and Powers,
     Princedoms, and Dominations, ministrant,
     Accompanied to Heaven-gate, from whence
     Eden and all the coast in prospect lay.
90 Down he descended straight; the speed of Gods
     Time counts not, though with swiftest minutes winged.
     Now was the Sun in western cadence° low
     From noon, and gentle airs° due at their hour
     To fan the Earth now waked, and usher in
95 The evening° cool,° when he, from wrath more cool,
     Came, the mild judge and intercessor both,
     To sentence Man: the voice of God they heard
     Now walking in the Garden, by soft winds
     Brought to their ears, while day declined; they heard,
100 And from his presence hid themselves among
     The thickest trees, both man and wife, till God,
     Approaching, thus to Adam called aloud:
     'Where art thou, Adam, wont with joy to meet
     My coming, seen far off? I miss thee here,
105 Not pleased, thus entertained with solitude,
     Where obvious duty erewhile appeared unsought.
     Or come I less conspicuous, or what change
     Absents thee, or what chance detains? Come forth.'

75 **thee and** elide to scan 77 **derived** turned aside 77–78 In
Portia's famous speech, "When mercy seasons justice"
(*Merchant of Venice,* IV, i, 197) 79 **Them** Justice and
Mercy **fully satisfied** cf. viii, 180 83 **Convíct** convicted 84
It is unnecessary to prove the serpent's guilt. 86 **collateral** see
viii, 426 **glory. Him** elide 92 **cadence** descent 93 **gentle airs**
cf. viii, 515 94–95 **usher . . . evening** cf. iv, 355 95 Genesis
gave the first "cool" (iii, 8); Milton could not resist the other.

He came, and with him Eve, more loth, though first
To offend, discountenanced both, and discomposed;   *110*
Love was not in their looks, either to God
Or to each other, but apparent guilt,
And shame, and perturbation, and despair,
Anger, and obstinacy, and hate, and guile.
Whence Adam, faltering long, thus answered brief: *115*
    'I heard thee in the garden, and, of thy voice
Afraid, being naked, hid myself.' To whom
The gracious Judge, without revile, replied:
    'My voice thou oft hast heard, and hast not feared,°
But still rejoiced; how is it now become   *120*
So dreadful to thee? That thou art naked who
Hath told thee? Hast thou eaten of the tree
Whereof I gave thee charge thou shouldst not eat?'
    To whom thus Adam, sore beset, replied:
'O Heaven! in evil strait this day I stand   *125*
Before my Judge, either to undergo
Myself the total crime, or to accuse
My other self,° the partner of my life,
Whose failing, while her faith to me remains,
I should conceal, and not expose to blame   *130*
By my complaint. But strict necessity°
Subdues me, and calamitous constraint,
Lest on my head both sin and punishment,
However insupportable, be all
Devolved; though, should I hold my peace, yet thou   *135*
Wouldst easily detect what I conceal.
This Woman, whom thou mad'st to be my help,
And gav'st me as thy perfect gift, so good,
So fit, so acceptable, so divine,
That from her hand I could suspect no ill,   *140*
And what she did, whatever in itself,
Her doing seemed to justify the deed—
She gave me of the tree, and I did eat.'°
    To whom the Sovran Presence thus replied:

119 Contrast the other "voice . . . heard so oft," associated
with "fears," i, 274–75. 128 **My other self** cf. viii, 450 131
strict necessity cf. v, 528. 131–32 is comparable to "Lycidas,"
6–7, and there is even rhyme: *complaint* and *constraint*. 143
Genesis, iii, 12.

145 'Was she thy God, that her thou didst obey
     Before his voice? or was she made thy guide,
     Superior, or but equal, that to her
     Thou didst resign thy manhood, and the place
     Wherein God set thee above her, made of thee
150 And for thee, whose perfection far excelled
     Hers in all real dignity? Adorned
     She was indeed, and lovely, to attract
     Thy love, not thy subjection, and her gifts
     Were such as under government well seemed,
155 Unseemly to bear rule,° which was thy part
     And person,° hadst thou known thyself aright.'
         So having said, he thus to Eve in few:
     'Say, Woman, what is this which thou hast done?'
         To whom sad Eve, with shame nigh overwhelmed,
160 Confessing soon, yet not before her Judge
     Bold or loquacious, thus abashed replied:
     'The Serpent me beguiled, and I did eat.'°
         Which when the Lord God heard, without delay
     To judgement he proceeded on the accused
165 Serpent, though brute, unable° to transfer
     The guilt on him who made him instrument
     Of mischief, and polluted from the end
     Of his creation—justly then accursed,
     As vitiated in nature: more to know
170 Concerned not Man (since he no further knew)
     Nor altered his offence, yet God at last
     To Satan, first in sin, his doom applied,
     Though in mysterious terms, judged as then best:
     And on the Serpent thus his curse let fall:
175   'Because thou hast done this, thou art accursed°
     Above all cattle, each beast of the field;°
     Upon thy belly grovelling thou shalt go,
     And dust shalt eat all the days of thy life.
     Between thee and the Woman I will put
180 Enmity, and between thine and her seed;
     Her seed shall bruise thy head, thou bruise his heel.'

155 **bear rule** cf. viii, 375   156 **person** role   162 Genesis, iii, 13,
except for a transposition for metrical reasons.   165 **unable**
uncertain reference—to the Serpent, or to the Son?   175–81
There is some metrical lameness here because of the poet's close
adherence to Genesis, iii, 14–15.   176 **beast of the field** cf. vii, 522

So spake his oracle, then verified
When Jesus, son of Mary, second Eve,°
Saw Satan fall like lightning down from Heaven,
Prince of the Air,° then, rising from his grave,   185
Spoiled Principalities and Powers, triumphed
In open show, and, with ascension bright,°
Captivity led captive through the Air,°
The realm itself of Satan, long usurped,
Whom he shall tread at last under our feet,°   190
Even he who now foretold his fatal bruise,
And to the Woman thus his sentence turned:
   'Thy sorrow I will greatly multiply
By thy conception; children thou shalt bring
In sorrow forth, and to thy husband's will   195
Thine shall submit; he over thee shall rule.'
   On Adam last thus judgement he pronounced:
'Because thou hast hearkened to the voice of thy wife,
And eaten of the tree° concerning which
I charged thee, saying, *Thou shalt not eat thereof,*   200
Cursed is the ground for thy sake; thou in sorrow
Shalt eat thereof all the days of thy life;
Thorns also and thistles it shall bring thee forth
Unbid; and thou shalt eat the herb of the field;
In the sweat of thy face shalt thou eat bread,   205
Till thou return unto the ground; for thou
Out of the ground wast taken: know thy birth,
For dust thou art, and shalt to dust return.'
   So judged he Man, both Judge and Saviour sent,
And the instant stroke of death, denounced that day,   210
Removed far off, then, pitying how they stood
Before him naked to the air, that now
Must suffer change, disdained not to begin
Thenceforth the form of servant to assume,°
As when he washed his servants' feet, so now,°   215
As father of his family, he clad

183 **Mary, second Eve** as at v, 387   185 **Prince of the Air** "the
prince of the power of the air" (Eph. ii, 2)   186–87 "And, having
spoiled principalities and powers, he made a show of them
openly, triumphing over them in it" (Col. ii, 15).   188 Based on
Ps. lxviii, 18   190 Romans, xvi, 20 (where margin has
"tread")   199 **eaten of the tree** cf. 122   214 cf. Philippians, ii,
7   215 John, xiii, 5

Their nakedness with skins of beasts, or slain
Or, as the snake, with youthful coat repaid;
And thought not much to clothe his enemies.
220 Nor he their outward only with the skins
Of beasts,° but inward nakedness, much more
Opprobrious, with his robe of righteousness°
Arraying, covered from his Father's sight.
To him with swift ascent he up returned,
225 Into his blissful bosom reassumed
In glory as of old; to him, appeased,
All, though all-knowing, what had passed with Man
Recounted, mixing intercession sweet.
  Meanwhile, ere thus was sinned and judged on Earth,
230 Within the gates of Hell sat Sin and Death,
In counterview° within the gates, that now
Stood open wide, belching outrageous flame
Far into Chaos, since the Fiend passed through,
Sin opening, who thus now to Death began:
235 'O Son, why sit we here, each other viewing
Idly, while Satan, our great author,° thrives
In other worlds, and happier seat provides
For us, his offspring dear? It cannot be
But that success attends him; if mishap,
240 Ere this he had returned, with fury driven
By his avengers, since no place like this
Can fit this punishment or their revenge.
Methinks I feel new strength within me rise,
Wings growing, and dominion given° me large
245 Beyond this Deep—whatever draws me on,
Or sympathy or some connatural force,
Powerful at greatest distance to unite
With secret amity things of like kind
By secretest conveyance. Thou, my shade°
250 Inseparable, must with me along,
For Death from Sin no power can separate.
But, lest the difficulty of passing back

220–21 **with . . . skins/ Of beasts** cf. 217 222 **robe of
righteousness** Isaiah, lxi, 10 231 **In counterview** opposite each
other; cf. 235 236 **great author** cf. v, 188 244 **dominion given**
cf. iv, 430–31; viii, 545–46; vi, 887 249 **shade** shadow, with a
pun on the classical meaning of shade

Stay his return perhaps over this gulf
Impassable, impervious, let us try
Adventurous work, yet to thy power and mine   255
Not unagreeable, to found° a path
Over this main° from Hell to that new World
Where Satan now prevails—a monument
Of merit high to all the infernal host,
Easing their passage hence, for intercourse   260
Or transmigration, as their lot shall lead.
Nor can I miss the way, so strongly drawn
By this new-felt attraction and instinct.'
    Whom thus the meagre Shadow answered soon:
'Go whither fate and inclination strong   265
Leads thee; I shall not lag behind nor err
The way, thou leading: such a scent I draw
Of carnage, prey innumerable, and taste
The savour of death from all things there that live.
Nor shall I to the work thou enterprisest   270
Be wanting, but afford thee equal aid.'
    So saying, with delight he snuffed the smell
Of mortal change on Earth. As when a flock
Of ravenous fowl, though many a league° remote,
Against the day of battle to a field   275
Where armies lie encamped come flying, lured
With scent of living carcases designed
For death the following day in bloody fight:
So scented the grim Feature° and upturned
His nostril wide into the murky air,   280
Sagacious° of his quarry from so far.
Then both, from out Hell-gates, into the waste
Wide anarchy of Chaos, damp and dark,
Flew diverse, and, with power (their power was great)
Hovering upon the waters, what they met°   285
Solid or slimy, as in raging sea
Tossed up and down, together crowded drove,
From each side shoaling, towards the mouth of Hell;

---

256 **found** construct   257 **this main** chaos   274 **many a league**
cf. ii, 929; iv, 164   279 **Feature** shape   281 **Sagacious** keen-
scented   285 ff. Note, as Tillyard points out, the ways in which
this passage is a "parody" of "God's creative act in the
seventh book."

As when two polar winds,° blowing adverse
290 Upon the Cronian Sea,° together drive
Mountains of ice, that stop the imagined way°
Beyond Petsora° eastward to the rich
Cathaian° coast. The aggregated soil
Death with his mace petrific, cold and dry,
295 As with a trident smote, and fixed as firm
As Delos,° floating once; the rest his look
Bound with Gorgonian° rigour not to move,
And with asphaltic slime; broad as the gate,
Deep to the roots of Hell the gathered beach
300 They fastened, and the mole° immense wrought on
Over the foaming Deep high-arched, a bridge
Of length prodigious, joining to the wall
Immovable of this now fenceless World,
Forfeit to Death—from hence a passage broad,
305 Smooth, easy, inoffensive,° down to Hell.
So, if great things to small may be compared,
Xerxes,° the liberty of Greece to yoke,
From Susa, his Memnonian palace high,
Came to the sea, and, over Hellespont
310 Bridging his way, Europe with Asia joined,
And scourged with many a stroke the indignant waves.
Now had they brought the work by wondrous art
Pontifical°—a ridge of pendent rock
Over the vexed abyss, following the track
315 Of Satan, to the selfsame place where he

289 **polar winds** cf. v, 269   290 **Cronian Sea** Arctic Ocean   291 **the imagined way** the northeast passage, the undiscoverable goal of so many Renaissance explorers   292 **Petsora** The author's *History of Muscovia* identifies as a "river . . . holding his course through Siberia, how far, the Russians thereabouts know not, runneth into the sea at 72 mouths, full of ice."   293 **Cathaian** Mongolian, distinguished from Chinese as more northerly   296 **Delos** cf. v, 265   297 **Gorgonian** petrifying; cf. ii, 611   300 **mole** causeway   305 **inoffensive** without obstacle   307 **Xerxes** On succeeding to the throne of Persia (486 B.C.), he thought it necessary to carry on the tradition of his father, Darius, in preparing a punitive expedition against Greece. Herodotus tells how the emperor ordered the waves to be scourged when they broke his bridge of ships.   313 **Pontifical** a pun that (1) means literally bridge-building and (2) hits at pontiffs

First lighted° from his wing and landed safe
From out of Chaos to the outside bare
Of this round World. With pins of adamant
And chains they made all fast, too fast they made
And durable; and now in little space   320
The confines met of empyrean Heaven
And of this World, and on the left hand Hell,
With long reach interposed; three several ways
In sight to each of these three places led.
And now their way to Earth they had descried,   325
To Paradise first tending, when, behold
Satan, in likeness of an Angel bright,°
Betwixt the Centaur and the Scorpion steering
His zenith, while the Sun in Aries rose;°
Disguised he came, but those his children dear   330
Their parent soon discerned, though in disguise.
He, after Eve seduced, unminded slunk
Into the wood fast by, and, changing shape
To observe the sequel, saw his guileful act
By Eve, though all unweeting, seconded   335
Upon her husband—saw their shame that sought
Vain covertures; but, when he saw descend
The Son of God to judge them, terrified
He fled, not hoping to escape, but shun
The present, fearing, guilty, what his wrath   340
Might suddenly inflict; that past, returned
By night, and, listening where the hapless pair
Sat in their sad discourse and various plaint,
Thence gathered his own doom, which understood
Not instant, but of future time. With joy   345
And tidings fraught to Hell he now returned,
And at the brink of Chaos, near the foot
Of this new wondrous pontifice,° unhoped
Met who to meet him came, his offspring dear.
Great joy was at their meeting, and at sight   350
Of that stupendious bridge his joy increased.
Long he admiring stood, till Sin, his fair

315–16 **where he/ First lighted** cf. iv, 570   327 **Angel bright** cf.
iii, 645   328–29 In order not to be detected, Satan goes by
constellations that are far from the region where the sun (with
Uriel) is rising.   348 **pontifice** bridge

Enchanting daughter,° thus the silence broke:
    'O Parent, these are thy magnific deeds,
355 Thy trophies, which thou view'st as not thine own;
    Thou art their author and prime architect.
    For I no sooner in my heart divined—
    My heart, which by a secret harmony
    Still moves with thine, joined in connection sweet—
360 That thou on Earth hadst prospered, which thy looks
    Now also evidence, but straight I felt,
    Though distant from thee worlds between, yet felt
    That I must after thee with this thy son;
    Such fatal consequence unites us three;
365 Hell could no longer hold us in her bounds,
    Nor this unvoyageable gulf obscure
    Detain from following thy illustrious track.
    Thou hast achieved our liberty, confined
    Within Hell-gates till now, thou us empowered
370 To fortify thus far, and overlay
    With this portentous bridge the dark abyss.°
    Thine now is all this World; thy virtue° hath won
    What thy hands builded not; thy wisdom gained,
    With odds, what war hath lost, and fully avenged
375 Our foil in Heaven. Here thou shalt monarch reign,°
    There didst not; there let him still victor sway,
    As battle hath adjudged, from this new World°
    Retiring, by his own doom° alienated,
    And henceforth monarchy with thee divide
380 Of all things, parted by the empyreal bounds,
    His quadrature° from thy orbicular World,
    Or try thee now more dangerous to his throne.'
        Whom thus the Prince of Darkness answered glad:
    'Fair daughter, and thou, son and grandchild both,
385 High proof ye now have given to be the race
    Of Satan (for I glory in the name,
    Antagonist of Heaven's Almighty King),
    Amply have merited of me, of all

352–53 **his fair/ Enchanting daughter** cf. *Samson Agonistes*,
934   371 **the dark abyss** cf. ii, 1027   372 **virtue** courage   375
monarch reign cf. v, 832; also i, 637–38   377 **new World** a fixed
reference, as at 257; i, 650; ii, 403, 867; iv, 34, 113, 391; vii,
209   378 **doom** sentence   381 **quadrature** Heaven is four-
square like the Heavenly Jerusalem (of Rev. xxi, 16)

The Infernal Empire, that so near Heaven's door
Triumphal with triumphal act have met,   390
Mine with this glorious work, and made one realm
Hell and this World—one realm, one continent
Of easy thoroughfare. Therefore, while I
Descend through Darkness, on your road with ease,
To my associate Powers, them to acquaint   395
With these successes and with them rejoice,
You two this way, among those numerous orbs,
All yours, right down to Paradise descend;
There dwell, and reign in bliss; thence on the Earth
Dominion exercise and in the air,   400
Chiefly on Man, sole lord of all declared;
Him first make sure your thrall, and lastly kill.
My substitutes I send ye, and create
Plenipotent on Earth, of matchless might
Issuing from me. On your joint vigour now   405
My hold of this new kingdom all depends,
Through Sin to Death exposed by my exploit.
If your joint power prevail,° the affairs of Hell
No detriment need fear; go, and be strong.'
    So saying,° he dismissed them; they with speed   410
Their course through thickest constellations held,
Spreading their bane; the blasted stars looked wan,
And planets, planet-struck, real eclipse
Then suffered. The other way Satan went down
The causey° to Hell-gate; on either side°   415
Disparted Chaos overbuilt exclaimed,
And with rebounding surge the bars assailed
That scorned his indignation. Through the gate,
Wide open° and unguarded, Satan passed,
And all about found desolate, for those   420
Appointed to sit there had left their charge,
Flown to the upper World; the rest were all
Far to the inland retired about the walls

408 **prevail** 1674 adds *s*. 410 **So saying** one of the many
formulae of speech that mark this epic, as others: this
participial expression has occurred a dozen times before, varied
by "Thus saying" four times. In the last two books there is
"To whom thus Michael" eight times, "To whom Michael
thus" once, etc. 415 **causey** causeway **on either side** cf. ii,
649; vi, 221, 844 418–19 **gate/ Wide open** cf. 231–32; ii, 884

Of Pandemonium, city and proud seat
425 Of Lucifer, so by allusion called
Of that bright star to Satan paragoned.°
There kept their watch the legions, while the Grand
In council sat, solicitous what chance
Might intercept their Emperor sent; so he
430 Departing gave command,° and they observed.°
As when the Tartar° from his Russian foe,
By Astracan,° over the snowy plains,
Retires, or Bactrian° Sophi, from the horns°
Of Turkish crescent, leaves all waste beyond
435 The realm of Aladule° in his retreat
To Tauris or Casbeen:° so these, the late
Heaven-banished host, left desert utmost Hell
Many a dark league, reduced in careful watch
Round their metropolis, and now expecting
440 Each hour their great Adventurer from the search
Of foreign worlds; he through the midst unmarked,
In show plebeian Angel militant
Of lowest order, passed, and, from the door
Of that Plutonian hall, invisible
445 Ascended his high throne, which, under state
Of richest texture spread, at the upper end
Was placed in regal lustre. Down a while
He sat, and round about him saw, unseen.
At last, as from a cloud, his fulgent head
450 And shape star-bright appeared, or brighter, clad
With what permissive glory since his fall
Was left him, or false glitter. All amazed
At that so sudden blaze,° the Stygian throng
Bent their aspéct, and whom they wished beheld,

426 **paragoned** compared 429–30 **so he/ Departing gave command** *namque ita discedens praeceperat* (*Aen.* IX, 40) 430 **observed** obeyed 431 **the Tartar** cf. iii, 432 432 **Astracan** at the mouth of the Volga 433 **Bactrian** Persian (the *Sophi* was the ruler of Persia) **horns** the two wings of an army, as well as the ends of the "crescent" or half-moon of the Turkish ensign 435 **The realm of Aladule** Armenia (named after King Aladeules, renowned for his stout resistance to the Turks) 436 **Tauris or Casbeen** Persian cities 453 The use of *sudden blaze* at "Lycidas" (74) may be viewed as sufficiently implying a craving for glory to warrant its being mentioned in the note.

Their mighty Chief° returned; loud was the acclaim:°   455
Forth rushed° in haste the great consulting Peers,
Raised from their dark Divan,° and with like joy
Congratulant approached him, who with hand
Silence, and with these words attention, won:°
'Thrones, Dominations, Princedoms, Virtues,
    Powers—   460
For in possession such, not only of right,
I call ye, and declare ye now, returned,
Successful beyond hope, to lead ye forth
Triumphant out of this infernal pit°
Abominable, accursed, the house of woe,°   465
And dungeon of our tyrant: Now possess,
As lords,° a spacious World, to our native Heaven°
Little inferior, by my adventure hard
With peril great° achieved. Long were to tell°
What I have done, what suffered, with what pain   470
Voyaged the unreal,° vast, unbounded Deep
Of horrible confusion, over which
By Sin and Death a broad way now is paved,
To expedite your glorious march; but I
Toiled out my úncouth° passage, forced to ride   475
The untractable Abyss, plunged in the womb
Of unoriginal° Night and Chaos° wild,
That, jealous of their secrets, fiercely opposed
My journey strange, with clamorous uproar
Protesting Fate supreme;° thence how I found   480
The new-created World,° which fame in Heaven°
Long had foretold, a fabric wonderful,

---

455 **Their mighty Chief** cf. i, 566   **loud . . . acclaim** cf. ii, 520; iii,
397; vi, 23   456 **Forth rushed** cf. vi, 749   457 **Divan** continuing
the Turkish comparison—council of state; cf. *Sultan*, i, 348.
458–59 The silent effectiveness of this leader is like Julius Caesar's
in Lucan's *Pharsalia*, I, 297.   464 **this infernal pit** cf. i, 657; ii, 850;
iv, 965   465 **the house of woe** cf. vi, 877   466–67 **possess/ As lords**
cf. viii, 339–40   467 **our native Heaven** cf. v, 863   469 **peril great**
cf. ix, 922   **Long were to tell** cf. i, 507 (a Spenserian formula)
471 **unreal** i.e., uncreated, formless   475 **úncouth** cf. ii, 407   477
unoriginal without origin or beginning (since nothing existed
before Night, "eldest of things," ii, 962)   **Night and Chaos** paired
at ii, 894–95   478–80 a lie   481 **The new-created World** cf. iii,
89; iv, 937; vii, 554   **fame in Heaven** cf. i, 651; ii, 346

Of absolute perfection; therein Man
Placed in a paradise, by our exile
485 Made happy. Him by fraud I have seduced
From his Creator, and, the more to increase
Your wonder, with an apple; He, thereat
Offended, worth your laughter, hath given up
Both his beloved Man and all his World
490 To Sin and Death a prey, and so to us,
Without our hazard, labour or alarm,
To range in, and to dwell, and over Man
To rule, as over all he should have ruled.
True is, me also he hath judged; or rather
495 Me not, but the brute Serpent, in whose shape
Man I deceived. That which to me belongs
Is enmity, which he will put between
Me and Mankind: I am to bruise his heel;
His seed—when is not set—shall bruise my head:
500 A world who would not purchase with a bruise,
Or much more grievous pain? Ye have the account
Of my performance; what remains, ye Gods,
But up and enter now into full bliss.'
    So having said, a while he stood, expecting
505 Their universal shout and high applause
To fill his ear, when, contrary, he hears,
On all sides, from innumerable tongues
A dismal universal hiss, the sound
Of public scorn; he wondered, but not long
510 Had leisure, wondering at himself now more;
His visage drawn he felt to sharp and spare,
His arms clung to his ribs, his legs entwining
Each other, till, supplanted,° down he fell,
A monstrous serpent on his belly prone,
515 Reluctant,° but in vain; a greater power
Now ruled him, punished in the shape he sinned,
According to his doom: he would have spoke,
But hiss for hiss returned with forkèd tongue
To forkèd tongue; for now were all transformed
520 Alike, to serpents all, as accessories
To his bold riot: dreadful was the din°

---

513 **supplanted** (Latin) tripped up by the heels   515 **Reluctant**
struggling   521–28 Note the hissing sibilance.

Of hissing through the hall, thick-swarming now
With complicated° monsters, head and tail,
Scorpion, and Asp, and Amphisbaena° dire,
Cerastes horned, Hydrus, and Ellops drear,°   *525*
And Dipsas° (not so thick swarmed° once the soil°
Bedropped with blood of Gorgon, or the isle
Ophiusa°), but still greatest he the midst,
Now Dragon° grown, larger than whom the Sun
Engendered in the Pythian vale on slime,   *530*
Huge Python; and his power no less he seemed
Above the rest still to retain; they all
Him followed, issuing forth° to the open field,
Where all yet left of that revolted rout,
Heaven-fallen, in station stood or just array,   *535*
Sublime with expectation when to see
In triumph issuing forth their glorious Chief;
They saw, but other sight instead—a crowd
Of ugly serpents; horror on them fell,
And horrid sympathy, for what they saw   *540*
They felt themselves now changing; down their arms,
Down fell both spear and shield; down they as fast,
And the dire hiss renewed, and the dire form
Catched by contagion, like in punishment
As in their crime. Thus was the applause they meant   *545*
Turned to exploding° hiss, triumph to shame°
Cast on themselves from their own mouths. There stood
A grove hard by, sprung up with this their change,
His will who reigns above,° to aggravate

---

523 **complicated** twisted   524 **Amphisbaena** (Greek, "going both ways") a fabulous serpent able to go forwards or backwards because it had a head at each end   525 Serpents all (*Hydrus,* as its name indicates, being a water snake)   526 **Dipsas** (Greek) called the "Thirst Snake" from the deadly consequences of its bite   **thick swarmed** cf. i, 767   **the soil** of Libya in Africa   528 **Ophiusa** ("Snake-abounding") Greek name for one of the islands near Minorca   529 "And the great dragon was cast out . . ." (Rev. xii, 9)   533 **issuing forth** another formula, as at 537; ii, 786; viii, 233; ix, 447   546 **exploding** this meant to drive off the stage by hissing   **triumph to shame** "therefore will I change their glory into shame" (Hos., iv, 7)   549 **who reigns above** cf. ii, 814

550 Their penance, laden with fair° fruit, like that
      Which grew in Paradise, the bait of Eve
      Used by the Tempter. On that prospect strange
      Their earnest eyes they fixed, imagining
      For one forbidden tree° a multitude
555 Now risen, to work them further woe or shame,
      Yet, parched with scalding thirst and hunger fierce,
      Though to delude them sent, could not abstain,
      But on they rolled in heaps, and, up the trees
      Climbing, sat thicker than the snaky locks
560 That curled Megaera.° Greedily they plucked
      The fruitage fair to sight, like that which grew
      Near that bituminous lake° where Sodom flamed;
      This, more delusive, not the touch, but taste
      Deceived; they, fondly thinking to allay
565 Their appetite with gust, instead of fruit
      Chewed bitter ashes, which the offended taste
      With spattering noise rejected; oft they assayed,°
      Hunger and thirst° constraining; drugged° as oft,
      With hatefulest disrelish writhed their jaws
570 With soot and cinders filled; so oft they fell
      Into the same illusion, not as Man
      Whom they triúmphed once lapsed. Thus were they plagued,
      And, worn with famine, long and ceaseless hiss,
      Till their lost shape, permitted, they resumed—
575 Yearly enjoined, some say, to undergo
      This annual humbling certain numbered days,
      To dash their pride, and joy for Man seduced.
      However, some tradition they dispersed
      Among the heathen of their purchase got,
580 And fabled how the Serpent, whom they called

550 **fair** was omitted in 1674. Actually it is applied to the
forbidden fruit nine times, including 561; first as "this fair
fruit," ix, 731, 763, 972.   554 **forbidden tree** cf. i, 2   560
Megaera One of the Furies, avenging goddesses; assigned
"snaky locks" by Claudian   562 **that bituminous lake** the
Dead Sea. Keightley reports the following tradition of the
apples of Sodom: "This fruit, when ripe, if it be pressed,
explodes, leaving in the hand only the shreds of the rind and
a few fibres."   567–70 onomatopoeia   568 **Hunger and thirst**
called "Powerful persuaders," ix, 586–87   **drugged** nauseated
as by pills

Ophion,° with Eurynome° (the wide-
Encroaching Eve perhaps), had first the rule
Of high Olympus, thence by Saturn driven
And Ops,° ere yet Dictaean° Jove was born.
   Meanwhile in Paradise the hellish pair   585
Too soon arrived—Sin, there in power before
Once actual, now in body, and to dwell
Habitual habitant; behind her Death,
Close following pace for pace, not mounted yet
On his pale horse;° to whom Sin thus began: 590
   'Second of Satan sprung, all-conquering Death,
What think'st thou of our empire now, though earned,
With travail difficult, not better far
Than still at Hell's dark threshold to have sat watch,
Unnamed, undreaded, and thyself half-starved?'   595
   Whom thus the Sin-born Monster answered soon:
'To me, who with eternal famine pine,
Alike is Hell, or Paradise, or Heaven,
There best where most with ravin I may meet:
Which here, though plenteous, all too little seems   600
To stuff this maw, this vast unhidebound° corpse.'
   To whom the incestuous Mother thus replied:
'Thou, therefore, on these herbs and fruits and flowers,°
Feed first; on each beast next, and fish, and fowl—
No homely morsels; and whatever thing   605
The scythe of Time mows down devour unspared,
Till I, in Man residing through the race,
His thoughts, his looks, words, actions, all infect,
And season him thy last and sweetest prey.'
   This said, they both betook them several ways,   610
Both to destroy, or unimmortal make
All kinds, and for destruction to mature
Sooner or later; which the Almighty seeing,
From his transcendent seat the Saints among,

---

581 **Ophion** "The Serpent," Titan, who was forced to yield
Olympus to Cronus (Saturn). The Renaissance followed Origen
in making an identification with the serpent of Eden **Eurynome**
Her Greek name is immediately translated. 584 **Ops** fertility
goddess made wife of Saturn by Romans **Dictaean** referring to
Mount Dicte in Crete, the island where Jupiter was brought
up. 590 **his pale horse** cf. Revelation, vi, 8 601 **unhidebound**
loose-skinned (famished) 603 **fruits and flowers** cf. viii, 44

615 To those bright Orders uttered thus his voice:
    'See with what heat these dogs of Hell advance
To waste and havoc yonder World, which I
So fair and good created, and had still
Kept in that state, had not the folly of Man
620 Let in these wasteful furies, who impute
Folly to me (so doth the Prince of Hell
And his adherents), that with so much ease
I suffer them to enter and possess°
A place so heavenly, and, conniving, seem
625 To gratify my scornful enemies,
That laugh, as if, transported with some fit
Of passion I to them had quitted all,
At random yielded up to their misrule,
And know not that I called and drew them thither,
630 My Hell-hounds, to lick up the draff and filth
Which Man's polluting sin with taint hath shed
On what was pure; till, crammed and gorged, nigh burst
With sucked and glutted offal, at one sling°
Of thy victorious arm, well-pleasing Son,
635 Both Sin and Death, and yawning Grave, at last
Through Chaos hurled, obstruct the mouth of Hell
Forever, and seal up his ravenous jaws.
Then Heaven and Earth, renewed, shall be made pure°
To sanctity that shall receive no stain:
640 Till then the curse pronounced on both precedes.'
    He ended, and the Heavenly audience loud°
Sung Halleluiah, as the sound of seas,°
Through multitude that sung: 'Just are thy ways,°
Righteous are thy decrees on all thy works;
645 Who can extenuate° thee? Next, to the Son,
Destined restorer of Mankind, by whom
New Heaven and Earth shall to the ages rise,

---

623 **enter and possess** legal terminology 633 **at one sling** "and
the souls of thine enemies, them shall he sling out, as out of
the middle of a sling" (1 Sam. xxv, 29) 638 i.e., the world
will be burned at the Last Judgment 641 **loud** functions both
as adjective and as adverb 642–43 "And I heard as it were
the voice of a great multitude, and as the voice of many
waters, . . . saying, Alleluia!" (Rev. xix, 6) 643 **'Just are thy
ways'** "Just and true are thy ways" (Rev. xv, 3) 645 **extenuate**
disparage, reduce

Or down from Heaven descend.' Such was their song,°
While the Creator, calling forth by name
His mighty Angels, gave them several charge,   650
As sorted best with present things. The Sun
Had first his precept so to move, so shine,
As might affect the Earth with cold and heat
Scarce tolerable, and from the north to call
Decrepit winter, from the south to bring   655
Solstitial summer's heat. To the blank° Moon
Her office they prescribed; to the other five
Their planetary motions and aspécts,
In sextile, square, and trine, and opposite,°
Of noxious efficacy, and when to join   660
In synod unbenign; and taught the fixed°
Their influence malignant when to shower—
Which of them, rising with the Sun or falling,°
Should prove tempestuous. To the winds they set
Their corners, when with bluster to confound   665
Sea, air, and shore; the thunder when to roll
With terror through the dark aerial hall.
Some say he bid his Angels turn askance
The poles of Earth twice ten degrees and more
From the Sun's axle; they with labour pushed   670
Oblique the centric Globe:° some say the Sun
Was bid turn reins from the equinoctial road
Like distant breadth to Taurus° with the seven
Atlantic Sisters° and the Spartan twins
Up to the Tropic Crab, thence down amain   675
By Leo, and the Virgin, and the Scales,°
As deep as Capricorn, to bring in change
Of seasons to each clime: else had the spring
Perpetual smiled on Earth with vernant flowers,
Equal in days and nights, except to those   680
Beyond the polar circles; to them day
Had unbenighted shone, while the low Sun,
To recompense his distance, in their sight

647–48 cf. Revelation, xxi, 1, 2   656 **blank** pale   659 alter-
nating prosperous and malignant positions   661 **the fixed**
stars   663 **rising . . . or falling** said of mists, v, 191   671 **the
centric Globe** the Earth   673 **Taurus** cf. i, 769   674 **Atlantic
Sisters** the Pleiades   676 **the Scales** Libra (cf. iv, 997)

Had rounded still the horizon, and not known
685 Or east or west, which had forbid the snow
From cold Estotiland,° and south as far
Beneath Magellan. At that tasted fruit,
The Sun, as from Thyestean banquet,° turned
His course intended; else how had the world
690 Inhabited, though sinless, more than now
Avoided pinching cold and scorching heat?
These changes in the heavens, though slow, produced
Like change on sea and land—sidereal blast,°
Vapour, and mist, and exhalation hot,
695 Corrupt and pestilent. Now from the north
Of Norumbega,° and the Samoed° shore,
Bursting their brazen dungeon, armed with ice,
And snow and hail, and stormy gust and flaw,°
Boreas and Caecias and Argestes loud
700 And Thrascias° rend the woods, and seas upturn;
With adverse blast upturns them from the south
Notus, and Afer° black with thundrous clouds
From Serraliona;° thwart of these, as fierce
Forth rush the Levant and the Ponent° winds,
705 Eurus and Zephyr,° with their lateral noise,
Sirocco and Libecchio.° Thus began
Outrage from lifeless things; but Discord first,
Daughter of Sin, among the irrational,
Death introduced through fierce antipathy:
710 Beast now with beast 'gan war, and fowl with fowl,
And fish with fish; to graze the herb all leaving
Devoured each other, nor stood much in awe

686 **Estotiland** an island off Labrador, according to Mercator maps. 688 **Thyestean banquet** Atreus slew the children of his brother Thyestes and served them to him at a banquet—a transgression from which the sun averted his face and reversed his course for one day. 693 **sidereal** (in the original *sideral*) **blast** from the stars 696 **Norumbega** roughly, the New England area **Samoed** "Northeast of Russia lieth Samoedia by the river Ob" (Milton's *History of Muscovia*) 698 **flaw** a blast of wind 699–700 northern winds 702 southern winds 703 **Serraliona** Sierra Leone, West African cape with a six-month-long rainy season 704 **the Levant and the Ponent** the East (sun-rising) and the West 705 as above 706 **Sirocco and Libecchio** Italian names for the southeast and southwest winds

Of Man, but fled him, or with countenance grim
Glared on him passing. These were from without
The growing miseries, which Adam saw   715
Already in part, though hid in gloomiest shade,
To sorrow abandoned, but worse felt within,
And, in a troubled sea of passion tossed,°
Thus to disburden sought with sad complaint:
  'O miserable of happy! is this the end   720
Of this new glorious World, and me so late
The glory of that glory? who now, become
Accursed of blessed, hide me from the face
Of God, whom to behold was then my height
Of happiness; yet well, if here would end   725
The misery, I deserved it, and would bear
My own deserving; but this will not serve:
All that I eat or drink, or shall beget,
Is propagated curse. O voice, once heard
Delightfully, *"Increase and multiply,"*°   730
Now death to hear! for what can I increase
Or multiply but curses on my head?
Who of all ages to succeed, but, feeling
The evil on him brought by me, will curse
My head? "Ill fare our ancestor impure;   735
For this we may thank Adam," but his thanks
Shall be the execration. So, besides
Mine own that bide upon me, all from me
Shall with a fierce reflux on me redound—
On me, as on their natural centre, light   740
Heavy, though in their place. O fleeting joys
Of Paradise, dear bought with lasting woes!
Did I request thee, Maker, from my clay
To mould me Man? did I solicit thee
From darkness to promote me, or here place   745
In this delicious garden? As my will
Concurred not to my being, it were but right

718 "But the wicked are like the troubled sea, when it cannot
rest, whose waters cast up mire and dirt" (Is. lvii, 20). "in . . .
sea/ Tossed" was literal at 286–87, and "'a troubled sea of
noises and hoarse disputes" is a personal allusion at the end
of the preface to Book II of *The Reason of Church
Government.* 730 Genesis, i, 28

And equal° to reduce me to my dust,
Desirous to resign and render back
750 All I received, unable to perform
Thy terms too hard, by which I was to hold
The good I sought not. To the loss of that,
Sufficient penalty, why hast thou added
The sense of endless woes? Inexplicable
755 Thy justice seems, yet, to say truth, too late
I thus contest; then should have been refused
Those terms, whatever, when they were proposed.
Thou didst accept them: wilt thou enjoy the good,
Then cavil the conditions? and, though God
760 Made thee without thy leave, what if thy son
Prove disobedient, and, reproved, retort,
,"Wherefore didst thou beget me? I sought it not."°
Wouldst thou admit for his contempt of thee
That proud excuse? yet him not thy election,°
765 But natural necessity, begot.
God made thee of choice his own, and of his own°
To serve him; thy reward was of his grace;
Thy punishment, then, justly is at his will.
Be it° so, for I submit; his doom is fair
770 That dust I am, and shall to dust return.°
O welcome hour whenever! why delays
His hand to execute what his decree
Fixed on this day? why do I overlive?
Why am I mocked with death, and lengthened out
775 To deathless pain? how gladly would I meet
Mortality, my sentence, and be earth
Insensible! how glad would lay me down
As in my mother's lap!° there I should rest
And sleep secure; his dreadful voice no more
780 Would thunder in my ears; no fear of worse
To me and to my offspring would torment me
With cruel expectation. Yet one doubt°
Pursues me still—lest all I cannot die;°

748 **equal** equitable 762 cf. Isaiah, xlv, 10 764 **election** choice
766 cf. 759–60 769 **Be it** elide 770 cf. 208 778 **As in my mother's
lap** cf. xi, 536 and "But on their mother Earth's dear lap did lie" (*F.
Q.*, V, vii, 9) 782 ff. The mortalist or soul-sleeper heresy—Milton's
own belief and reasoning in his *Christian Doctrine* (I, xiii) 783 **all
I cannot die** *non omnis moriar* (Horace, *Carm.* III, 30, 63)

Lest that pure breath of life, the Spirit of Man
Which God inspired, cannot together perish 785
With this corporeal clod; then, in the grave,
Or in some other dismal place, who knows
But I shall die a living death?° O thought
Horrid, if true! yet why? It was but breath
Of life that sinned:° what dies but what had life 790
And sin? the body properly hath neither.
All of me, then, shall die: let this appease°
The doubt, since human reach no further knows.
For, though the Lord of all be infinite,
Is his wrath also? be it,° Man is not so, 795
But mortal doomed. How can he exercise
Wrath without end° on Man, whom death must end?
Can he make deathless death? that were to make
Strange contradictions; which to God himself
Impossible is held, as argument 800
Of weakness, not of power. Will he draw out,
For anger's sake, finite to infinite
In punished Man, to satisfy his rigour,
Satisfied never? that were to extend
His sentence beyond dust and Nature's law, 805
By which all causes else, according still
To the reception of their matter, act,
Not to the extent of their own sphere. But say
That death be not one stroke, as I supposed,
Bereaving sense, but endless misery° 810
From this day onward, which I feel begun
Both in me and without° me, and so last
To perpetuity, ay me, that fear
Comes thundering back with dreadful revolution
On my defenceless head; both Death and I 815
Am found eternal, and incorporate both,
Nor I on my part single; in me all
Posterity stands cursed. Fair patrimony
That I must leave ye, sons; oh, were I able
To waste it all myself, and leave ye none! 820

788 **a living death** cf. *Samson Agonistes,* 100 789–90 cf.
784 792 Cf. 783 and iii, 246 795 **be it** elide, as at 769 797
without end used eight times previously 810 **endless misery**
cf. i, 142 812 **without** outside

So disinherited, how would ye bless
Me, now your curse! Ah, why should all Mankind,
For one man's fault thus guiltless be condemned,
If guiltless? But from me what can proceed
825 But all corrupt, both mind and will depraved
Not to do only, but to will the same
With me? How can they, then, acquitted stand
In sight of God? Him, after all disputes,
Forced I absolve: all my evasions vain
830 And reasonings, though through mazes, lead me still
But to my own conviction: first and last°
On me, me only, as the source and spring
Of all corruption, all the blame lights due.
So might the wrath. Fond wish! couldst thou support
835 That burden, heavier than the Earth to bear—
Than all the world much heavier, though divided
With that bad Woman? Thus, what thou desir'st
And what thou fear'st alike destroys all hope
Of refuge, and concludes thee miserable
840 Beyond all past example and future,
To Satan only like, both crime and doom.
O Conscience, into what abyss of fears
And horrors hast thou driven me; out of which
I find no way, from deep to deeper plunged!'
845   Thus Adam to himself lamented loud
Through the still night, not now, as ere Man fell,
Wholesome and cool and mild, but with black air
Accompanied, with damps and dreadful gloom;
Which to his evil conscience represented
850 All things with double terror. On the ground
Outstretched he lay, on the cold ground, and oft
Cursed his creation, Death as oft accused
Of tardy execution, since denounced
The day of his offence. 'Why comes not Death,'°
855 Said he, 'with one thrice acceptable stroke
To end me? Shall Truth fail to keep her word,
Justice divine not hasten to be just?
But Death comes not at call;° Justice divine

831 **first and last** cf. ii, 324; iii, 134   854 **Why comes not Death**
an echo of Sophocles' *Philoctetes*, 793 ff.   858 cf. xi, 491–93

Mends not her slowest pace for prayers or cries.
O woods, O fountains, hillocks, dales, and bowers,   860
With other echo late I taught your shades
To answer, and resound far other song.'°
Whom, thus afflicted, when sad Eve° beheld,
Desolate where she sat, approaching nigh,
Soft words to his fierce passion she assayed,   865
But her, with stern regard,° he thus repelled:
    'Out of my sight, thou serpent; that name best
Befits thee with him leagued, thyself as false
And hateful: nothing wants, but that thy shape
Like his, and colour serpentine, may show   870
Thy inward fraud, to warn all creatures from thee
Henceforth, lest that too heavenly form,° pretended°
To hellish falsehood, snare them. But for thee
I had persisted happy, had not thy pride
And wandering vanity, when least was safe,   875
Rejected my forewarning and disdained
Not to be trusted—longing to be seen,
Though by the Devil himself; him overweening
To overreach; but, with the Serpent meeting,
Fooled and beguiled; by him thou, I by thee,   880
To trust thee from my side, imagined wise,
Constant, mature, proof against all assaults,
And understood not all was but a show,
Rather than solid virtue, all but a rib
Crooked by nature—bent, as now appears,   885
More to the part sinister°—from me drawn;
Well if thrown out, as supernumerary
To my just number found.° Oh, why did God,°
Creator wise,° that peopled highest Heaven°

861–62 verbal echoes here of Virgil's *Eclogues*, I, 4–5, which also
influenced "Lycidas" (68)   863 **sad Eve** as at 159   866 **with stern
regard** cf. iv, 877   872 **heavenly form** cf. ix, 457   **pretended** Latin,
stretched out (like a screen)   886 **sinister** in Latin, left   887–88
Tradition had it that Adam had had an extra, thirteenth rib, from
which Eve was formed.   888 ff. Euripides' Hippolytus was like-
minded (616 ff.): "Great Zeus, why didst thou, to man's sorrow, put
woman, evil counterfeit, to dwell where shines the sun? If thou wert
minded that the human race should multiply, it was not from
women they should have drawn their stock. . . ."   888–89 **God./
Creator wise** cf. ix, 938   **highest Heaven** cf. i, 517; iii, 657; viii, 178

890 With Spirits masculine, create at last
     This novelty on Earth, this fair defect
     Of Nature, and not fill the World at once
     With men as Angels, without feminine;
     Or find some other way to generate
895 Mankind? this mischief had not then befallen,
     And more that shall befall—innumerable
     Disturbances on Earth through female snares,
     And strait conjunction with this sex: for either
     He never shall find out fit mate, but such
900 As some misfortune brings him, or mistake,
     Or whom he wishes most shall seldom gain,
     Through her perverseness, but shall see her gained
     By a far worse, or, if she love, withheld
     By parents, or his happiest choice too late
905 Shall meet, already linked and wedlock-bound°
     To a fell adversary, his hate or shame,
     Which infinite calamity shall cause
     To human life, and household peace confound.'
       He added not, and from her turned, but Eve,
910 Not so repulsed, with tears that ceased not flowing
     And tresses all disordered, at his feet
     Fell humble, and, embracing them, besought
     His peace, and thus proceeded in her plaint:
     'Forsake me not thus, Adam, witness Heaven
915 What love sincere and reverence in my heart
     I bear thee, and unweeting have offended,
     Unhappily deceived; thy suppliant
     I beg, and clasp thy knees; bereave me not
     Whereon I live, thy gentle looks, thy aid,
920 Thy counsel in this uttermost distress,
     My only strength and stay. Forlorn of thee,
     Whither shall I betake me, where subsist?
     While yet we live, scarce one short hour perhaps,
     Between us two let there be peace; both joining,
925 As joined in injuries, one enmity

905 **already linked and wedlock-bound** It is uncertain whether
these participles refer to the man or to the woman, "his
happiest choice." Milton after his first wife left him considered
marrying a Miss Davis; 910–13 describe what that first wife did
to win his forgiveness.

Against a foe by doom express assigned us,
That cruel Serpent. On me exercise not
Thy hatred for this misery befallen,
On me already lost, me than thyself
More miserable; both have sinned, but thou   930
Against God only, I against God and thee,
And to the place of judgement will return,
There with my cries importune Heaven, that all
The sentence, from thy head removed, may light
On me, sole cause to thee of all this woe,   935
Me, me only, just object of His ire.'
    She ended, weeping, and her lowly plight,
Immoveable° till peace obtained from fault
Acknowledged and deplored, in Adam wrought
Commiseration: soon his heart relented   940
Towards her, his life so late, and sole delight,°
Now at his feet submissive in distress—
Creature so fair° his reconcilement seeking,
His counsel whom she had displeased, his aid;
As one disarmed, his anger all he lost,   945
And thus with peaceful words upraised her soon:
    'Unwary, and too desirous, as before
So now, of what thou know'st not, who desir'st
The punishment all on thyself; alas!
Bear thine own first, ill able to sustain   950
His full wrath whose thou feel'st as yet least part,
And my displeasure bear'st so ill. If prayers
Could alter high decrees,° I to that place°
Would speed before thee and be louder heard,
That on my head all might be visited,   955
Thy frailty and infirmer sex forgiven,
To me committed and by me exposed.
But rise; let us no more contend, nor blame
Each other, blamed enough elsewhere, but strive
In offices of love how we may lighten   960
Each other's burden in our share of woe;
Since this day's death denounced,° if aught I see,

938 **Immoveable** best taken as modifying Eve rather than
Adam 941 **sole delight** cf. i, 160   943 **Creature so fair** cf. iv,
468 953 **high decrees** cf. iii, 126; v, 717 **that place** cf.
932 962 **death denounced** cf. 49, 210, 852–53; ix, 695

Will prove no sudden, but a slow-paced evil,
A long day's dying, to augment our pain,
965 And to our seed (O hapless seed!) derived.'
　　To whom thus Eve, recovering heart, replied:
'Adam, by sad experiment I know
How little weight my words with thee can find,
Found so erroneous, thence by just event
970 Found so unfortunate; nevertheless,
Restored by thee, vile as I am, to place
Of new acceptance, hopeful to regain
Thy love, the sole contentment of my heart,
Living or dying from thee I will not hide
975 What thoughts in my unquiet breast are risen,
Tending to some relief of our extremes,
Or end, though sharp and sad, yet tolerable,
As in our evils,° and of easier choice.
If care of our descent° perplex us most,
980 Which must be born to certain woe, devoured
By Death at last, and miserable it is
To be to others cause of misery,
Our own begotten, and of our loins to bring
Into this cursèd world a woeful race,
985 That, after wretched life, must be at last
Food for so foul a monster, in thy power
It lies, yet ere conception, to prevent
The race unblest, to being yet unbegot.
Childless thou art, childless remain: so Death
990 Shall be deceived his glut, and with us two
Be forced to satisfy his ravenous maw.
But, if thou judge it hard and difficult,
Conversing, looking, loving, to abstain
From love's due rites, nuptial embraces sweet,
995 And with desire to languish without hope
Before the present object languishing
With like desire, which would be misery
And torment less than none of what we dread,
Then, both ourselves and seed at once to free
1000 From what we fear for both, let us make short;
Let us seek Death, or, he not found, supply

978 **As in our evils** considering our plight   979 **descent**
descendants

With our own hands his office on ourselves.
Why stand we longer shivering under fears
That show no end but death, and have the power,
Of many ways to die the shortest choosing,   *1005*
Destruction with destruction to destroy?'
   She ended here, or vehement despair
Broke off the rest; so much of death her thoughts
Had entertained as dyed her cheeks with pale.
But Adam, with such counsel nothing swayed,   *1010*
To better hopes his more attentive mind
Labouring had raised, and thus to Eve replied:
   'Eve, thy contempt of life and pleasure seems
To argue in thee something more sublime
And excellent than what thy mind contemns,   *1015*
But self-destruction therefore sought refutes
That excellence thought in thee, and implies
Not thy contempt, but anguish and regret
For loss of life and pleasure overloved.
Or, if thou covet death, as utmost end   *1020*
Of misery, so thinking to evade
The penalty pronounced, doubt not but God
Hath wiselier armed his vengeful ire° than so
To be forestalled: much more I fear lest death
So snatched will not exempt us from the pain   *1025*
We are by doom to pay; rather such acts
Of contumacy will provoke the Highest
To make death in us live: Then let us seek
Some safer resolution, which methinks
I have in view, calling to mind with heed   *1030*
Part of our sentence, that thy seed shall bruise
The Serpent's head—piteous amends, unless
Be meant, whom I conjecture, our grand foe,°
Satan, who in the Serpent hath contrived
Against us this deceit: to crush his head   *1035*
Would be revenge indeed, which will be lost
By death brought on ourselves, or childless days
Resolved as thou proposest; so our foe
Shall 'scape his punishment ordained, and we
Instead shall double ours upon our heads.   *1040*

1023 **his vengeful ire** cf. i, 148   1033 **our grand foe** cf. i, 122;
vi, 149

No more be mentioned, then, of violence
Against ourselves, and wilful barrenness,
That cuts us off from hope, and savours only
Rancour and pride, impatience and despite,
1045 Reluctance° against God and his just yoke
Laid on our necks. Remember with what mild
And gracious temper he both heard and judged,°
Without wrath or reviling. We expected
Immediate dissolution, which we thought
1050 Was meant by death that day; when, lo! to thee
Pains only in child-bearing were foretold,
And bringing forth, soon recompensed with joy,
Fruit of thy womb. On me the curse aslope
Glanced on the ground: with labour I must earn
1055 My bread—what harm? Idleness had been worse;°
My labour will sustain me; and, lest cold
Or heat should injure us, his timely care
Hath, unbesought, provided, and his hands
Clothed us unworthy, pitying while he judged.
1060 How much more, if we pray him, will his ear
Be open, and his heart to pity incline,°
And teach us further by what means to shun
The inclement seasons, rain, ice, hail, and snow,
Which now the sky, with various face, begins
1065 To show us in this mountain, while the winds
Blow moist and keen, shattering the graceful locks
Of these fair spreading trees, which bids us seek
Some better shroud, some better warmth to cherish
Our limbs benumbed, ere this diurnal star
1070 Leave cold the night, how we his gathered beams
Reflected may with matter sere foment,
Or by collision of two bodies grind
The air attrite° to fire, as late the clouds,
Justling, or pushed with winds, rude in their shock,
Tine° the slant lightning, whose thwart flame,
1075   driven down,
Kindles the gummy bark of fir or pine,

1045 **Reluctance** struggling (cf. 515)   1046–47 **mild . . . judged**
cf. "the mild judge," 96.   1055 **Idleness had been worse** The
strenuous Puritan emerges.   1061 **to pity incline** cf. iii, 402,
405   1073 **attrite** worn by friction   1075 **Tine** kindle

And sends a comfortable heat from far,
Which might supply the sun; such fire to use,
And what may else be remedy or cure
To evils which our own misdeeds have wrought,   *1080*
He will instruct us praying, and of grace
Beseeching him, so as we need not fear
To pass commodiously this life, sustained
By him with many comforts till we end
In dust, our final rest and native home.   *1085*
What better can we do than, to the place
Repairing where he judged us, prostrate fall
Before him reverent, and there confess
Humbly our faults, and pardon beg, with tears
Watering the ground,° and with our sighs the air   *1090*
Frequenting,° sent from hearts contrite, in sign
Of sorrow unfeigned and humiliation meek?
Undoubtedly he will relent, and turn
From his displeasure, in whose look serene,
When angry most he seemed and most severe,   *1095*
What else but favour, grace, and mercy shone?'
    So spake our Father penitent, nor Eve
Felt less remorse: they, forthwith to the place
Repairing where he judged them, prostrate fell°
Before him reverent, and both confessed   *1100*
Humbly their faults, and pardon begged, with tears
Watering the ground, and with their sighs the air
Frequenting, sent from hearts contrite, in sign
Of sorrow unfeigned and humiliation meek.

1089–90 **tears/ Watering the ground** *spargitur et tellus lacrimis*
(*Aen.* XI, 191)   1091 **Frequenting** filling   1099–1104 A daring
repetition of 1087–92

BOOK XI

THE ARGUMENT

*The Son of God presents to his Father the prayers of our first
parents now repenting, and intercedes for them. God accepts
them, but declares that they must no longer abide in Paradise;
sends Michael with a band of Cherubim to dispossess them,
but first to reveal to Adam future things; Michael's coming
down. Adam shows to Eve certain ominous signs: he discerns Michael's approach; goes out to meet him; the Angel
denounces their departure. Eve's lamentation. Adam pleads,
but submits; the Angel leads him up to a high hill; sets
before him in vision what shall happen till the Flood.*

THUS they, in lowliest plight, repentant stood°
Praying, for from the mercy-seat above
Prevenient grace descending had removed
The stony from their hearts and made new flesh°
5   Regenerate grow instead, that sighs now breathed
Unutterable which the Spirit of prayer
Inspired, and winged for Heaven with speedier flight
Than loudest oratory; yet their port
Not of mean suitors, nor important less
10   Seemed their petition than when the ancient pair
In fables old, less ancient yet than these,
Deucalion and chaste Pyrrha, to restore
The race of mankind drowned, before the shrine
Of Themis stood devout.° To Heaven their prayers
15   Flew up, nor missed the way, by envious winds

1 **stood** in apparent contradiction to x, 1099. Some take as
meaning "continued," but cf. the punning 8–9 and note 14,
where this interpretation is scarcely possible. Ovid has Pyrrha
and Deucalion act as at 1099 ff.; the Puritan in *Christian
Doctrine* allows for standing to pray.   4 Based on Ezekiel, xi,
19   10–14 After a deluge from Zeus like the biblical one,
Deucalion and Pyrrha received the advice from the oracle of
Themis, goddess of justice, to cast stones behind them, which
turned into men and women, a new race called the Stone
People.

Blown vagabond or frustrate:° in they passed
Dimensionless° through heavenly doors, then, clad
With incense, where the golden altar fumed
By their great Intercessor, came in sight
Before the Father's throne. Them the glad Son   20
Presenting, thus to intercede began:
  'See, Father, what firstfruits on Earth are sprung
From thy implanted grace in Man—these sighs
And prayers, which in this golden censer, mixed°
With incense, I, thy priest, before thee bring;   25
Fruits of more pleasing savour, from thy seed
Sown with contrition in his heart, than those
Which, his own hand manuring,° all the trees
Of Paradise could have produced, ere fallen
From innocence. Now, therefore, bend thine ear   30
To supplication; hear his sighs, though mute;
Unskilful with what words to pray, let me
Interpret for him, me his advocate
And propitiation;° all his works on me,
Good or not good, ingraft; my merit those   35
Shall perfect, and for these my death shall pay.
Accept me, and in me from these receive
The smell of peace toward Mankind; let him live,
Before thee reconciled, at least his days
Numbered, though sad, till death, his doom (which I   40
To mitigate° thus plead, not to reverse),
To better life shall yield him, where with me
All my redeemed may dwell in joy and bliss,
Made one with me, as I with thee am one.'
  To whom the Father, without cloud, serene: 45
'All thy request for Man, accepted Son,
Obtain; all thy request was my decree,
But longer in that Paradise to dwell
The law I gave to Nature him forbids;
Those pure immortal elements, that know   50
No gross, no unharmonious mixture foul,
Eject him, tainted now, and purge him off,
As a distemper gross, to air as gross

15–16 Contrast the Paradise of Fools, iii, 485–89.   17 **Dimensionless** incorporeal   24 cf. Revelation, viii, 3   28 **manuring** cultivating   34 **propitiation** a word from 1 John, ii, 2   40–41 **doom . . . mitigate** cf. x, 76

And mortal food as may dispose him best
55 For dissolution wrought by sin, that first
Distempered all things, and of incorrupt
Corrupted. I at first with two fair gifts
Created him endowed—with Happiness
And Immortality; that fondly lost,
60 This other served but to eternize woe,
Till I provided Death; so Death becomes
His final remedy, and after life
Tried in sharp tribulation, and refined
By faith and faithful works, to second life,°
65 Waked in the renovation of the just,
Resigns him up with Heaven and Earth renewed.°
But let us call to synod all the Blest
Through Heaven's wide bounds; from them I will
         not hide
My judgements, how with Mankind I proceed,
70 As how with peccant Angels late they saw,
And in their state, though firm, stood more confirmed.'
    He ended, and the Son gave signal high
To the bright Minister that watched; he blew
His trumpet, heard in Oreb° since perhaps
75 When God descended, and perhaps once more
To sound at general doom. The angelic blast
Filled all the regions: from their blissful bowers
Of amaranthine° shade, fountain or spring,
By the waters of life, where'er they sat
80 In fellowships of joy, the Sons of Light°
Hasted, resorting to the summons high,
And took their seats, till from his throne supreme°
The Almighty thus pronounced his sovran will:
    'O Sons, like one of us Man is become
85 To know both good and evil, since his taste
Of that defended° fruit; but let him boast
His knowledge of good lost and evil got;°
Happier had it sufficed him to have known
Good by itself and evil not at all.
90 He sorrows now, repents, and prays contrite—

64 cf. xii, 427   66 **Heaven and Earth renewed** cf. x, 638   74 **Oreb**
cf. i, 7   78 **amaranthine** cf. iii, 352 ff.   80 cf. "Lycidas" 177–79.   82
throne supreme cf. x, 28   86 **defended** in the French sense of
forbidden   87 cf. vii, 543; ix, 697, 723; also iv, 222; viii, 324

My motions in him; longer than they move,
His heart I know how variable and vain,
Self-left. Lest, therefore, his now bolder hand
Reach also of the Tree of Life, and eat,
And live forever, dream at least to live   95
Forever, to remove him I decree,
And send him from the Garden forth, to till
The ground whence he was taken, fitter soil.
     'Michael, this my behest have thou in charge:
Take to thee from among the Cherubim   100
Thy choice of flaming warriors, lest the Fiend,
Or in behalf of° Man or to invade
Vacant possession, some new trouble raise;
Haste thee, and from the Paradise of God
Without remorse drive out the sinful pair,   105
From hallowed ground the unholy, and denounce
To them, and to their progeny, from thence
Perpetual banishment. Yet, lest they faint
At the sad sentence rigorously urged
(For I behold them softened, and with tears   110
Bewailing their excess°), all terror hide.
If patiently thy bidding they obey,
Dismiss them not disconsolate; reveal
To Adam what shall come in future days,
As I shall thee enlighten; intermix   115
My covenant in the Woman's seed renewed.
So send them forth, though sorrowing, yet in peace;
And on the east side of the Garden place,
Where entrance up from Eden easiest climbs,
Cherubic watch,° and of a sword the flame   120
Wide-waving, all approach far off to fright,
And guard all passage to the Tree of Life,
Lest Paradise a réceptácle prove
To Spirits foul, and all my trees their prey,
With whose stolen fruit Man once more to delude.' 125
     He ceased, and the Archangelic Power prepared
For swift descent; with him the cohort bright
Of watchful Cherubim. Four faces each°

102 **in behalf of** with regard to   111 **excess** transgression   120
Cherubic watch cf. ix, 68, and below, 128   128 **Four faces each**
cf. vi, 753

Had, like a double Janus;° all their shape
130 Spangled with eyes more numerous than those
Of Argus,° and more wakeful than to drowse,
Charmed with Arcadian pipe, the pastoral reed
Of Hermes, or his opiate rod. Meanwhile,
To resalute the World with sacred light,°
135 Leucothea° waked, and with fresh dews° embalmed
The Earth, when Adam and first matron Eve
Had ended now their orisons, and found,
Strength added from above, new hope to spring
Out of despair, joy, but with fear yet linked;
140 Which thus to Eve his welcome words renewed:
'Eve, easily may faith admit that all
The good which we enjoy from Heaven descends;
But that from us aught should ascend to Heaven
So prevalent as to concern the mind
145 Of God° high-blest, or to incline his will,
Hard to belief may seem; yet this will prayer,
Or one short sigh of human breath, upborne
Even to the seat of God. For, since I sought
By prayer the offended Deity to appease,
150 Kneeled and before him humbled all my heart,
Methought I saw him placable and mild,
Bending his ear; persuasion in me grew
That I was heard with favour; peace returned
Home to my breast, and to my memory
155 His promise that thy seed shall bruise our Foe;
Which, then not minded in dismay, yet now
Assures me that the bitterness of death°
Is past, and we shall live. Whence hail to thee,

129 **a double Janus** Roman divinity presiding over gates and the beginning of everything, such as the year (thus January) and seasons. Usually represented with two heads looking east and west, he sometimes had four, signifying power in the four quarters of the earth. 131 **Argus** who, in words from *Of Reformation*, had "a hundred eyes of jealousy" with which to watch Juno's rival Io, but Hermes succeeded in putting them all to sleep 134 **sacred light** cf. ix, 192 135 **Leucothea** "Shining goddess," on Ovid's authority the Roman Matuta, goddess of the dawn **fresh dews** cf. i, 771 144–145 **the mind/ Of God** cf. v, 117 157 **the bitterness of death** phrase from 1 Samuel xv, 32

Eve rightly called, Mother of all Mankind,°
Mother of all things living,° since by thee   160
Man is to live, and all things live for Man.'
    To whom thus Eve, with sad demeanour meek:
'Ill-worthy I such title should belong
To me transgressor, who, for thee ordained
A help, became thy snare; to me reproach   165
Rather belongs, distrust and all dispraise:
But infinite in pardon was my Judge,
That I, who first brought death on all, am graced
The source of life; next favourable thou,
Who highly thus to entitle me vouchsaf'st,   170
Far other name deserving. But the field
To labour calls us, now with sweat imposed,
Though after sleepless night; for see, the Morn,
All unconcerned with our unrest, begins
Her rosy progress smiling; let us forth,   175
I never from thy side henceforth to stray,
Where'er our day's work lies, though now enjoined
Laborious, till day droop; while here we dwell,
What can be toilsome in these pleasant walks?
Here let us live, though in fallen state, content.'   180
    So spake, so wished, much-humbled Eve; but Fate
Subscribed not; Nature first gave signs, impressed
On bird, beast, air—air suddenly eclipsed,°
After short blush of morn; nigh in her sight°
The bird of Jove,° stooped from his aery tour,°   185
Two birds of gayest plume before him drove;
Down from a hill the beast that reigns in woods,
First hunter then, pursued a gentle brace,
Goodliest of all the forest, hart and hind;
Direct to the eastern gate was bent their flight.   190
Adam observed, and, with his eye the chase
Pursuing, not unmoved, to Eve thus spake:
    'O Eve, some further change awaits us nigh,

---

159 **Mother of all Mankind** cf. i, 36; v, 388   160 "And Adam
called his wife's name Eve; because she was the mother of all
living" (Gen. iii, 20).   183 **eclipsed** a bad sign; cf. "Lycidas,"
101.   184–86 modeled on an omen in the twelfth book of the
Aeneid   185 **The bird of Jove** the eagle   **tour** perhaps to be
spelled *tower* and meaning lofty flight, but the ambiguity is to
the good

Which Heaven by these mute signs in Nature shows,
195 Forerunners of his purpose, or to warn
Us, haply too secure of our discharge
From penalty because from death released
Some days: how long, and what till then our life,
Who knows, or more than this, that we are dust,
200 And thither must return, and be no more.
Why else this double object in our sight
Of flight pursued in the air and o'er the ground
One way the selfsame hour? why in the east
Darkness ere day's mid-course, and morning-light
205 More orient in yon western cloud, that draws
O'er the blue firmament a radiant white,
And slow descends, with something heavenly fraught?'
    He erred not, for by this the heavenly bands
Down from a sky of jasper lighted now
210 In Paradise, and on a hill made halt,
A glorious apparition, had not doubt
And carnal fear that day dimmed Adam's eye.
Not that more glorious when the Angels met°
Jacob in Mahanaim, where he saw
215 The field pavilioned with his guardians bright,°
Nor that which on the flaming mount° appeared°
In Dothan, covered with a camp of fire,
Against the Syrian king, who, to surprise
One man,° assassinlike, had levied war,
220 War unproclaimed. The princely Hierarch
In their bright stand there left his Powers to seize
Possession of the Garden; he alone,
To find where Adam sheltered, took his way,
Not unperceived of Adam, who to Eve,
225 While the great visitant approached, thus spake:
    'Eve, now expect great tidings, which perhaps
Of us will soon determine, or impose
New laws° to be observed, for I descry,
From yonder blazing cloud that veils the hill,
230 One of the heavenly host,° and, by his gait,°

213–15 Genesis, xxxvii, 1–2 215 **guardians bright** cf. iii,
512 216–20 2 Kings, vi, 13–17 216 **flaming mount** cf. v,
598 219 **One man** Elisha 228 **New laws** cf. v, 679, 680 230
the heavenly host cf. ii, 824 **by his gait** cf. iv, 870

None of the meanest—some great Potentate,°
Or of the Thrones above, such majesty
Invests him coming, yet not terrible,
That I should fear, nor sociably mild,
As Raphael, that I should much confide,   235
But solemn and sublime; whom not to offend,
With reverence I must meet, and thou retire.'
    He ended; and the Archangel soon drew nigh,
Not in his shape celestial, but as man
Clad to meet man; over his lucid° arms   240
A military vest of purple flowed,
Livelier than Meliboean,° or the grain
Of Sarra,° worn by kings and heroes old°
In time of truce; Iris° had dipped the woof;
His starry helm unbuckled showed him prime   245
In manhood where youth ended; by his side,
As in a glistering zodiac, hung the sword,
Satan's dire dread, and in his hand the spear.
Adam bowed low; he, kingly, from his state°
Inclined not, but his coming thus declared: 250
    'Adam, Heaven's high behest no preface needs;
Sufficient that thy prayers are heard, and Death,
Then due by sentence when thou didst transgress,
Defeated of his seizure many days,
Given thee of grace, wherein thou may'st repent,   255
And one bad act with many deeds well done
May'st cover: well may then thy Lord, appeased,
Redeem thee quite from Death's rapacious claim;
But longer in this Paradise to dwell
Permits not—to remove thee I am come,   260
And send thee from the garden forth, to till
The ground whence thou wast taken, fitter soil.'°
    He added not; for Adam, at the news
Heart-struck, with chilling gripe of sorrow stood,
That all his senses bound; Eve, who unseen   265
Yet all had heard, with audible lament

231 **great Potentate** cf. v, 706 240 **lucid** shining 242
Meliboean a rich purple dye ("grain") from the maritime
Thessalian town of Meliboea (cf. *Aen.* V, 251) 243 **Sarra**
Tyre, Phoenician seaport famous for its dyes **heroes old** cf. i,
552 244 **Iris** the rainbow goddess 249 **state** stateliness
259–62 largely repeats 48, 96–98

Discovered soon the place of her retire:
　'O unexpected stroke, worse than of Death!
　Must I thus leave thee, Paradise? thus leave
270　Thee, native soil, these happy walks and shades,
　Fit haunt of Gods? where I had hope to spend,
　Quiet, though sad, the respite of that day
　That must be mortal to us both. O flowers,
　That never will in other climate grow,
275　My early visitation, and my last
　At even, which I bred up with tender hand
　From the first opening bud and gave ye names,
　Who now shall rear ye to the Sun, or rank
　Your tribes, and water from the ambrosial fount?
280　Thee, lastly, nuptial bower,° by me adorned
　With what to sight or smell was sweet, from thee
　How shall I part, and whither wander down
　Into a lower world, to this obscure
　And wild? how shall we breathe in other air
285　Less pure, accustomed to immortal fruits?'
　　Whom thus the Angel interrupted mild:
　'Lament not, Eve, but patiently resign
　What justly thou hast lost, nor set thy heart,
　Thus overfond, on that which is not thine.
290　Thy going is not lonely; with thee goes
　Thy husband; him to follow thou art bound;
　Where he abides, think there thy native soil.'°
　　Adam, by this from the cold sudden damp°
　Recovering, and his scattered spirits returned,
295　To Michael thus his humble words addressed:
　　'Celestial, whether among the Thrones, or named
　Of them the highest—for such of shape may seem
　Prince above princes—gently hast thou told
　Thy message, which might else in telling wound,
300　And in performing end us;° what besides
　Of sorrow, and dejection, and despair,
　Our frailty can sustain, thy tidings bring:
　Departure from this happy place,° our sweet

280 **nuptial bower** cf. viii, 510　292 **native soil** cf. 270　293
damp depression of spirits; cf. 544　298–300 Compare the
Messenger's delicacy towards Manoa, *Samson Agonistes*,
1565–68.　303 **this happy place** cf. iv, 562; v, 364

Recess,° and only consolation left
Familiar to our eyes; all places else   305
Inhospitable appear, and desolate,
Nor knowing us, nor known; and if by prayer
Incessant I could hope to change the will
Of him who all things can, I would not cease
To weary him with my assiduous cries,   310
But prayer against his absolute decree°
No more avails than breath against the wind,
Blown stifling back on him that breathes it forth:
Therefore to his great bidding I submit.
This most afflicts me, that, departing hence,   315
As from his face I shall be hid,° deprived
His blessed countenance; here I could frequent,
With worship, place by place where he vouchsafed
Presence Divine,° and to my sons relate,
"On this mount he appeared; under this tree   320
Stood visible; among these pines his voice
I heard; here with him at this fountain talked."
So many grateful altars I would rear
Of grassy turf,° and pile up every stone
Of lustre from the brook, in memory   325
Or monument to ages, and thereon
Offer sweet-smelling gums, and fruits, and flowers.
In yonder nether world where shall I seek
His bright appearances or footstep trace?
For, though I fled him angry, yet, recalled   330
To life prolonged and promised race, I now
Gladly behold though but his utmost skirts
Of glory,° and far off his steps adore.'
    To whom thus Michael, with regard benign:
'Adam, thou know'st Heaven his, and all the Earth, 335
Not this rock only; his omnipresence fills
Land, sea, and air, and every kind that lives,
Fomented by his virtual power and warmed.
All the Earth he gave thee to possess and rule,°

303–04 **sweet/ Recess** cf. ix, 456   311 **absolute decree** cf. iii,
115 316 Closer than *Samson Agonistes,* 1749, are Cain's
words, "and from thy face shall I be hid" (Gen. iv, 14). 319
Presence Divine cf. viii, 314 324 **Of grassy turf** cf. v,
391 332–33 **skirts/ Of glory,** cf. iii, 388 339 **gave . . . to . . .
rule** cf. i, 736

340 No despicable gift; surmise not, then,
His presence to these narrow bounds confined
Of Paradise or Eden: this had been
Perhaps thy capital seat, from whence had spread
All generations, and had hither come,
345 From all the ends of ° the Earth, to celebrate
And reverence thee their great progenitor.°
But this pre-eminence thou hast lost, brought down
To dwell on even ground now with thy sons;
Yet doubt not but in valley and in plain
350 God is as here, and will be found alike
Present, and of his presence many a sign
Still following thee, still compassing thee round
With goodness and paternal love, his face
Express, and of his steps the track divine.
355 Which that thou may'st believe, and be confirmed
Ere thou from hence depart, know I am sent
To show thee what shall come in future days°
To thee and to thy offspring; good with bad
Expect to hear, supernal grace° contending
360 With sinfulness of men, thereby to learn
True patience, and to temper joy with fear
And pious sorrow, equally inured
By moderation either state to bear,
Prosperous or adverse: so shalt thou lead
365 Safest thy life, and best prepared endure
Thy mortal passage when it comes. Ascend
This hill; let Eve (for I have drenched her eyes)
Here sleep below while thou to foresight wak'st,
As once thou slept'st while she to life was formed.'
370   To whom thus Adam gratefully replied:
'Ascend; I follow thee, safe guide, the path
Thou lead'st me, and to the hand of Heaven submit,
However chastening, to the evil turn
My obvious° breast, arming to overcome
375 By suffering, and earn rest from labour won,
If so I may attain.' So both ascend

345 **From all the ends of** cf. v, 586   346 **great progenitor** cf.
v, 544   357 **what shall come in future days** cf. 114; also vi,
502   359 **supernal grace** cf. vii, 573   374 **obvious** literally, lying
in the way

In the visions of God:° It was a hill,
Of Paradise the highest, from whose top
The hemisphere of Earth in clearest ken
Stretched out to the° amplest reach of prospect lay.   380
Not higher that hill, nor wider looking round,
Whereon for different cause the Tempter set
Our second Adam,° in the wilderness,
To show him all Earth's kingdoms and their glory.
His eye might there command wherever stood   385
City of old or modern fame, the seat
Of mightiest empire, from the destined walls
Of Cambalu,° seat of Cathaian Can,
And Samarcand° by Oxus, Temir's throne,
To Paquin° of Sinaean° kings, and thence   390
To Agra° and Lahor° of Great Mogul,
Down to the golden Chersonese,° or where
The Persian in Ecbatan° sat, or since
In Hispahan,° or where the Russian Tsar
In Moscow, or the Sultan in Bizance,°   395
Turkestan-born; nor could his eye not ken
The empire of Negus° to his utmost port
Ercoco,° and the less maritime kings,
Mombaza,° and Quiloa, and Melind,

377 "Now I am come to make thee understand what shall
befall thy people in the latter days: for yet the vision is for
many days". (Dan. x, 14).   380 **the** omitted in 1667   383 **Our
second Adam** Jesus (the subject of *Paradise Regained*)   388
Cambalu built by Kubla Khan   389 **Samarcand** oldest city of
central Asia, the capital of Tamberlane (*Temir*)   390 **Paquin**
Peking **Sinaean** Chinese   391 **Agra** in northwestern India,
formerly a great Mogul capital; site of the famous mid-
seventeenth-century construction the Taj Mahal **Lahor**
another Mogul center, in western Pakistan   392 **the golden
Chersonese** "Aurea Chersonesus . . . the same which is now
called Sumatra" (Purchas); or possibly the Malay
Peninsula   393 **Ecbatan** capital of ancient Media, residence of
Cyrus   394 **Hispahan** Ispahan became the capital of Persia in
the sixteenth century.   395 **Bizance** Constantinople   397
Negus the title of the king of Abyssinia (Ethiopia)   398
Ercoco Abyssinian port on the west shore of the Red Sea   399
Mombaza Kenyan port, an early center of Arab trade, held by
Portuguese in Milton's time. "This kingdom lyeth between the
borders of Quiloa and Melind (Purchas).

400 And Sofala° (thought Ophir°), to the realm
  Of Congo, and Angola farthest south;°
  Or thence from Niger flood° to Atlas mount,°
  The kingdoms of Almansor,° Fez° and Sus,°
  Marocco, and Algiers, and Tremisen;°
405 On Europe thence, and where Rome was to sway
  The world; in spirit perhaps he also saw
  Rich Mexico, the seat of Motezume,
  And Cusco° in Peru, the richer seat
  Of Atabalipa,° and yet unspoiled
410 Guiana, whose great city Geryon's sons°
  Call El Dorado; but to nobler sights
  Michael from Adam's eyes the film removed,°
  Which that false fruit° that promised clearer sight
  Had bred, then purged with euphrasy° and rue°
415 The visual nerve, for he had much to see,
  And from the well of life three drops instilled.°
  So deep the power of these ingredients pierced,
  Even to the inmost seat of mental sight,
  That Adam, now enforced to close his eyes,
420 Sunk down, and all his spirits became entranced;
  But him the gentle Angel by the hand
  Soon raised, and his attention thus recalled:
    'Adam, now ope thine eyes, and first behold

400 **Sofala** a rich seaport in Portuguese East Africa   **Ophir** the region where King Solomon obtained gold   401 **Angola farthest south** (of the Congo) Portuguese West Africa   402 **Niger flood** the 2600-mile river of western Africa   **Atlas mount** in northwest Africa   403 **Almansor** tenth-century Mohammedan rulers of Andalusia and North Africa, some of whose subject towns Milton names   **Fez** in Morocco, one of the sacred places of Islam and trade source of the red hat, the fez   **Sus** a province of Morocco   404 **Tremisen** modern Tlemcen, in Algeria; one of the five Barbary States and capital of the Moslem Berber dynasty   408 **Cusco** Inca capital   409 **Atabalipa** Atahualpa (d. 1533), last Inca king of Peru, overthrown and condemned to death by Pizarro   410 **Geryon's sons** Spaniards   412 **the film removed** Michael does the same in Tasso, and there were precedents in Homer and Virgil.   413 **that false fruit** cf. ix, 1011   414 **euphrasy** the plant eye-bright (from Greek *to cheer*)   **rue** an herb supposedly effective against snake bite   416 "For with thee is the fountain of life: in thy light shall we see light" (Ps. xxxvi, 9).

The effects which thy original crime hath wrought
In some to spring from thee, who never touched   *425*
The excepted tree, nor with the Snake conspired,
Nor sinned thy sin, yet from that sin° derive
Corruption to bring forth more violent deeds.'
    His eyes he opened, and beheld a field,°
Part arable and tilth,° whereon were sheaves   *430*
New-reaped, the other part sheep-walks and folds;
I' the midst an altar as the landmark stood,
Rustic, of grassy sward; thither anon
A sweaty reaper from his tillage brought
Firstfruits, the green ear and the yellow sheaf,   *435*
Unculled, as came to hand; a shepherd next,
More meek, came with the firstlings of his flock,
Choicest and best; then, sacrificing, laid
The inwards° and their fat, with incense strewed,
On the cleft wood, and all due rites performed.   *440*
His offering soon propitious fire from Heaven
Consumed with nimble glance and grateful steam:
The other's not, for his was not sincere;°
Whereat he inly raged, and, as they talked,
Smote him into the midriff with a stone   *445*
That beat out life; he fell, and, deadly pale,
Groaned out his soul, with gushing blood effused.°
Much at that sight was Adam in his heart
Dismayed, and thus in haste to the Angel cried:
    'O Teacher, some great mischief hath befallen   *450*
To that meek man, who well had sacrificed;
Is piety thus and pure devotion paid?'
    To whom Michael thus, he also moved, replied:
'These two are brethren, Adam, and to come
Out of thy loins; the unjust the just hath slain,   *455*
For envy that his brother's offering found
From Heaven acceptance; but the bloody fact°
Will be avenged, and the other's faith° approved
Lose no reward, though here thou see him die,

427 **from that sin** *sin* omitted in 1674   429 ff. the story of Cain
and Abel   430 **tilth** land that is tilled   439 **The inwards** the
entrails   443 Milton, whose function it is to justify God's ways,
supplies a reason for God's discrimination that is missing in
Genesis, iv, 4–5.   447 imitative of *Aeneid,* IX, 349 and X, 908
457 **fact** deed   458 **faith** cf. Hebrews, xi, 4

460 Rolling in dust and gore.' To which our Sire:
      'Alas, both for the deed and for the cause!
     But have I now seen Death? Is this the way
     I must return to native dust? O sight
     Of terror, foul and ugly to behold,
465 Horrid to think, how horrible to feel!'
         To whom thus Michael: 'Death thou hast seen
     In his first shape on Man; but many shapes
     Of Death, and many are the ways that lead
     To his grim cave, all dismal, yet to sense
470 More terrible at the entrance than within.°
     Some, as thou saw'st, by violent stroke shall die,
     By fire, flood, famine; by intemperance more
     In meats and drinks, which on the Earth shall bring
     Diseases dire, of which a monstrous crew
475 Before thee shall appear, that thou may'st know
     What misery the inabstinence of Eve
     Shall bring on men.' Immediately a place
     Before his eyes appeared, sad, noisome, dark;
     A lazar-house° it seemed, wherein were laid,
480 Numbers of all diseased, all maladies
     Of ghastly spasm or racking torture, qualms
     Of heart-sick agony; all feverous kinds,
     Convulsions, epilepsies, fierce catarrhs,
     Intestine stone and ulcer, colic pangs,
485 Demoniac frenzy, moping melancholy,°
     And moon-struck madness,° pining atrophy,
     Marasmus,° and wide-wasting pestilence,
     Dropsies and asthmas, and joint-racking rheums.
     Dire was the tossing, deep the groans; Despair
490 Tended the sick, busiest from couch to couch;
     And over them triumphant Death his dart
     Shook, but delayed to strike, though oft invoked
     With vows, as their chief good and final hope.°
     Sight so deform what heart of rock could long
495 Dry-eyed behold? Adam could not, but wept,

470 Bacon in "Of Death" quoted from Seneca to this effect,
"Pompa mortis magis terret," etc.   479 **A lazar-house** a pest
house or hospital   485–87 added in the second edition   486
moon-struck madness lunacy   487 **Marasmus** consumption, the
"wasting" sickness   493 **final hope** cf. ii, 142

Though not of woman born: compassion quelled
His best of man, and gave him up to tears°
A space, till firmer thoughts restrained excess,
And, scarce recovering words, his plaint renewed:
   'O miserable Mankind, to what fall   *500*
Degraded, to what wretched state reserved!
Better end here unborn. Why is life given
To be thus wrested from us? rather why
Obtruded on us thus? who, if we knew
What we receive, would either not accept   *505*
Life offered, or soon beg to lay it down,
Glad to be so dismissed in peace. Can thus
The image of God in Man, created once
So goodly and erect, though faulty since,
To such unsightly sufferings be debased   *510*
Under inhuman pains? Why should not Man,
Retaining still divine similitude°
In part, from such deformities be free,
And for his Maker's image sake exempt?'
   'Their Maker's image,' answered Michael, 'then   *515*
Forsook them, when themselves they vilified
To serve ungoverned appetite, and took
His image whom they served, a brutish vice,
Inductive mainly to the sin of Eve.
Therefore so abject is their punishment,   *520*
Disfiguring not God's likeness, but their own,
Or, if his likeness, by themselves defaced,
While they pervert pure Nature's healthful rules
To loathsome sickness, worthily, since they
God's image did not reverence in themselves.'   *525*
   'I yield it just,' said Adam, 'and submit.
But is there yet no other way, besides
These painful passages, how we may come
To death, and mix with our connatural dust?'
   'There is,' said Michael, 'if thou well observe   *530*
The rule of *Not too much*, by temperance taught°
In what thou eat'st and drink'st, seeking from thence
Due nourishment, not gluttonous delight,
Till many years over thy head return;

496–97 echoes of *Macbeth* here, V, viii, 18, 30–31   512 **divine
similitude** cf. 508 and iii, 384   531 classic advice

535 So may'st thou live, till, like ripe fruit, thou drop
Into thy mother's lap,° or be with ease
Gathered, not harshly plucked, for death mature:°
This is old age; but then thou must outlive
Thy youth, thy strength, thy beauty, which will change
540 To withered, weak, and grey; thy senses then
Obtuse, all taste of pleasure must forgo
To what thou hast; and, for the air of youth,
Hopeful and cheerful, in thy blood will reign
A melancholy damp of cold and dry,°
545 To weigh thy spirits down, and last consume
The balm of life.' To whom our Ancestor:
   'Henceforth I fly not death, nor would prolong
Life much, bent rather how I may be quit,
Fairest and easiest, of this cumbrous charge,
550 Which I must keep till my appointed day°
Of rendering up, and patiently attend
My dissolution.'° Michael replied:
   'Nor love thy life nor hate, but what thou liv'st°
Live well; how long or short permit to Heaven:
555 And now prepare thee for another sight.'
   He looked, and saw a spacious plain, whereon
Were tents of various hue; by some were herds
Of cattle grazing: others whence the sound
Of instruments that made melodious chime
560 Was heard, of harp and organ, and who° moved
Their stops and chords was seen: his volant° touch,
Instinct through all proportions low and high,
Fled and pursued transverse the resonant fugue.
In other part stood one who, at the forge
565 Labouring, two massy clods of iron and brass
Had melted (whether found where casual fire

536 **Into thy mother's lap** cf. x, 778   537 Milton has in mind
a passage in Cicero's *De Senectute,* the title he translates in
the next line   544 **cold and dry** cf. x, 294   550 cf. Job, xiv,
14   551–52 **and patiently attend/ My dissolution** added in
second edition   553 Martial, X, 47   560 **who** Jubal. His half
bother was Tubal-cain—564; see Genesis, iv, 20–22.   561
volant flying. James Whaler contends, "Milton's unsurpassable
definition of fugue at PL XI, 561–563, is surely meant by him
to apply to the rhythmic method of his epic style as well as to
polyphonic music."

Had wasted woods, on mountain or in vale,
Down to the veins of earth, thence gliding hot
To some cave's mouth, or whether washed by stream
From underground); the liquid ore he drained   570
Into fit moulds prepared, from which he formed
First his own tools, then what might else be wrought
Fusil° or graven in metal. After these,
But on the hither side,° a different sort°
From the high neighbouring hills,° which was their seat, 575
Down to the plain descended: by their guise
Just men they seemed, and all their study bent
To worship God aright, and know his works
Not hid, nor those things last which might preserve
Freedom and peace to men; they on the plain   580
Long had not walked, when from the tents behold
A bevy of fair women, richly gay°
In gems and wanton dress; to the harp they sung
Soft amorous ditties,° and in dance came on;
The men, though grave, eyed them, and let their eyes 585
Rove without rein, till, in the amorous net
Fast caught, they liked, and each his liking chose;
And now of love they treat, till the evening-star,
Love's harbinger, appeared, then, all in heat,
They light the nuptial torch, and bid invoke   590
Hymen, then first to marriage rites° invoked:
With feast and music all the tents resound.
Such happy interview, and fair event
Of love and youth not lost, songs, garlands, flowers,
And charming symphonies,° attached the heart   595
Of Adam, soon inclined to admit delight,
The bent of Nature; which he thus expressed:
   'True opener of mine eyes, prime Angel blest,
Much better seems this vision, and more hope
Of peaceful days portends, than those two past: 600
Those were of hate and death, or pain much worse;
Here Nature seems fulfilled in all her ends.'
   To whom thus Michael: 'Judge not what is best

573 **Fusil** formed by melting or casting, molten   574 **hither side** cf. iii, 722   **a different sort** the descendants of Seth   575 **neighbouring hills** cf. v, 547; vi, 663   581–82 Genesis, vi, 1–2   584 **amorous ditties** cf. i, 449   591 **marriage rites** cf. viii, 487   595 **charming symphonies** cf. iii, 368

By pleasure, though to Nature seeming meet,
605 Created, as thou art, to nobler end,
Holy and pure, conformity divine.
Those tents thou saw'st so pleasant were the tents
Of wickedness,° wherein shall dwell his race
Who slew his brother; studious they appear
610 Of arts that polish life, inventors rare,
Unmindful of their Maker, though his Spirit
Taught them; but they his gifts acknowledged none.
Yet they a beauteous offspring shall beget,
For that fair female troop thou saw'st, that seemed
615 Of goddesses, so blithe, so smooth, so gay,
Yet empty of all good wherein consists
Woman's domestic honour and chief praise,
Bred only and completed to the taste
Of lustful appetence, to sing, to dance,
620 To dress, and troll° the tongue, and roll the eye—
To these that sober race of men, whose lives
Religious titled them the Sons of God,
Shall yield up all their virtue, all their fame,
Ignobly, to the trains° and to the smiles
625 Of these fair atheists, and now swim in joy
(Erelong to swim at large°) and laugh; for which
The world erelong a world of tears must weep.'
    To whom thus Adam, of short joy bereft:
'O pity and shame, that they who to live well
630 Entered so fair should turn aside to tread
Paths indirect, or in the midway faint!
But still I see the tenor of Man's woe
Holds on the same, from Woman to begin.'°
    'From Man's effeminate slackness it begins,'
635 Said the Angel, 'who should better hold his place
By wisdom, and superior gifts received.
But now prepare thee for another scene.'
    He looked, and saw wide territory spread
Before him, towns, and rural works between,

607–608 **the tents/ Of wickedness** Psalms, lxxxiv, 10   620 **troll**
wag   624 **trains** snares   626 **Erelong to swim at large** A similar
punning reference to the Flood is at 756–57.   632–33 play on the
traditional derivation of *Woman*—Woe to man!

Cities of men with lofty gates and towers,   640
Concourse in arms, fierce faces threatening war,
Giants of mighty bone and bold emprise.
Part wield their arms, part curb the foaming steed,°
Single, or in array of battle ranged,
Both horse and foot, nor idly mustering stood.   645
One way a band select from forage drives°
A herd of beeves, fair oxen and fair kine,
From a fat meadow-ground, or fleecy flock,
Ewes and their bleating lambs, over the plain,
Their booty; scarce with life the shepherds fly,   650
But call in aid, which makes° a bloody fray:
With cruel tournament the squadrons join;
Where cattle pastured late, now scattered lies
With carcases and arms the ensanguined field
Deserted: others to a city strong   655
Lay siege, encamped, by battery, scale,° and mine,
Assaulting; others from the wall defend
With dart and javelin, stones and sulphurous fire;
On each hand slaughter and gigantic deeds.
In other part the sceptred heralds call   660
To council in the city-gates; anon
Grey-headed men and grave, with warriors mixed,
Assemble, and harangues are heard, but soon
In factious opposition, till at last
Of middle age one rising,° eminent   665
In wise deport, spake much of right and wrong,
Of justice, or religion, truth, and peace,
And judgement from above: him old and young
Exploded,° and had seized with violent hands,
Had not a cloud descending snatched him thence,   670
Unseen amid the throng. So violence
Proceeded, and oppression, and sword-law,
Through all the plain, and refuge none was found.
Adam was all in tears, and to his guide

643 **part curb the foaming steed** a mixture of ii, 531 and vi,
391 646 ff. Milton is following closely the description of
Achilles' shield in *Iliad* XVIII. 651 **makes** 1667 has *tacks* 656
scale ladder 665 **Of middle age one rising** Enoch, who lived to
age 365 (Gen. v, 23)—not half so long as such patriarchs as
Methuselah and Lamech, who follow next in Genesis 669
Exploded hissed (as at x, 546)

675 Lamenting turned full sad: 'O, what are these?
     Death's ministers, not men, who thus deal death
     Inhumanly to men, and multiply
     Ten thousandfold the sin of him who slew
     His brother; for of whom such massacre
680 Make they but of their brethren, men of men?
     But who was that just man, whom had not Heaven
     Rescued, had in his righteousness been lost?'
        To whom thus Michael: 'These are the product
     Of those ill-mated marriages thou saw'st,
685 Where good with bad were matched, who of themselves
     Abhor to join, and, by imprudence mixed,
     Produce prodigious births of body or mind.
     Such were these giants, men of high renown,
     For in those days might only shall be admired,
690 And valour and heroic virtue called;
     To overcome in battle, and subdue
     Nations, and bring home spoils with infinite
     Manslaughter, shall be held the highest pitch
     Of human glory, and, for glory done,
695 Of triumph to be styled great conquerors,
     Patrons of mankind, gods, and sons of gods—
     Destroyers rightlier called, and plagues of men.
     Thus fame shall be achieved, renown on earth,°
     And what most merits fame in silence hid.
     But he, the seventh from thee, whom thou
700   beheld'st°
     The only righteous in a world perverse,
     And therefore hated, therefore so beset
     With foes, for daring single to be just
     And utter odious truth that God would come
705 To judge them with his Saints—him the Most High,
     Rapt in a balmy cloud, with wingèd steeds,°
     Did, as thou saw'st,° receive, to walk with God
     High in salvation and the climes of bliss,
     Exempt from death, to show thee what° reward

698 Compare the disquisition on fame in "Lycidas,"
70–84   700 "And Enoch also, the seventh from Adam,
prophesied of these, saying, Behold, the Lord cometh with ten
thousand of his saints" (Jude, 14)   706 Compare the variant,
iii, 522.   707 **as thou saw'st** a formula here not true: cf. ii, 796;
viii, 446   709 **to show thee what** cf. 357

Awaits the good, the rest what punishment;   *710*
Which now direct thine eyes and soon behold.'
   He looked, and saw the face of things quite changed.
The brazen throat of war had ceased to roar;
All now was turned to jollity and game,
To luxury° and riot, feast and dance,   *715*
Marrying or prostituting, as befell,
Rape or adultery, where passing fair
Allured them; thence from cups to civil broils.
At length a reverend sire° among them came,
And of their doings great dislike declared,   *720*
And testified against their ways; he oft
Frequented their assemblies, whereso met,
Triumphs or festivals, and to them preached
Conversion and repentance, as to souls
In prison under judgements imminent,°   *725*
But all in vain: which when he saw, he ceased
Contending, and removed his tents far off;
Then, from the mountain hewing timber tall,
Began to build a vessel of huge bulk,°
Measured by cubit, length, and breadth, and height   *730*
Smeared round with pitch, and in the side a door
Contrived, and of provisions laid in large
For man and beast; when lo, a wonder strange!
Of every beast, and bird, and insect small,
Came sevens and pairs, and entered in, as taught   *735*
Their order; last, the sire and his three sons,
With their four wives; and God made fast the door.
Meanwhile the south wind rose, and, with black wings
Wide-hovering, all the clouds together drove
From under heaven; the hills, to their supply,   *740*
Vapour, and exhalation dusk and moist,
Sent up amain; and now the thickened sky
Like a dark ceiling° stood: down rushed the rain
Impetuous, and continued till the earth

---

715 **luxury** lust   719 **reverend sire** the phrase from "Lycidas,"
103, the reference Noah   724–25 In the words of St. Peter,
Noah "went and preached unto the spirits in prison" (1 Peter,
iii, 19).   729 **huge bulk** always a floating reference, i, 196; vii,
410   743 **ceiling** a recollection of the derivation from *caelum*,
heaven

745   No more was seen; the floating vessel swum
      Uplifted, and secure with beakéd prow
      Rode tilting o'er the waves; all dwellings else
      Flood overwhelmed, and them with all their pomp
      Deep under water rolled; sea covered sea,
750   Sea without shore,° and in their palaces,
      Where luxury late reigned, sea-monsters whelped
      And stabled: of mankind, so numerous late,
      All left in one small bottom swum embarked.
      How didst thou grieve then, Adam, to behold
755   The end of all thy offspring, end so sad,
      Depopulation; thee another flood,
      Of tears and sorrow a flood, thee also drowned,
      And sunk thee as thy sons, till, gently reared
      By the Angel, on thy feet thou stood'st at last,
760   Though comfortless, as when a father mourns
      His children, all in view destroyed at once,
      And scarce to the Angel utter'dst thus thy plaint:
        'O visions ill foreseen! better had I
      Lived ignorant of future, so had borne
765   My part of evil only, each day's lot
      Enough to bear; those now that were dispensed
      The burden of many ages on me light
      At once, by my foreknowledge gaining birth
      Abortive, to torment me, ere their being,
770   With thought that they must be. Let no man seek
      Henceforth to be foretold what shall befall
      Him or his children—evil, he may be sure,
      Which neither his foreknowing can prevent,
      And he the future evil shall no less
775   In apprehension than in substance feel,
      Grievous to bear. But that care now is past;
      Man is not whom to warn; those few escaped
      Famine and anguish will at last consume,
      Wandering that watery desert:° I had hope,
780   When violence was ceased and war on Earth,
      All would have then gone well, peace would have
          crowned
      With length of happy days the race of Man,

750 **Sea without shore** cf. ii, 912, 939–40; also ix, 117   779 cf.
ii, 973

But I was far deceived, for now I see
Peace to corrupt no less than war to waste.
How comes it thus? Unfold, Celestial Guide,   785
And whether here the race of Man° will end.'
  To whom thus Michael: 'Those whom last thou saw'st
In triumph and luxurious wealth are they
First seen in acts of prowess eminent
And great exploits, but of true virtue void;   790
Who, having spilt much blood, and done much waste,
Subduing nations, and achieved thereby
Fame in the world, high titles, and rich prey,
Shall change their course to pleasure, ease, and sloth,
Surfeit, and lust, till wantonness and pride   795
Raise out of friendship hostile deeds in peace.
The conquered, also, and enslaved by war,
Shall, with their freedom lost, all virtue lose,
And fear of God, from whom their piety feigned
In sharp contést of battle found no aid   800
Against invaders; therefore, cooled in zeal,
Thenceforth shall practise how to live secure,
Worldly or dissolute, on what their lords
Shall leave them to enjoy, for the Earth shall bear
More than enough, that temperance may be tried.   805
So all shall turn degenerate, all depraved,
Justice and temperance, truth and faith, forgot;
One man except,° the only son of light
In a dark age, against example good,
Against allurement, custom, and a world   810
Offended; fearless of reproach and scorn,
Or violence, he of their wicked ways
Shall them admonish, and before them set
The paths of righteousness, how much more safe
And full of peace,° denouncing wrath to come   815
On their impenitence, and shall return
Of them derided, but of God observed
The one just man alive: by his command
Shall build a wondrous ark, as thou beheld'st,
To save himself and household from amidst   820

786 **the race of Man** cf. 13, 782, and ii, 382; iii, 161, 280, 679;
vii, 155 808 **One man except** cf. ix, 545 815 **And full of
peace** cf. ix, 1126

A world devote to universal wrack.
No sooner he, with them of man and beast
Select for life, shall in the ark be lodged
And sheltered round, but all the cataracts
825 Of Heaven set open on the Earth shall pour
Rain day and night; all fountains of the deep,
Broke up, shall heave the ocean to usurp
Beyond all bounds, till inundation rise
Above the highest hills: then shall this Mount
830 Of Paradise by might of waves be moved
Out of his place, pushed by the hornèd flood,
With all his verdure spoiled, and trees adrift,
Down the great river to the opening Gulf,
And there take root, an island salt and bare,
835 The haunt of seals, and orcs,° and sea-mews' clang,°
To teach thee that God áttribútes to place
No sanctity, if none be thither brought
By men who there frequent or therein dwell.
And now what further shall ensue behold.'
840   He looked, and saw the ark hull° on the flood,
Which now abated, for the clouds were fled,
Driven by a keen north wind, that, blowing dry,
Wrinkled the face of deluge, as decayed;
And the clear sun on his wide watery glass
845 Gazed hot, and of the fresh wave largely drew,
As after thirst; which made their flowing shrink
From standing lake to tripping ebb, that stole
With soft foot towards the deep, who now had stopped
His sluices, as the Heaven his windows shut.°
850 The ark no more now floats, but seems on ground,
Fast on the top of some high mountain fixed.
And now the tops of hills as rocks appear;
With clamour thence the rapid currents° drive
Towards the retreating sea their furious tide.
855 Forthwith from out the ark a raven flies,
And, after him, the surer messenger,
A dove, sent forth once and again to spy
Green tree or ground whereon his foot may light;

835 **orcs** whales **clang** cf. vii, 422   840 **hull** to drift to and
fro   849 "the windows of heaven were stopped" (Gen. viii,
2)   853 **rapid currents** cf. iv, 227

The second time returning, in his bill
An olive-leaf he brings, pacific sign.   *860*
Anon dry ground appears, and from his ark
The ancient sire descends, with all his train;
Then, with uplifted hands and eyes devout,
Grateful to Heaven, over his head beholds
A dewy cloud, and in the cloud a bow   *865*
Conspicuous with three listed° colours gay,
Betokening peace from God, and covenant new.
Whereat the heart of Adam, erst so sad,
Greatly rejoiced, and thus his joy broke forth:
  'O thou, who° future things canst represent   *870*
As present, Heavenly Instructor, I revive
At this last sight, assured that Man shall live,
With all the creatures, and their seed preserve.
Far less I now lament for one whole world
Of wicked sons destroyed than I rejoice   *875*
For one man found so perfect and so just
That God vouchsafes to raise another world°
From him, and all his anger to forget.
But say, what mean those coloured streaks in Heaven,
Distended as the brow of God appeased?   *880*
Or serve they as a flowery verge to bind
The fluid skirts of that same watery cloud,
Lest it again dissolve and shower the Earth?'
  To whom the Archangel: 'Dextrously thou aim'st.
So willingly doth God remit his ire: *885*
Though late° repenting him of Man depraved,
Grieved at his heart, when, looking down, he saw
The whole Earth filled with violence, and all flesh
Corrupting each their way, yet, those removed,
Such grace shall one just man° find in his sight   *890*
That he relents, not to blot out mankind,
And makes a covenant never to destroy
The Earth again by flood, nor let the sea
Surpass his bounds, nor rain to drown the world
With man therein or beast; but, when he brings   *895*

866 **listed** striped (the three colors being red, yellow, and
blue)   870 **who** *that*, 1667   877 **another world** cf. ii, 347, 1004;
v, 569; vii, 155   886 **late** lately   890 **just man** a theme of this
book, 577, 681, 818; also, vii, 570

Over the Earth a cloud, will therein set
His triple-coloured bow, whereon to look
And call to mind his covenant. Day and night,
Seed-time and harvest, heat and hoary frost,
900 Shall hold their course, till fire purge all things new,
Both Heaven and Earth, wherein the just shall dwell.'

BOOK XII

THE ARGUMENT

The Angel Michael continues, from the Flood, to relate what shall succeed: then, in the mention of Abraham, comes by degrees to explain who that Seed of the Woman shall be which was promised Adam and Eve in the Fall: his incarnation, death, resurrection, and ascension; the state of the Church till his second coming. Adam, greatly satisfied and recomforted by these relations and promises, descends the hill with Michael; wakens Eve, who all this while had slept, but with gentle dreams composed to quietness of mind and submission. Michael in either hand leads them out of Paradise, the fiery sword waving behind them, and the Cherubim taking their stations to guard the place.

As one who, in his journey, baits at noon,
Though bent on speed, so here the Archangel paused
Betwixt the world destroyed and world restored,
If Adam aught perhaps might interpose,
Then, with transition sweet, new speech resumes:°   5
    'Thus thou hast seen one world begin and end,
And Man as from a second stock proceed.
Much thou hast yet to see; but I perceive
Thy mortal sight to fail; objects divine
Must needs impair and weary human sense:°   10
Henceforth what is to come I will relate;
Thou, therefore, give due audience, and attend.
    'This second source of men, while yet but few,
And while the dread of judgement past remains
Fresh in their minds, fearing the Deity,   15
With some regard to what is just and right
Shall lead their lives, and multiply apace,

1–5 added for the 1674 edition, and thus the last poetry Milton wrote   10 **human sense** cf. iv, 206; v, 565, 572; ix, 554, 871

Labouring the soil, and reaping plenteous crop,
Corn, wine, and oil; and, from the herd or flock
20 Oft sacrificing bullock, lamb, or kid,
With large wine-offerings poured, and sacred feast,
Shall spend their days in joy unblamed, and dwell
Long time in peace, by families and tribes,
Under paternal rule, till one° shall rise,
25 Of proud, ambitious heart, who, not content
With fair equality, fraternal state,
Will arrogate dominion undeserved
Over his brethren, and quite dispossess
Concord and law of Nature from the Earth—
30 Hunting (and men, not beasts, shall be his game)
With war and hostile snare such as refuse
Subjection to his empire tyrannous:
A mighty hunter thence he shall be styled
Before the Lord, as in despite of Heaven,
35 Of from Heaven claiming second sovranty,
And from rebellion shall derive his name,
Though of rebellion others he accuse.
He, with a crew whom like ambition joins
With him or under him to tyrannize,
40 Marching from Eden towards the west, shall find
The plain wherein a black bituminous gurge
Boils out from under ground, the mouth of Hell.°
Of brick, and of that stuff, they cast to build
A city and tower, whose top may reach to Heaven,
45 And get themselves a name, lest, far dispersed
In foreign lands, their memory be lost,
Regardless whether good or evil fame.
But God, who oft descends to visit° men
Unseen, and through their habitations walks
50 To mark their doings, them beholding soon,
Comes down to see their city, ere the tower
Obstruct Heaven-towers, and in derision sets

24 **one** Nimrod, noted as "the first that founded monarchy" in
Eikonoklastes and a type of pride (25) in Dante's *Purgatorio*.
Milton had ample nonbiblical authority for making him the
builder of Babel—44 ("ikon for Satan and Pandemonium"—
Broadbent, cf. 42).   42 **the mouth of Hell** ends x, 288, 636   48
oft . . . to visit cf. *to visit oft,* iii, 532, 661; vii, 570

Upon their tongues a various° spirit, to rase
Quite out their native language, and, instead,
To sow a jangling noise of words unknown;   55
Forthwith a hideous gabble rises loud
Among the builders; each to other calls,
Not understood, till, hoarse and all in rage,
As mocked they storm; great laughter was in Heaven,
And looking down to see the hubbub strange   60
And hear the din: thus was the building left
Ridiculous, and the work *Confusion* named.'
    Whereto thus Adam, fatherly displeased:
'O execrable son, so to aspire
Above his brethren, to himself assuming   65
Authority usurped, from God not given:
He gave us only over beast, fish, fowl,
Dominion absolute; that right we hold
By his donation, but man over men
He made not lord, such title to himself   70
Reserving, human left from human free.
But this usurper his encroachment proud
Stays not on Man; to God his tower intends
Siege and defiance. Wretched man! what food°
Will he convey up thither, to sustain   75
Himself and his rash army, where thin air
Above the clouds will pine his entrails gross,
And famish him of breath, if not of bread?'
    To whom thus Michael: 'Justly thou abhorr'st
That son, who on the quiet state of men   80
Such trouble brought, affecting to subdue
Rational liberty; yet know withal,
Since thy original lapse, true liberty
Is lost, which always with right reason dwells
Twinned, and from her hath no dividual being.   85
Reason in Man obscured, or not obeyed,
Immediately inordinate desires
And upstart passions catch the government

---

53 **various** quarrelsome 74 ff. A hit, so to speak, at
skyscrapers. Josephus quotes Nimrod as saying "he would be
avenged on God, if he should have a mind to drown the world
again; for that he would build a tower too high for the waters
to be able to reach!"

From Reason, and to servitude reduce
90 Man, till then free. Therefore, since he permits
Within himself unworthy powers to reign
Over free reason, God, in judgement just,
Subjects him from without to violent lords,
Who oft as undeservedly enthral
95 His outward freedom. Tyranny must be,
Though to the tyrant thereby no excuse.
Yet sometimes nations will decline so low
From virtue, which is reason, that no wrong,
But justice, and some fatal curse annexed,
100 Deprives them of their outward liberty,
Their inward lost: witness the irreverent son°
Of him who built the ark, who, for the shame
Done to his father, heard this heavy curse,
Servant of servants,° on his vicious race.
105 Thus will this latter, as the former world,°
Still tend from bad to worse, till God at last,
Wearied with their iniquities, withdraw
His presence from among them, and avert
His holy eyes, resolving from thenceforth
110 To leave them to their own polluted ways,
And one peculiar nation to select
From all the rest, of whom to be invoked—
A nation from one faithful man° to spring:
Him on this side Euphrates yet residing,
115 Bred up in idol-worship. Oh, that men
(Canst thou believe?) should be so stupid grown,
While yet the patriarch lived who 'scaped the Flood,°
As to forsake the living God,° and fall

101 **irreverent son** Ham, father of Canaan 104 Noah "said,
Cursed be Canaan; a servant of servants shall he be unto his
brethren" (Gen. ix, 25). 105 ff. Interesting is the parallel with
Theseus' speech (Europides, *Hippolytus*, 938 ff.), "O the mind of
mortal man! to what lengths will it proceed? What limit will its
bold assurance have? for if it goes on growing as man's life
advances, and each successor outdo the man before him in
villainy, the gods will have to add another sphere unto the
world, which shall take in the knaves and villains." But *vicious
race,* 104, is Horace's *progeniem vitiosiorem* (*Carm.* III, vi,
48). 113 **one faithful man** Abraham, cf. 152 117 **'scaped the
Flood** cf. i, 239 118 cf. *Samson Agonistes,* 1140 ("The living
God" is a phrase that occurs two dozen times in the Bible.)

To worship their own work in wood and stone
For gods!—yet him God the Most High vouchsafes   *120*
To call by vision from his father's house,
His kindred, and false gods, into a land
Which he will show him and from him will raise
A mighty nation, and upon him shower
His benediction so, that in his seed   *125*
All nations shall be blessed; he straight obeys,
Not knowing to what land, yet firm believes.
I see him, but thou canst not, with what faith°
He leaves his gods, his friends, and native soil,
Ur of Chaldaea, passing now the ford   *130*
To Haran,° after him a cumbrous train
Of herds and flocks, and numerous servitude,°
Not wandering poor, but trusting all his wealth
With God, who called him, in a land unknown.
Canaan he now attains; I see his tents   *135*
Pitched about Shechem and the neighbouring plain
Of Moreh. There, by promise, he receives
Gift to his progeny of all that land,
From Hamath northward to the Desert south
(Things by their names I call, though yet unnamed),   *140*
From Hermon° east to the great western sea;°
Mount Hermon, yonder sea, each place behold
In prospect, as I point them: on the shore,
Mount Carmel; here, the double-founted° stream,
Jordan, true limit eastward; but his sons°   *145*
Shall dwell to Senir, that long ridge of hills.
This ponder, that all nations of the Earth
Shall in his seed be blessed; by that seed
Is meant thy great Deliverer, who shall bruise

128 Michael, having employed visions in Book XI, is now using
direct narrative (as explained, xii, 8–12). **with what faith** cf.
Hebrews, xi, 8   131 **Haran** a town in Mesopotamia on an
affluent of the Euphrates, where Abraham settled on leaving
Ur and where he received God's bidding to journey to Canaan
(Gen. xii, 1–4)   132 **servitude** abstract for concrete—servants
141 **Hermon** the highest mountain of Palestine   **the great
western sea** the Mediterranean   144 **double-founted** It was
Jerome's mistaken belief that two streams, a Jor and a Dan,
joined to make the Jordan.   145 **his sons** 1 Chronicles, v, 23

150 The Serpent's head;° whereof to thee anon
Plainlier shall be revealed. This patriarch blessed,
Whom *faithful Abraham* due time shall call,
A son, and of his son a grandchild,° leaves,
Like him in faith, in wisdom, and renown,
155 The grandchild, with twelve sons increased, departs
From Canaan to a land hereafter called
Egypt, divided by the river Nile;
See where it flows, disgorging at seven mouths
Into the sea; to sojourn in that land
160 He comes, invited by a younger son°
In time of dearth, a son whose worthy deeds
Raise him to be the second in that realm
Of Pharaoh; there he dies, and leaves his race
Growing into a nation, and now grown
165 Suspected to a sequent king, who seeks
To stop their overgrowth, as inmate guests
Too numerous; whence of guests he makes them slaves
Inhospitably, and kills their infant males:
Till, by two brethren (those two brethren call
170 Moses and Aaron) sent from God to claim
His people from enthralment, they return,
With glory and spoil, back to their promised land.
But first the lawless tyrant, who denies°
To know their God, or message to regard,
175 Must be compelled by signs and judgements dire:
To blood unshed the rivers must be turned;
Frogs, lice, and flies must all his palace fill
With loathed intrusion, and fill all the land;
His cattle must of rot and murrain die;
180 Botches and blains must all his flesh emboss,
And all his people; thunder mixed with hail,
Hail mixed with fire, must rend the Egyptian sky,
And wheel on the earth, devouring where it rolls;
What it devours not, herb, or fruit, or grain,
185 A darksome cloud of locusts° swarming down
Must eat, and on the ground leave nothing green;

149–50 **shall bruise/ The Serpent's head** cf. x, 1031–32   153
grandchild Jacob   160 **a younger son** Joseph   173–90 Exodus,
vii–xii   185 **A darksome cloud of locusts** cf. "a pitchy cloud/
Of locusts," i, 340–41

Darkness must overshadow all his bounds,
Palpable° darkness, and blot out three days;
Last, with one midnight-stroke, all the first-born
Of Egypt must lie dead. Thus with ten wounds   *190*
This river-dragon,° tamed at length, submits
To let his sojourners depart, and oft
Humbles his stubborn heart, but still as ice
More hardened after thaw; till, in his rage
Pursuing whom he late dismissed, the sea   *195*
Swallows him with his host, but them lets pass,
As on dry land,° between two crystal walls,°
Awed by the rod of Moses so to stand
Divided till his rescued gain their shore:
Such wondrous power God to his saint will lend,   *200*
Though present in his Angel, who shall go
Before them in a cloud, and pillar of fire—
By day a cloud, by night a pillar of fire—
To guide them in their journey, and remove
Behind them, while the obdúrate king pursues: *205*
All night he will pursue, but his approach
Darkness defends° between till morning-watch,
Then through the fiery pillar, and the cloud,
God looking forth will trouble all his host,
And craze° their chariot-wheels, when, by command,   *210*
Moses once more his potent rod° extends
Over the sea; the sea his rod obeys,
On their embattled ranks the waves return
And overwhelm their war: the race elect
Safe towards Canaan, from the shore, advance   *215*
Through the wild Desert—not the readiest way,
Lest, entering on the Canaanite alarmed,
War terrify them inexpert, and fear
Return them back to Egypt, choosing rather
Inglorious life with servitude, for life°   *220*
To noble and ignoble is more sweet
Untrained in arms, where rashness leads not on.

---

188 **Palpable** cf. Exodus, x, 21   191 **This** (*The*, 1674) **river-dragon** Pharaoh   197 **dry land** cf. i, 227; vii, 307   **crystal walls** cf. vi, 860; vii, 293   207 **defends** forbids, as at ix, 86   210 **craze** break to pieces   211 **potent rod** cf. i, 338   220 Compare *Samson Agonistes*, 268–71, and contrast ii, 255–57; xi, 798–99.

This also shall they gain by their delay
In the wide wilderness; there they shall found
225 Their government, and their great Senate choose
Through the twelve tribes, to rule by laws ordained.
God, from the Mount of Sinai, whose grey top
Shall tremble, he descending, will himself,
In thunder, lightning, and loud trumpet's sound,°
230 Ordain them laws, part, such as appertain
To civil justice; part, religious rites
Of sacrifice, informing them, by types°
And shadows, of that destined Seed to bruise
The Serpent, by what means he shall achieve
235 Mankind's deliverance. But the voice of God
To mortal ear is dreadful: they beseech
That Moses might report to them his will,
And terror cease; he grants what they besought,°
Instructed that to God is no access
240 Without Mediator, whose high office now
Moses in figure bears, to introduce
One greater, of whose day he shall foretell,
And all the Prophets, in their age, the times
Of great Messiah° shall sing. Thus laws and rites
245 Established, such delight hath God in men
Obedient to his will, that he vouchsafes
Among them to set up his tabernacle,
The Holy One with mortal men° to dwell;
By his prescript a sanctuary is framed
250 Of cedar, overlaid with gold, therein
An ark, and in the ark his testimony,
The records of his covenant; over these
A mercy-seat of gold, between the wings
Of two bright Cherubim; before him burn
255 Seven lamps, as in a zodiac representing
The heavenly fires; over the ten a cloud
Shall rest by day, a fiery gleam by night,
Save when they journey; and at length they come,
Conducted by his Angel, to the land°

229 **trumpet's sound** cf. i, 754 232 **types** Old Testament
prefigurations (cf. 303) 238 **what they besought** *them their
desire* first edition 244 **great Messiah** cf. v, 691 248 **mortal
men** cf. i, 51; iii, 268 (a Homeric expression) 259 "For mine
Angel shall go before thee" (Ex. xxiii, 23).

Promised to Abraham and his seed—the rest 260
Were long to tell: how many battles fought,
How many kings destroyed, and kingdoms won,
Or how the sun shall in mid-heaven° stand still°
A day entire, and night's due course adjourn,
Man's voice commanding, "Sun, in Gibeon stand, 265
And thou, Moon, in the vale of Ajalon,°
Till Israel overcome"—so call the third
From Abraham, son of Isaac, and from him
His whole descent, who thus shall Canaan win.'
    Here Adam interposed: 'O sent from Heaven, 270
Enlightener of my darkness, gracious things
Thou hast revealed, those chiefly which concern
Just Abraham and his seed; now first I find
Mine eyes true opening, and my heart much eased,
Erewhile perplexed with thoughts what would become 275
Of me and all mankind; but now I see
His day, in whom all nations shall be blessed—
Favour unmerited by me, who sought
Forbidden knowledge° by forbidden means.
This yet I apprehend not, why to those 280
Among whom God will deign to dwell on Earth
So many and so various laws are given;
So many laws argue° so many sins
Among them; how can God with such reside?'
    To whom thus Michael: 'Doubt not but that sin 285
Will reign among them, as of thee begot;
And therefore was law given them, to evince
Their natural pravity, by stirring up
Sin against Law to fight, that, when they see
Law can discover sin, but not remove, 290
Save by those shadowy expiations weak,
The blood of bulls and goats, they may conclude
Some blood more precious must be paid for Man,
Just for unjust, that in such righteousness,
To them by faith imputed, they may find 295
Justification towards God, and peace

263 **in mid-heaven** cf. iii, 729; vi, 889; ix, 468   263–67 Joshua,
x, 12–13   266 A line borrowed from Sylvester's *Du Bartas* (as
was iii, 373)   279 **Forbidden knowledge** cf. iv, 515   283
argue indicate

Of conscience, which the law by ceremonies
Cannot appease, nor Man the moral part
Perform, and, not performing, cannot live.°
300 So law appears imperfect, and but given
With purpose to resign them, in full time,
Up to a better covenant, disciplined
From shadowy types to truth, from flesh to spirit,
From imposition of strict laws° to free
305 Acceptance of large grace, from servile fear
To filial, works of law to works of faith.
And therefore shall not Moses, though of God
Highly beloved, being but the minister
Of Law, his people into Canaan lead;
310 But Joshua,° whom the Gentiles Jesus call,
His name and office bearing who shall quell
The adversary Serpent, and bring back
Through the world's wilderness long-wandered Man
Safe to eternal Paradise of rest.
315 Meanwhile they, in their earthly Canaan placed,
Long time shall dwell and prosper, but when sins
National interrupt their public peace,
Provoking God to raise them enemies,
From whom as oft he saves them penitent,
320 By Judges first, then under Kings; of whom
The second, both for piety renowned
And puissant deeds, a promise shall receive
Irrevocable, that his regal throne
For ever shall endure; the like shall sing
325 All Prophecy—that of the royal stock
Of David (so I name this king) shall rise
A son, the Woman's Seed to thee foretold,
Foretold to Abraham, as in whom shall trust
All nations, and to kings foretold of kings
330 The last, for of his reign shall be no end.
But first a long succession must ensue;
And his next son,° for wealth and wisdom famed,
The clouded ark of God, till then in tents

299 Romans, x, 5   304 **strict laws** cf. ii, 241   310 **Joshua,**
whose name means the Saviour (like Greek *Jesus*), led the
Israelites in the invasion and settlement of Canaan.   332 **son**
Solomon, the son of David

Wandering, shall in a glorious temple enshrine.
Such follow him as shall be registered   *335*
Part good, part bad; of bad the longer scroll,
Whose foul idolatries° and other faults,
Heaped to the popular sum,° will so incense
God as to leave them, and expose their land,
Their city, his temple, and his holy ark,   *340*
With all his sacred things, a scorn and prey
To that proud city° whose high walls thou saw'st
Left in confusion, Babylon thence called.
There in captivity he lets them dwell
The space of seventy years, then brings them back, *345*
Remembering mercy, and his covenant sworn
To David, stablished as the days of Heaven.
Returned from Babylon by leave of kings,
Their lords, whom God disposed, the house of God
They first re-edify,° and for a while   *350*
In mean estate live moderate, till, grown
In wealth and multitude, factious they grow.
But first among the priests dissension springs—
Men who attend the altar and should most
Endeavour peace; their strife pollution brings   *355*
Upon the temple itself; at last they seize
The sceptre, and regard not David's sons,
Then lose it to a stranger,° that the true
Anointed King° Messiah might be born
Barred of his right; yet at his birth a star,   *360*
Unseen before in Heaven, proclaims him come,
And guides the eastern sages, who inquire
His place, to offer incense, myrrh, and gold;
His place of birth a solemn Angel tells
To simple shepherds, keeping watch by night;   *365*
They gladly thither° haste, and by a choir
Of squadroned Angels hear his carol sung.
A Virgin is his mother, but his sire
The Power of the Most High; he shall ascend

---

337 **foul idolatries** cf. "idols foul," i, 446   338 **the popular sum**
the sins of the common people   342 **proud city** cf. ii,
533   348–50 see Ezra   358 **a stranger** Antipater the Edomite,
father of Herod the Great   359 **Anointed King** cf. v, 664, 777,
870; vi, 718   366 **thither** to Bethlehem

370 The throne hereditary, and bound his reign
 With Earth's wide bounds, his glory with the Heavens.'
   He ceased, discerning Adam with such joy
 Surcharged as had, like grief, been dewed in tears,°
 Without the vent of words; which these he breathed:
375   'O prophet of glad tidings, finisher
 Of utmost hope! now clear I understand
 What oft my steadiest thoughts have searched in vain—
 Why our great Expectation should be called
 The Seed of Woman: Virgin Mother, hail,
380 High in the love of Heaven, yet from my loins
 Thou shalt proceed, and from thy womb the Son
 Of God Most High; so God with Man unites.
 Needs must the Serpent now his capital° bruise
 Expect with mortal pain: say where and when
385 Their fight, what stroke shall bruise the Victor's heel.'
   To whom thus Michael: 'Dream not of their fight
 As of a duel, of the local wounds
 Of head or heel; not therefore joins the Son
 Manhood to Godhead, with more strength to foil
390 Thy enemy, nor so is overcome
 Satan, whose fall from Heaven, a deadlier bruise,
 Disabled not to give thee thy death's wound,°
 Which he who comes thy Saviour shall recure,
 Not by destroying Satan, but his works
395 In thee and in thy seed; nor can this be,
 But by fulfilling that which thou didst want,
 Obedience to the law of God, imposed
 On penalty of death, and suffering death,
 The penalty to thy transgression due,
400 And due to theirs which out of thine will grow:
 So only can high justice rest appaid.
 The law of God° exact he shall fulfil
 Both by obedience and by love, though love
 Alone fulfil the Law; thy punishment
405 He shall endure, by coming in the flesh

373 cf. *Samson Agonistes,* 728   383 **capital** (two syllables) fatal,
with perhaps some reference (despite Michael's admonition,
386–88) to *caput,* head, where Satan first felt pain as Sin was
born (ii, 752 ff.) and where the Serpent was to be
"bruised"   392 **death's wound** cf. iii, 252   402 **The law of God**
cf. 397

To a reproachful life and cursèd death,
Proclaiming life to all who shall believe
In his redemption, and that his obedience
Imputed becomes theirs by faith, his merits
To save them, not their own, though legal, works.   410
For this he shall live hated, be blasphemed,
Seized on by force, judged, and to death condemned
A shameful and accursed, nailed to the cross
By his own nation, slain for bringing life;
But to the cross he nails thy enemies: 415
The Law that is against thee, and the sins°
Of all mankind, with him there crucified,
Never to hurt them more who rightly trust
In this his satisfaction; so he dies,
But soon revives; Death over him no power   420
Shall long usurp; ere the third dawning light
Return, the stars of morn shall see him rise
Out of his grave, fresh as the dawning light,
Thy ransom paid, which Man from Death redeems—
His death for Man, as many as offered life   425
Neglect not, and the benefit embrace
By faith not void of works. This godlike act
Annuls thy doom, the death thou shouldst have died,
In sin forever lost from life; this act
Shall bruise the head of Satan, crush his strength,   430
Defeating Sin and Death, his two main arms,
And fix far deeper in his head their stings
Than temporal death shall bruise the Victor's heel,
Or theirs whom he redeems—a death like sleep,
A gentle wafting to immortal life.   435
Nor after resurrection shall he stay
Longer on Earth than certain times to appear
To his disciples, men who in his life
Still followed him; to them shall leave in charge
To teach all nations what of him they learned   440
And his salvation, them who shall believe
Baptizing in the profluent° stream—the sign

415–16 Colossians, ii, 14   442 **profluent** flowing. Milton uses
in *Christian Doctrine* (I, 28) the expression "*in profluentem
aquam*" to signify his belief that baptism should take place in
running water.

Of washing them from guilt of sin to life
Pure, and in mind prepared, if so befall,
445 For death like that which the Redeemer died.
Not only to the sons of Abraham's loins
Salvation shall be preached, but to the sons
Of Abraham's faith wherever through the world;
So in his seed all nations shall be blessed.°
450 Then to the Heaven of Heavens he shall ascend
With victory, triúmphing through the air·
Over his foes and thine; there shall surprise
The Serpent, Prince of Air, and drag in chains
Through all his realm, and there confounded leave;
455 Then enter into glory, and resume
His seat at God's right hand, exalted high
Above all names in Heaven; and thence shall come,
When this World's dissolution shall be ripe,
With glory and power, to judge both quick and dead°—
460 To judge the unfaithful dead, but to reward
His faithful and receive them into bliss,
Whether in Heaven or Earth, for then the Earth
Shall all be Paradise, far happier place
Than this of Eden, and far happier days.'
465 　So spake the Archangel Michael, then paused,
As at the World's great period,° and our Sire,
Replete with joy and wonder, thus replied:
'O goodness infinite,° goodness immense,
That all this good of evil° shall produce,
470 And evil turn° to good, more wonderful
Than that by which creation first brought forth
Light out of darkness! full of doubt I stand,
Whether I should repent me now of sin°
By me done and occasioned, or rejoice
475 Much more that much more good thereof shall spring—
To God more glory, more good-will to men
From God—and over wrath grace shall abound.
But say, if our Deliverer up to Heaven

449 Galatians, iii, 8　459 adapted from the Apostles'
Creed　466 **period** end　468 **goodness infinite** cf. i, 218; iv, 734;
also iv, 414; vii, 76　469 **good of evil** cf. i, 163; vii, 188　470 **evil
turn** cf. xi, 373　473 the doctrine of the happy fall—*felix culpa*,
cf. 587

Must reascend, what will betide the few,
His faithful, left among the unfaithful herd,°   480
The enemies of truth; who then shall guide
His people, who defend? will they not deal
Worse with his followers than with him they dealt?'
　'Be sure they will,' said the Angel; 'but from Heaven
He to his own a Comforter will send,   485
The promise of the Father, who shall dwell,
His Spirit, within them, and the law of faith
Working through love upon their hearts shall write,
To guide them in all truth, and also arm
With spiritual armour,° able to resist   490
Satan's assaults, and quench his fiery darts,
What man can do against them, not afraid,
Though to the death; against such cruelties
With inward consolations recompensed,
And oft supported so as shall amaze   495
Their proudest persecutors: for the Spirit,°
Poured first on his Apostles, whom he sends
To evangelize the nations, then on all
Baptized, shall them with wondrous gifts endue
To speak all tongues, and do all miracles,   500
As did their Lord before them. Thus they win
Great numbers of each nation to receive
With joy the tidings brought from Heaven; at length,
Their ministry performed, and race well run,°
Their doctrine and their story written left,   505
They die, but in their room, as they forewarn,°
Wolves shall succeed for teachers, grievous wolves,
Who all the sacred mysteries of Heaven
To their own vile advantages shall turn
Of lucre and ambition, and the truth   510
With superstitions and traditions taint,
Left only in those written records pure,
Though not but by the Spirit understood.
Then shall they seek to avail themselves of names,
Places, and titles, and with these to join   515

---

480 compare Abdiel, v, 897   490 Ephesians, vi, 11–17
496–501 Acts, ii   504 **race . . . run** a Pauline expression found
also in *Samson Agonistes,* 597   506 **forewarn** Acts, xx, 29

Secular power, though feigning still to act°
By spiritual, to themselves appropriating
The Spirit of God, promised alike and given
To all believers, and, from that pretence,
520 Spiritual laws by carnal power shall force
On every conscience—laws which none shall find
Left them enrolled, or what the Spirit within°
Shall on the heart engrave. What will they then
But force the Spirit of Grace itself, and bind
525 His consort, Liberty; what but unbuild°
His living temples, built by faith to stand°—
Their own faith, not another's, for on Earth
Who against faith and conscience can be heard
Infallible? Yet many will presume,
530 Whence heavy persecution shall arise
On all who in the worship persevere
Of Spirit and Truth; the rest, far greater part,°
Will deem in outward rites and specious forms°
Religion satisfied; Truth shall retire
535 Bestuck with slanderous darts, and works of Faith°
Rarely be found: so shall the World go on,
To good malignant, to bad men benign,
Under her own weight groaning,° till the day
Appear of respiration° to the just
540 And vengeance to the wicked, at return
Of him so lately promised to thy aid,
The Woman's Seed, obscurely then foretold,
Now amplier known thy Saviour and thy Lord;
Last in the clouds from Heaven to be revealed
545 In glory of the Father, to dissolve°
Satan with his perverted World; then raise
From the conflágrant° mass, purged and refined,

515–16 **to join/ Secular power** one of the causes of the Civil War in England. Milton is carrying on the protests he made as a pamphleteer. 522 **Spirit within** cf. 487; viii, 440 524–25 2 Corinthians, iii, 17 526 "For the temple of God is holy, which temple ye are" (1 Cor. iii, 17) 531–32 John, iv, 23 532 **far greater part** cf. vii, 145, 359 533 Michael reveals himself a Puritan (rejecting the 1674 reading of *Well* for *Will*). 535 **works of Faith** cf. 306 538 "The whole creation groaneth" (Rom. viii, 22) 539 **respiration** in the Anglican version of Acts, iii, 19, "refreshing" 544–45 Matthew, xxiv, 30 547 **conflágrant** burning together

New Heavens, new Earth, Ages of endless date
Founded in righteousness and peace and love,
To bring forth fruits, joy and eternal bliss.'° 550
   He ended, and thus Adam last replied:
'How soon hath thy prediction, Seer blest,
Measured this transient World, the race of Time,
Till Time stand fixed: beyond is all abyss,
Eternity, whose end no eye can reach. 555
Greatly instructed I shall hence depart,
Greatly in peace of thought, and have my fill
Of knowledge, what this vessel° can contain,
Beyond which was my folly to aspire.
Henceforth I learn that to obey is best, 560
And love with fear the only God, to walk
As in his presence, ever to observe
His providence, and on him sole depend,
Merciful over all his works, with good
Still overcoming evil, and by small 565
Accomplishing great things, by things deemed weak
Subverting worldly-strong, and worldly-wise
By simply meek, that suffering for Truth's sake
Is fortitude to highest victory,
And to the faithful death the gate of life; 570
Taught this by his example whom I now
Acknowledge my Redeemer ever blest.'
   To whom thus also the Angel last replied:
'This having learned, thou hast attained the sum
Of wisdom; hope no higher, though all the stars 575
Thou knew'st by name, and all the ethereal powers,
All secrets of the deep, all Nature's works,
Or works of God in heaven, air, earth, or sea,
And all the riches of this world enjoy'dst,
And all the rule, one empire. Only add 580
Deeds to thy knowledge answerable; add faith;
Add virtue, patience, temperance; add love,
By name to come called Charity, the soul
Of all the rest: then wilt thou not be loth
To leave this Paradise, but shalt possess 585
A Paradise within thee, happier far.°

550 **joy and . . . bliss** cf. xi, 43   558 **vessel** 1 Thessalonians, iv, 4
586 cf. iv, 20, 75, and i, 254–55

Let us descend now, therefore, from this top
Of speculation;° for the hour precise
Exacts our parting hence; and see, the guards,
590 By me encamped on yonder hill, expect
Their motion, at whose front a flaming sword,°
In signal of remove, waves fiercely round.°
We may no longer stay: go, waken Eve;
Her also I with gentle dreams have calmed,
595 Portending good, and all her spirits composed
To meek submission: thou, at season fit,
Let her with thee partake what thou hast heard,
Chiefly what may concern her faith to know,
The great deliverance by her seed to come
600 (For by the Woman's Seed°) on all mankind,
That ye may live, which will be many days,°
Both in one faith unanimous, though sad
With cause for evils past, yet much more cheered
With meditation on the happy end.'
605   He ended, and they both descend the hill;
Descended, Adam to the bower where Eve
Lay sleeping ran before, but found her waked,°
And thus with words not sad she him received:
        'Whence thou return'st and whither went'st I know;
610 For God is also in sleep,° and dreams advise,
Which he hath sent propitious, some great good
Presaging, since, with sorrow and heart's distress
Wearied, I fell asleep: but now lead on;
In me is no delay;° with thee to go
615 Is to stay here; without thee here to stay
Is to go hence unwilling; thou to me
Art all things under Heaven, all places thou,
Who for my wilful crime art banished hence.
This further consolation yet secure
620 I carry hence: though all by me is lost,
Such favour I unworthy am vouchsafed,
By me the Promised Seed shall all restore.'

588 **speculation** observation 591 **flaming sword** cf. i,
664 591–92 cf. xi, 120–21 600 **the Woman's Seed** cf. 327,
542; xi, 116 601 930 years (Gen. v, 5) 607 **but found her
waked** contrast the Argument, "wakens Eve" 610 **For God
is also in sleep** a translation of *Iliad,* I, 63 614 **In me is no
delay** a translation of Virgil, *Eclogues,* III, 52

So spake our Mother Eve; and Adam heard
Well pleased, but answered not, for now too nigh
The Archangel stood, and from the other hill   625
To their fixed station, all in bright array°
The Cherubim descended, on the ground
Gliding meteorous, as evening mist,
Risen from a river, o'er the marish° glides,
And gathers ground fast at the labourer's heel   630
Homeward returning. High in front advanced,
The brandished sword of God before them blazed,
Fierce as a comet, which° with torrid heat,
And vapour° as the Libyan air adust,°
Began to parch that temperate clime; whereat   635
In either hand the hastening Angel caught
Our lingering parents, and to the eastern gate°
Led them direct, and down the cliff as fast
To the subjected° plain; then disappeared.
They, looking back, all the eastern side beheld   640
Of Paradise, so late their happy seat,°
Waved over by that flaming brand, the gate
With dreadful faces thronged and fiery arms:
Some natural tears they dropped, but wiped them soon;
The world was all before them,° where to choose   645
Their place of rest, and Providence their guide;
They, hand in hand, with wandering steps and slow,°
Through Eden took their solitary way.

626 **in bright array** cf. vi, 801   629 marish marsh   633 **which**
the sword   634 **vapour** waves of heat   **adust** burnt   636–37
cf. Genesis, xix, 16   637 **to the eastern gate** xi, 190; also iv,
542   639 **subjected** literally, underlying   641 **happy seat** cf. ii,
347; iii, 632; iv, 247; vi, 226   645 This famous line was perhaps
suggested by Mowbray's words on being exiled (*Richard II,* I,
iii, 206-07):

"Farewell, my liege. Now no way can I stray;
    Save back to England, all the world's my way."
647 Harking back to iv, 321, 689

SAMSON AGONISTES

The main, very likely the only, source of *Samson Agonistes* is Judges, xiii–xvi, with emphasis on 21–30 of xvi. It is impressive what a transformation has been wrought in the rather oafish folk-tale character of the Old Testament to give him tragic stature worthy of the two Greek plays Milton had most in mind as models, Aeschylus' *Prometheus Bound* and Sophocles' *Oedipus at Colonus*. For instance, the episode of the foxes' tails used as fire-brands (xv, 4–5) is beneath Milton's notice, and "the jawbone of an ass" (xv, 16) strikes him as "a trivial weapon" (*Samson Agonistes,* 142, 263).

Self-identification must have lent its heightening or deepening force. The parallels are numerous—a champion of his people, "my breeding ordered and prescribed/ As of a person separate to God,/ Designed for great exploits" (30–32), who, betrayed by a wife from the enemy side, languishes blind and helpless in the midst of a ruined cause. It is almost too easy to see Mary Powell Milton in Dalila (as in Eve), and correspondences present themselves between Harapha and Salmasius, Milton's own father and Manoa, one chosen but relapsing people and another. Lines 693–96 look like a topical allusion (see The Life of Milton, p. xliii); 697 ff. comes from a gout-sufferer; 566–71 corroborates Richardson's picture of "Milton sitting in an elbow chair, black clothes and neat enough, pale but not cadaverous, his hands and fingers gouty and with chalk stones. Among other discourse he expressed himself to this purpose: that was he free from the pain this gave him, his blindness would be tolerable."

Agonistes in Greek means a contestant in the games: that is, Milton was dealing with the last phase of Samson's career (what he once titled in manuscript "Dagonalia"), the blind *wrestler* or *athlete* at the public games of the Philistines. *Agonize* in the seventeenth century meant to *play the champion* and had nothing to do with inner torment. Milton was defining the scope of his play (in the 1640s he had listed other phases of Samson's history as possible subjects), even as Aeschylus distinguished *Prometheus Bound* from *Prometheus Unbound*.

Note that all the names are recessive, that is, accented on the first syllable.

SAMSON AGONISTES

OF THAT SORT OF DRAMATIC POEM WHICH IS CALLED TRAGEDY

TRAGEDY, as it was anciently composed, hath been ever held the gravest, moralest, and most profitable of all other poems, therefore said by Aristotle° to be of power by raising pity and fear, or terror, to purge the mind of those and such-like passions, that is, to temper and reduce them to just measure with a kind of delight, stirred up by reading or seeing those passions well imitated. Nor is Nature wanting in her own effects to make good his assertion; for so, in physic,° things of melancholic hue and quality are used against melancholy, sour against sour, salt to remove salt humours. Hence philosophers and other gravest writers, as Cicero, Plutarch, and others, frequently cite out of tragic poets, both to adorn and illustrate their discourse. The Apostle Paul himself thought it not unworthy to insert a verse of Euripides into the text of Holy Scripture, 1 Corinthians xv, 33; and Paraeus,° commenting on the Revelation, divides the whole book, as a tragedy, into acts, distinguished each by a Chorus of heavenly harpings and song between. Heretofore men in highest dignity have laboured not a little to be thought able to compose a tragedy. Of that honour Dionysius the elder° was no less ambitious than before of his attaining to the tyranny. Augustus Caesar also had begun his *Ajax,* but, unable to please his own judgement with what he had begun, left it unfinished. Seneca the philosopher is by some thought the author

---

Aristotle in his *Poetics,* VI **physic** homeopathic medicine **Paraeus** David (1548–1622), German Calvinist **Dionysius the elder** (C. 430–367 B.C.) Tyrant of Syracuse from 405, he won first prize in tragedy at Athens the year he died.

of those tragedies (at least the best of them) that go under that name. Gregory Nazianzen,° a Father of the Church, thought it not unbeseeming the sanctity of his person to write a tragedy, which he entitled *Christ Suffering*. This is mentioned to vindicate Tragedy from the small esteem, or rather infamy, which in the account of many it undergoes at this day, with other common interludes; happening through the poet's error of intermixing comic stuff with tragic sadness and gravity,° or introducing trivial and vulgar persons, which by all judicious hath been counted absurd, and brought in without discretion, corruptly to gratify the people. And, though ancient Tragedy use no Prologue,° yet using sometimes, in case of self-defence or explanation, that which Martial calls an Epistle; in behalf of this tragedy, coming forth after the ancient manner, much different from what among us passes for best,° thus much beforehand may be *epistled*—that Chorus is here introduced after the Greek manner, not ancient only but modern, and still in use among the Italians. In the modelling therefore of this poem, with good reason the Ancients and Italians are rather followed, as of much more authority and fame. The measure of verse used in the Chorus is of all sorts, called by the Greeks *Monostrophic*, or rather *Apolelymenon,*° without regard had to Strophe, Antistrophe, or Epode; which were a kind of stanzas framed only for the music, then used with the Chorus that sung; not essential to the poem, and therefore not material; or, being divided into stanzas or pauses, they may be called *Allaeostropha.*° Division into act and scene, referring chiefly to the stage (to which this work never was intended), is here omitted.

It suffices if the whole drama be found not produced beyond the fifth act. Of the style and uniformity, and that commonly called the plot, whether intricate or explicit—which is nothing indeed but such economy, or

Gregory Nazianzen now thought to be by a twelfth-century Byzantine Greek, though the fourth-century "Father of the Church" wrote poems **gravity** an Elizabethan mixture **Prologue** preface **best** e.g., Shakespearean tragedy. *Apolelymenon* a Greek word meaning *freed* (that is, from the obligation to follow a set pattern) *Allaeostropha* having irregular strophes or stanzas

disposition of the fable, as may stand best with verisimil-
itude and decorum—they only will best judge who are
not unacquainted with Aeschylus, Sophocles, and Euripides, the three tragic poets unequalled yet by any, and
the best rule to all who endeavour to write Tragedy. The
circumscription of time, wherein the whole drama begins
and ends, is, according to ancient rule and best example,
within the space of twenty-four hours.

THE ARGUMENT

Samson, made captive, blind, and now in the prison at Gaza, there to labour as in a common workhouse, on a festival day, in the general cessation from labour, comes forth into the open air to a place nigh, somewhat retired, there to sit a while and bemoan his condition, where he happens at length to be visited by certain friends and equals of his tribe, which make the Chorus, who seek to comfort him what they can; then by his old father, Manoa, who endeavours the like, and withal tells him his purpose to procure his liberty by ransom; lastly, that this feast was proclaimed by the Philistines as a day of thanksgiving for their deliverance from the hands of Samson—which yet more troubles him. Manoa then departs to prosecute his endeavour with the Philistian lords for Samson's redemption; who, in the meanwhile, is visited by other persons, and, lastly, by a public officer to require his coming to the feast before the lords and people, to play or show his strength in their presence; he at first refuses, dismissing the public officer with absolute denial to come; at length, persuaded inwardly that this was from God, he yields to go along with him, who came now the second time with great threatenings to fetch him; the Chorus yet remaining on the place, Manoa returns full of joyful hope to procure ere long his son's deliverance; in the midst of which discourse an Hebrew comes in haste, confusedly at first, and afterwards more distinctly, relating the catastrophe, what Samson had done to the Philistines, and by accident to himself; wherewith the Tragedy ends.

THE PERSONS

SAMSON
MANOA, the father of Samson
DALILA, his wife
HARAPHA of Gath
Public Officer
Messenger
Chorus of Danites

The Scene before the Prison in GAZA

Sam. A little onward lend thy guiding hand
To these dark steps, a little further on,
For yonder bank hath choice of sun or shade;
There I am wont to sit, when any chance
5 Relieves me from my task of servile toil,
Daily in the common prison else enjoined me,
Where I, a prisoner chained, scarce freely draw
The air, imprisoned also, close and damp,
Unwholesome draught: but here I feel amends,
10 The breath of Heaven fresh blowing, pure and sweet,
With day-spring born; here leave me to respire.
This day a solemn feast the people hold
To Dagon,° their sea-idol, and forbid
Laborious works, unwillingly this rest
15 Their superstition yields me; hence, with leave
Retiring from the popular noise, I seek
This unfrequented place to find some ease,
Ease to the body some, none to the mind
From restless thoughts, that, like a deadly swarm
20 Of hornets armed, no sooner found alone
But rush upon me thronging, and present
Times past, what once I was, and what am now.
Oh, wherefore was my birth from Heaven foretold
Twice by an Angel, who at last, in sight
25 Of both my parents, all in flames ascended
From off the altar, where an offering burned,
As in a fiery column charioting
His godlike presence, and from some great act
Or benefit revealed to Abraham's race?
30 Why was my breeding ordered and prescribed
As of a person separate° to God,

13 **Dagon** half fish (so the etymology), as described in *Paradise Lost,* i, 462 ff., deity of the Philistines that had a famous temple at Gaza, their southern border city   31 **separate** the etymological meaning of Nazarite, which Samson was (cf. 318)

Designed for great exploits, if I must die
Betrayed, captíved, and both my eyes put out,
Made of my enemies the scorn and gaze,
To grind in brazen fetters under task   35
With this heaven-gifted strength? O glorious strength
Put to the labour of a beast, debased
Lower than bond-slave! Promise was that I
Should Israel from Philistian yoke deliver;
Ask for this great deliverer now, and find him   40
Eyeless in Gaza at the mill with slaves,
Himself in bonds under Philistian yoke;
Yet stay, let me not rashly call in doubt
Divine prediction; what if all foretold
Had been fulfilled but through mine own default?   45
Whom have I to complain of but myself
Who this high gift° of strength committed to me,
In what part lodged, how easily bereft me,
Under the seal of silence could not keep,
But weakly to a woman must reveal it,   50
O'ercome with importunity and tears?
O impotence of mind, in body strong!
But what is strength without a double share
Of wisdom? vast, unwieldy, burdensome,
Proudly secure,° yet liable to fall°   55
By weakest subtleties; not made to rule,
But to subserve where wisdom bears command.
God, when he gave me strength, to show withal
How slight the gift was, hung it in my hair.
But peace, I must not quarrel with the will   60
Of highest dispensation, which herein
Haply had ends above my reach to know;°
Suffices that to me strength is my bane,
And proves the source of all my miseries,
So many, and so huge, that each apart   65
Would ask a life to wail, but chief of all,
O loss of sight, of thee I most complain!

47 **gift** object of *keep* (49) 53–55 **strength without . . .
wisdom . . . unwieldy . . . liable to fall** These words can serve
as a translation of Horace's *Carmina,* III, iv, 65: *Vis consili
expers mole ruit sua.* A traveler in Milton's day said that
"Gaza . . . signifieth strong." 55 **secure** heedless of
danger 62 the ultimate message

Blind among enemies, O worse than chains,
Dungeon, or beggary, or decrepit age!
70 Light, the prime work of God, to me is° extinct,
And all her various objects of delight
Annulled, which might in part my grief have eased;
Inferior to the vilest now become
Of man or worm, the vilest here excel me,
75 They creep, yet see; I, dark in light, exposed
To daily fraud, contempt, abuse, and wrong,
Within doors, or without, still as a fool,
In power of others, never in my own,
Scarce half I seem to live, dead more than half.
80 O dark, dark, dark, amid the blaze of noon,°
Irrecoverably dark, total eclipse,
Without all° hope of day!
O first-created beam, and thou great Word,
'Let there be light, and light was over all,'°
85 Why am I thus bereaved thy prime decree?
The Sun to me is dark
And silent° as the Moon,
When she deserts the night,
Hid in her vacant° interlunar cave.
90 Since light so necessary is to life,
And almost life itself, if it be true
That light is in the soul,
She all in every part, why was the sight
To such a tender ball as the eye confined,
95 So obvious and so easy to be quenched,
And not, as feeling, through all parts diffused,
That she might look at will through every pore?
Then had I not been thus exiled from light,
As in the land of darkness, yet in light,
100 To live a life half dead, a living death,°
And buried; but, O yet more miserable!

70 **me is** contract   80 ff. compare "East Coker," III, of T. S. Eliot's *Four Quartets*   82 **all** any   84 cf. *Paradise Lost*, vii, 243   87 **silent** i.e., withdrawn   89 **vacant** a word related to vacation: the Moon has withdrawn into a cave (so the ancients accounted for her disappearance: compare the Endymion myth) and is not performing her usual duties.   100 **a living death** a common phrase in authors before Milton and used by him in *Paradise Lost*, x, 788

Myself my sepulchre, a moving grave,
Buried, yet not exempt
By privilege of death and burial
From worst of other evils, pains, and wrongs,   105
But made hereby obnoxious° more
To all the miseries of life,
Life in captivity
Among inhuman foes.
But who are these? for with joint pace I hear   110
The tread of many feet steering this way;
Perhaps my enemies, who come to stare
At my affliction, and perhaps to insult,
Their daily practice to afflict me more.
   Chor. This, this is he; softly a while;   115
Let us not break in upon him.
O change beyond report, thought, or belief!
See how he lies at random, carelessly diffused,°
With languished head unpropped,
As one past hope, abandoned,   120
And by himself given over,
In slavish habit,° ill-fitted weeds°
O'erworn and soiled;
Or do my eyes misrepresent? Can this be he,
That heroic, that renowned,   125
Irresistible Samson? whom, unarmed,
No strength of man or fiercest wild beast could withstand,
Who tore the lion as the lion tears the kid,
Ran on embattled armies clad in iron,
And, weaponless himself,   130
Made arms ridiculous, useless the forgery
Of brazen shield and spear, the hammered cuirass,°
Chalybean-tempered° steel, and frock of mail
Adamantean proof,°
But safest he who stood aloof   135
When insupportably his foot advanced,
In scorn of their proud arms and warlike tools,

106 **obnoxious** exposed, like *obvious* (95) 118 **diffused**
"poured out" 122 **habit** dress **weeds** garments 132 **cuirass**
breastplate 133 **Chalybean-tempered** The Chalybes were
renowned ironworkers, who dwelt on the southern shore of
the Black Sea 134 **Adamantean proof** made of adamant, the
hardest substance, or proof against weapons of adamant

Spurned them to death by troops. The bold Ascalonite°
Fled from his lion ramp;° old warriors turned
140 Their plated backs under his heel,
Or grovelling soiled their crested helmets in the dust.
Then with what trivial weapon° came to hand,
The jaw of a dead ass, his sword of bone,
A thousand foreskins fell, the flower of Palestine,°
145 In Ramath-lechi, famous to this day;°
Then by main force pulled up and on his shoulders bore
The gates of Azza,° post and massy bar,
Up to the hill by Hebron,° seat of giants° old,
No journey of a sabbath-day, and loaded so,
150 Like whom the Gentiles feign to bear up Heaven.°
Which shall I first bewail,
Thy bondage or lost sight,
Prison within prison
Inseparably dark?
155 Thou art become (O worst imprisonment!)
The dungeon of thyself; thy soul
(Which men enjoying sight oft without cause complain)
Imprisoned now indeed,
In real darkness of the body dwells,
160 Shut up from outward light
To incorporate with gloomy night;
For inward light, alas!
Puts forth no visual beam.
O mirror of our fickle state,°
165 Since man on earth, unparalleled,°
The rarer thy example stands,
By how much from the top of wondrous glory,
Strongest of mortal men,
To lowest pitch of abject fortune thou art fallen.°

138 **The bold Ascalonite** see Judges, xiv, 19   139 **ramp** fiercely
rearing   142 **trivial weapon** (cf. 263); "the jawbone of an ass"
of Judges, xv, 16.   144 a reference to the uncircumcised
Philistines (cf. 260) 145 Judges, xv, 17 (with marginal
note)   147 **Azza** Gaza   148 **Hebron** one of the oldest cities in
the world, twenty miles south of Jerusalem   **seat of giants** see
Numbers, xiii, 33   150 the Atlas myth   164 **fickle state** cf.
Paradise Lost, ix, 948   165 cf. *Paradise Lost*, i, 573   167–69 A
fall from a great height was the figurative basis of Greek
tragedy as analyzed by Aristotle.

For him I reckon not in high estate   170
Whom long descent of birth
Or the sphere of fortune raises;
But thee, whose strength, while virtue was her mate,
Might have subdued the Earth,
Universally crowned with highest praises.   175
   Sam. I hear the sound of words; their sense the air
Dissolves unjointed ere it reach my ear.
   Chor. He speaks: let us draw nigh. Matchless in might,°
The glory late of Israel, now the grief,
We come, thy friends and neighbours not unknown,   180
From Eshtaol and Zora's° fruitful vale,
To visit or bewail thee; or, if better,
Counsel or consolation we may bring,
Salve to thy sores: apt words have power to 'suage
The tumours of a troubled mind,   185
And are as balm to festered wounds.°
   Sam. Your coming, friends, revives me, for I learn
Now of my own experience, not by talk,
How counterfeit a coin they are who 'friends'
Bear in their superscription (of the most   190
I would be understood); in prosperous days
They swarm, but in adverse withdraw their head,°
Not to be found, though sought. Ye see, O friends,
How many evils have enclosed me round;°
Yet that which was the worst now least afflicts me,   195
Blindness; for, had I sight, confused with shame,
How could I once look up, or heave the head,
Who, like a foolish pilot, have shipwrecked
My vessel trusted to me from above,
Gloriously rigged, and for a word, a tear,   200
Fool! have divulged the secret gift of God
To a deceitful woman: tell me, friends,
Am I not sung° and proverbed for a fool
In every street? do they not say, 'How well
Are come upon him his deserts'? yet why?   205

178 **Matchless in might** cf. *Paradise Lost,* x, 404   181 **Eshtaol and Zora** neighbouring towns "in the camp of Dan" (Judg. xiii, 25), the latter being Samson's birthplace   184–86 a sentiment found in Aeschylus, Euripides, Horace, and Spenser   191–92 a thought found in Ovid and Shakespeare   194 cf. *Paradise Lost*, vii, 27   203 **sung** see Job, xxx, 9; Psalms, lxix, 12

Immeasurable strength they might behold
In me; of wisdom nothing more than mean.°
This with the other should at least have paired;
These two, proportioned ill, drove me transverse.°
210   *Chor.* Tax not divine disposal.° Wisest men
Have erred, and by bad women° been deceived;
And shall again, pretend they ne'er so wise.
Deject not, then, so overmuch thyself,
Who hast of sorrow thy full load besides.
215 Yet, truth to say, I oft have heard men wonder
Why thou shouldst wed Philistian women rather
Than of thine own tribe fairer, or as fair,
At least of thy own nation, and as noble.
    Sam. The first I saw at Timna, and she pleased
220 Me, not my parents, that I sought to wed
The daughter of an infidel: they knew not
That what I motioned° was of God; I knew
From intimate impulse, and therefore urged
The marriage on, that, by occasion hence,
225 I might begin Israel's deliverance,
The work to which I was divinely called.
She proving false, the next I took to wife
(O that I never had! fond wish° too late)
Was in the vale of Sorec,° Dalila,
230 That specious° monster, my accomplished snare.
I thought it lawful from my former act,
And the same end, still watching to oppress
Israel's oppressors: of what now I suffer
She was not the prime cause, but I myself,
235 Who, vanquished with a peal of words (O weakness!),
Gave up my fort of silence to a woman.
    Chor. In seeking just occasion to provoke

207 **mean** average   209 cf. 199   210 In the *Doctrine and Discipline of Divorce* (II, xx) Milton warns the man "in misery" not to "open his lips against the providence of Heaven, or tax the ways of God and his divine truth." The ease with which "wisest men" err in matrimonial matters is also a recurring theme—in the prose and below, 759, 1034.   211 **bad women** cf. *Paradise Lost,* x, 837   222 **motioned** proposed (cf. *Paradise Lost,* ix, 229)   228 **fond wish** cf. x, 834   229 **Sorec** the Philistine city nearest Gaza in Palestine   230 **specious** attractive and false

The Philistine, thy country's enemy,
Thou never wast remiss, I bear thee witness;
Yet Israel still serves with all his sons.   240
   Sam. That fault I take not on me, but transfer
On Israel's governors, and heads of tribes,
Who, seeing those great acts which God had done
Singly by me against their conquerors,
Acknowledged not, or not at all considered   245
Deliverance offered: I, on the other side,
Used no ambition° to commend my deeds;
The deeds themselves, though mute, spoke loud the
    doer;
But they persisted deaf, and would not seem
To count them things worth notice, till at length   250
Their lords, the Philistines, with gathered powers,
Entered Judea seeking me, who then
Safe to the rock of Etham° was retired,
Not flying, but forecasting in what place
To set upon them, what advantaged best;   255
Meanwhile the men of Judah, to prevent
The harass of their land, beset me round;
I willingly on some conditions came
Into their hands, and they as gladly yield me
To the uncircumcised a welcome prey,   260
Bound with two cords; but cords to me were threads
Touched with the flame: on their whole host I flew
Unarmed, and with a trivial weapon felled
Their choicest youth; they only lived who fled.
Had Judah that day joined, or one whole tribe,   265
They had by this possessed the towers of Gath
And lorded over them whom now they serve;
But what more oft, in nations grown corrupt,
And by their vices brought to servitude,
Than to love bondage more than liberty,   270
Bondage with ease than strenuous liberty;
And to despise, or envy, or suspect,
Whom God hath of his special favour raised
As their deliverer; if he aught begin,

247 **ambition** "going around" for public support 253 **Etham**
Etam (Judg. xv, 8) a natural stronghold in Judah, perhaps in
the neighborhood of Bethlehem

275 How frequent to desert him, and at last
To heap ingratitude on worthiest deeds?
   Chor. Thy words to my remembrance bring
How Succoth° and the fort of Penuel°
Their great deliverer° contemned,
280 The matchless Gideon, in pursuit
Of Madian° and her vanquished kings,
And how ingrateful Ephraim
Had dealt with Jephtha,° who by argument,
Not worse than by his shield and spear,
285 Defended Israel from the Ammonite,
Had not his prowess quelled their pride
In that sore battle when so many died
Without reprieve adjudged to death,
For want of well pronouncing *Shibboleth.*
290   *Sam.* Of such examples add me to the roll;
Me easily indeed mine° may neglect,
But God's proposed deliverance not so.
   Chor. Just are the ways of God,
And justifiable to men,°
295 Unless there be who think not God at all.
If any be, they walk obscure;
For of such doctrine never was there school,
But the heart of the fool,°
And no man therein doctor but himself.
300   Yet more there be who doubt his ways not just,
As to his own edicts found contradicting,
Then give the reins to wandering thought,
Regardless of his glory's diminution,
Till, by their own perplexities involved,
305 They ravel more, still less resolved,
But never find self-satisfying solution.
   As if they would confine the interminable°

278 **Succoth** "Booths," a town between Penuel and Sechem **Penuel** east of Jordan; see Judges, viii, 8–9   279 **Their great deliverer** cf. 40   281 **Madian** a spelling of Midian found in Acts, vii, 29; a nomadic Arabian tribe whose *vanquished kings* were Zebah and Zalmunna   283 **Jephtha** who freed Israel from the Ammonites (see Judg., xi–xii)   291 **mine** my people (cf. *thine*, 1169)   293–94 Cf. i, 26 and Revelation, xv, 3: "just and true are thy ways, thou King of saints."   298 "The fool hath said in his heart, There is no God" (Ps. xiv, 1; liii, 1).   307 **interminable** infinite (God)

And tie him to his own prescript
Who made our laws to bind us, not himself,
And hath full right to exempt   310
Whom so it pleases him by choice
From national obstriction,° without taint
Of sin or legal debt,
For with his own laws he can best dispense.
He would not else, who never wanted means,   315
Nor in respect of the enemy just cause,
To set his people free,
Have prompted this heroic Nazarite,°
Against his vow of strictest purity,°
To seek in marriage that fallacious bride,   320
Unclean, unchaste.
   Down, Reason, then; at least, vain reasonings down;
Though Reason here aver
That moral verdict quits her of unclean:
Unchaste was subsequent, her stain, not his.   325
   But see, here comes thy reverend sire,
With careful° step, locks white as down,
Old Manoa: advise
Forthwith how thou ought'st to receive him.
   Sam. Ay me! another inward grief, awaked   330
With mention of that name, renews the assault.
   Man. Brethren and men of Dan, for such ye seem,
Though in this uncouth place, if old respect,
As I suppose, towards your once gloried friend,
My son, now captive, hither hath informed   335
Your younger feet, while mine, cast back with age
Came lagging after, say if he be here.
   Chor. As signal now in low dejected state
As erst in highest, behold him where he lies.
   Man. O miserable change! is this the man,   340
That invincible Samson, far renowned,°
The dread of Israel's foes, who with a strength
Equivalent to Angels' walked their streets,

312 **obstriction** legal obligation   318 **Nazarite** the name given to
Samson in the Bible as one bound by a vow of a peculiar kind
to be set apart from others for the service of God (cf. Num. vi,
1–21)   319 against intermarriage   327 **careful** full of care. Old
Manoa has been slower, as he explains (336–37), than the Chorus
in coming the same distance.   341 **far renowned** cf. i, 507

None offering fight; who, single combatant,
345 Duelled° their armies ranked in proud array,
Himself an army, now unequal match
To save himself against a coward armed
At one spear's length. O ever-failing trust
In mortal strength! and, oh, what not in man
350 Deceivable and vain? Nay, what thing good
Prayed for but often proves our woe, our bane?
I prayed for children, and thought barrenness
In wedlock a reproach; I gained a son,
And such a son as all men hailed me happy:
355 Who would be now a father in my stead?
O wherefore did God grant me my request,
And as a blessing with such pomp adorned?
Why are his gifts desirable, to tempt
Our earnest prayers, then given with solemn hand
360 As graces,° draw a scorpion's tail behind?
For this did the Angel twice descend? for this
Ordained thy nurture holy, as of a plant;°
Select and sacred? glorious for a while,
The miracle of men, then in an hour
365 Ensnared, assaulted, overcome, led bound,
Thy foes' derision, captive, poor, and blind,
Into a dungeon thrust, to work with slaves?
Alas! methinks whom God hath chosen once
To worthiest deeds,° if he through frailty err,
370 He should not so o'erwhelm, and as a thrall
Subject him to so foul indignities,
Be it but for honour's sake of former deeds.
    Sam. Appoint not heavenly disposition, Father.°
Nothing of all these evils hath befallen me
375 But justly; I myself have brought them on;
Sole author I, sole cause:° if aught seem vile,
As vile hath been my folly, who have profaned°
The mystery of God, given me under pledge

345 **Duelled** took on single-handed   360 **graces** favors. "If [a son] shall ask an egg, will he offer him a scorpion?" (Luke, xi, 12)   362 "For the vineyard of the Lord of hosts is the house of Israel, and the men of Judah his pleasant plant" (Is. v, 7). "For he shall grow up before him as a tender plant" (liii, 2).   369 **worthiest deeds** cf. 276   373 The meaning is: Do not judge God.   376 **sole cause** cf. x, 935   377 **profaned** revealed a sacred secret

Of vow, and have betrayed it to a woman,
A Canaanite,° my faithless enemy.   380
This well I knew, nor was at all surprised,
But warned by oft experience: did not she
Of Timna first betray me, and reveal
The secret wrested from me in her height
Of nuptial love professed, carrying it straight   385
To them who had corrupted her, my spies
And rivals? In this other was there found
More faith? who, also in her prime of love,
Spousal embraces, vitiated with gold,
Though offered only, by the scent° conceived,   390
Her spurious first-born, treason against me?
Thrice she assayed, with flattering prayers and sighs
And amorous reproaches, to win from me
My capital° secret, in what part my strength
Lay stored, in what part summed, that she might know;   395
Thrice I deluded her and turned to sport
Her importunity, each time perceiving
How openly and with what impudence
She purposed to betray me, and (which was worse
Than undissembled hate) with what contempt   400
She sought to make me traitor to myself;
Yet, the fourth time, when, mustering all her wiles,
With blandished parleys, feminine assaults,
Tongue-batteries, she surceased not day nor night
To storm me, overwatched and wearied out,   405
At times when men seek most repose and rest,
I yielded, and unlocked her all my heart,
Who, with a grain of manhood well resolved,
Might easily have shook off all her snares,
But foul effeminacy held me yoked   410
Her bond-slave; O indignity,° O blot
To honour and religion! servile mind
Rewarded well with servile punishment!
The base degree to which I now am fallen,
These rags, this grinding, is not yet so base   415

380 **A Canaanite** a special usage for "a Philistine" (referring
to the first conquerors of Canaan)   390 **by the scent** of
money   394 **capital** meaning both principal and pertaining to
the *caput*, head (cf. xii, 383)   411 **O indignity** cf. ix, 154

As was my former servitude, ignoble,
Unmanly, ignominious, infamous,
True slavery; and that blindness worse than this,
That saw not how degenerately I served.

420   *Man.* I cannot praise thy marriage-choices, son,°
Rather approved them not; but thou didst plead
Divine impulsion prompting how thou might'st
Find some occasion to infest our foes.
I state not that; this I am sure, our foes

425 Found soon occasion thereby to make thee
Their captive, and their triumph; thou the sooner
Temptation found'st, or overpotent charms
To violate the sacred trust of silence
Deposited within thee, which to have kept

430 Tacit was in thy power, true, and thou bear'st
Enough, and more, the burden of that fault;
Bitterly hast thou paid, and still art paying,
That rigid score. A worse thing yet remains:
This day the Philistines a popular feast

435 Here celebrate in Gaza and proclaim
Great pomp, and sacrifice, and praises loud
To Dagon, as their god who hath delivered
Thee, Samson, bound and blind, into their hands;°
Them out of thine, who slew'st them° many a slain.

440 So Dagon shall be magnified, and God,
Besides whom is no god, compared with idols,
Disglorified, blasphemed, and had in scorn
By the idolatrous rout amidst their wine;
Which to have come to pass by means of thee,

445 Samson, of all thy sufferings think the heaviest,
Of all reproach the most with shame that ever
Could have befallen thee and thy father's house.
   Sam. Father, I do acknowledge and confess
That I this honour, I this pomp, have brought

450 To Dagon, and advanced his praises high

420 Perhaps the most famous understatement in English
literature. 436–38 "Then the lords of the Philistines gathered
them together for to offer a great sacrifice unto Dagon their
god, and to rejoice: for they said, Our god hath delivered
Samson our enemy into our hand" (Judg. xvi, 23). 439 The
first *Them* is direct object (of *delivered* [437]), the second, a
Greek dative of disadvantage.

Among the Heathen round; to God have brought
Dishonour, obloquy, and oped the mouths
Of idolists and atheists; have brought scandal
To Israel, diffidence of God, and doubt
In feeble hearts, propense° enough before   *455*
To waver, or fall off and join with idols:
Which is my chief affliction, shame and sorrow,
The anguish of my soul, that suffers not
Mine eye to harbour sleep or thoughts to rest.
This only hope relieves me, that the strife   *460*
With me hath end; all the contest is now
'Twixt God and Dagon; Dagon hath presumed,
Me overthrown,° to enter lists with God,
His deity comparing and preferring
Before the God of Abraham. He, be sure,   *465*
Will not connive,° or linger, thus provoked,
But will arise, and his great name assert:
Dagon must stoop, and shall ere long receive
Such a discomfit as shall quite despoil him
Of all these boasted trophies won on me,   *470*
And with confusion blank his worshippers.

   Man. With cause this hope relieves thee; and these
      words°
I as a prophecy receive, for God,
Nothing more certain, will not long defer
To vindicate the glory of his name   *475*
Against all competition, nor will long
Endure it doubtful whether God be Lord,
Or Dagon. But for thee what shall be done?
Thou must not in the meanwhile, here forgot,
Lie in this miserable loathsome plight   *480*
Neglected. I already have made way
To some Philistian lords, with whom to treat
About thy ransom: well they may by this
Have satisfied their utmost of revenge,
By pains and slaveries, worse than death, inflicted *485*
On thee, who now no more canst do them harm.

   Sam. Spare that proposal, Father; spare the trouble
Of that solicitation; let me here,

455 **propense** inclined to   463 **Me overthrown**, an ablative
absolute—after my downfall   466 **connive** literally, shut the
eyes   472 cf. 460

As I deserve, pay on my punishment,
490 And expiate, if possible, my crime,
Shameful garrulity. To have revealed
Secrets of men, the secrets of a friend,
How heinous had the fact been, how deserving
Contempt and scorn of all—to be excluded
495 All friendship, and avoided as a blab,
The mark of fool set on his front!
But I God's counsel have not kept, his holy secret
Presumptuously have published, impiously,
Weakly at least and shamefully—a sin
500 That Gentiles in their parables condemn
To their abyss and horrid pains confined.°
    Man. Be penitent and for thy fault contrite,
But act not in thy own affliction, son.
Repent the sin, but if the punishment
505 Thou canst avoid, self-preservation bids:
Or the execution leave to high disposal
And let another hand, not thine, exact
Thy penal forfeit from thyself; perhaps
God will relent and quit thee all his debt;
510 Who evermore approves and more accepts
(Best pleased with humble and filial submission)
Him who, imploring mercy, sues for life,
Than who, self-rigorous, chooses death as due,
Which argues overjust,° and self-displeased
515 For self-offence more than for God offended.
Reject not, then, what offered means who knows
But God hath set before us to return
Home to thy country and his sacred house,
Where thou may'st bring thy offerings, to avert
520 His further ire, with prayers and vows renewed.
    Sam. His pardon I implore, but as for life
To what end should I seek it? when in strength
All mortals I excelled, and great in hopes,
With youthful courage and magnanimous thoughts
525 Of birth from Heaven foretold and high exploits,°
Full of divine instinct, after some proof

500–01 possibly a reference both to Tantalus and Prometheus,
punished revealers of divine secrets   514 **Which argues over-**
just which demand (of death for oneself) indicates the person
to be excessively scrupulous   525 cf. 23

Of acts indeed heroic, far beyond
The sons of Anak,° famous now and blazed,
Fearless of danger, like a petty god
I walked about, admired of all, and dreaded   530
On hostile ground, none daring my affront.
Then, swollen with pride, into the snare I fell
Of fair fallacious looks, venereal trains,°
Softened with pleasure and voluptuous life,
At length to lay my head and hallowed pledge   535
Of all my strength in the lascivious lap
Of a deceitful concubine, who shore me,°
Like a tame wether,° all my precious fleece,
Then turned me out ridiculous, despoiled,
Shaven, and disarmed among my enemies.   540
   Chor. Desire of wine and all delicious drinks,
Which many a famous warrior overturns,
Thou couldst repress; nor did the dancing ruby,°
Sparkling outpoured, the flavour, or the smell,
Or taste, that cheers the heart of gods and men,°   545
Allure thee from the cool crystálline stream.
   Sam. Wherever fountain or fresh current flowed
Against the eastern ray, translucent, pure
With touch ethereal of Heaven's fiery rod,
I drank, from the clear milky juice° allaying   550
Thirst, and refreshed; nor envied them the grape
Whose heads that turbulent liquor fills with fumes.
   Chor. O madness, to think use of strongest wines
And strongest drinks our chief support of health,
When God with these forbidden made choice to rear   555
His mighty champion, strong above compare,

---

528 **The sons of Anak** a race of giants   533 **venereal trains**
snares of love   535–37 Compare Spenser's Cymochles and
Phaedria: She sat beside, laying his head disarmed /In her loose
lap, it softly to sustain, /Where soon he slumbered, fearing not
be harmed, /The whiles with a love lay she thus him sweetly
charmed.   (*Faerie Queene,* II, vi, 14)   538 **wether** a castrated
ram   543 **the dancing ruby** "Look not thou upon the wine
when it is red, when it giveth his colour in the cup, when it
moveth itself aright" (Prov. xxiii, 31); compare "rubied nectar
flows" (*Paradise Lost,* v, 633)   545 "wine, which cheers gods
and men" (Judg. ix, 13, Revised Standard Version)   550 **clear
milky juice** so water was "milky stream" at v, 306

Whose drink was only from the liquid° brook.
   Sam. But what availed this temperance, not complete
Against another object more enticing?
560 What boots it° at one gate to make defence,
And at another to let in the foe,
Effeminately vanquished? by which means,
Now blind, disheartened, shamed, dishonoured,
     quelled,
To what can I be useful? wherein serve
565 My nation, and the work from Heaven imposed,
But to sit idle on the household hearth,
A burdenous drone; to visitants a gaze,
Or pitied object; these redundant locks,
Robustious to no purpose, clustering down,
570 Vain monument of strength, till length of years
And sedentary numbness craze my limbs
To a contemptible old age obscure.
Here rather let me drudge and earn my bread,
Till vermin, or the draff° of servile food,
575 Consume me, and oft-invocated death
Hasten the welcome end of all my pains.
   Man. Wilt thou then serve the Philistines with that gift
Which was expressly given thee to annoy them?
Better at home lie bed-rid, not only idle,
580 Inglorious, unemployed, with age outworn.
But God, who caused a fountain at thy prayer
From the dry ground° to spring, thy thirst to allay
After the brunt of battle, can as easy
Cause light again within thy eyes to spring,
585 Wherewith to serve him better than thou hast;
And I persuade me so—why else this strength
Miraculous yet remaining in those locks?
His might continues in thee not for naught,
Nor shall his wondrous gifts° be frustrate thus.
590   *Sam.* All otherwise to me my thoughts portend,
That these dark orbs no more shall treat with light,
Nor the other light of life continue long,
But yield to double darkness nigh at hand;

557 **liquid** transparent; see the prescription for the Nazarite's
abstinence in Numbers vi, 3–4   560 **What boots it** see "Lycidas,"
64.   574 **draff** refuse   582 **dry ground** cf. xi, 861   589 **wondrous
gifts** cf. xii, 500

So much I feel my genial spirits° droop,
My hopes all flat: nature within me seems   595
In all her functions weary of herself;
My race of glory run, and race of shame,
And I shall shortly be with them that rest.
   Man. Believe not these suggestions, which proceed
From anguish of the mind and humours black°   600
That mingle with thy fancy. I, however,
Must not omit a father's timely care°
To prosecute the means of thy deliverance
By ransom or how else; meanwhile be calm,
And healing words° from these thy friends admit.   605
   Sam. Oh, that torment should not be confined
To the body's wounds and sores
With maladies innumerable
In heart, head, breast, and reins,°
But must secret passage find   610
To the inmost mind,
There exercise all his fierce accidents,
And on her purest spirits° prey,
As on entrails, joints, and limbs,
With answerable pains, but more intense,   615
Though void of corporal sense.
   My griefs not only pain me
As a lingering disease,
But, finding no redress, ferment and rage;
Nor less than wounds immedicable°   620
Rankle, and fester, and gangrene,
To black mortification.
Thoughts, my tormentors, armed with deadly stings,
Mangle my apprehensive tenderest parts,
Exasperate, exulcerate, and raise   625
Dire inflammation, which no cooling herb
Or med'cinal liquor can assuage,
Nor breath of vernal air° from snowy alp.°
Sleep hath forsook and given me o'er

---

594 **my genial spirits** my special energies   600 **humours black**
melancholy   602 **timely care** cf. x, 1057   605 **healing words** cf. ix,
290   609 **reins** kidneys   613 **purest spirits** cf. v, 406   620 **wounds
immedicable** *immedicabile vulnus* (Ovid, *Met.* X, 189)   628
vernal air cf. iv, 264   **alp** used in Late Latin poetry for any high
mountain; cf. ii, 620

630 To death's benumbing opium as my only cure;
    Thence faintings, swoonings of despair,
    And sense of Heaven's desertion.
      I was his nursling once and choice delight,
    His destined from the womb,
635 Promised by heavenly message° twice descending.
    Under his special eye
    Abstemious I grew up and thrived amain;
    He led me on to mightiest deeds,
    Above the nerve° of mortal arm,
640 Against the uncircumcised, our enemies;
    But now hath cast me off as never known,
    And to those cruel enemies,
    Whom I by his appointment had provoked,
    Left me all helpless, with the irreparable° loss
645 Of sight, reserved alive to be repeated
    The subject of their cruelty or scorn.
    Nor am I in the list of them that hope;
    Hopeless are all my evils, all remediless;
    This one prayer yet remains, might I be heard,
650 No long petition—speedy death,
    The close of all my miseries and the balm.
      Chor. Many are the sayings of the wise,
    In ancient and in modern books enrolled,
    Extolling patience as the truest fortitude,
655 And to the bearing well of all calamities,
    All chances incident to man's frail life,
    Consolatories writ
    With studied argument, and much persuasion sought,
    Lenient of° grief and anxious thought,
660 But with the afflicted in his pangs their sound
    Little prevails, or rather seems a tune
    Harsh and of dissonant mood° from his complaint,
    Unless he feel within
    Some source of consolation from above,
665 Secret refreshings that repair his strength
    And fainting spirits uphold.
      God of our fathers, what is Man!°

635 **message** messenger   639 **nerve** Latin *nervus,* sinew.   644
irreparable loss cf. ii, 330–31.   659 **Lenient of** alleviating   662
mood a musical term, mode   667 "What is man, that thou art
mindful of him" (Ps. viii, 4; cf. Job, vii, 17).

That thou towards him with hand so various,
Or might I say contrarious,
Temper'st thy providence through his short course,   *670*
Not evenly, as thou rul'st
The angelic orders, and inferior creatures mute,
Irrational and brute.
Nor do I name of men the common rout,
That, wandering loose about,   *675*
Grow up and perish as the summer fly,
Heads° without name, no more remembered;
But such as thou hast solemnly elected,
With gifts and graces eminently adorned,
To some great work, thy glory,   *680*
And people's safety, which in part they effect:
Yet toward these, thus dignified, thou oft,
Amidst their height of noon,
Changest thy countenance and thy hand, with no regard
Of highest favours past   *685*
From thee on them, or them to thee of service.
     Nor only dost degrade them, or remit°
To life obscured, which were a fair dismission,
But throw'st them lower than thou didst exalt them high;
Unseemly falls in human eye,   *690*
Too grievous for the trespass or omission;
Oft leav'st them to the hostile sword
Of heathen and profane, their carcases
To dogs and fowls a prey,° or else captíved;
Or to the unjust tribunals, under change of times,   *695*
And condemnation of the ingrateful multitude.
If these they 'scape, perhaps in poverty
With sickness and disease thou bow'st them down,
Painful diseases and deformed,
In crude° old age;   *700*
Though not disordinate,° yet causeless suffering
The punishment of dissolute days, in fine,
Just or unjust alike seem miserable,
For oft alike both come to evil end.
     So deal not with this once thy glorious champion,   *705*
The image of thy strength, and mighty minister.

677 **Heads** people (a Latinism)   687 **remit** send back   694 **To
dogs and fowls a prey** *Iliad*, I, 4–5   700 **crude** possibly,
premature, as in "Lycidas," 3.   701 **disordinate** intemperate

What do I beg? how hast thou dealt already?
Behold him in this state calamitous, and turn
His labours, for thou canst, to peaceful end.
710   But who is this, what thing of sea or land?
Female of sex it seems,
That, so bedecked, ornate, and gay,
Comes this way sailing,
Like a stately ship
715 Of Tarsus,° bound for the isles
Of Javan° or Gadire°
With all her bravery° on and tackle trim,
Sails filled and streamers waving,
Courted by all the winds that hold them play;°
720 An amber scent° of odorous perfume
Her harbinger, a damsel train behind;
Some rich Philistian matron she may seem,
And now, at nearer view, no other certain
Than Dalila, thy wife.
    Sam. My wife, my traitress, let her not come
725   near me.
    Chor. Yet on she moves; now stands and eyes thee
      fixed,
About to have spoke; but now, with head declined,
Like a fair flower surcharged with dew, she weeps,
And words addressed seem into tears dissolved,
730 Wetting the borders of her silken veil;
But now again she makes address to speak.
    Dal. With doubtful feet and wavering resolution
I came, still dreading thy displeasure, Samson,
Which to have merited, without excuse,
735 I cannot but acknowledge; yet, if tears
May expiate (though the fact more evil drew

715 **Tarsus** equated with Tarshish, the ships of which are so
often mentioned in the Old Testament as symbols of pride and
affluence (e.g., 1 Kings, x, 22) as to suggest any distant place,
whether the port on the Guadalquivir in Spain or the thriving
capital of Cilicia   716 **Javan** the son of Japhet, identified with
Ion, ancestor of the Ionians or Greeks, so that *the isles* (715)
are Greece   **Gadire** Cádiz in Spain   717 **bravery** finery   719
compare Gratiano's speech, which here has "Hugg'd and
embraced by the strumpet wind!" (*Merchant of Venice,* II, vi,
16)   720 **amber scent** derived probably from the ambergris of
the whale rather than from the equally fragrant amber tree

In the perverse event than I foresaw),
My penance° hath not slackened, though my pardon
No way assured. But conjugal affection,
Prevailing over fear and timorous doubt,   740
Hath led me on, desirous to behold
Once more thy face, and know of thy estate,
If aught in my ability may serve
To lighten what thou suffer'st and appease
Thy mind with what amends is in my power,   745
Though late, yet in some part to recompense
My rash but more unfortunate misdeed.
    Sam. Out, out, hyaena;° these are thy wonted arts,
And arts of every woman false like thee,
To break all faith, all vows, deceive, betray,   750
Then, as repentant, to submit, beseech,
And reconcilement move with feigned remorse,
Confess, and promise wonders in her change,
Not truly penitent, but chief to try
Her husband, how far urged his patience bears,   755
His virtue or weakness which way to assail;
Then with more cautious and instructed skill
Again transgresses, and again submits;
That wisest and best men, full oft beguiled,
With goodness principled not to reject   760
The penitent but ever to forgive,
Are drawn to wear out miserable days,
Entangled with a poisonous bosom snake,
If not by quick destruction soon cut off,
As I by thee, to ages an example.   765
    Dal. Yet hear me, Samson; not that I endeavour
To lessen or extenuate my offence,
But that, on the other side, if it be weighed
By itself, with aggravations not surcharged,
Or else with just allowance counterpoised,   770
I may, if possible, thy pardon find
The easier towards me, or thy hatred less.
First granting, as I do, it was a weakness

738 **penance** penitence   748 Pliny reported of the *hyaena* that
"he will feign man's speech, and, coming to the shepherds'
cottages, will call one of them forth whose name he hath
. learned, and when he hath him without, all to worry and tear
him to pieces."

In me, but incident to all our sex,
775 Curiosity, inquisitive, importune
Of secrets, then with like infirmity
To publish them, both common female faults;
Was it not weakness also to make known
For importunity, that is for naught,
780 Wherein consisted all thy strength and safety?
To what I did thou show'dst me first the way.
But I to enemies revealed, and should not.
Nor shouldst thou have trusted that to woman's frailty:
Ere I to thee, thou to thyself wast cruel.
785 Let weakness, then, with weakness come to parle,
So near related, or the same of kind;°
Thine forgive mine, that men may censure thine
The gentler, if severely thou exact not
More strength from me than in thyself was found.
790 And what if love, which thou interpret'st hate,
The jealousy of love, powerful of sway
In human hearts, nor less in mine towards thee,
Caused what I did? I saw thee mutable
Of fancy;° feared lest one day thou wouldst leave me
795 As her at Timna; sought by all means, therefore,
How to endear, and hold thee to me firmest:
No better way I saw than by importuning
To learn thy secrets, get into my power
Thy key of strength and safety: thou wilt say,
800 'Why, then, revealed?' I was assured by those
Who tempted me that nothing was designed
Against thee but safe custody and hold:°
That made for me, I knew that liberty
Would draw thee forth to perilous enterprises,
805 While I at home sat full of cares and fears,
Wailing thy absence in my widowed bed;
Here I should still enjoy thee, day and night,
Mine and love's prisoner, not the Philistines',
Whole to myself, unhazarded abroad,
810 Fearless at home of partners in my love.

786 **kind** nature   793–94 **mutable/ Of fancy** fancy-free   800–02
A lie: Dalila knew the Philistines' purpose was to "bind him
to afflict him" (Judg. xvi, 5). Nor does Dalila care to mention
the "Philistian gold," 831.

These reasons in Love's law have passed for good,
Though fond and reasonless to some perhaps;
And love hath oft, well meaning, wrought much woe,
Yet always pity or pardon hath obtained.
Be not unlike all others, not austere   815
As thou art strong, inflexible as steel.
If thou in strength all mortals dost exceed,°
In uncompassionate anger do not so.
   Sam. How cunningly the sorceress displays
Her own transgressions, to upbraid me mine!   820
That malice, not repentance, brought thee hither
By this appears: I gave, thou say'st, the example,
I led the way—bitter reproach, but true;
I to myself was false ere thou to me.
Such pardon, therefore, as I give my folly   825
Take to thy wicked deed; which° when thou seest
Impartial, self-severe, inexorable,
Thou wilt renounce thy seeking, and much rather
Confess it feigned: weakness is thy excuse,
And I believe it; weakness to resist   830
Philistian gold. If weakness may excuse,
What murderer, what traitor, parricide,
Incestuous, sacrilegious, but may plead it?
All wickedness is weakness; that plea, therefore,
With God or man will gain thee no remission.   835
But love constrained thee; call it furious rage°
To satisfy thy lust: Love seeks to have love;
My love how couldst thou hope, who took'st the way
To raise in me inexpiable hate,
Knowing, as needs I must, by thee betrayed?   840
In vain thou striv'st to cover shame with shame,
Or by evasions thy crime uncover'st more.
   Dal. Since thou determin'st weakness for no plea°
In man or woman, though to thy own condemning,
Hear what assaults I had, what snares besides,   845
What sieges girt me round, ere I consented,
Which might have awed the best-resolved of men,
The constantest, to have yielded without blame.
It was not gold, as to my charge thou lay'st,

817 cf. 522–23 826 **which** The antecedent is "pardon,"
825. 836 **furious rage** cf. viii, 244 843 cf. 834

850 That wrought with me: thou know'st the magistrates
     And princes of my country came in person,
     Solicited, commanded, threatened, urged,
     Adjured by all the bonds of civil duty
     And of religion, pressed how just it was,
855 How honourable, how glorious to entrap
     A common enemy, who had destroyed
     Such numbers of our nation; and the priest
     Was not behind, but ever at my ear,
     Preaching how meritorious with the gods
860 It would be to ensnare an irreligious
     Dishonourer of Dagon:° what had I
     To oppose against such powerful arguments?
     Only my love of thee held long debate,°
     And combated in silence all these reasons
865 With hard contést. At length, that grounded maxim,
     So rife and celebrated in the mouths
     Of wisest men, that to the public good
     Private respects° must yield, with grave authority
     Took full possession of me and prevailed;
870 Virtue, as I thought, truth, duty, so enjoining.
         Sam. I thought where all thy circling wiles would end:
     In feigned religion, smooth hypocrisy;
     But, had thy love, still odiously pretended,
     Been, as it ought, sincere, it would have taught thee
875 Far other reasonings, brought forth other deeds.
     I before all the daughters of my tribe
     And of my nation chose thee from among
     My enemies, loved thee, as too well thou knew'st,
     Too well, unbosomed all my secrets to thee,
880 Not out of levity, but overpowered
     By thy request, who could deny thee nothing,
     Yet now am judged an enemy. Why, then,
     Didst thou at first receive me for thy husband?
     Then, as since then, thy country's foe professed:
885 Being once a wife, for me thou wast to leave

857–61 As F. T. Prince remarks, "The Old Testament makes
no mention of priestly influence on Dalila; Milton is colouring
the story with his own anti-clerical convictions."   863 **long
debate** cf. ii, 390; ix, 87   868 **respects** considerations or
interests

Parents and country; nor was I their subject,
Nor under their protection, but my own;
Thou mine, not theirs: if aught against my life
Thy country sought of thee, it sought unjustly,
Against the law of nature, law of nations;°   890
No more thy country, but an impious crew
Of men conspiring to uphold their state
By worse than hostile deeds, violating the ends
For which our country is a name so dear,
Not therefore to be obeyed. But zeal moved thee;   895
To please thy gods thou didst it; gods unable
To acquit themselves and prosecute their foes
But by ungodly deeds, the contradiction
Of their own deity, gods cannot be:
Less therefore to be pleased, obeyed, or feared.   900
These false pretexts and varnished colours failing,
Bare in thy guilt, how foul must thou appear?
    Dal. In argument with men a woman ever
Goes by the worse, whatever be her cause.
    Sam. For want of words, no doubt, or lack of breath;   905
Witness when I was worried with thy peals.
    Dal. I was a fool, too rash, and quite mistaken
In what I thought would have succeeded best.
Let me obtain forgiveness of thee, Samson;
Afford me place to show what recompense°   910
Towards thee I intend for what I have misdone,
Misguided; only what remains past cure
Bear not too sensibly,° nor still insist
To afflict thyself in vain: though sight be lost,
Life yet hath many solaces, enjoyed   915
Where other senses want not their delights,
At home, in leisure and domestic ease,
Exempt from many a care and chance to which
Eyesight exposes, daily, men abroad.
I to the lords will intercede, not doubting   920
Their favourable ear, that I may fetch thee

890 Here Milton translates the title of a book he had used
both for *Areopagitica* and the *Doctrine and Discipline of
Divorce: De Jure Naturali et Gentium,* by the learned John
Selden (1584–1654).   910 Esau "found no place of repentance,
though he sought it carefully with tears" (Heb. xii, 17).   913
sensibly acutely

From forth this loathsome prison-house, to abide
With me, where my redoubled love and care,
With nursing diligence, to me glad office,
925 May ever tend about thee to old age
With all things grateful cheered, and so supplied
That what by me thou hast lost thou least shalt miss.
    Sam. No, no, of my condition take no care;
It fits not; thou and I long since are twain;
930 Nor think me so unwary or accursed
To bring my feet again into the snare
Where once I have been caught; I know thy trains,°
Though dearly to my cost, thy gins,° and toils;
Thy fair enchanted cup and warbling charms
935 No more on me have power—their force is nulled;
So much of adder's wisdom I have learnt
To fence my ear against thy sorceries.°
If in my flower of youth and strength, when all men
Loved, honoured, feared me, thou alone could hate me,
940 Thy husband, slight me, sell me, and forgo me,
How wouldst thou use me now, blind, and thereby
Deceivable, in most things as a child
Helpless, thence easily contemned and scorned,
And last neglected? How wouldst thou insult,
945 When I must live uxorious to thy will
In perfect thraldom, how again betray me,
Bearing my words and doings to the lords
To gloss upon, and, censuring, frown or smile?
This jail I count the house of liberty
950 To thine, whose doors my feet shall never enter.
    Dal. Let me approach at least, and touch thy hand.
    Sam. Not for thy life, lest fierce remembrance wake
My sudden rage to tear thee joint by joint.
At distance I forgive thee; go with that;
955 Bewail thy falsehood, and the pious works
It hath brought forth to make thee memorable
Among illustrious women, faithful wives;

932 **trains** cf. 533   933 **gins** traps (short for engines)   936–37
"Their poison is like the poison of a serpent: they are like
the deaf adder that stoppeth her ear; Which will not hearken
to the voice of charmers, charming never so wisely" (Ps.
lviii, 4–5).

Cherish thy hastened widowhood with the gold
Of matrimonial treason: so farewell.
   Dal. I see thou art implacable, more deaf   960
To prayers than winds and seas; yet winds to seas
Are reconciled at length, and sea to shore:
Thy anger, unappeasable, still rages,
Eternal tempest never to be calmed,
Why do I humble thus myself, and, suing   965
For peace, reap nothing but repulse and hate?
Bid go with evil omen, and the brand
Of infamy upon my name denounced?
To mix with thy concernments I desist
Henceforth, nor too much disapprove my own.   970
Fame, if not double-faced, is double-mouthed,
And with contrary blast proclaims most deeds;
On both his wings, one black, the other white,
Bears greatest names in his wild aery flight:
My name, perhaps, among the circumcised   975
In Dan, in Judah, and the bordering tribes,
To all posterity may stand defamed,
With malediction mentioned, and the blot
Of falsehood most unconjugal traduced.
But in my country, where I most desire,   980
In Ecron, Gaza, Asdod, and in Gath,°
I shall be named among the famousest
Of women, sung at solemn festivals,
Living and dead recorded, who, to save
Her country from a fierce destroyer, chose   985
Above the faith of wedlock-bands, my tomb
With odours° visited and annual flowers.
Not less renowned than in Mount Ephraim°
Jael, who, with inhospitable guile,°
Smote Sisera sleeping, through the temples nailed.   990
Nor shall I count it heinous to enjoy

---

981 Dalila names four of the five (omitting Ascalon) chief cities
of the Philistines to illustrate how widespread her fame will
be, the first two being respectively northernmost and southern-
most. 987 **odours** incense 988 **Mount Ephraim** in the hilly
district of central Palestine inhabited by the tribe of Ephraim
that had been "ingrateful" (282) to Jephtha 989 ff. see
Judges, iv, 21

The public marks of honour and reward
Conferred upon me for the piety
Which to my country I was judged to have shown.
995 At this whoever envies or repines,
  I leave him to his lot, and like my own.
    Chor. She's gone, a manifest serpent by her sting
Discovered in the end, till now concealed.
    Sam. So let her go; God sent her to debase me,
1000 And aggravate my folly, who committed
To such a viper his most sacred trust°
Of secrecy, my safety, and my life.
    Chor. Yet beauty, though injurious, hath strange
      power,°
After offence returning, to regain
1005 Love once possessed, nor can be easily
Repulsed, without much inward passion felt,
And secret sting of amorous remorse.
    Sam. Love-quarrels oft in pleasing concord end;°
Not wedlock-treachery endangering life.
1010   *Chor.* It is not virtue, wisdom, valour, wit,
Strength, comeliness of shape, or amplest merit,
That woman's love can win, or long inherit;
But what it is, hard is to say,
Harder to hit
1015 (Which way soever men refer it),
Much like thy riddle, Samson, in one day
Or seven though one should musing sit;
  If any of these, or all, the Timnian bride
Had not so soon preferred
1020 Thy paranymph,° worthless to thee compared,
Successor in thy bed,
Nor both so loosely disallied
Their nuptials, nor this last so treacherously
Had shorn the fatal harvest of thy head.
1025 Is it for that° such outward ornament
Was lavished on their sex, that inward gifts
Were left for haste unfinished, judgement scant,
Capacity not raised to apprehend

1001 **sacred trust** cf. 428   1003 compare beseeching Eve, x, 910
ff   1008 a translation of a famous line: *Amantium irae amoris
integratio est* (Terence, *Andria,* III, iii, 23)   1020 **paranymph**
best man   1025 **for that** because

Or value what is best
In choice, but oftest to affect the wrong?   1030
Or was too much of self-love mixed,
Of constancy no root infixed,
That either they love nothing, or not long?
   Whate'er it be, to wisest men and best,°
Seeming at first all heavenly under virgin veil,   1035
Soft, modest, meek, demure,
Once joined, the contrary she proves—a thorn
Intestine,° far within defensive arms
A cleaving mischief,° in his way to virtue
Adverse and turbulent; or by her charms   1040
Draws him awry, enslaved
With dotage, and his sense depraved
To folly and shameful deeds, which ruins ends.
What pilot so expert but needs must wreck,
Embarked with such a steers-mate at the helm?   1045
   Favoured of Heaven° who finds
One virtuous, rarely found,
That in domestic good combines:
Happy that house! his way to peace is smooth:
But virtue which breaks through all opposition,   1050
And all temptation can remove,
Most shines and most is acceptable above.
   Therefore God's universal law
Gave to the man despotic power
Over his female in due awe,   1055
Nor from that right to part an hour,
Smile she or lower:
So shall he least confusion draw
On his whole life, not swayed
By female usurpation, nor dismayed.   1060
   But had we best retire? I see a storm.
   Sam. Fair days have oft contracted wind and rain.
   Chor. But this another kind of tempest brings.
   Sam. Be less abstruse; my riddling days are past.

1034 cf. 210, 759, 867   1037–38 "a thorn in the flesh" (2 Cor.
xii, 7)   1039 **A cleaving mischief** taken by the eighteenth-
century commentator Meadowcourt as referring "to the
poisoned shirt sent to Hercules by his wife Deianira"; cf. ii,
542–43   1046 **Favoured of Heaven** cf. i, 30

1065   *Chor.* Look now for no enchanting voice, nor fear
       The bait of honeyed words; a rougher tongue
       Draws hitherward; I know him by his stride,
       The giant Harapha° of Gath, his look
       Haughty, as is his pile° high-built and proud.
1070 Comes he in peace? what wind hath blown him hither
       I less conjecture than when first I saw
       The sumptuous Dalila floating this way:
       His habit carries peace, his brow defiance.
       Sam. Or peace or not, alike to me he comes.
1075   *Chor.* His fraught° we soon shall know: he now arrives.
       Har. I come not, Samson, to condole thy chance,
       As these perhaps, yet wish it had not been,
       Though for no friendly intent. I am of Gath;
       Men call me Harapha, of stock renowned
1080 As Og, or Anak, and the Emims old°
       That Kiriathaim° held; thou know'st me now,
       If thou at all art known.° Much I have heard
       Of thy prodigious might and feats performed,
       Incredible to me, in this displeased,
1085 That I was never present on the place
       Of those encounters, where we might have tried
       Each other's force in camp or listed field;
       And now am come to see of whom such noise
       Hath walked about, and each limb to survey,
1090 If thy appearance answer loud report.
       Sam. The way to know were not to see, but taste.
       Har. Dost thou already single me? I thought
       Gyves and the mill had tamed thee. Oh, that fortune
       Had brought me to the field where thou art famed
1095 To have wrought such wonders with an ass's jaw;
       I should have forced thee soon with° other arms,
       Or left thy carcase where the ass lay thrown;
       So had the glory of prowess been recovered

1068 **Harapha** a name meaning *the giant* (the marginal note in the Anglican version has Rapha for giant in 2 Sam. xxi, 16; the Vulgate—Regum, 2, xxi, 16—Arapha) 1069 **his pile** his huge body 1075 **fraught** freight or message 1080 giants 1081 **Kiriathaim** a town east of the Jordan; see Genesis, xiv, 5 1081–82 cf. iv, 830 1096 **with** the emendation *wish* is popular

To Palestine, won by a Philistine
From the unforeskinned race, of whom thou bear'st 1100
The highest name for valiant acts; that honour,
Certain to have won by mortal duel from thee,
I lose, prevented by thy eyes put out.°
   Sam. Boast not of what thou wouldst have done,
     but do
What then thou wouldst; thou seest it in thy hand. 1105
   Har. To combat with a blind man I disdain,
And thou hast need much washing to be touched.
   Sam. Such usage as your honourable lords
Afford me, assassinated° and betrayed,
Who durst not with their whole united powers 1110
In fight withstand me single and unarmed,
Nor in the house with chamber ambushes
Close-banded durst attack me, no, not sleeping,
Till they had hired a woman with their gold,
Breaking her marriage faith, to circumvent me. 1115
Therefore, without feigned shifts, let be assigned
Some narrow place enclosed, where sight may give thee,
Or rather flight, no great advantage on me;
Then put on all thy gorgeous arms, thy helmet
And brigandine° of brass, thy broad habergeon,° 1120
Vant-brass° and greaves° and gauntlet; add thy spear,
A weaver's beam, and seven-times-folded shield:°
I only with an oaken staff will meet thee,
And raise such outcries on thy clattered iron,
Which long shall not withhold me from thy head, 1125
That in a little time, while breath remains thee,
Thou oft shalt wish thyself at Gath, to boast
Again in safety what thou wouldst have done
To Samson, but shalt never see Gath more.
   Har. Thou durst not thus disparage glorious arms 1130
Which greatest heroes have in battle worn,
Their ornament and safety, had not spells

1103 **thy eyes put out** cf. 33 1109 **assassinated** attacked by
treachery 1120 **brigandine** metal-plated body armor
habergeon a coat of mail 1121 **Vant-brass** armor for the
forearm **greaves** armor for the lower leg 1121–22 A
deliberate reminiscence (as the armor was above) of the
equipage of Goliath: "And the staff of his spear was like a
weaver's beam" (1 Sam. xvii, 7).

And black enchantments, some magician's art,
Armed thee or charmed thee strong, which thou
    from Heaven
1135 Feign'dst at thy birth was given thee in thy hair,
Where strength can least abide, though all thy hairs
Were bristles ranged like those that ridge the back
Of chafed wild boars or ruffled porcupines.°
    Sam. I know no spells, use no forbidden arts;°
1140 My trust is in the living God who gave me,
At my nativity, this strength, diffused
No less through all my sinews, joints, and bones,
Than thine, while I preserved these locks unshorn,
The pledge of my unviolated vow.
1145 For proof hereof, if Dagon be thy god,
Go to his temple, invocate his aid
With solemnest devotion, spread before him
How highly it concerns his glory now
To frustrate and dissolve these magic spells,
1150 Which I to be the power of Israel's God
Avow, and challenge Dagon to the test,
Offering to combat thee, his champion bold,
With the utmost of his godhead seconded:
Then thou shalt see, or rather to thy sorrow
1155 Soon feel, whose God is strongest, thine or mine.
    Har. Presume not on thy God; whate'er he be,
Thee he regards not, owns not, hath cut off
Quite from his people, and delivered up
Into thy enemies' hand; permitted them
1160 To put out both thine eyes, and fettered send thee
Into the common prison, there to grind,
Among the slaves and asses, thy comrádes,
As good for nothing else, no better service
With those thy boisterous locks, no worthy match
1165 For valour to assail, nor by the sword
Of noble warrior, so to stain his honour,
But by the barber's razor best subdued.
    Sam. All these indignities, for such they are
From thine, these evils I deserve and more,

1137–38 More famous is "each particular hair to stand an end/
Like quills upon the fretful porpentine" (*Hamlet*, I, v,
19–20). 1139 So jousters were supposed to swear, in the
Middle Ages.

Acknowledge them from God inflicted on me   *1170*
Justly, yet despair not of his final pardon,
Whose ear is ever open, and his eye
Gracious to readmit the suppliant;
In confidence whereof I once again
Defy thee to the trial of mortal fight,   *1175*
By combat to decide whose god is God,
Thine, or whom I with Israel's sons adore.
  Har. Fair honour that thou dost thy God, in trusting
He will accept thee to defend his cause,
A murderer, a revolter, and a robber.   *1180*
  Sam. Tongue-doughty giant, how dost thou prove
       me these?
  Har. Is not thy nation subject to our lords?
Their magistrates confessed it when they took thee
As a league-breaker and delivered bound
Into our hands, for hadst thou not committed   *1185*
Notorious murder on those thirty men
At Ascalon, who never did thee harm,
Then, like a robber, stripp'dst them of their robes?
The Philistines, when thou hadst broke the league,
Went up with armèd powers thee only seeking,   *1190*
To others did no violence nor spoil.
  Sam. Among the daughters of the Philistines
I chose a wife, which argued me no foe,
And in your city held my nuptial feast;
But your ill-meaning politician lords,   *1195*
Under pretence of bridal friends and guests,
Appointed to await me thirty spies,
Who, threatening cruel death, constrained the bride
To wring from me, and tell to them, my secret,
That solved the riddle which I had proposed.   *1200*
When I perceived all set on enmity,
As on my enemies, where ever chanced,
I used hostility, and took their spoil
To pay my underminers in their coin.
My nation was subjected to your lords.   *1205*
It was the force of conquest; force with force
Is well ejected when the conquered can.
But I, a private person, whom my country
As a league-breaker gave up bound, presumed°

1209 cf. 1184

1210 Single rebellion, and did hostile acts.
     I was no private, but a person raised,
     With strength sufficient and command from Heaven,
     To free my country; if their servile minds
     Me, their deliverer sent, would not receive,
1215 But to their masters gave me up for nought,
     The unworthier they; whence to this day they serve.
     I was to do my part from Heaven assigned,
     And had performed it if my known offence
     Had not disabled me, not all your force.
1220 These shifts refuted, answer thy appellant,°
     Though by his blindness maimed for high attempts,
     Who now defies thee thrice to single fight,
     As a petty enterprise of small enforce.
        Har. With thee, a man condemned, a slave enrolled,
1225 Due by the law to capital punishment?
     To fight with thee no man of arms will deign.
        Sam. Cam'st thou for this, vain boaster, to survey me,
     To descant on my strength, and give thy verdict?
     Come nearer; part not hence so slight informed;
1230 But take good heed my hand survey not thee.
        Har. O Baal-zebub! can my ears unused
     Hear these dishonours, and not render death?
        Sam. No man withholds thee; nothing from thy hand
     Fear I incurable; bring up thy van;
1235 My heels are fettered, but my fist is free.
        Har. This insolence other kind of answer fits.
        Sam. Go, baffled coward, lest I run upon thee,
     Though in these chains, bulk without spirit vast,
     And with one buffet lay thy structure low,
1240 Or swing thee in the air, then dash thee down
     To the hazard of thy brains and shattered sides.
        Har. By Astaroth,° ere long thou shalt lament
     These braveries, in irons loaden on thee.
        Chor. His giantship is gone somewhat crestfallen,
1245 Stalking with less unconscionable strides
     And lower looks, but in a sultry chafe.
        Sam. I dread him not, nor all his giant-brood,

1220 **appellant** challenger (who "calls out" the defendant)
1242 **Astaroth** Syro-Phoenician goddess identified variously
with Aphrodite, Selene, and Artemis

Though fame divulge him father of five sons,
All of gigantic size, Goliah chief.
   Chor. He will directly to the lords, I fear,   *1250*
And with malicious counsel stir them up
Some way or other yet further to afflict thee.
   Sam. He must allege some cause, and offered fight
Will not dare mention, lest a question rise
Whether he durst accept the offer or not,   *1255*
And that he durst not plain enough appeared.
Much more affliction than already felt
They cannot well impose, nor I sustain,
If they intend advantage of my labours,
The work of many hands, which earns my keeping, *1260*
With no small profit daily to my owners.
But come what will; my deadliest foe will prove
My speediest friend, by death to rid me hence;
The worst that he can give, to me the best.
Yet so it may fall out; because their end   *1265*
Is hate, not help to me, it may with mine
Draw their own ruin who attempt the deed.
   Chor. Oh, how comely it is, and how reviving
To the spirits of just men long opprest,
When God into the hands of their deliverer   *1270*
Puts invincible might,
To quell the mighty of the earth, the oppressor,
The brute and boisterous force of violent men,
Hardy and industrious to support
Tyrannic power, but raging to pursue   *1275*
The righteous, and all such as honour Truth!
He all their ammunition
And feats of war defeats°
With plain heroic magnitude of mind
And celestial vigour armed;   *1280*
Their armouries and magazines contemns,
Renders them useless, while
With wingèd expedition
Swift as the lightning glance he executes
His errand on the wicked, who, surprised,   *1285*
Lose their defence, distracted and amazed.
   But patience is more oft the exercise

1278 a jingle like i, 642

Of saints, the trial of their fortitude,
Making them each his own deliverer,
1290 And victor over all
That tyranny or fortune can inflict.
Either of these is in thy lot,
Samson, with might endued
Above the sons of men; but sight bereaved
1295 May chance to number thee with those
Whom patience finally must crown.
      This Idol's day hath been to thee no day of rest,
Labouring thy mind
More than the working day thy hands;
1300 And yet, perhaps, more trouble is behind.
For I descry this way
Some other tending; in his hand
A sceptre or quaint staff he bears,
Comes on amain, speed in his look.
1305 By his habit I discern him now
A public officer, and now at hand.
His message will be short and voluble.°
      Off. Hebrews, the prisoner Samson here I seek.
      Chor. His manacles remark° him; there he sits.
1310   *Off.* Samson, to thee our lords thus bid me say:
This day to Dagon is a solemn feast,°
With sacrifices, triumph,° pomp, and games;
Thy strength they know surpassing human rate,
And now some public proof thereof require
1315 To honour this great feast, and great assembly;
Rise, therefore, with all speed, and come along,
Where I will see thee heartened and fresh clad,
To appear as fits before the illustrious lords.
      Sam. Thou know'st I am an Hebrew, therefore tell
            them
1320 Our law forbids at their religious rites°
My presence; for that cause I cannot come.
      Off. This answer, be assured, will not content them.
      Sam. Have they not sword-players,° and every sort

1307 **voluble** rolled out fast   1309 **remark** distinguish   1311 **a
solemn feast** cf. 12 (a biblical phrase)   1312 **triumph** festivity
or public exhibition, as at xi, 723   1320 **religious rites** cf. xii,
231   1323 **sword-players** fencers

Of gymnic artists,° wrestlers, riders, runners,
Jugglers and dancers, antics, mummers, mimics,°   1325
But they must pick me out, with shackles tired,
And overlaboured at their public mill,
To make them sport with blind activity?
Do they not seek occasion of new quarrels,
On my refusal, to distress me more,   1330
Or make a game of my calamities?
Return the way thou cam'st; I will not come.
   Off. Regard thyself; this will offend them highly.
   Sam. Myself? my conscience, and internal peace.
Can they think me so broken, so debased   1335
With corporal servitude, that my mind ever
Will condescend to such absurd commands?
Although their drudge, to be their fool or jester,
And, in my midst of sorrow and heart-grief,
To show them feats, and play before their god—   1340
The worst of all indignities, yet on me
Joined with extreme contempt? I will not come.
   Off. My message was imposed on me with speed,
Brooks no delay: is this thy resolution?
   Sam. So take it with what speed thy message needs.   1345
   Off. I am sorry what this stoutness will produce.°
   Sam. Perhaps thou shalt have cause to sorrow indeed.
   Chor. Consider, Samson; matters now are strained
Up to the height, whether to hold or break.
He's gone, and who knows how he may report   1350
Thy words by adding fuel to the flame?
Expect another message, more imperious,
More lordly thundering than thou well wilt bear.
   Sam. Shall I abuse this consecrated gift
Of strength, again returning with my hair   1355
After my great transgression, so requite
Favour renewed, and add a greater sin
By prostituting holy things to idols,
A Nazarite, in place abominable,
Vaunting my strength in honour to their Dagon?   1360
Besides, how vile, contemptible, ridiculous,

1324 **gymnic artists** gymnasts   1325 **mimics** actors (misprinted
mimirs—as if mimers?—in the first ed.)   1346 I am sorry to
think what this stubbornness will lead to.

What act more execrably unclean, profane?
    Chor. Yet with this strength thou serv'st the Philistines,
Idolatrous, uncircumcised, unclean.
1365   *Sam.* Not in their idol-worship, but by labour
Honest and lawful to deserve my food
Of those who have me in their civil power.
    Chor. Where the heart joins not, outward acts
      defile not.
    Sam. Where outward force constrains, the
      sentence holds;
1370 But who constrains me to the temple of Dagon,
Not dragging? the Philistian lords command.
Commands are no constraints. If I obey them,
I do it freely, venturing to displease
God for the fear of man, and man prefer,
1375 Set God behind, which, in his jealousy,
Shall never, unrepented, find forgiveness.
Yet that he may dispense with me or thee,
Present in temples at idolatrous rites
For some important cause, thou need'st not doubt.
    Chor. How thou wilt here come off surmounts
1380   my reach.
    Sam. Be of good courage; I begin to feel
Some rousing motions in me, which dispose
To something extraordinary my thoughts.
I with this messenger will go along,
1385 Nothing to do, be sure, that may dishonour
Our Law, or stain my vow of Nazarite.
If there be aught of presage in the mind,
This day will be remarkable in my life
By some great act, or of my days the last.
1390   *Chor.* In time thou hast resolved: the man returns.
    Off. Samson, this second message from our lords
To thee I am bid say. Art thou our slave,
Our captive, at the public mill° our drudge,
And dar'st thou, at our sending and command,
1395 Dispute thy coming? come without delay,
Or we shall find such engines to assail
And hamper thee as thou shalt come of force
Though thou wert firmlier fastened than a rock.

1393 **at the public mill** cf. 1327 (and back to 41)

Sam. I could be well content to try their art,
Which to no few of them would prove pernicious.   *1400*
Yet, knowing their advantages too many,
Because they shall not trail me through their streets
Like a wild beast, I am content to go.
Masters' commands come with a power resistless
To such as owe them absolute subjection,   *1405*
And for a life who will not change his purpose?
(So mutable are all the ways of men°)
Yet this be sure, in nothing to comply
Scandalous or forbidden in our Law.

Off. I praise thy resolution; doff these links: *1410*
By this compliance thou wilt win the lords
To favour, and perhaps to set thee free.

Sam. Brethren, farewell; your company along
I will not wish, lest it perhaps offend them
To see me girt with friends, and how the sight   *1415*
Of me, as of a common enemy,°
So dreaded once, may now exasperate them
I know not. Lords are lordliest in their wine,
And the well-feasted priest then soonest fired
With zeal, if aught religion seem concerned;   *1420*
No less the people, on their holy-days,
Impetuous, insolent, unquenchable;
Happen what may, of me expect to hear
Nothing dishonourable, impure, unworthy
Our God, our Law, my nation, or myself;   *1425*
The last of me or no, I cannot warrant.

Chor. Go, and the Holy One
Of Israel be thy guide
To what may serve his glory best, and spread his name
Great among the Heathen round;°   *1430*
Send thee the Angel of thy birth, to stand
Fast by thy side, who from thy father's field
Rode up in flames after his message told
Of thy conception, and be now a shield
Of fire; that Spirit that first rushed on thee   *1435*
In the camp of Dan,
Be efficacious in thee now at need.

1407 **the ways of men** cf. iii, 46   1416 **a common enemy** cf.
856   1430 **among the Heathen round** cf. 451 (also x, 579)

For never was from Heaven imparted
Measure of strength so great to mortal seed
1440 As in thy wondrous actions hath been seen.
But wherefore comes old Manoa in such haste
With youthful steps? much livelier than erewhile
He seems: supposing here to find his son,
Or of him bringing to us some glad news?
1445   *Man.* Peace with you, brethren; my inducement hither
Was not at present here to find my son,
By order of the lords new parted hence
To come and play before them at their feast.
I heard all as I came; the city rings,
1450 And numbers thither flock: I had no will,
Lest I should see him forced to things unseemly.
But that which moved my coming now was chiefly
To give ye part with me what hope I have
With good success to work his liberty.
1455   *Chor.* That hope would much rejoice us to partake
With thee; say, reverend sire;° we thirst to hear.
   Man. I have attempted,° one by one, the lords,
Either at home, or through the high street passing,
With supplication prone and father's tears,
1460 To accept of ransom for my son, their prisoner;
Some much averse I found, and wondrous harsh,
Contemptuous, proud, set on revenge and spite;
That part most reverenced Dagon and his priests:
Others more moderate seeming, but their aim
1465 Private reward, for which both God and State
They easily would set to sale; a third
More generous far and civil, who confessed
They had enough revenged, having reduced
Their foe to misery beneath their fears;
1470 The rest was magnanimity to remit,
If some convenient ransom were proposed.
What noise or shout was that? it tore the sky.°
   Chor. Doubtless the people shouting to behold
Their once great dread, captive and blind before them,
1475 Or at some proof of strength before them shown.
   Man. His ransom, if my whole inheritance
May compass it, shall willingly be paid

1456 **reverend sire** cf. 326; ix, 719; "Lycidas," 103 1457
attempted approached 1472 **it tore the sky** cf. i, 542

And numbered down: much rather I shall choose
To live the poorest in my tribe than richest,
And he in that calamitous prison left.   *1480*
No, I am fixed not to part hence without him.
For his redemption all my patrimony,
If need be, I am ready to forgo
And quit: not wanting him, I shall want nothing.
   Chor. Fathers are wont to lay up for their sons,   *1485*
Thou for thy son art bent to lay out all;
Sons wont to nurse their parents in old age,°
Thou in old age car'st how to nurse thy son,
Made older than thy age through eyesight lost.
   Man. It shall be my delight to tend his eyes,   *1490*
And view him sitting in the house, ennobled
With all those high exploits° by him achieved,
And on his shoulders waving down those locks
That of a nation armed the strength contained;
And I persuade me God had not permitted   *1495*
His strength again to grow up with his hair°
Garrisoned round about him like a camp
Of faithful soldiery were not his purpose
To use him further yet in some great service,
Not to sit idle° with so great a gift   *1500*
Useless, and thence ridiculous, about him.
And, since his strength with eyesight was not lost,
God will restore him eyesight to his strength.
   Chor. Thy hopes are not ill founded, nor seem vain,
Of his delivery, and thy joy thereon   *1505*
Conceived, agreeable to a father's love,
In both which we, as next, participate.
   Man. I know your friendly minds, and—O, what noise!
Mercy of Heaven! what hideous noise was that?
Horribly loud, unlike the former shout.   *1510*
   Chor. Noise call you it, or universal groan,
As if the whole inhabitation° perished?
Blood, death, and deathful deeds are in that noise,
Ruin, destruction at the utmost point.
   Man. Of ruin° indeed methought I heard the noise. *1515*

1487 **old age** cf. 572, 700, 925 (used only here in Milton's
poetry) 1492 **high exploits** cf. 525 1496 cf. 1355 1500 **to
sit idle** cf. 566 1512 **the whole inhabitation** the world 1515
ruin collapse

Oh! it continues; they have slain my son.
   Chor. Thy son is rather slaying them: that outcry
From slaughter of one foe could not ascend.
   Man. Some dismal accident it needs must be;
1520 What shall we do—stay here, or run and see?
   Chor. Best keep together here, lest, running thither,
We unawares run into danger's mouth.
This evil on the Philistines is fallen:
From whom could else a general cry be heard?
1525 The sufferers, then, will scarce molest us here:
From other hands we need not much to fear.
What if his eyesight (for to Israel's God°
Nothing is hard) by miracle restored,
He now be dealing dole among his foes,
1530 And over heaps of slaughtered walk his way?
   Man. That were a joy presumptuous to be thought.
   Chor. Yet God hath wrought things as incredible
For his people of old; what hinders now?°
   Man. He can, I know, but doubt to think he will:
1535 Yet hope would fain subscribe, and tempts belief.
A little stay will bring some notice hither.
   Chor. Of good or bad so great, of bad the sooner;
For evil news rides post,° while good news baits.°
And to our wish I see one hither speeding,
1540 A Hebrew, as I guess, and of our tribe.
   Messenger. O, whither shall I run, or which way fly
The sight of this so horrid spectacle
Which erst° my eyes beheld, and yet behold?
For dire imagination still pursues me.
1545 But providence or instínct of nature seems,
Or reason, though disturbed and scarce consulted,
To have guided me aright, I know not how,
To thee first, reverend Manoa, and to these
My countrymen, whom here I knew remaining,
1550 As at some distance from the place of horror,
So in the sad event too much concerned.

1527 **Israel's God** cf. 1150 1532–33 Lines (rough as
representing a sort of stammer of hope) that someone ventured
to smooth by transposition: For God of old hath for his people
wrought/ Things as incredible: what hinders now? 1538 **post**
post-haste **baits** halts, for rest and refreshment (cf. xii,
1) 1543 **erst** lately

Man. The accident was loud, and here before thee
With rueful cry; yet what it was we hear not.
No preface needs; thou seest we long to know.
    Mess. It would burst forth, but I recover breath,   *1555*
And sense distract, to know well what I utter.
    Man. Tell us the sum; the circumstance° defer.
    Mess. Gaza yet stands, but all her sons are fallen,
All in a moment overwhelmed and fallen.
    Man. Sad, but thou know'st to Israelites not saddest *1560*
The desolation of a hostile city.
    Mess. Feed on that first, there may in grief be surfeit.°
    Man. Relate by whom.
    Mess.   By Samson.
    Man.   That still lessens
The sorrow, and converts it nigh to joy.
    Mess. Ah! Manoa, I refrain too suddenly   *1565*
To utter what will come at last too soon,
Lest evil tidings, with too rude irruption
Hitting thy aged ear, should pierce too deep.
    Man. Suspense in news is torture; speak them out.
    Mess. Then take the worst in brief: Samson is dead. *1570*
    Man. The worst indeed! Oh, all my hope's° defeated
To free him hence! but Death, who sets all free,
Hath paid his ransom now and full discharge.
What windy joy this day had I conceived,
Hopeful of his delivery, which now proves   *1575*
Abortive as the first-born bloom of spring
Nipped with the lagging rear of winter's frost.°
Yet, ere I give the reins to grief, say first
How died he? death to life is crown or shame.
All by him fell, thou say'st; by whom fell he,   *1580*
What glorious hand gave Samson his death's wound?
    Mess. Unwounded of his enemies he fell.
    Man. Wearied with slaughter, then, or how? explain.

1557 **the circumstance** the circumstances or details   1562 "O,
I have fed upon this woe already, / And now excess of it will
make me surfeit" (*Two Gentlemen of Verona*, III, i, 220
f.).   1571 **hope's** some modern editors drop the apostrophe
1576–77 A burst of "Shakespeare," as can be illustrated from
a simile in *Love's Labour's Lost:* "an envious sneaping frost /
That bites the first-born infants of the spring" (I, i, 100 f.).

    Mess. By his own hands.
    Man.   Self-violence? What cause
1585 Brought him so soon at variance with himself
Among his foes?
    Mess.   Inevitable cause
At once both to destroy and be destroyed;
The edifice, where all were met to see him,
Upon their heads and on his own he pulled.
1590   *Man.* Oh, lastly overstrong against thyself!
A dreadful way thou took'st to thy revenge.
More than enough we know, but, while things yet
Are in confusion, give us, if thou canst,
Eye-witness of what first or last was done,
1595 Relation more particular and distinct.
    Mess. Occasions drew me early to this city;
And, as the gates I entered with sun-rise,
The morning trumpets festival proclaimed
Through each high street; little I had dispatched,
1600 When all abroad was rumoured that this day
Samson should be brought forth, to show the people
Proof of his mighty strength in feats and games;
I sorrowed at his captive state, but minded
Not to be absent at that spectacle.
1605 The building was a spacious theatre,
Half round on two main pillars vaulted high,
With seats where all the lords, and each degree
Of sort,° might sit in order to behold;
The other side was open, where the throng
1610 On banks° and scaffolds under sky might stand:
I among these aloof obscurely stood.
The feast and noon grew high, and sacrifice
Had filled their hearts with mirth, high cheer, and wine,
When to their sports they turned. Immediately
1615 Was Samson as a public servant brought,
In their state livery clad, before him pipes
And timbrels; on each side went armed guards,
Both horse and foot before him and behind,
Archers, and slingers, cataphracts° and spears.
1620 At sight of him the people with a shout

1608 **Of sort** of quality 1610 **banks** benches (French
bancs) 1619 **cataphracts** men in armor on horses in armor

Rifted the air, clamouring their god with praise
Who had made their dreadful enemy their thrall.
He, patient but undaunted, where they led him
Came to the place; and what was set before him,
Which without help of eye might be assayed,   *1625*
To heave, pull, draw, or break, he still performed
All with incredible, stupendious force,
None daring to appear antagonist.
At length for intermission sake they led him
Between the pillars; he his guide requested   *1630*
(For so from such as nearer stood we heard),
As overtired, to let him lean a while
With both his arms on those two massy pillars,
That to the arched roof° gave main support.
He unsuspicious led him; which when Samson   *1635*
Felt in his arms, with head a while inclined,
And eyes fast fixed, he stood, as one who prayed,
Or some great matter° in his mind revolved.
At last, with head erect, thus cried aloud:
'Hitherto, Lords, what your commands imposed   *1640*
I have performed, as reason was, obeying,
Not without wonder or delight beheld.
Now, of my own accord, such other trial
I mean to show you of my strength, yet greater,
As with amaze shall strike all who behold.'°   *1645*
This uttered, straining all his nerves, he bowed;
As with the force of winds and waters pent,°
When mountains tremble, those two massy pillars°
With horrible convulsion to and fro
He tugged, he shook, till down they came, and drew *1650*
The whole roof after them with burst of thunder
Upon the heads of all who sat beneath,
Lords, ladies, captains, counsellors, or priests,
Their choice nobility and flower, not only
Of this, but each Philistine city round,   *1655*
Met from all parts to solemnize this feast.
Samson, with these immixed, inevitably

1634 **the arched roof** cf. i, 726 1638 **some great matter** cf.
ix, 669 1645 punning like Satan's and Belial's, vi, 619
ff. 1647 a simile resembling vi, 195–97; also i, 230–37 1648
those two massy pillars cf. 1633

Pulled down the same destruction on himself;
The vulgar only 'scaped, who stood without.
1660   *Chor.* O dearly-bought revenge, yet glorious!
Living or dying° thou hast fulfilled
The work for which thou wast foretold
To Israel, and now ly'st victorious
Among thy slain self-killed,
1665 Not willingly, but tangled in the fold
Of dire Necessity,° whose law in death conjoined
Thee with thy slaughtered foes, in number more
Than all thy life had slain before.°
    Semichor. While their hearts were jocund and
        sublime,°
1670 Drunk with idolatry, drunk with wine,
And fat regorged of bulls and goats,°
Chanting their idol, and preferring
Before our living Dread, who dwells
In Silo,° his bright sanctuary:
1675 Among them he a spirit of frenzy sent
Who hurt their minds,
And urged them on with mad desire
To call in haste for their destroyer;
They, only set on sport and play,
1680 Unweetingly importuned
Their own destruction to come speedy upon them.
So fond are mortal men,
Fallen into wrath divine,
As their own ruin on themselves to invite,
1685 Insensate left, or to sense reprobate,
And with blindness internal struck.
    Semichor. But he, though blind of sight,

1661 **Living or dying** cf. x, 974   1666 **dire Necessity** *dira Necessitas*, Horace, *Carmina,* III, xxiv, 6   1667–68 "The dead which he slew at his death were more than they which he slew in his life" (Judg. xvi, 30).   1669 **sublime** elated   1671 **of bulls and goats** cf. xii, 292   1674 **Silo** (Anglican Version Shiloh, but Milton always avoids the "Sh" sound in names) a town of Palestine north of Bethel where "the whole congregation of the children of Israel . . . set up the tabernacle of the congregation" after the conquest of Canaan (Josh. xviii, 1) "where it remained till taken by the Philistines at the death of Eli" (marginal note)— 300 to 400 years (cf. Jer. vii, 12).

Despised, and thought extinguished quite,
With inward eyes illuminated,
His fiery virtue roused   *1690*
From under ashes into sudden flame,
And as an evening dragon° came,
Assailant on the perchèd roosts
And nests in order ranged
Of tame villatic° fowl, but as an eagle   *1695*
His cloudless thunder bolted on their heads.
So Virtue, given for lost,
Depressed and overthrown, as seemed,
Like that self-begotten bird°
In the Arabian woods embost,°   *1700*
That no second knows nor third,
And lay erewhile a holocaust,°
From out her ashy womb now teemed,
Revives, reflourishes, then vigorous most
When most inactive deemed,   *1705*
And, though her body die, her fame survives,
A secular° bird, ages of lives.
    Man. Come, come; no time for lamentation now,
Nor much more cause; Samson hath quit himself
Like Samson, and heroicly hath finished   *1710*
A life heroic, on his enemies
Fully revenged—hath left them years of mourning,
And lamentation to the sons of Caphtor°
Through all Philistian bounds. To Israel
Honour hath left and freedom, let but them   *1715*
Find courage to lay hold on this occasion;
To himself and father's house eternal fame,°

1692 **dragon** serpent   1695 **villatic** farmyard   1699 **that self-begotten bird** the phoenix. In the words of Sir Thomas Browne, "That there is but one phoenix in the world, which after many hundred years burneth itself and from the ashes thereof ariseth up another, is a conceit not new or altogether popular, but of great antiquity; not only delivered by humane authors, but frequently expressed also by holy writers."   1700 **embost** embosked, hidden in the woods   1702 **holocaust** a sacrifice wholly consumed by the fire (Greek, *entirely burnt*)   1707 **secular** living for ages (*saecula*) or centuries   1713 **the sons of Caphtor** the Philistines (Jer. xlvii, 4; Deut. ii, 23)   1717 **eternal fame** cf. vi, 240

And, which is best and happiest yet, all this
With God not parted from him, as was feared,
1720 But favouring and assisting to the end.
Nothing is here for tears, nothing to wail
Or knock the breast; no weakness, no contempt,
Dispraise, or blame; nothing but well and fair,
And what may quiet us in a death so noble.
1725 Let us go find the body where it lies
Soaked in his enemies' blood, and from the stream
With lavers pure and cleansing herbs wash off
The clotted gore. I, with what speed° the while
(Gaza is not in plight to say us nay)
1730 Will send for all my kindred, all my friends,
To fetch him hence, and solemnly attend,
With silent obsequy and funeral train,
Home to his father's house; there will I build him
A monument, and plant it round with shade
1735 Of laurel ever green° and branching palm,°
With all his trophies hung, and acts enrolled
In copious legend, or sweet lyric song.
Thither shall all the valiant youth resort,
And from his memory inflame their breasts
1740 To matchless valour and adventures high;
The virgins also shall, on feastful days,
Visit his tomb with flowers, only bewailing
His lot unfortunate in nuptial choice,
From whence captivity and loss of eyes.
1745   *Chor.* All is best, though we oft doubt
What the unsearchable dispose
Of Highest Wisdom brings about,
And ever best found in the close.
Oft he seems to hide his face,°
1750 But unexpectedly returns,
And to his faithful champion hath in place
Bore witness gloriously; whence Gaza mourns,
And all that band them to resist
His uncontrollable intent:

1728 **with what speed** add possible   1735 **laurel ever green**
compare the opening of "Lycidas"   **branching palm** cf. i, 139;
vi, 885.   1749 "Hide not thy face far from me; put not thy
servant away in anger" (Ps. xxvii, 9).

His servants he, with new acquist°   *1755*
Of true experience from this great event,
With peace and consolation hath dismissed,
And calm of mind all passion spent.

1755 **acquist** acquisition

LYCIDAS

The circumstances of the composition and publication of "Lycidas" are related on pages xxi-xxii.

The problem in reading Milton is not so much the extent of his learning as its now unfamiliar area. Up through the nineteenth century the classically educated Englishman was found in sufficient numbers reading his Milton without footnotes. Mark Pattison said that the full enjoyment of "Lycidas" was a final fruit of literary culture. Macaulay issued his impromptu definition of an educated man: one who reads Plato with his feet on the fender. He meant, of course, reads Plato in Greek (and perhaps it would be well to add that he meant by a fender something that goes around a fireplace). But those days are gone, though the Greek and Roman classics have been returning through a wider (and often paperbacked) door of late—that of translation. This is the way for the average reader now, and it is a question of making the minimum suggestions as to what works to be especially aware of while reading "Lycidas" (and again for *Paradise Lost* and *Samson Agonistes*).

Theocritus' *First Idyl,* the *Lament for Bion* attributed to Moschus, and Virgil's *Fifth* and *Tenth Eclogues* are basic. These few pages will serve to bring glints of recognition for which the ordinary school curriculum once laid the basis. One will understand that Milton has a procession of lamenting figures largely because Theocritus and Virgil had one, or asks a question ("Where were ye, Nymphs?") that actually is a translation from the Greek. There is no major strand in the poem for which a precedent cannot be found. One must know, like the author, what kind of poem a pastoral elegy is. It is barbarous to be, like Dr. Johnson, impatient with its allegory and its devices: "Nothing can less display knowledge, or less exercise invention, than to tell how a shepherd has lost his companion, and must now feed his flocks alone, without any judge of his skill in piping; and how one god asks another god what is become of Lycidas, and how neither god can tell." Nothing can less display knowledge than such prejudice as this against the forms and ceremonies of centuries of great poetry, including Shelley's "Adonais" and Matthew Arnold's "Thyrsis." "Lycidas" flaunts its artifice, pulls the stops of all the conventions. Like Spenser's "Shepheards Calender" or his memorial stanzas on Sidney, "Astrophel," it delights to make something new of something old. In verse form it is a free improvisation—but modeled on the Italian *canzone*. Even where we are most prone to suspect a personal note, as in the dedicated man's allusion to girls, 67–69, it may be that note comes in because Bion's famous "Lament for Adonis" has an erotic tone; the names of the girls derive demonstrably from Horace and Virgil. Just as important literarily as the fact that Edward King drowned is the fiction that Daphnis drowned in Theocritus' *First Idyl*. Feelings are disguised, given esthetic distance; antique guises become charged with emotion. One sees the realization of Emily Dickinson's statement: "Nature is a haunted house/Art is a house that tries to be haunted."

*In this Monody the Author bewails a learned Friend, un-
fortunately drowned in his passage from Chester on the
Irish Seas, 1637; and, by occasion, foretells the ruin of
our corrupted Clergy, then in their height.*

YET once more, O ye laurels, and once more,°
Ye myrtles brown,° with ivy never sere,°
I come to pluck your berries harsh and crude,°
And with forced fingers rude
Shatter your leaves before the mellowing year.°   *5*
Bitter constraint and sad occasion dear°
Compels me to disturb your season due,
For Lycidas is dead, dead ere his prime,
Young Lycidas, and hath not left his peer.°
Who would not sing for Lycidas?° he knew°   *10*
Himself to sing, and build the lofty rhyme.°
He must not float upon his watery bier

1–5 Milton, writing around the time of his twenty-ninth
birthday, had done no verse for three years—not since
"Comus" (1634). Previously in English or Latin verses he had
mourned no fewer than seven persons, not counting his lines
"On Shakespeare" for the Second Folio. 2 **brown** dark
never sere All three plants are evergreens (the first two grow
on Parnassus) and thus symbols of immortality.   3 **crude** Latin
crudus, unripe   5 A protest of unreadiness that is ironic in the
light of the claims that can be—and have been—advanced for
"Lycidas" as the greatest poem in the English language.   6
dear of intimate concern   8–9 a figure of repetition called
epanalepsis combined with another called epizeuxis—one of a
number of artful devices to be found within the 193 lines   10
The question is patterned after Virgil's *neget quis carmina
Gallo? (Ecl.* X, 3).   **knew** i.e., knew how. The manuscript and
a presentation copy at Cambridge have "well" inserted before
knew. 11 **build the lofty rhyme** an expression like Horace's
condis amabile carmen and with closer Greek analogues.

Unwept, and welter° to the parching wind,
Without the meed° of some melodious tear.°
15   Begin, then, Sisters of the sacred well°
That from beneath the seat of Jove doth spring,
Begin, and somewhat loudly sweep the string.
Hence with denial vain and coy° excuse:
So may some gentle Muse°
20 With lucky° words favour my° destined urn,
And as he passes turn
And bid fair peace be to my° sable shroud!
For we were nursed upon the selfsame hill,
Fed the same flock, by fountain, shade, and rill;°
25   Together both, ere the high lawns° appeared
Under the opening eyelids of the Morn,
We drove a-field, and both together heard
What time° the grey-fly° winds° her sultry horn,
Battening° our flocks with the fresh dews of night,
30 Oft till the star that rose at evening, bright,°
Toward heaven's descent had sloped his westering
      wheel.
Meanwhile the rural ditties were not mute,
Tempered° to the oaten flute,
Rough Satyrs danced, and Fauns with cloven heel
35 From the glad sound would not be absent long,
And old Damaetas° loved to hear our song.
    But, oh! the heavy change now thou art gone,
Now thou art gone, and never must return!
Thee, Shepherd, thee the woods and desert caves,
40 With wild thyme and the gadding vine o'ergrown,
And all their echoes, mourn.
The willows and the hazel copses green

13 **welter** toss or roll about   14 **meed** recompense   **tear** one
meaning was dirge, funeral poem   15 **Sisters of the sacred well**
the Muses with their poetic springs   18 **coy** modest   19 **Muse**
poet   20 **lucky** propitious   20, 22 **my** as if italicized   23–24
i.e., Milton and Edward King had the same alma mater.   25
high lawns pastures   28 **What time** when (*quo tempore*) **the
grey-fly** also known as the trumpet-fly and heard at hot
midday **winds** blows   29 **Battening** feeding, fattening   30
Hesperus   33 **Tempered** attuned   36 **old Damaetas** in the
pastoral allegory this might stand for a tutor, such as Joseph
Mede, fellow of Christ's College, who died in 1638 at the age
of fifty-two.

Shall now no more be seen,
Fanning their joyous leaves to thy soft lays.
As killing as the canker° to the rose,   45
Or taint-worm° to the weanling herds that graze,
Or frost to flowers, that their gay wardrobe wear,
When first the white-thorn° blows,
Such, Lycidas, thy loss to shepherd's ear.
    Where were ye, Nymphs, when the remorseless deep   50
Closed o'er the head of your loved Lycidas?
For neither were ye playing on the steep
Where your old bards, the famous Druids,° lie,
Nor on the shaggy top of Mona° high,
Nor yet where Deva° spreads her wizard stream.   55
Ay me! I fondly° dream
Had ye been there, . . . for what could that have done?
What could the Muse herself° that Orpheus bore,
The Muse herself for her enchanting son,
Whom universal nature did lament,   60
When, by the rout that made the hideous roar,
His gory visage down the stream was sent,
Down the swift Hebrus to the Lesbian shore?°
    Alas! what boots it° with uncessant° care
To tend the homely, slighted, shepherd's trade,°   65

45 **canker** cankerworm 46 **taint-worm** a worm or crawling
larva noxious to cattle 48 **the white-thorn** the hawthorn 53
Druids the priests and bards of the ancient Britons, thought of
as buried in northern Wales 54 **Mona** same as Anglesey,
island off the northwest coast of Wales 55 **Deva** the river
Dee runs through Chester, whence King set sail; called *wizard*
because, as Giraldus Cambrensis wrote, the waters "change
their fords every month, and as it inclines more towards
England or Wales" makes it possible to "prognosticate which
nation will be successful or unfortunate during the year" 56
fondly both foolishly and affectionately 58 **the Muse herself**
Calliope was the mother of Orpheus 61–63 This ideal poet,
indifferent to womankind after his failure to bring back
Eurydice from Hades, was set upon by a "wild rout" (*Paradise
Lost*, vii, 34 ff.) of Thracian women, angry maenads in the
midst of their Bacchanalian orgies, who tore him to pieces. His
head was tossed into the Hebrus river and, still lamenting,
floated across the Aegean to the island of Lesbos. 64 **what
boots it** what does it avail (as at *Samson Agonistes*, 560)
uncessant MS. has *incessant*. 65 **shepherd's trade** poet's craft

And strictly meditate° the thankless Muse?
Were it not better done, as others use,
To sport with Amaryllis° in the shade,
Or with° the tangles of Neaera's hair?
70 Fame is the spur° that the clear° spirit° doth raise
(That last infirmity of noble mind)
To scorn delights, and live laborious days;
But the fair guerdon° when we hope to find,
And think to burst out into sudden blaze,
75 Comes the blind Fury° with the abhorrèd shears,
And slits the thin-spun life. 'But not the praise,'
Phoebus replied, and touched my trembling ears:°
'Fame is no plant that grows on mortal soil,
Nor in the glistering foil°
80 Set off to the world nor in broad rumour lies,
But lives and spreads aloft by those pure eyes
And perfect witness of all-judging Jove;
As he pronounces lastly on each deed,
Of so much fame in heaven expect thy meed.'
85   O fountain Arethuse,° and thou honoured flood,
Smooth-sliding Mincius,° crowned with vocal reeds,
That strain I heard was of a higher mood.
But now my oat° proceeds,
And listens to the Herald of the Sea°

66 **meditate** practice (Virgil has *musam meditaris, Ecl.* I,
2) 68–69 The names of these girls—standing for various
youthful pleasures—come respectively from Virgil (continuing
Ecl. I above and including the *shade, in umbra*) and Horace
(who mentions the locks, *Carm.* III, xiv, 21–22). 69 **Or with** The
first reading was *Hid in* (!). It has been suggested that *with* is a
verb, *withe*, to twist. 70 **Fame is the spur** *gloria calcar habet*
(Ovid, *Ex Ponto,* IV, ii, 36) **clear** pure, but in the ambience is
the Latin word for famous, *clarus* **spirit** object of "doth
raise" 73 **guerdon** reward 75 **the blind Fury** actually one of
the Fates, Atropos the "inflexible" 77 **touched my trembling
ears** a mode of reminder not strange to a classicist, since the
same god does this to the poet in Virgil's *Eclogues,* VI, 3–4 79
glistering foil glittering setting (of a gem) 85 **Arethuse** in Sicily,
and standing for Greek pastoral poetry, since Theocritus was a
native of Syracuse 86 **Mincius** mentioned by Virgil and
associated with him, as it is a tributary of the Po, which it joins
near his native city of Mantua 88 **oat** the oaten pipe of pastoral
poetry 89 **the Herald of the Sea** Triton

That came in Neptune's plea. 90
He asked the waves, and asked the felon winds,
What hard mishap hath doomed this gentle swain?
And questioned every gust of rugged wings
That blows from off each beaked promontory;
They knew not of his story, 95
And sage Hippotades° their answer brings,
That not a blast was from his dungeon strayed:
The air was calm, and on the level brine
Sleek Panope° with all her sisters played.
It was that fatal and perfidious bark, 100
Built in the eclipse, and rigged with curses dark,
That sunk so low that sacred head of thine.
  Next Camus,° reverend sire, went footing° slow,
His mantle hairy and his bonnet sedge,
Inwrought with figures dim, and on the edge 105
Like to that sanguine flower° inscribed with woe.
'Ah! who hath reft,'° qouth he, 'my dearest pledge?'°
Last came, and last did go,
The Pilot of the Galilean Lake;°
Two massy° keys he bore of metals twain 110
(The golden opes,° the iron shuts amain°).
He shook his mitred locks,° and stern bespake:
'How well could I have spared for thee, young swain,

96 **Hippotades** Aeolus (son of Hippotas), deity in charge of
the winds 99 **Panope** "all-seeing," a sea nymph, one of the
Nereids 103 **Camus** the personification or patron god of the
river Cam, as representative of Cambridge University in reedy
academic garb **footing** A Latin-French pun has been
conjectured here, pedant. 106 **that sanguine flower** the
hyacinth, named after Apollo's favorite companion who was
accidentally killed by the god's discus. His blood turned into
the flower marked AI, AI in sign of Apollo's mourning, thus
inscribed with woe, since an alumnus has reported that "the
sedge of the Cam, when dry, shows markings like a palm-leaf
MS. (or like the traditional marks of the hyacinth)." 107 **reft**
snatched away **pledge** child 109 Winding up the procession is
St. Peter, the keeper of "the keys of the kingdom of heaven"
(Matt. xvi, 19). 110 **massy** bulky. Ancient keys were very
large; cf. Isaiah, xxii, 22. 111 **The golden opes** "that golden
key/ That opes the palace of eternity" ("Comus,"
13–14) **amain** with force 112 **mitred locks** wearing a mitre
as the prime example of a good bishop

Enow of such as, for their bellies' sake,
115 Creep, and intrude, and climb into the fold!°
Of other care they little reckoning make
Than how to scramble at the shearer's feast
And shove away the worthy bidden guest.
Blind mouths!° that scarce themselves know how to hold
120 A sheep-hook, or have learned aught else the least
That to the faithful herdman's art belongs!
What recks it them?° What need they? They are sped,°
And when they list° their lean and flashy songs°
Grate on their scrannel° pipes of wretched straw;
125 The hungry sheep look up, and are not fed,
But, swollen with wind and the rank mist they draw,
Rot inwardly, and foul contagion spread:

115 Ruskin commented (in *Sesame and Lilies*): "Do not think
Milton uses those three words to fill up his verse, as a loose
writer would. He needs all the three; specially those three, and
no more than those—'creep,' and 'intrude,' and 'climb'; no
other words would or could serve the turn, and no more could
be added. For they exhaustively comprehend the three classes,
correspondent to the three characters, of men who dishonestly
seek ecclesiastical power. First, those who *'creep'* into the fold;
who do not care for office, nor name, but for secret influence,
and do all things occultly and cunningly, consenting to any
servility of office or conduct, so only that they may intimately
discern, and unawares direct, the minds of men. Then those
who 'intrude' (thrust, that is) themselves into the fold, who by
natural insolence of heart, and stout eloquence of tongue, and
fearlessly perseverant self-assertion, obtain hearing and authority
with the common crowd. Lastly, those who 'climb,' who, by
labour and learning, both stout and sound, but selfishly exerted
in the cause of their own ambition, gain high dignities and
authorities, and become 'lords over the heritage,' though not
'ensamples to the flock.' " 119 **Blind mouths** A metaphor which
Ruskin also illuminates: "Those two monosyllables express the
precisely accurate contraries of right character, in the two great
offices of the Church—those of bishop and pastor. A Bishop
means a person who sees [Greek]. A Pastor means one who
feeds. The most unbishoply character a man can have is therefore
to be Blind. The most unpastoral is, instead of feeding, to want
to be fed—to be a Mouth." 122 **What recks it them?** what do
they care? **They are sped** They prosper. 123 **list** wish **flashy
songs** poor (literally, watery) sermons 124 **scrannel** shriveled
and thin and harsh (a word possibly of Milton's invention)

Besides what the grim wolf with privy paw°
Daily devours apace, and nothing said.
But that two-handed engine at the door   130
Stands ready to smite once, and smite no more.'°
  Return, Alpheus, the dread voice is past
That shrunk thy streams; return, Sicilian Muse,°
And call the vales and bid them hither cast
Their bells and flowerets of a thousand hues.   135
Ye valleys low, where the mild whispers use°
Of shades, and wanton winds, and gushing brooks,
On whose fresh lap the swart star° sparely looks,
Throw hither all your quaint enamelled eyes,°
That on the green turf suck the honied showers,   140
And purple all the ground with vernal flowers.

128 **the grim wolf with privy paw** doubtless a reference to
the Church of Rome, with its secret proselytizing agents, the
Jesuits   130–31 The most famous crux in English literature, of
which not fewer than forty different explanations can be traced
in print. The *door* should be the door of the sheepfold, 115,
which is the door of the church (which is, in turn, the way to
heaven, opened by the golden key—111). It would be
consistent with the verse paragraph—"the iron shuts amain"
(111)—if the two-handed threat had to do with death and
damnation, the simultaneous fate that impends over the
corrupt priest (see Milton's headnote to his poem). Judging
from Milton's only other use of "two-handed" (*Paradise Lost,*
vi, 250–53), the *engine* is a two-handed sword, a perfectly
normal meaning once, where the modern reader thinks only
of a battery engine or a machine with moving parts. The Lord
wields it—or possibly the militant archangel Michael of the
next verse paragraph (161 ff.); 131 has its parallel in vi,
317–18.   132–33 The river referred to literally does go
underground, as readers of Coleridge's "Kubla Khan" will
remember: "Where Alph the sacred river ran/ Through caverns
measureless to man/ Down to a sunless sea." The mythological
explanation was that the river-god Alpheus dived under the
sea from the Peloponnesus in pursuit of the nymph Arethusa
(cf. 85) and came up in Sicily, where his beloved was turned
into a fountain and their waters mingled.   136 **use** are
accustomed (as at 67)   138 **the swart star** Sirius, the Dog Star,
so called because at the time of its appearance the complexion
or grass is turned to a swart, or dark, color   139 **quaint
enamelled eyes** pretty varicolored blossoms

Bring the rathe° primrose that forsaken dies,
The tufted crow-toe° and pale jessamine,
The white pink, and the pansy freaked° with jet,
145 The glowing violet,
The musk-rose, and the well-attired woodbine,
With cowslips wan that hang the pensive head,
And every flower that sad embroidery wears;
Bid amaranthus° all his beauty shed,
150 And daffadillies fill their cups with tears,
To strew the laureate hearse where Lycid lies.
For so, to interpose a little ease,
Let our frail thoughts dally with false surmise,
Ay me! whilst thee the shores and sounding seas
155 Wash far away, where'er thy bones are hurled;
Whether beyond the stormy Hebrides,°
Where thou perhaps under the whelming tide
Visit'st the bottom of the monstrous° world,
Or whether thou, to our moist vows° denied,
160 Sleep'st by the fable of Bellerus° old,
Where the great Vision of the guarded mount°
Looks toward Namancos and Bayona's hold.°
Look homeward, Angel, now, and melt with ruth,

142 **rathe** early 143 **crow-toe** the crowfoot or wild hyacinth;
tufted describes the plant when in flower. 144 **freaked**
streaked 149 **amaranthus** not, of course, the mythical flower of
Paradise Lost, iii, 352, but probably love-lies-bleeding. 156 A
northern reference, to be followed by extreme southern
references. The Hebrides are the islands on the west coast of
Scotland. 158 **monstrous** full of monsters of the deep 159
moist vows tearful prayers 160 **Bellerus** Bellerium was the
Roman name of Land's End (the southwestern tip of Cornwall).
The fable is probably that told in Milton's *History of Britain* of
a battle between giants. 161 **mount** St. Michael's Mount, near
Penzance in Cornwall, described in a 1906 Baedeker as "a curious
rocky islet, rising precipitously to a height of 230 ft., and
connected with the shore by a natural causeway . . . a miniature
copy of Mont St. Michel in Normandy. Its earliest occupant,
according to the legend, was the Giant Cormoran, slain by Jack
the Giant-killer. The priory at the top was dedicated to St.
Michael, who is said to have appeared to some hermits here very
early in the Christian era." Thus Milton, as so often, mingles
Christian and non-Christian elements. 162 **Namancos and
Bayona's hold** Spanish strongholds faced by the guardian angel
Michael, who in the next line is bid to look back "homeward."

And, O ye dolphins, waft the hapless youth.
    Weep no more, woeful shepherds, weep no more,   *165*
For Lycidas, your sorrow, is not dead,
Sunk though he be beneath the watery floor.
So sinks the day-star° in the ocean bed,
And yet anon repairs his drooping head,
And tricks° his beams, and with new-spangled ore   *170*
Flames in the forehead of the morning sky:
So Lycidas, sunk low but mounted high,
Through the dear might of Him that walked the waves,
Where, other groves and other streams along,
With nectar pure his oozy locks he laves,   *175*
And hears the unexpressive nuptial song°
In the blest kingdoms meek of joy and love.
There entertain him all the Saints above,
In solemn troops and sweet societies,
That sing, and singing in their glory move,   *180*
And wipe the tears forever from his eyes.°
Now, Lycidas, the shepherds weep no more;
Henceforth thou art the Genius of the shore,°
In thy large recompense, and shalt be good
To all that wander in that perilous flood.   *185*
    Thus sang the uncouth° swain to the oaks and rills,°
While the still morn went out with sandals grey;
He touched the tender stops of various quills,°
With eager thought warbling his Doric lay;°
And now the sun had stretched out all the hills,   *190*
And now was dropt into the western bay;
At last he rose, and twitched his mantle blue:
To-morrow to fresh woods, and pastures new.

---

168 **the day-star** the sun (the analogy will be with the Sun of
Righteousness) 170 **tricks** decks out 176 **the unexpressive
nuptial song** the inexpressible marriage song ("Blessed are they
which are called unto the marriage supper of the Lamb." Rev. xix,
9). 181 "And God shall wipe away all tears from their eyes" (Rev.
vii, 17; xxi, 4; cf. Is. xxv, 8). 183 **the Genius of the shore** Lycidas
is seen as a tutelary deity or presiding spirit, *genius loci* or patron
saint. 186 **uncouth** rustically unknown to fame 186–93 An
ottava rima stanza (ababbcc), either in commemoration of the
influence of the Italian Renaissance or by way of glancing at the
poet's imminent trip to Italy, the "fresh woods, and pastures
new" 188 **quills** reeds of a Pan's pipe 189 **Doric lay** Theocritus,
Bion, and Moschus wrote in the Doric dialect.

SELECTED BIBLIOGRAPHY

Editions

Hughes, Merritt Y., ed. *John Milton: The Complete Poems and Major Prose*. New York: Odyssey Press, 1957.

Patterson, F. A. and others, eds. *The Complete Works of John Milton* (18 vols.). New York: Columbia University Press, 1931–38.

Shawcross, John T., ed. *The Complete Poetry of John Milton*. New York: Doubleday, 1971.

Biography

Brown, Cedric C. *John Milton: A Literary Life*. London: Macmillan, 1995.

Bush, Douglas. *John Milton: A Sketch of His Life and Writings*. New York: Macmillan, 1964.

Hill, Christopher. *Milton and the English Revolution*. London: Faber and Faber, 1977.

Levi, Peter. *Eden Renewed: The Public and Private Life of John Milton*. London: Macmillan, 1996.

Lewalski, Barbara Kiefer. *The Life of John Milton: A Critical Biography*. Blackwell Critical Biographies. Oxford: Blackwell, 2000.

Parker, William Riley. *Milton: A Biography*. 2nd ed. Revised by Gordon Campbell. Oxford: Clarendon Press, 1996.

Shawcross, John T. *John Milton: The Self and the World*. Lexington: University of Kentucky Press, 1993.

Wilson, A. N. *The Life of John Milton*. New York: Oxford University Press, 1983.

General

Barker, Arthur, ed. *Milton: Modern Essays in Criticism*. New York: Oxford University Press, 1965.

Bennett, Joan S. *Reviving Liberty: Radical Christian Hu-*

manism in Milton's Great Poems. Cambridge, MA: Harvard University Press, 1989.

Bloom, Harold, ed. *John Milton: Modern Critical Views.* New York: Chelsea House, 1986.

Danielson, Dennis, ed. *The Cambridge Companion to Milton.* 2nd ed. Cambridge: Cambridge University Press, 1999.

Eliot, T. S. "Milton I and II." In his *On Poets and Poetry.* New York: Farrar, Straus and Giroux, 1957.

Empson, William. *Milton's God.* 2nd ed. London: Chatto and Windus, 1965.

Fish, Stanley Eugene. *How Milton Works.* Cambridge, MA: Harvard University Press, 2001.

Grose, Christopher. *Milton and the Sense of Tradition.* New Haven, CT: Yale University Press, 1988.

Hanford, James Holly, and James G. Taaffe. *A Milton Handbook.* 5th ed. New York: Appleton-Century-Crofts, 1970.

Hunter, Jr., William B., gen. ed. *A Milton Encyclopedia* (9 vols.). Lewisburg, PA: Bucknell University Press, 1978–83.

Kendrick, Christopher, ed. *Critical Essays on John Milton.* New York: G. K. Hall, 1995.

Ricks, Christopher. *Milton's Grand Style.* Oxford: Clarendon Press, 1963.

Gender and Sexuality in Milton's Works

Abate, Corinne S. "The Mischief Making of Raphael upon Adam and Eve in *Paradise Lost.*" *English Language Notes* 36 (1999): 41–54.

Interdanto, Deborah. "Render Me More Equal: Gender Inequality and the Fall in *Paradise Lost.*" *Milton Quarterly* 29 (1995): 95–106.

Labriola, Albert C. "Milton's Eve and the Cult of Elizabeth I." *Journal of English and German Philology* 95 (1996): 38–51.

Le Comte, Edward. *Milton and Sex.* New York: Columbia University Press, 1978.

Rumrich, John P. "The Erotic Milton." *Texas Studies in Literature and Language* 41 (1999): 128–41.

Smith, Greg. "Binary Opposition and Sexual Power in

Paradise Lost." The Midwest Quarterly 38 (1996): 383–99.

Turner, James Grantham. *One Flesh: Paradisal Marriage and Sexual Relations in the Age of Milton.* Oxford: Clarendon Press, 1987.

Walker, Julia M. *Milton and the Idea of Woman.* Urbana: University of Illinois Press, 1988.

Webber, Joan M. "The Politics of Poetry: Feminism and *Paradise Lost." Milton Quarterly* 14 (1980): 3–24.

Wittreich, Jr., Joseph A. *Feminist Milton.* Ithaca, NY: Cornell University Press, 1987.

Paradise Lost

Blamires, Harry. *Milton's Creation: A Guide Through* Paradise Lost. London: Methuen, 1971.

Bloom, Harold, ed. *John Milton's* Paradise Lost: *Modern Critical Interpretations.* New York: Chelsea House, 1987.

Bush, Douglas. Paradise Lost *in Our Time: Some Comments.* Ithaca, NY: Cornell University Press, 1945. Rpt. Gloucester, MA: Peter Smith, 1967.

Fish, Stanley Eugene. *Surprised by Sin: The Reader in* Paradise Lost. 2nd ed. Cambridge, MA: Harvard University Press, 1998.

Gardner, Helen. *A Reading of* Paradise Lost. New York: Oxford University Press, 1965.

Lewalski, Barbara Kiefer. Paradise Lost *and the Rhetoric of Literary Forms.* Princeton, NJ: Princeton University Press, 1985.

Lewis, C. S. *A Preface to* Paradise Lost. New York: Oxford University Press, 1942. [Frequently reprinted.]

MacCaffrey, Isabel G. Paradise Lost *as "Myth."* Cambridge, MA: Harvard University Press, 1959.

Martz, Louis. *Milton,* Paradise Lost: *A Collection of Critical Essays.* Englewood Cliffs, NJ: Prentice-Hall, 1966.

Patrides, C. A. *Milton and the Christian Tradition.* Oxford: Clarendon Press, 1966.

——, ed. *Milton's Epic Poetry: Essays on* Paradise Lost *and* Paradise Regained. Harmondsworth, England: Penguin, 1967.

Roston, Murray. *Milton and the Baroque*. Pittsburgh: University of Pittsburgh Press, 1980.

Shawcross, John T. *With Mortal Voice: The Creation of Paradise Lost*. Lexington: University of Kentucky Press, 1982.

Webber, Joan M. *Milton and His Epic Tradition*. Seattle: University of Washington Press, 1979.

"Lycidas"

Alpers, Paul. "*Lycidas* and Modern Criticism." *English Literary History* 49 (1982): 468–96.

Baier, Lee. "Sin and Repentance in *Lycidas*." *Philological Quarterly* 67 (1988): 291–302.

Bourdette, Jr., Robert E. "Mourning *Lycidas*: The Poem of the Mind in the Act of Finding What Will Suffice." *Essays in Literature* 11 (1984): 11–20.

Fish, Stanley. "*Lycidas*: A Poem Finally Anonymous." *Glyph* 8 (1981): 1–18.

Graham, Jean E. "Ay Me: Selfishness and Empathy in *Lycidas*." *Early Modern Literary Studies* 2.3 (1996): 1–21.

Hanson, Elizabeth. "To Smite Once and Yet Once More: The Transaction of Milton's *Lycidas*." *Milton Studies* 25 (1989): 69–88.

Hughes, Merritt Y., gen. ed. *A Variorum Commentary on the Poems of John Milton*. Vol. II, eds. A.S.P. Woodhouse and Douglas Bush, *The Minor English Poems*. New York: Columbia University Press, 1972: 554–734 on *Lycidas*.

Johnson, Barbara A. "Fiction and Grief: The Pastoral Idiom of Milton's *Lycidas*." *Milton Quarterly* 18 (1984): 69–76.

Le Comte, Edward, ed. and translator. *Justa Edovardo King: A Facsimile Edition of the Memorial Volume in which Milton's* Lycidas *First Appeared*. Norwood, PA: Norwood Editions, 1978.

Patrides, C. A., ed. *Milton's* Lycidas: *The Tradition and the Poem*. New York: Holt, Rinehart & Winston, 1961. [Collection of Essays]

Pecheux, Mother M. Christopher. "The Dread Voice in *Lycidas*." *Milton Studies* 9 (1976): 221–41.

Snyder, Susan. "Nature, History, and the Waters of *Lycidas*." *Huntington Library Quarterly* 50 (1987): 323–35.

Watterson, William Collins. " 'Once More, O ye Laurels': *Lycidas* and the Psychology of Pastoral." *Milton Quarterly* 27 (1993): 48–57.

Samson Agonistes

Bennett, Joan S. "A Reading of *Samson Agonistes*" in *The Cambridge Companion to Milton*, Dennis Danielson, ed. 2nd ed. Cambridge: Cambridge University Press, 1999.

Crump, G. M., ed. *20th Century Interpretations of* Samson Agonistes. Englewood Cliffs, NJ: Prentice-Hall, 1968.

Duran, Angelica. "The Last Stages of Education: *Paradise Regained* and *Samson Agonistes*." *Milton Quarterly* 34 (2000).

Krouse, F. Michael. *Milton's Samson and the Christian Tradition*. Princeton, NJ: Princeton University Press, 1949.

Lewalski, Barbara K. "Milton on Women—Yet Again." In *Problems with Feminist Criticism*, ed. Sally Minogue. New York: Routledge, 1990.

Low, Anthony. *The Blaze of Noon: A Reading of* Samson Agonistes. New York: Columbia University Press, 1974.

Mason, John B. "Multiple Perspectives in *Samson Agonistes*: Critical Attitudes Toward Dalila." *Milton Studies* 10 (1977): 23–33.

Radzinowicz, Mary Ann. *Toward* Samson Agonistes: *The Growth of Milton's Mind*. Princeton, NJ: Princeton University Press, 1978.

Stollman, S. "Milton's Samson and the Jewish Tradition." *Milton Studies* 3 (1971).

Wittreich, Joseph. *Interpreting* Samson Agonistes. Princeton, NJ: Princeton University Press, 1999.